NIGHTFALL OVER SHANGHAI

BY DANIEL KALLA
FROM TOM DOHERTY ASSOCIATES

Blood Lies
Cold Plague
Of Flesh and Blood
Pandemic
Rage Therapy
Resistance
The Far Side of the Sky
Rising Sun, Falling Shadow
Nightfall Over Shanghai

NIGHTFALL OVER SHANGHAI

A Novel

Daniel Kalla

A TOM DOHERTY ASSOCIATES BOOK
NEW YORK

This is a work of fiction. All of the characters, organizations, and events portrayed in this novel are either products of the author's imagination or are used fictitiously.

NIGHTFALL OVER SHANGHAI

A Forge Book
Published by Tom Doherty Associates, LLC
175 Fifth Avenue
New York, NY 10010

www.tor-forge.com

Forge® is a registered trademark of Tom Doherty Associates, LLC.

The Library of Congress Cataloging-in-Publication Data is available upon request.

ISBN 978-0-7653-8380-8 (hardcover)
ISBN 978-1-4668-9334-4 (e-book)

Our books may be purchased in bulk for promotional, educational, or business use. Please contact your local bookseller or the Macmillan Corporate and Premium Sales Department at (800) 221-7945, extension 5442, or by e-mail at MacmillanSpecialMarkets@macmillan.com.

First published in Canada by HarperCollins Publishers Ltd

First U.S. Edition: January 2016

Printed in the United States of America

0 9 8 7 6 5 4 3 2 1

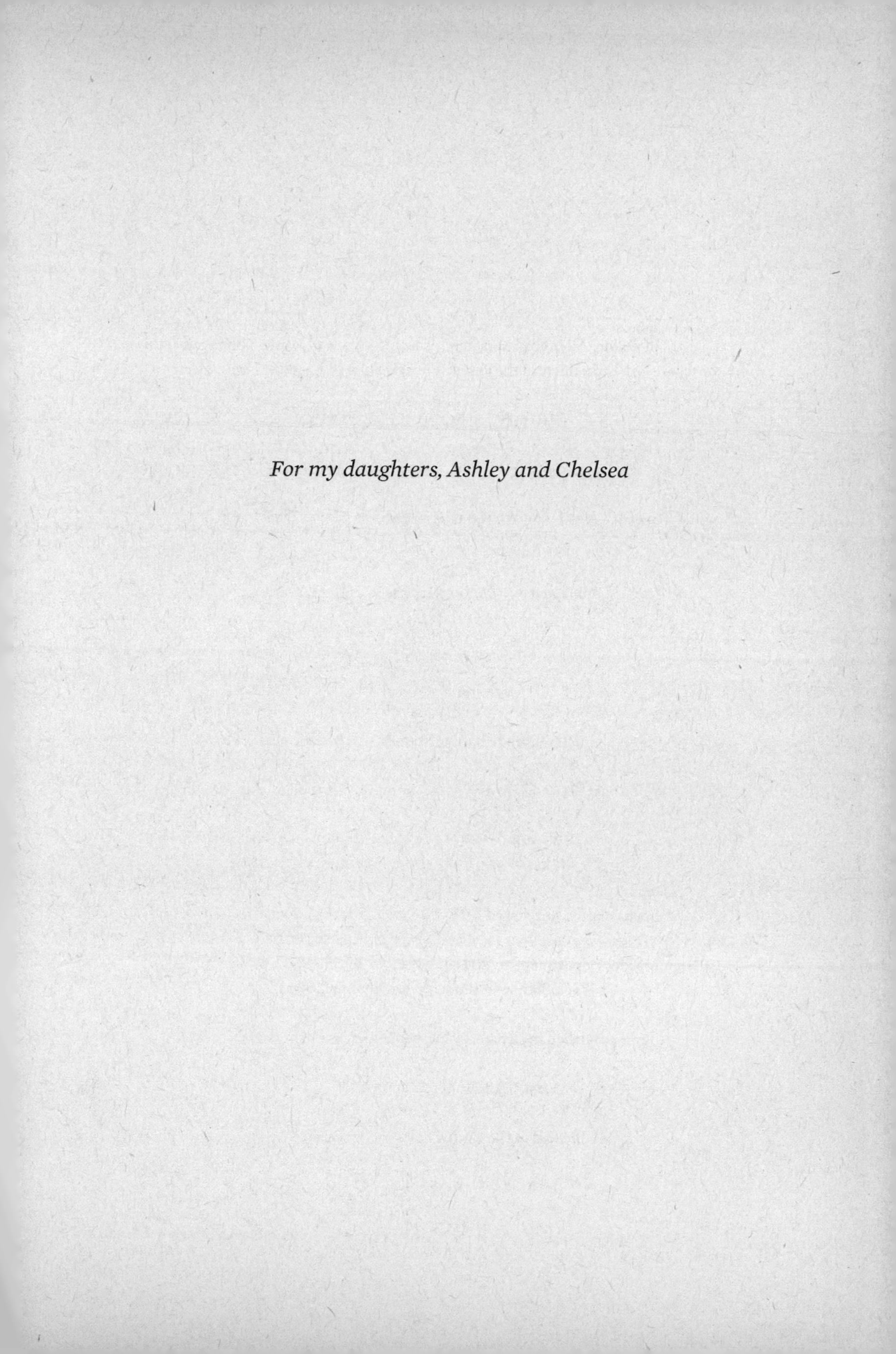

For my daughters, Ashley and Chelsea

I

CHAPTER 1

April 15, 1944, Shanghai

Soon Yi "Sunny" Adler found the quiet disconcerting. Normally, the tiny apartment was a hive of activity. But Sunny's stepdaughter, Hannah, was in school while her husband, Franz, was busy tending to patients at the refugee hospital, where Sunny also spent most of her time. And her sister-in-law, Esther, had taken her one-year-old, Jakob, to scour the local grocers, looking for anything to accompany the mouldy rice in the pot. There was no money, so perhaps Esther planned to barter the pair of socks that she had knitted earlier in the afternoon?

Sunny tidied up the cramped sitting room that doubled as Esther and Jakob's bedroom at night. She pushed the chairs in under the wobbly table where the family spent most of their evenings. She picked up the worn wooden blocks that Jakob loved to bang for hours at a time off the couch. The ratty sofa, which Sunny had reclaimed from the dump and recovered with an old blanket, was one of the few pieces of furniture inside the dingy flat. And yet, Sunny was acutely aware of how lucky her family was compared with many of the Jewish refugees who had been forced by the Japanese to reside inside the Shanghai ghetto. Some twenty thousand of them lived among a hundred thousand native Chinese, all crammed into one square mile of rundown apartments set in a confusing network of narrow alleys known as *longtangs*. The Adlers' indoor plumbing alone was an extravagance that was viewed by many of the other refugees with open envy.

Still, in her low moments, like this one, Sunny found it hard to feel grateful for their relative good fortune. Her past year had been defined by loss. So many loved ones had either been killed or were interned in the squalid prison camps scattered across the city. Over the past fifteen months, the Japanese had incarcerated tens of thousands of American and British Shanghailanders, several of her friends included. But she missed her old amah, Yang, the most, and in some ways felt responsible for the woman's fate. Yang had been caught sheltering fugitive friends of Sunny's and was now rotting away inside one of the worst of the camps.

Sunny appreciated that Shanghai could be even more dangerous for those living outside the camps than inside. With each military setback in the Pacific Theatre—as the radio announcers referred to it on the banned Voice of America broadcasts that still found a way into several of the refugees' homes—the Japanese grew more unpredictable. Every day seemed to bring new waves of unprovoked roundups and disappearances among the Chinese and the refugee Jews. Lately, the Japanese hadn't even bothered with public floggings, opting usually just to execute the accused on sight.

The rattling of the door drew Sunny's attention. It flew open and Hannah stood at the threshold with an arm draped over the shoulders of a young Chinese girl, hunched forward and clutching at her belly.

A month shy of her fourteenth birthday, Hannah had sprouted over the previous winter. She shared her father's hazel eyes and dimpled chin, but Sunny knew from old photographs that Franz had brought with him from Austria that her stepdaughter had inherited her mother's fair complexion and oval face. Despite her physical self-consciousness—Hannah's left arm and leg had been weakened and mildly disfigured since birth—she was developing into a beautiful young woman.

"Where's Papa?" Hannah demanded.

"At the hospital." Sunny rushed over to meet them. "What's going on?"

"Feng Wei." Hannah nodded to the bent-over girl. "Something is wrong with her stomach."

Sunny hadn't even recognized Feng Wei, whose features were contorted in agony. The shy young girl was no more than a year or two older than Hannah and lived with her large family in one of the neighbouring *longtangs*.

Sunny slipped in between the two girls and ushered Feng Wei toward the couch. Even before she ran her hand over her tense belly, Sunny could tell what was happening from Feng Wei's stilted breathing and not-fully-concealed bulge. "How many months?" she demanded in Shanghainese.

"Wie viele Monate?" Frowning, Hannah echoed the question in German. "Months? This only happened today."

But Feng Wei understood. "Last summer," she whimpered. "Before monsoon season."

Hannah whipped her head in her friend's direction. "Feng Wei, you are not with child?"

Grimacing, Feng Wei looked away, embarrassment only compounding her pain.

Sunny helped Feng Wei onto the couch. The girl's face relaxed as the discomfort appeared to pass. "And the contractions—these painful spasms—when did they begin?"

"I have had the pains for the past month," Feng Wei said, still avoiding eye contact. "This morning, they were so much stronger."

"And do the pains come regularly now, every few minutes or so?" Sunny asked, and Feng Wei nodded slightly. "Do you feel the urge to bear down? As if you have to go the bathroom?"

Feng Wei nodded more vigorously. "Yes, dear lady. I have such strong—" Another contraction seized her. She lurched forward and grabbed hold of her belly with both hands, crunching herself into the shape of a bean. Her mouth opened but no sound emerged.

Sunny turned to her stepdaughter. "Hannah, get me a pail of water. And bring me some cloths and sheets, please. Strip the bed, if need be. Oh, and bring me your aunt's thread and the scissors from her knitting kit."

Feng Wei's head fell back onto the couch and her breathing eased. This was familiar territory for Sunny, who had delivered countless babies over the past few years. Despite all the mentoring her father, an eminent doctor, had provided, Sunny had begun the war as a ward nurse. Even after she met Franz at the refugee hospital and fell in love with him, she would never have dreamed that her future husband would train her to become a surgeon almost as capable as he was. It still astounded her to think of the medical responsibilities she had since assumed and the complex surgeries she had performed. But she also knew too well that war changes everything and everyone, very occasionally and only inadvertently for the better.

Sunny reached for the hem of Feng Wei's traditional grey dress. "I need to check you. From below. You understand, little one?"

The girl's cheeks flushed deeply, but she nodded her consent. Kneeling at the foot of the couch, Sunny lifted the hem up past Feng Wei's waist and then wriggled her cotton bloomers down her legs. The ammonia-tinged odour of urine intermingled with amniotic fluid drifted to Sunny's nose as she gently bent the girl's knees and positioned her bare feet on the couch so that the ankles were touching. Sunny attempted to push her thighs apart, but Feng Wei resisted, keeping her knees clamped tightly together.

Sunny relaxed the pressure. "It's time, little Wei," she said in a soft but firm tone.

Feng Wei hesitated and then slowly separated her legs until they were partway open. Sunny could see dark hair beneath Feng Wei's dress and, looking carefully, spotted another source of black hair protruding between the girl's legs. "The baby is crowning," she said. "He's ready to come out."

"I . . . I don't know how," Feng Wei whispered.

Sunny squeezed the girl's calf reassuringly. "When the contraction comes, you just have to push. Let your body guide you. It will not take long."

"I brought the . . ." Hannah stopped midsentence.

Sunny glanced over her shoulder to see her stepdaughter standing behind her with mouth open and eyes wide, a pail of water dangling from one hand and a stack of folded sheets and cloths supporting a spool of thread and pair of scissors balanced on the other. Hannah closed her mouth and made her way over to the couch, her eyes fixed with new-found determination.

Sunny fought back a smile, proud of her stepdaughter's show of bravery. "Pass me the water and a cloth, Hannah. And one of the sheets, please."

Sunny ran the sheet under Feng Wei's legs and slipped it up underneath her buttocks. Then she rested her hands against the inside of Feng Wei's knees and pushed. This time, Feng Wei allowed her legs to part wider so Sunny could gently swab between the girl's legs with a damp cloth. Just as she began the second stroke, Feng Wei tensed her neck and panted through another contraction.

"Push, Feng Wei," Sunny encouraged. "Push."

Hannah squeezed Feng Wei's hand and chanted, "Push, push, push."

Sunny watched the baby's head emerge a few inches further. "Good," Sunny said. "Keep pushing!"

"Keep going, Feng Wei, you are doing so well," Hannah urged in nearly accent-free Chinese.

The contraction passed and Feng Wei's head flopped back once more onto the couch. Sunny ran her fingers over the baby's wet, spongy scalp. "You must push through the pain, little Wei," Sunny instructed. "The baby will come with the next contraction with one big push. Do you understand?"

"A baby," Hannah sang. "Only one more big push and you will have a baby!"

Except for her laboured breathing, Feng Wei remained silent and still. After another minute or two, she tensed her hips and thrust her head up again. "Push hard, Feng Wei," Sunny commanded. "*Now.*"

Suddenly, the baby's entire head was free. Sunny gently held it with her fingers placed over each ear, then slowly guided it downward until the shoulders cleared Feng Wei's pelvis and the rest of the body slipped out. Holding him under the armpits, Sunny lifted the baby clear of the dangling umbilical cord. She studied his colour, relieved by the healthy pinkish hue. She could feel his heart beating, and she felt her own pulse pound in exhilaration. The baby opened his eyes, grunted and then uttered more of a mew than a cry.

Unexpectedly moved, Sunny laughed. "Look at him. The little angel."

"A boy," Hannah cried excitedly, still holding Feng Wei's hand. "It's a beautiful boy. A friend for Jakob."

Feng Wei squeezed her eyes shut. Her shoulders trembled and she began to sob silently.

Sunny folded a sheet and used it to swaddle the baby before lowering him onto the couch next to his mother. She reached for the scissors, cut off a long piece of thread and then wrapped it three times around the umbilical cord close to the baby's belly. She tied it off with multiple knots and then repeated the step three times, leaving a small gap between the two sets of ties. She looked over at Hannah, who was watching with rapt attention. "Would my able assistant like to cut the cord?" Sunny asked.

Hannah's eyes brimmed with eagerness. "Could I?"

Sunny held out the scissors for her. Hannah tucked her mildly contracted left hand against her side, and accepted the tool with her right. The scissors shook slightly as she moved the open blades toward the cord. She turned uncertainly to Sunny. "Will this hurt him?"

"No, not at all." Sunny grinned.

Hannah hesitated, then squeezed the blades together. She had to cut three or four times before the cord was sliced through. Once it fell away, Sunny lifted the baby and brought him close to her own face. The distinct smell of new life almost brought tears to her eyes. "It must be time to feed you, gorgeous," she murmured close to his cheek.

Sunny lowered him toward Feng Wei, but the girl recoiled, turning her head and rolling onto her side. Taken aback, Sunny brought the baby to her own chest and nestled him there. "Is there someone we should notify, Feng Wei? Your parents, perhaps?"

With her back still turned, Feng Wei shook her head. "Not a soul. Please, dear lady."

"Do your parents not know?" Hannah asked.

"No one can know," Feng Wei whimpered.

"And the baby's father?" Sunny asked.

"No! Especially not him." Feng Wei's shoulders trembled again, and this time her sobs were audible. "I do not even know his name."

A chill ran down Sunny's spine. With her free hand, she reached out and touched the girl's shoulder. "The father–is he Japanese? A soldier?"

Feng Wei shot her hands up to cover her face, and her sobs grew louder. Finally, she nodded.

Sunny's mind flashed back to an evening five years before, the night she had been forced up against a shop window by a knife-wielding, drunken Japanese sailor, her blouse ripped open and her legs spread apart by the pressure of his knee. She had willed him to plunge the blade into her throat, preferring that over another moment of pain or debasement. That was when her father had intervened, sacrificing his life to save hers or, at least, preventing her from knowing the terrible dilemma that Feng Wei now faced–giving birth to a baby that was also the child of the man who had raped her.

"Sunny, may I?" Hannah asked, easing the baby out of Sunny's arms.

Hannah studied the baby. "He even looks like you, Feng Wei," she said with an encouraging smile. "Those same puffy cheeks."

Feng Wei still wouldn't look at either of them. "Father will never allow it," she muttered.

Sunny caressed Feng Wei's shoulder again. "Perhaps with time—"

"To lose face in such a way?" Feng Wei cried. "Never, ever. Not until the end of time. I could never bring such shame to the family."

The baby stirred in Hannah's arms and uttered another croaky cry.

"We will figure something out," Sunny said emptily. "Meantime, your baby is hungry."

But Feng Wei remained on her side. "Are there no bottles?"

"He needs his mother's milk," Sunny said, squeezing her shoulder more firmly.

Reluctantly, Feng Wei rolled onto her back. She still didn't reach for the child, but instead, with a blank expression and no sign of her previous modesty, raised her dress to expose her breasts. Sunny took the baby from Hannah and lowered him to the closest breast and repositioned his head until he rooted around and found a nipple. "That's it, little darling," she said with satisfaction as she watched him latch.

Feng Wei made no move to embrace her son. She kept her arms at her side and stared up at the ceiling while the baby nursed. Sunny was alarmed at the sight of a mother neglecting her newborn. Finally, she lifted up Feng Wei's arm and positioned it to support the baby. The girl held her son to her chest but kept her eyes fixed on the ceiling.

The door opened again and Esther stepped in, holding Jakob in her arms. In Vienna, Esther had been married to Franz's younger brother, who had been murdered on Kristallnacht. Even though she had since remarried, Franz still considered her to be his sister-in-law. Sunny thought of her as one too. Esther had always been skinny, but after a year of forced separation from her second husband, Simon, she had lost so much weight that she swam in her simple grey dress. Her narrow features and deep-set eyes were more sunken than ever, making her look older than her thirty-eight years.

As soon as Jakob saw Sunny and Hannah, the toddler struggled free of his mother's grip and tottered over to greet them. Hannah swept him up in her arms. "Look, Jakob, you're not the youngest anymore."

"Baby, baby," Jakob repeated.

Esther turned to Sunny with a look of quiet concern.

"I was as surprised as you." Sunny went on to explain what had just happened, safe in the knowledge that Feng Wei couldn't understand German. "Look at her, Essie. I've never seen anything like this. She is resisting the maternal instinct."

Esther nodded in an understanding way. "Under the circumstances, I don't think the girl has much choice."

"So what will become of him?"

Esther sighed. "An orphanage?"

Sunny had no idea which, if any, of the orphanages in the city were still operating since the Japanese occupation had begun. She thought, with a shudder, of those little packages wrapped in bamboo that she had passed on the streets over the years—babies who died at birth or were abandoned soon after. *Never*, she vowed to herself. She would never let that happen to this precious one.

"What then?" Esther eyed her quizzically. "Sunny, you're not suggesting . . ."

All her exhilaration and wonder drained away. Sunny felt utterly defeated. "How could I . . . we?" *What would Franz say?*

But she kept that thought to herself. "Besides, what would I even feed him?"

Esther studied the nursing baby for a long moment without comment. Finally, she nodded to herself. "I'm still feeding Jakob. I have plenty of milk to share."

CHAPTER 2

Dr. Franz Adler shot out a hand and grabbed the stretcher's railing, fighting off another wave of light-headedness. Lately, the episodes had been striking more often. Back in Vienna, he'd been able to stay up for nights on end performing surgeries with little difficulty. But nowadays, a single sleepless night in the refugee hospital was guaranteed to incite multiple bouts of dizziness.

Franz's approach to his own symptoms, like that of so many other doctors he knew, was to minimize or to ignore them. After all, he was almost forty-three years old. How could he possibly expect to possess the stamina he once had as a young surgeon? He considered telling Sunny, but he couldn't bring himself to compound her worries.

Franz glanced around the open ward, the hospital's only one, to see if anyone had witnessed his spell. The two nurses—the dependable and maternal head nurse, Berta Abeldt, and the sweet but skittish Miriam Weinstein—were busy tending to patients, oblivious to his struggles. None of the patients paid him any attention either. Franz had no concern that the man on the stretcher below him might have noticed. Herr Steinmann's glassy and unfocused gaze suggested that he was still drifting somewhere between consciousness and coma. Franz was surprised that the seventy-year-old lawyer had even survived surgery.

Steinmann had stumbled into the hospital the night before, his skin the colour of slate and his belly as rigid as a board. In the operating theatre, Franz had a found a coin-sized hole where an ulcer had eaten through the stomach's lining and leaked acid throughout the abdominal cavity. Surely only willpower and obstinacy had kept the old lawyer alive.

Franz had come to know Steinmann through the Refugee Council, a loosely organized association of representative refugees that helped support the ghetto's three *heime*, or hostels, where the poorest Jewish families lived. Franz had felt an immediate kinship with the elegant and fastidious Berliner—no doubt because, as Esther had pointed out, Steinmann bore so many similarities to Franz's father, who had died in Vienna shortly before the outbreak of war, not long after Franz, Hannah and Esther had fled the city. Not only did Steinman physically resemble Adler senior, he also shared his profession, his meticulousness and his dim view of all religions. Steinmann even possessed the same fatalistic sense of humour.

Franz's dizziness passed and was replaced by elation. He was relieved, of course, that Herr Steinmann had survived the surgery and now had a legitimate chance of recovering, though it would be a long and challenging road. But there was more to Franz's upbeat mood. In the past two weeks, he had rediscovered a sense of professional purpose. For months, the hospital had been hopelessly low on almost all supplies, including ether for general anesthesia. Without these resources, Franz had felt neutered—a surgeon with nothing to offer his patients but stopgaps and half measures. But a few weeks earlier, several Russian Jews had arrived at the hospital unannounced, bearing cartons full of supplies. The boxes were all marked in Cyrillic, but it hadn't taken Franz long to dig through them and find five bottles of ether buried at the bottom of one.

Shanghai's Russian Jewish community, which numbered over five thousand, still enjoyed rare personal and economic freedoms because of the neutrality pact between the Soviets and Japanese. The attack on Pearl Harbor had made it impossible for any British and American financial aid to reach Shanghai's expatriate communities, so the Russian Jews were the only potential benefactors the refugees had left. The Russians had proved to be a fickle and unpredictable group, separated by tradition, language and, for the most part, culture from the other European Jews in the ghetto. Almost a year earlier, Franz had appeared before a group of Russian elders and appealed for medical supplies and financial aid. He had long since given up hope of their help, so he was shocked and delighted when the provisions materialized.

Franz gently smoothed the bandages down over his patient's abdomen. "All things considered, the surgery went better than expected, Herr Steinmann," he said, more to himself than to the unconscious patient. He was about to step over to the next bed when he heard a commotion somewhere down the hallway. His shoulders and neck tensed. More than the frantic voices, it was the sound of boots pounding the floor that set off his internal alarm. He would never mistake those footfalls for anything other than the harbinger of a raid.

Seconds later, the first soldier stormed down the corridor. A half dozen or so others followed after in their brimmed caps and khakis. The only two who didn't have rifles slung over their shoulders carried bulky wicker boxes in their arms.

Steadying his breathing, Franz went out to meet them at the

ward's entry. They breezed past him without a word of explanation. On the ward, the soldiers split up. The two with the boxes headed straight for the small supply closet at the back. Franz followed after, but Berta reached the closet first. The head nurse filled the doorway, so Franz had to peer over her shoulder to watch the soldiers inside. They stood back to back, facing the shelves. Each man swept an arm along a shelf, knocking the bottles into the waiting boxes. Within seconds, they had emptied half of the cupboard.

Berta put her hands on her hips. "What is the meaning of this?" she demanded. "You have no right to—"

The soldier nearest to her dropped his box, spun and punched Berta so hard in the chest that she toppled backwards. Franz caught her out of reflex, but her substantial weight almost knocked him off his own feet. He struggled to right the heavy woman in his arms. When she was finally supporting her own weight, he grabbed her by the shoulders and asked, "Are you all right, Berta?"

Face flushed and struggling for air, she buried her distress behind a stoic expression. "I only need a moment, Herr Doktor," she gasped.

Just then, shouting from within the ward drew his attention. Franz looked over to see a white-haired patient, Frau Adelmann, waving her right arm desperately while her left limb lay stiff and unresponsive on the mattress. A stocky soldier was shrieking at her in Japanese while he yanked a blanket away from her body.

"I cannot get up," Frau Adelmann cried. "I have suffered a stroke only last week."

Undeterred, the soldier grabbed the sheet underneath her and jerked it off the bed, hauling Frau Adelmann along with it, until she rolled off and landed on the floor with a sickening thud.

She screamed in pain, but it had no effect on the infantryman. He bunched up a corner of the sheet and dragged her along with it toward the hallway. All around the ward, soldiers were scaring, prodding and dumping patients out of their beds. Those who could walk were herded toward the exit in their gowns. Those who couldn't, like Frau Adelmann, were being dragged out—in the case of one man, by his ankle.

When Franz spotted a soldier pulling the sheet out from underneath Herr Steinmann, he rushed over to him. He had managed only two or three strides before another soldier stuck out his leg, sending Franz sprawling to the ground. Just as he started to push himself up, a jolt of pain ripped through the right side of his chest. The soldier kicked him a second time, harder, and Franz heard his rib crack before he even felt the stab of pain. Air whooshed out of his lungs. Desperate for breath, he pushed himself up by the elbows. Then a boot slammed into his jaw, throwing him onto his side. The taste of blood filled his mouth, and he felt his jaw agonizingly snap out of place before clunking back in with a grinding crunch.

The soldier grabbed Franz by the collar of his shirt and started to pull. Breathless and in pain, Franz had no strength to resist. All he could do was pant for every molecule of oxygen as he was hauled along the floor and heaved out the front door onto the ground in front of the hospital.

He lay on his side on the cold, damp dirt and gasped for breath as patients accumulated around him. Some were seated on the ground, others curled in heaps, including Herr Steinmann. A few of the more robust patients stood up, leaning against one another for support. Out of the corner of his eye, Franz saw two soldiers nailing boards across the hospital's entrance while the men carrying boxes walked down the short pathway to trucks at the curb. After a minute or two, a panicky voice asked from somewhere above him, "Herr Doktor Adler, please, can you hear me?"

He nodded to Miriam but regretted it immediately as pain shot up the side of his jaw and into his ear.

Berta knelt down beside him, looking remarkably composed. "Say something, Dr. Adler. Are you all right?"

"Yes," he croaked. "The soldiers?"

"They have left," Berta said. "Can you stand?"

"I think so. Yes."

"Let's try, shall we," she encouraged as she placed a hand gently under his shoulder and began to lift.

Franz managed to get to his knees and, holding on to Berta, rose shakily to his feet. He was terrified that an inopportune dizzy spell might topple him back to the ground, but thankfully none came, so he released Berta's arm.

Miriam stared at him, panic-stricken. "What now, Herr Doktor? The hospital is closed. Finished."

Finished. The word hurt Franz more than his injuries. He and Sunny had dedicated the past five years of their life to the refugee hospital. Somehow, the chronically undersupplied, decrepit old site had always defied the odds. Franz had saved Sunny's life there after she had been attacked by a Japanese sailor. Sunny had nursed Hannah through a near-fatal bout of cholera. Together, they had rescued Esther and her baby from certain peril with an emergency Caesarean section. How many other lives had been saved inside the hospital? How many people had been allowed to die in dignity, their pain mitigated through medication and compassion? Too many to remember them all.

"The patients, Dr. Adler." Berta sighed. "Where shall we take them?"

Franz looked around at the patients piled on the ground or standing in clusters, shivering in their light gowns. Earlier in the day, he had counted twenty-one. Some were recuperating, but others were in the throes of illness.

Berta was talking again, but Franz couldn't concentrate on her words. His eyes fixed on the ramshackle grey building across the street, its front windows still boarded up more than five years after a Japanese aerial bombardment had blown them out. He raised his hand toward it but pain in his ribcage stopped him halfway. Instead, he motioned with his head. "There. We will take them there."

"That old heim?" Berta asked.

"There are several rooms inside."

"But they use every last bed and then some," Miriam said with a wild shake of her head. "The families, they sleep in bunks on top of one another."

"They will have to make space," Franz said.

"And what about supplies? The Japanese—they took everything."

"We've coped with our cupboards bare before, Berta." But Franz doubted the head nurse believed his reassurance any more than he did.

Berta eyed him silently before she finally nodded. "It's the only way. *Ja.* I'll go gather some young men from the heim to help us carry the patients."

Franz nodded. "See if you also can find some boards to carry them on."

With a crisp nod, Berta marched off toward the heim, as composed as if she had never been attacked. Franz hobbled over to

Herr Steinmann, who lay on the ground, his hips bent and rotated and his gown pulled halfway up his thigh, exposing veiny legs. His eyes were open and more focused than earlier. He appeared to be mouthing words, but Franz couldn't make him out.

Splinting his own chest with his elbow, Franz carefully crouched down beside the man.

"The operation, Dr. Adler," Steinmann breathed. "It's over?"

"Yes, Herr Steinmann. It went well."

"My back, it feels so wet and so cold." His lips curled slightly, but Franz couldn't tell if they formed a grimace or a smile. "Am I . . . am I still alive?"

Franz nodded. "You are, yes. The Japanese raided the hospital. They dragged us outside."

Steinmann's only response was to shut his eyes and mutter "I see."

Franz looked over to the door of the hospital. It was nailed shut with at least four boards. Something caught his eye: a single sheet of paper that had been tacked onto the planks. He rose gingerly to his feet and shuffled over. Scanning past the Japanese writing, he read the German words printed at the bottom of the page: "By the decree of the Empire of Japan, these premises have been order closed. No one is permitted to enter. Anyone breaching this order will be considered as to be trespassing. Such trespassers will be treated with the heaviest and most immediate of responses."

The proclamation was unsigned, but Franz had no doubt who had drafted it. He could think of only one person who could be behind such flowery, non-grammatical phrasing. The man who lorded over the ghetto, and the Jews inside it, like the raja of some remote Indian province. The same little tyrant who was responsible for the scars that criss-crossed Franz's back. *Ghoya.*

CHAPTER 3

Hannah was eager to tell Herschel Zunder all about the baby, but she could barely squeeze a word in edgewise. "They are all such appeasers," the boy cried.

"Who are?" Hannah asked.

"The ones who call themselves Zionist but aren't willing to rock the boat. They would wait forever for a Jewish homeland rather than offend the British or any other goys who oppose us in Palestine."

Hannah realized that Herschel was parroting the words of Rabbi Hiltmann, one of the most outspoken Zionists in Shanghai, but she held her tongue.

"Both sides of the Jordan River, like in the days of King David," Herschel railed on. "Every last acre of Eretz Yisrael, just as the Torah promises. It's the only way forward. Nowhere else will we be able to live in peace. The Nazis have proven it. The Japanese too." He waved a finger at the crowded street, where clusters of Jewish refugees milled among the native Chinese on Tong Shan Road.

Nothing seemed out of the ordinary to Hannah, who had lived in Shanghai for more than five years. Her memories of Vienna had begun to blur and what she did remember—that visceral sense of alienation and terror of living under the heel of the Nazis—she wished she could forget. The Tong Shan street market, even in its current rundown state, was as good a reflection of the refugee life as any Hannah could imagine. The storefronts, once all Chinese, had been reclaimed by refugees and turned into doctors' offices, a delicatessen, a pharmacy, a café and even the headquarters of a Yiddish newspaper. German Jews, many dressed in the same suits they had arrived in Shanghai wearing (and continued to wear regardless of the temperature or season), stood huddled in conversation or bartering with Chinese merchants, who hawked everything from rice and produce to street dentistry. Gaunt rickshaw drivers stood hunched over their empty carts, dejectedly soliciting anyone who passed, with dim hope of ever landing a fare.

Japanese soldiers in khakis and puttees, their distinctive lower-leg coverings, marched self-importantly through the streets. Hannah spotted one soldier at the end of the block berating a Chinese merchant for some perceived infraction. The infantryman shoved the merchant, who fell backwards into his cart, knocking it over and scattering heads of lettuce, or possibly cabbage, along the road. Hannah turned away with hardly a second thought. She had witnessed so much worse.

And yet, as familiar as the scene was, Hannah noticed subtle differences too. Despite the open businesses with their welcoming signs, few refugees were prospering. She could see men now wearing rags tied around their feet, their shoes destroyed from years of pounding the same broken pavement. Most people's suits and dresses looked a size or two too large for them, despite having likely been already taken in, as her father's suit had been. The Chinese had fared no better, particularly not the children, many of whom appeared emaciated. Hunger was a constant in the ghetto. Hannah knew that her family was among the luckier ones—Esther somehow managed to ensure that there was something on the table almost every dinner, if only a bowl of wet rice—but she couldn't remember what it felt like to fall asleep with a full belly.

Herschel was carrying on about the kibbutzim and the need to cultivate land in Palestine, but Hannah tuned him out. She had heard this speech too many times already. She sighed heavily. "You sound like a scratched phonograph record. You've convinced me, Herschel. We need a homeland. I agree. But can't we talk about something else?"

Herschel grimaced as though she had suggested they stop breathing for a while. "It's so very important, Hannah. We need to convince the others. We need solidarity."

"Solidarity, yes." She nodded distractedly. "Do you remember my friend Feng Wei? That girl from my neighbourhood?"

"Yes, I do," Herschel said warily. He crossed him arms and then uncrossed them, tucking his hands into his pockets, seeming uncertain of what to do with them.

Hannah suppressed a grin. At fifteen, Herschel Zunder was as gangly as a baby giraffe and as graceless, not at all accustomed to his long limbs. Paradoxically, Herschel was also an old soul, as serious as a middle-aged rabbi with a solemn narrow face and a long forehead that was almost always creased in a frown. And when he wasn't inveighing against the obstacles to Zionism, he could be remarkably shy and awkward.

Herschel squinted at her. "Why did you ask me about Feng Wei?"

"She had a baby."

His mouth fell open. "A . . . a baby? But how?"

Hannah looked around to ensure nobody was in earshot before

speaking in a low tone. "No one knew. Feng Wei hadn't told anyone, not even her own family. She hid her stomach under baggy clothes. I don't know what she would have done if I hadn't found her crouched in the alley."

Herschel gawked at her. "But that girl is no older than you or me, surely?"

Feeling sudden misgivings, Hannah grabbed his wrist. "You can't tell a soul," she implored. "Feng Wei didn't keep the baby. No one in her family knows. Promise me, Herschel."

Nodding, he looked down to her fingers wrapped around his wrist. She realized it was probably the first time she had ever touched him, but she liked the feeling of his slender arm in her hand, so she kept her fingers where they were. He reddened slightly before looking back up at her with a timid smile. "What will become of the baby?"

"My stepmother, Sunny, is looking after him right now. She says they will find him a suitable home but—" Hannah took another quick glance around her. "I think she wants to keep him."

Herschel nodded understandingly. "I have a little brother. They can drive you crazy."

Hannah hadn't even considered it. She would actually have a baby brother, or half-brother, at least. It seemed surreal. Her own mother had died from an infection only days after her birth. For her first eight years of life, Hannah had lived alone with her father. As a younger child, she used to pretend that her beloved rag doll, Schweizer Fräulein, was her little sister. As foreign as the idea of a brother now seemed, it also excited her.

Herschel cleared his throat. "Are you hungry, Hannah?"

Hannah squeezed his wrist a little tighter and laughed. "Who isn't, around here?"

"Yes, of course. I mean . . ." Herschel blushed deeper. He dug his free hand into his pocket and opened his palm to show her two coins, both Japanese military yens. "A few of us have worked the last two weeks for Rabbi Hiltmann, cleaning the synagogue. Painting a little too."

"You should save your money, Herschel. Your family must need it."

"Zeyde took the other three coins," he said, referring to his grandfather.

Hannah liked Herschel's paternal grandparents. She knew he and his brother had accompanied them to Shanghai on one of the last ocean liners to leave Italy for the Orient in the summer of 1939. His parents had been scheduled to follow within a month, but the outbreak of war in Europe had blocked their departure, leaving them stranded in Berlin. Herschel never spoke of his parents, and Sunny had only learned their fate from a classmate who had known the family in Berlin.

"Zeyde told me I could keep these. He said I earned them." Herschel pointed to a bamboo stall where an old woman stood cooking at a stove. Hannah had loitered near the same stand before just to inhale the delectable aroma. "I think I would really enjoy some of those dumplings."

Hannah's mouth watered at the prospect. "They're not kosher, Herschel." Her father had never kept their home kosher, but she wasn't sure if the same was true for Herschel. "They're probably made with pork."

Herschel gently laid his other hand on the top of hers. "I won't tell, if you won't."

She laughed. And, for the first time since Freddy Herzberg, someone set butterflies loose inside her chest.

CHAPTER 4

Ernst Muhler nonchalantly waved his yellow-stained fingers around the room, a lazy tail of smoke following behind. "Personally, I would have opted for a cheerful throw rug." He shrugged. "But no doubt a baby will brighten up the room too."

Sunny bit back a smile; the cheekiness was typical of her flamboyant friend. "This is only temporary, Ernst. Until we can find a safe home for him."

His eyes twinkled. "Ah, temporary, naturally. What was I thinking?" He pointed to the couch where, only hours earlier, Feng Wei had given birth to the baby. Esther now held the infant to her breast, discreetly tucked under a blanket, while Jakob sprawled out next to her fast asleep, his head in her lap. "That sight could melt a statue's heart, couldn't it?" Ernst said.

Sunny felt her own heart melting. She felt a glimmer of something else too—a sense of inadequacy. She knew it was irrational, but she couldn't help herself. She wished she could provide for the child, instead of watching helplessly while another woman nursed him.

Esther viewed Ernst plaintively. "Ernst, my Simon . . ."

"A thousand apologies, Essie. Sometimes, I forget that my sole purpose here is as your mailman," he said in an amused tone as he dug his free hand into his pocket and extracted a crumpled envelope. "Another letter from your beloved."

"Oh." Esther brought a finger to her lips. Her husband, Simon Lehrer, was an American Jew who had been swept up in the Japanese wave of internments of Allied citizens. He had been a prisoner in one of the camps before escaping to be nearer to his family, and now lived in hiding with Ernst on the other side of the city.

It had been more than a year since Simon had gone underground, but he was still considered a saviour among the refugees. He had arrived in Shanghai in 1937, allegedly to avoid the obligation of running his family's furniture business in New York, but he had quickly fallen into a far more responsible role, running the city's major charitable organization, the Committee for Assistance of European Refugees. With a compassion that was matched only by his energy level, Simon had spearheaded the building of the refugee hospital while helping to find food and housing for the penniless German Jews who had arrived at the harbour by the boatload almost daily in the late 1930s. It was in this capacity that Simon had first met the Adlers, and Esther.

Simon had also introduced Sunny to Franz and the refugee hospital, changing her life completely and forever. To say she felt indebted to the easygoing New Yorker would have been a massive understatement. Sunny was heartsick to see Simon and Esther separated by Ghoya's cruel order. Ghoya had banned the entire family, including Esther, from leaving the ghetto. Simon could only see his son whenever Sunny—who wasn't confined to the ghetto like the German refugees—had time to sneak Jakob out to Ernst's flat, where Simon lived. Ironically, Ernst was actually the more wanted fugitive of the two men. Sunny could still see in her mind his haunting oil paintings of the rape and murder victims of the Nanking Massacre. They had enraged the Japanese authorities and sent Ernst fleeing to the countryside. Since returning to Shanghai, he had chosen to hide in plain sight. He lived in an enclave known as Germantown, behind wild whorls of hair, a beard and the assumed name of Gustav Klimper, a cheeky homage to the great Viennese painter Gustav Klimt. He made a living selling his non-controversial paintings, mainly German landscapes that he disdained as conformist and unoriginal. Every few weeks, along with Simon's letters, Ernst brought the family a bag of groceries or rice. And, unbeknownst to Franz, who was too proud to accept anything he viewed as charity, Ernst was slipping Esther the few dollars he could spare, which she pretended to earn through sales of her knitting.

Esther's eyes lit up at the sight of the letter in his hand, but she nodded to the baby below the blanket. "In a minute or two, Ernst. Thank you." She cleared her throat. "Tell me, how he is?"

"The man is lovesick, Essie." Ernst sighed. "Speaks of you day and night. Frankly, it's a little tiresome."

"*Ach*, you talk such nonsense." Esther looked down to conceal her happy smile and the sudden colour in her cheeks.

Ernst lit another cigarette. "Where, I ask you, is a man like that for me?"

"In that mountain village, waiting," Sunny reassured. "Just where you left him." She had always liked Shan, whom Ernst had met soon after arriving in Shanghai. The two men had fled the city together after the scandal of Ernst's Nanking paintings.

"Why would Shan wait for me? After the way I absconded without so much as a goodbye."

"You did it for Charlie," Sunny said. In the countryside, Ernst and Shan had met Charlie, a charismatic Resistance leader and the youngest general in the Communist army. After Charlie had been shot through the leg, Ernst had taken the risk of dragging him to the city for medical attention at the refugee hospital. "Charlie was dying from that infected wound. You sacrificed everything to get him here."

"God only knows what has happened to that village or my poor Shan without Charlie. It's hard to believe that any of them might still be alive."

Esther shook her head vigorously. "You can't talk that way, Ernst. You must have faith."

He grimaced. "Oh, Essie, life has given me precious little reason for faith. And your people even less so. How do you Jews possibly sustain it?"

Esther repositioned the baby and adjusted the blanket. "Karl used to say that it takes no effort to believe during good times. That only in the worst of times can one demonstrate true faith."

Sunny had never known Franz's younger brother, Karl, but she still felt a kind of closeness to the man who had been Esther's first husband. "Karl paid for his faith with his life. What those monsters did to him . . ." Ernst shook his head in disgust. "Besides, he was a better man than I could ever hope to be."

"Nonsense, Ernst," Esther said with a gentle laugh. "You are a good man. And a brave one too. Looking after my Simon the way you do. You, an Austrian goy, who has always been a friend to—"

Esther was silenced by the unexpected opening of the door. Franz entered, his face ghostly pale and his hair dishevelled. Dirt marks criss-crossed the pant legs of his only suit. But it was his halting movement, and the way he kept his right arm clamped to his chest, that drew Sunny's attention. She hurried over and tried to wrap him in a hug but stopped when he gasped in pain. "What have they done to you, Franz?"

"My rib. It's broken."

"Oh, darling." Sunny lightly ran her fingers over his jacket. Just her touch caused Franz to wince and lean away. Then she noticed the bruising on his jaw and moved her hand up to carefully explore it. "And this?"

"It's nothing, Sunny." He pulled her hand from his face. "Only the chest."

Ernst marched over to the door. "Was it the Kempeitai?"

"No, not the military police. Just regular soldiers." Franz looked from Ernst to Sunny and then down to the floor. "After all these years, they have shut us down."

"The hospital?" Sunny took his left hand in her right and caressed his knuckles. "Tell me."

Franz described the raid, ending with the decree being pinned to the entrance.

"Why, Franz?" she asked. "Why would they do this?"

"Ghoya," he grunted. "He can't let us have anything."

"That horrid little man," Esther spat. The Japanese bureaucrat had kept her and Simon apart for the past six months by forbidding her an exit pass, but she was only one of thousands of refugees who had come to despise the man, who referred to himself as the "King of the Jews."

"Now what, Franz?" Sunny asked.

Franz freed his hand from Sunny's. "I am going to go see him."

"Ghoya?" Ernst frowned. "Not that I have ever been the epitome of caution or care but, Franz, do you really think that's wise?"

Franz turned on Ernst angrily, catching himself when he felt a stab of pain in his chest. "My patients are all over the hostel. Most of them suffering on the floor like stray cats. No medicine. No operating theatre. No supplies. What am I supposed to do for them, for God's sake?"

Ernst held up his hand as though the answer were obvious. "What the rest of us do. Accept it. Turn a blind eye. Look after yourself. And forget about everyone else."

Franz was about to respond when the baby, turning from Esther's chest, uttered a high-pitched gurgle. Something stirred inside Sunny, but she resisted the urge to go to him.

Franz looked over just as the baby's head emerged from beneath the blanket. Confused, he turned back to Sunny for an explanation.

"You remember Hannah's friend? The neighbour girl, Feng Wei?"

Franz squinted at her in disbelief. "The baby is Feng Wei's?"

"He was, yes." Sunny explained what had happened. Franz said nothing, but his impassive expression cut her to the bone. She felt she could read his mind: *How can we bring another baby into our overcrowded home? Another mouth to feed.*

Too hurt to even meet his gaze, she turned to Esther with her arms outstretched. "Let me burp him, Essie."

As she took the boy in her arms, it occurred to her that he still didn't have a name. Inhaling his sweet scent and feeling the warmth of his cheek against hers, she realized that she would never be able to let him go.

CHAPTER 5

The narrow corridor inside the Bureau of Stateless Refugee Affairs reeked of stale wool and sweat, a smell that Franz had come to associate with the futility and despair of the ghetto. Two or three of the other refugees in the queue shot him withering glances as he sidled past, but the rest appeared indifferent. Years in Shanghai living under Japanese occupation had eroded their sense of entitlement or even fairness. Most of the refugees just seemed resigned.

Most in the line were young or middle-aged men, but a few women and stooped old men were interspersed among them. They would have been queued for hours, ever since the curfew had lifted in the morning. They had come to beg Ghoya for one of the precious exit passes, which, for many, would determine whether or not their families would go hungry that day. Everyone knew that Ghoya relished his position as sole arbiter of the passes. He played the role like a lion trainer at the circus, with as much showmanship and cruelty.

Ghoya's high-pitched voice—more screech than shout—emerged from the open door at the end of the hallway. One young man standing near Franz flinched, but few others showed much of a reaction.

They were accustomed to Ghoya's mood swings, which were as erratic as the Shanghai winds in typhoon season.

A young woman bolted out of the office, clutching her face and running with her head down. Before Franz could move out of the way, she slammed into him, launching another thunder-clap of pain through his chest. The woman looked up at him with terrified eyes, angry welts on both cheeks. Franz recognized her as a former patient. Sunny had delivered her baby via an urgent Caesarian section several months earlier. He remembered how fragile the woman had seemed, both physically and emotionally. "Frau Kornfeld?"

"Ah, Dr. Adler, I'm so sorry," she said. "I'm so sorry, so very sorry."

Franz caught his breath. "It's fine," he said, trying to conceal his pain. "Are you all right?"

"I only came for my husband's pass because of his fever. He couldn't get out of bed," she mumbled, seeming in shock as she rubbed at one of her cheeks. "Mr. Ghoya, he said Felix was a coward for sending his wife. He slapped me so hard. Twice. And he told me that we could starve like the rest of the rats."

"Mr. Ghoya, he is prone to exaggerate," Franz said half-heartedly. "Tomorrow he will probably forget it altogether."

"You think so, Dr. Adler?" she asked, desperate for reassurance. "Felix, he sells wood carvings at the wharf. Without the passes, there will be no food. The baby . . ."

Franz nodded sympathetically, but her predicament was so commonplace that it had lost the capacity to move him. Besides, her mention of the baby reminded him of the infant in his own home. He could see how attached Sunny had already become to him. She desperately wanted a child. She deserved one. But not now, of all times.

"Tomorrow will be a different story, Frau Kornfeld," he said distractedly. "You will see."

"Yes. No doubt. Thank you, Dr. Adler," she said as she squeezed past him.

Franz shouldered his way down to the end of the hallway, giving rise to a few more half-hearted protests from those at the front of the line. Reaching the doorway, he peered into the office. Ghoya sat behind his desk, wearing the pinstriped suit he considered his uniform. His oversized head bobbed from side to side, a smile creasing his pockmarked face. "Yes, yes, Herr Friedmann," he was saying in his reedy, almost accent-free German. "Bring me more of that schnitzel your wife makes, and the ink on your exit pass will never dry."

Ghoya looked over to the door and noticed Franz. "Go, go, Herr Friedmann. Leave me now." He waved at the door, beckoning Franz. "Ah, Dr. Adler. It has been too long. Too long indeed."

Franz shared an empathetic glance with Friedmann as they passed, then bowed his head deeply and said, "Good day, Mr. Ghoya."

"And a good day to you, Dr. Adler," Ghoya said merrily without rising from his seat. "What brings you to my office? Not to request a pass, I hope. I could never grant you one of those." His smile faded and he shook his head grimly. "Not after your daughter was caught smuggling those cigarettes into the Designated Area. Such a foolish thing to do. A serious crime too. You were most fortunate I was so very lenient with you two." He tut-tutted. "Too soft. I'm always too soft on you people."

The skin on Franz's back crawled at the memory of the public flogging he had endured as punishment. "Yes, Mr. Ghoya, you were most benevolent."

Ghoya shrugged disinterestedly. "What brings you to me today?"

"It's the hospital, Mr. Ghoya."

Ghoya squinted, pretending he didn't have a clue what Franz was referring to. Then he snapped his fingers. "Yes, yes. Your hospital for the Jews. What about it?"

Franz shifted from foot to foot. "The soldiers, they closed it. There was a decree."

"Ah, yes, the decree." Ghoya laughed, clearly enjoying his deranged game. "That was my order. Yes, yes. I closed your hospital."

"Mr. Ghoya, the hospital cared for refugees who were ill. Who had nowhere else to turn. We were not expecting any help—"

Ghoya held up a hand to silence him. "You remember last autumn, when our leaders were ambushed by the cowardly Underground?"

Franz thought of the two colonels and admiral who had been rushed to the refugee hospital after being gravely wounded in a nearby Resistance surprise attack. "Yes . . ."

"Did your hospital save our brave leaders then?"

No, we didn't. And for good reason. In the case of Colonel Tanaka, the sadistic former chief of the Kempeitai, Franz's own scalpel had finished the job begun by the assassin's blade. "Those men were gravely ill, Mr. Ghoya. We did what we could, but it's such a basic hospital," Franz said, resisting the urge to speak his mind.

"It's a terrible hospital," Ghoya said dismissively.

"It's all we have in—"

Ghoya brushed away Franz's concerns with a sweep of his hand. "We will use the building for something else. Perhaps storage? I will think of something." Before Franz could respond,

Ghoya went on. "I would hate to see your medical skills go to waste, Dr. Alder."

Franz stiffened.

"Our Imperial Army is fighting on many fronts," Ghoya continued. "Eventually, we will win. Yes, yes, we will. But the cost of victory is high. There are many wounded men. We do not have enough field doctors to care for them all."

The hospital's closure made sudden sense to Franz. "Mr. Ghoya, are you asking me to work for the Japanese army?"

Ghoya jumped to his feet and stormed around the desk. He stopped so close that Franz picked up on the odour of schnitzel on his breath. "*Asking*?" he cried as he raised his open palm, ready to strike. "The King of the Jews does not ask anything of you. He tells you!"

Seconds passed in tense silence. Ghoya's hand still hovered over Franz's head, but when he finally spoke, his tone had calmed. "You will begin immediately."

Franz's mind raced. "I would be honoured to work for the Imperial Army, sir."

Ghoya eyed him skeptically. "Is that so?"

"In my humble opinion, there is an even larger opportunity here."

"What would that be?"

"We already have an operating room," Franz pointed out. "And I have such able assistants. Would it not be even more beneficial if we were to care for your wounded in our little hospital?"

Ghoya scoffed. "The same hospital that could not tend to our honourable officers' wounds?"

"Yes, but—"

"But nothing," Ghoya screamed and flicked his wrist. The sharp slap surprised Franz more than it hurt him. "You will work for us. Under the supervision of a proper Japanese surgeon. Yes, yes. You will!"

Franz lowered his gaze. "As you wish, Mr. Ghoya."

Ghoya turned and sauntered back to his desk, dropping into his chair. He casually reached for a form and began to fill in the blanks. "My men will come for you later today," he said.

"Today?" Franz sputtered. "Sir, my family . . ."

"Are they a distraction to you?" Ghoya flashed another of his crazed grins. "Perhaps it would be best if I relocated them elsewhere?"

The internment camps—or worse! The light-headedness struck again without warning, and Franz reached out to grab hold of the edge of the desk, his legs feeling as though they might buckle.

Still smiling, Ghoya studied Franz's fingers on the desk. "You disagree, Dr. Adler?"

"No." Franz fought off the spell. He pulled his hand from the desk, though his legs still felt rubbery. "My family is fine. They can take care of themselves. No need to relocate them."

"We shall see." Ghoya laughed. "Yes, yes. We shall."

Franz's dizziness abated but dread took its place. He couldn't leave his family so vulnerable. "Mr. Ghoya, I will dedicate myself to caring for the injured soldiers, but the hospital . . ."

"The hospital again?" Ghoya rolled his eyes and glanced from side to side, as though conferring with imaginary colleagues. "It's all this Jew ever thinks about."

"With or without me, refugees will continue to become sick or injured."

"They probably will, yes."

"And that burden will now fall to you, Mr. Ghoya. The King of the Jews. There will be no one else."

"That is life, Dr. Adler. People get sick. People die. Yes, yes. They die all the time."

"And if the cholera returns?" Franz asked. "Then someone will have to control the infection before it spreads through the homes of the Designated Area. What if it spreads beyond? And sickens your own soldiers? And even reaches this office?"

Ghoya sat up straighter. "What are you suggesting, Dr. Adler?"

"My wife, Sunny, is an educated nurse. For basic illnesses, she is almost as competent as I am." In many respects, Franz considered her to be a more capable doctor than himself, but he was desperate not to encourage Ghoya to enlist her as well.

"Your wife? The mongrel woman?" Ghoya squinted. "She could manage this hospital of yours?"

His heart felt incredibly heavy. "Yes, yes she can."

CHAPTER 6

Sunny had always lived in Shanghai. She had hardly ventured beyond the city's borders, leaving Shanghai only for short trips as an adult and twice as a child, when she and her father had visited Hong Kong. Growing up, she had watched, with more than a little pride, as her cosmopolitan city became known as the Paris of the East while most other metropolises withered under the shadow of the Great Depression. Shanghai's skyline had glimmered with new art deco skyscrapers that lined grand avenues such as the riverside Bund and Nanking Road. Celebrities, entrepreneurs and intelligentsia flocked to the city, which vibrated with an around-the-clock vitality that people often compared to New York. However, Sunny also knew too well the city's seedy and dangerous underbelly: the drugs, gambling and prostitution; the rampant crime, both petty and violent; and the simmering pot of conflicting politics and cultures that constantly threatened to boil over. Still, the city had been in its glory in the late 1930s, hitting a zenith that few people, and certainly not Sunny, had recognized at the time.

Now, after six years of war and almost three of complete occupation, Sunny saw Shanghai as a battered shell of its former self: a hobbled old woman, sadder for all the memories of the beautiful star she had once been. Sunny's dilemma had once been deciding what to eat among the abundance of international restaurants or where to go in a city that boasted more shops, parks, theatres and clubs than any other in Asia. But nowadays, simply finding food for her family or a safe route to navigate her day had become a challenge.

There were few places in Shanghai that had been untouched, or undamaged, by years of war. That was what made the Comfort Home so striking in comparison. The renowned brothel was located in the heart of the French Concession, or Frenchtown, in what had once been one of the city's most desirable neighbourhoods. As Sunny walked down the meandering pathway toward the grand, mustard-coloured Spanish villa, which perched on a slight slope, she saw that the grounds were as meticulously maintained as ever. Although the wildflowers had yet to bloom, the magnolias and gingko trees appeared more robust than most of the people on the street around her. The premises were unmarked, but anyone native to the city, not to mention most Japanese officers and many international businessmen before them, would have recognized the Comfort Home for the exclusive bordello it was.

Sunny hurried down to the end of the pathway, where a towering Chinese guard, at least six foot five and weighing over three hundred pounds, stood at the base of the ornate mahogany staircase, arms at his side, wearing a black suit and tie. She threw her arms around his massive chest in a very non-traditional embrace. Sunny had known Ushi since she was a teenager and had come to think of him as a guardian angel to her best friend, Jia-Li. They exchanged a few pleasantries, though Ushi was predictably unforthcoming. Sunny had never heard him utter a complaining or regretful word but she always sensed, behind his stoicism, a sadness that extended beyond his unrequited love for Jia-Li.

Ushi led Sunny up the staircase, through the imposing foyer and into the drawing room, which was furnished with baroque pieces and matching millwork, and smelled of leather and wood polish. Sunny could imagine its original owners, an aristocratic French couple—their sombre portraits still hung on the walls—entertaining elite Shanghailanders here, serving brandy and port after supper, the cigar smoke curling up to the ceiling. The owner, a major in the French army, had lost the family home as a gambling debt to the Green Gang, which had converted the mansion into the city's most successful brothel.

Sunny only had to wait a short while before Jia-Li swept into the room wearing a navy sequined cheongsam cut with a slit almost to the top of her thigh, exposing a glimpse of garter. Her purple eyeshadow and fire-engine-red lipstick had been applied thicker than Sunny had ever before seen. The whole ensemble was too much for Sunny, who at times like these couldn't help but wish her friend had chosen almost any other lifestyle. Despite her years of employment as a prostitute and intermittent drug abuser, Jia-Li was still the most gorgeous person Sunny had ever laid eyes on, and had the charisma to match. Even as Jia-Li neared the age of thirty, with her porcelain skin, magnetic eyes and commanding smile, her presence was arresting.

Jia-Li grabbed Sunny by the shoulders and kissed her lightly on either cheek, leaving behind the scent of cinnamon and tobacco. "What brings you to my humble home, Sister?" she asked in an airy tone.

Home. The word grated. Sunny appreciated that Jia-Li had

nowhere else to turn. She had lost her apartment and her husband four months earlier. Jia-Li and Charlie—the same wounded Resistance leader Ernst had secreted into the city—had fallen in love and hastily married, but Charlie's stay ended tragically when he was discovered and became a Japanese target. Jia-Li had survived, but her apartment had been destroyed and her husband killed in an explosion that he had triggered to facilitate her escape. Still, Sunny cringed at the idea of her best friend considering the brothel home. Jia-Li was supposed to have returned solely to be sheltered with the other fugitives in the basement hideaway, but she had insisted on returning to the life of an escort, over the protests of Sunny and even the madam, Chih-Nii, who normally prized profit over all else.

"I wanted to see you. It's been too long, *bǎo bèi*." Sunny used her best friend's Chinese nickname, which meant "precious." Something in her friend's demeanour discouraged Sunny from blurting out news of the baby, even though she wanted to.

"Yes, visit, lovely," Jia-Li said in the carefree manner that she had adopted in recent months. She grabbed Sunny by the hand and led her over to the chaise longue. They sat down, still holding hands, while Jia-Li casually draped her right leg over her left knee, exposing even more of her thigh. Her eyes held a faraway look, but Sunny was relieved to not see any constriction of her pupils, which would have suggested that her friend had fallen back onto the opium pipe.

"What is new, *bǎo bèi*?" Sunny asked.

"New? Nothing is ever new." Jia-Li laughed heartily. "The one advantage to this life of mine is that every day is exactly like the previous one, *xiǎo hè*." She used Sunny's nickname—"little lotus."

Sunny squeezed her friend's hand. "Honestly, *bǎo bèi*?"

"I am fine, Auntie," Jia-Li teased.

But Sunny saw through the cheery pretense. She had walked with Jia-Li through the Old City in the hours following her husband's death, her anguish so intense that the memory of it still chilled Sunny. Such heartbreak didn't mend in a matter of months, if ever. But Sunny also knew her friend too well to press her. Instead, she just gave her hand a reassuring squeeze. "Good."

"And you, *xiǎo hè*? How is that dashing husband of yours and the rest of the brood? What of all those lost Jews you single-handedly keep alive and well?" Laughing, she tossed a hand skyward. "Honestly, how you manage it all."

"They shut our hospital."

"Of course they did, the *Rìběn guǐzi*." Jia-Li used the Shanghainese pejorative—meaning "Japanese devils"—for the city's occupiers.

"Franz is devastated, *bǎo bèi*."

"Well, what did he expect?"

Sunny frowned. "Expect?"

"If Franz thought it would end any other way, then I'm afraid he's a fool," Jia-Li said dismissively.

"Is that not a little harsh?"

"It's the truth, Sister. Nothing more, nothing less." Her tone was devoid of sympathy. "Shanghai is like a garden that has been deprived of water and sunlight. Everything inside it eventually wilts and dies. Why would Franz think his precious little hospital would fare any differently?"

Sunny pulled her hand free of Jia-Li's. "It wasn't only *his* hospital."

Jia-Li threw an arm around Sunny's shoulder and pulled her in close, cheek to cheek, as though consoling her from a hurt that someone else had levelled. "I know, *xiǎo hè*. It was your hospital too." Sunny began to protest but Jia-Li continued. "And the other doctors and nurses. The Jewish refugees, also. But, surely you must see that it was inevitable? The *Rìběn guĭzi* would never allow something so . . . so constructive to survive."

"No. I suppose not."

They sat in silence, faces touching, for a few moments. "There's something else, *bǎo bèi*."

Jia-Li pulled her head back and arched an eyebrow. "Oh?"

"A baby."

Jia-Li's expression was opaque. "You are pregnant?"

"No. A girl in the neighbourhood. A friend of Hannah's." As Sunny described the birth, she realized how much she already missed the baby in the hour since she had left him.

"You're planning to keep this child, aren't you?" Jia-Li said quietly.

Sunny felt her face heating. "Only until I can find a suitable orphanage or another home to—"

"Who do you think you are fooling, Sister?" Jia-Li snapped. "You are planning to raise him as your own. I see it in your eyes."

Sunny knew it was hopeless to try to hide it from her friend. She leaned in to embrace her, but Jia-Li stood up quickly.

Sunny looked up at her. "You would be his auntie, *bǎo bèi*. If . . ."

"If what?"

"Franz doesn't want us to keep him."

"He told you so?"

"Not in so many words, no. But I can tell."

"No matter." Jia-Li folded her arms across her chest. "Franz will not be able to resist you. He never can."

Sunny didn't know how to interpret her friend's detached tone, but she was bursting inside and needed to share it with someone. "I want to name him Joey." She had thought immediately of the young Chinese man who had assisted Simon in setting up the hospital and had helped in innumerable other ways before being killed during a raid by the local Nazis.

"Why not?" Jia-Li said. "The other Joey was completely devoted to you."

"Such a good man he was," Sunny murmured. "Well, hardly much more than a boy, really."

"Good, bad, it doesn't really matter. He is dead. That's all you can say about him now," Jia-Li cried with sudden ferocity.

Sunny jumped to her feet. "That's not fair, *bǎo bèi*. Not to Joey, or to his memory."

"Joey was just another country orphan. One of millions." Jia-Li waved away the objection. "He died for you, trying to protect that hospital for Jews that neither of you had any business being involved in. And for what, in the end? To have some other unwanted baby named after him?"

Sunny bristled at the words but said nothing. Normally, Jia-Li had an endless capacity to share in Sunny's happiness, regardless of her own circumstances. Sunny had never seen such bitterness in her friend, not even during the worst of her opium withdrawals.

They stared at each for a moment, then Jia-Li's whole face seemed to transform into a loving smile. "Oh, *xiǎo hè*, you know I would love to chat longer, but duty calls."

Disoriented by her best friend's volatility and hurtful words, Sunny simply nodded. "Yes, I should let you go."

Jia-Li wrapped Sunny in another embrace, planting kisses on each of her cheeks. "We will talk more soon, no? Best wishes for you and little darling Joey."

Dazed, Sunny followed Jia-Li out of the room and into the corridor. At the far end, an older Japanese officer stood flanked by two younger soldiers. Sunny's heart leapt into her throat at the sight of the white bands encircling their upper arms, marking them as Kempeitai officers. She froze, terrified that they might somehow know that Jia-Li had been Charlie's wife, which would mean certain execution.

But rather than hiding her face or turning away, Jia-Li squealed in delight and cried "*Bà!*"—"Daddy!"—as she raced toward the senior officer.

Sunny spun away, unable to watch. How could Jia-Li even feign affection for those Kempeitai monsters after all they had done to her and Charlie?

As Sunny reached the front door, a familiar singsong voice called to her from behind. She inhaled an overpowering floral perfume as she turned to face the fleshy form of Chih-Nii, who was powdered and rouged, and wore an impossibly bright and ostentatiously flowing gown. Chih-Nii looked like the epitome of a pulp fiction madam, a role she inhabited deliberately and with gusto. Sunny knew that behind the facade was of one of Shanghai's most shrewd business people, a person who encouraged others to make the mistake of underestimating her.

"Ah, Soon Yi. My exotic little buttercup." The madam gave Sunny a quick once-over, then shook her head in exaggerated disappointment. "Oh, how you could have thrived in Chih-Nii's garden."

Sunny hugged the other woman, feeling her generous form through her silk dress. "How are you, Mama?" she asked.

"I do what I can to get by," Chih-Nii said happily as she picked at a flake of lipstick at the corner of her mouth. "The Comfort

Home is needed more than ever now. War or not, people have to live."

"Yes, they do," Sunny said, thinking of little Joey at home.

"You were visiting my special flower?"

"Yes."

Chih-Nii tilted her head. "And?"

"Jia-Li is not right. Not right at all."

"Not at all," Chih-Nii agreed.

"It's not the opium pipe again, is it, Mama?"

Chih-Nii sighed. "If only it were as simple as the pipe. We could fix that, like we have done many times before."

Sunny nodded. "But not a broken heart?"

Chih-Nii considered it, then shook her head. "It's not a broken heart either. Those heal too."

"What is it, then?"

"She can hide it from almost everyone, can't she? Behind all that cheerful bluster. But Mama sees right through it." The madam's voice caught in her throat. "My special flower has died inside."

CHAPTER 7

Franz had heard his wife speak Mandarin and Shanghainese often enough that he could tell one language from the other based on her inflection alone, but never before had he heard her sing in Chinese. Sunny was pacing back and forth in front of the couch, cradling the baby, who fussed gently in her arms. She sang a soothing, unfamiliar lullaby in a tinkling melody that Franz always associated with Chinese music.

Sunny looked up to Franz with a small smile but didn't stop singing or moving. After another minute or so, the baby stilled in her arms and her song faded. She stepped over to Franz almost on tiptoes and brushed her lips over his before twisting her torso to allow him a better view of the sleeping baby.

Franz still could remember those long evenings in Vienna when he had paced endlessly with Hannah, bouncing her in his arms while humming lullabies and praying that she would exhaust herself from crying. At the time, he had attributed Hannah's fits of colic to the absence of a mother in her life, but looking back he wondered if maybe his daughter had somehow detected the fog of grief that had enshrouded him in those months following Hilde's death. Ever since, Franz had always found a measure of contentment, even relief, in the sight of a sleeping baby. Until today.

"I would like to call him Joey," Sunny said in a hushed voice, her eyes searching his for approval. "Perhaps Joey Kun-Li Adler, after my father as well."

Franz tried to convey an enthusiasm he didn't feel. "That would be fitting, yes."

Sunny was too perceptive to be fooled. She rotated her body away, offering him only her shoulder in profile. "How was your meeting with Mr. Ghoya?" she asked distantly.

Franz reached out and touched her upper arm. "He is considering letting us open the hospital again."

She looked over her shoulder at him. "If?"

"If you run it, Sunny."

"Me? Ghoya requested that I run the hospital? That makes no sense, Franz."

He averted his gaze. "Where's Hannah?"

"Out with that boy Herschel."

He sighed. "The one who fills her head with all that Zionism nonsense?"

"He's a sweet boy."

"Where did they go?"

"The market, I believe. Hannah said she would be home to help with supper. Esther and Jakob should be back by then too."

He massaged his temples distractedly, struggling to conceal his anxiety. "So she still could be hours?"

Sunny's face clouded with alarm. "What is it, Franz? What did Ghoya tell you?"

He squeezed her arm and gently directed her to the couch. "Come. Sit with me."

They sat side by side. Franz remained still, but Sunny rocked back and forth in her seat, even though the newborn was already fast asleep. Her tempo increased as he recounted his conversation with Ghoya.

"Where does he intend for you to work?" she demanded.

"He didn't say."

"Surely it will be the Shanghai General? Where you operated on General Nogomi's stomach ulcer? I hear they still send many of their wounded there. Maybe Nogomi himself even suggested it."

"Probably the Shanghai General, yes," he muttered.

She placed her free hand on his thigh and squeezed it. "You don't think they might send you somewhere outside Shanghai?"

It was precisely what Franz had been wondering ever since Ghoya had announced that the soldiers would be coming for him. Why else would he require an escort? Certainly not to go to the Shanghai General, which was less than a mile outside the ghetto's border. "I have no idea where he will post me."

Staring into his eyes, Sunny tightened her grip on his thigh. "Franz . . ."

He ran his fingers along the smooth contour of her cheek. It occurred to him again that she often looked most beautiful in troubled moments. Her face was a delicate fusion of Western sharpness and Eastern delicacy: her straight nose and prominent cheekbones, inherited from her American mother, complemented by the soft milky complexion that was pure Chinese. Her almond-coloured eyes had a speckled texture that Franz loved, and that made them so expressive at times like this. "Ghoya probably means to keep me somewhere nearby." He reassured her with a forced laugh. "We refugees are dying off at an alarming rate, and the 'King of the Jews' would be loath to lose another subject in the ghetto, particularly one he loves to terrorize as much as me."

Sunny's expression held fast. "What if he takes you away from me . . . from the family?"

Ignoring the ache in his chest, Franz leaned forward over the sleeping child to kiss Sunny. She met his mouth hungrily, her tongue coursing along the inner contours of his lips. Franz reluctantly pulled free. "Ghoya was clear that I cannot set so much as one foot inside the hospital, Sunny."

She frowned. "What about Dr. Freiberg? Or Dr. Goldmann?"

He laughed sadly. "You would have a psychoanalyst or a skin specialist run our hospital?"

"They are doctors at least."

"And you are a surgeon, Sunny."

"No. I'm a nurse."

He shook his head. "Papers or not, your father trained you to be a doctor. And I trained you to be a surgeon. You operate better than most I've seen. That is not flattery either. It's the truth. You are the only one who can manage the hospital."

Sunny eyed him questioningly for another moment before sighing. "I will do what I can."

"Thank you." He reached for her free hand, caressing her fingers. "And if they do send me somewhere outside the city, the others . . ."

"I will take care of the family." She swallowed. "We will all still be right here when you come home."

He glanced down at the newborn in her arm and then back up at her.

She met his gaze with gentle defiance. "Joey too."

Franz motioned around the cramped quarters. "Darling, is this really the best place for him? To be raised in the ghetto? Surely, in

Frenchtown or the International Settlement, one of the churches still must run an orphanage of some—"

"No," she snapped, hugging the baby closer to her chest. "This is the best place for Joey. Right here."

"Are you thinking with your head or your heart now?"

Her hand went limp in his. "Both."

"Sunny, I want this for you. For us." He sighed. "But of all the terrible times to assume such responsibility, now when Ghoya is about to—"

Three heavy knocks rattled the door, cutting him off midsentence. There was no mistaking the sound. His mouth went dry and his neck tightened just as they had back in Vienna on the afternoon the SS had pounded so roughly at his door that he wondered if it might fly off its hinges.

Sunny leaned in toward him just as the baby stirred in her arms. He could feel her shoulders shaking. And the pain of his broken rib was no match for the deeper ache inside his chest.

* * *

The soldiers at the door had been unusually patient. Neither had laid a hand on Franz, and they had even allowed a moment for a tearful goodbye with Sunny. The older of the two was clearly in charge. He smelled of hair oil and spoke passable English but had said very little after escorting Franz outside. He hadn't uttered a word since the military vehicle had pulled away from the curb. When Franz tried to inquire after their destination, the man didn't acknowledge the question.

As they turned onto Chapoo Road, Franz spotted the sign for the Shanghai General Hospital through the window ahead. Flickers of relief settled over him. As long he remained in Shanghai, he could handle whatever Ghoya demanded of him. But the vehicle didn't slow down. Instead, they flew past the hospital's entrance. Franz turned to the older escort, but the cool look in the man's eyes was enough to crush any hope that the driver might have missed his stop.

They headed west down Great Western Road, away from the centre of town. Franz's fingers drummed faster against his thigh with every tree and telephone pole that passed by the car window. Each pothole that shook the car rattled him further. *I'll never see them again,* he thought.

As they neared the outskirts of the city, the car slowed. Franz resisted the spark of hope he felt, reluctant to have it ripped away again. Craning his neck to peer out the window, he could see the lavish columns and arches of a grand building. He hadn't seen the structure in well over two years, but he recognized it immediately. He had worked in the Country Hospital from the first week he had arrived in Shanghai, in December 1938, until the day the Japanese attacked Pearl Harbor.

His pulse slowed as the car rolled to a stop and they exited the vehicle. From the outside, the Country Hospital looked much as it had on his last visit. He knew the art deco marvel had been built in the mid-1920s, primarily to cater to wealthy Shanghailanders, the expats and tourists who used to flood into the cosmopolitan city. While the surroundings had suffered, the hospital still maintained its inviting elegance.

However, stepping through the main door, as he had done so many times before, provided no sense of nostalgia or even comfort. Despite having once been the youngest professor of surgery in the history of the University of Vienna, Franz had spent his days at the Country Hospital functioning at the level of an intern, condescended to and bullied by the chief of surgery, Dr. Samuel Reuben. Although he had complained to Sunny about his mistreatment at the time, as Franz glanced around the spacious foyer, now filled with uniformed Japanese, he had little doubt that he might soon be longing for those days under Reuben's reign.

The hospital still smelled faintly of iodine and sterility. The foyer's dark wooden furniture, wainscoting and crown mouldings provided a familiar sombre air. And yet Franz barely recognized the place. Gone were all the white nurses, clerks and wealthy Shanghailander women who came as volunteers and, according to the world-weary matron, were far more nuisance than help. Now the faces all belonged to Japanese men, most in military uniform—patients and staff alike.

Franz's two escorts ushered him through the waiting area, past a stretcher bearing a man whose entire body was encased from the collarbones down in plaster cast, a white bar holding his legs apart. Franz was whisked down the hallway and onto the men's surgical ward, where he had once spent so much time tending to Reuben's post-operative patients. The twenty-five beds were still arranged in a horseshoe shape around the open, high-ceilinged ward. Every bed was occupied. More than half of the patients had their heads bandaged, some so that the faces were beyond recognition.

Franz was guided to a bed in the far corner, where a balding Japanese doctor in a lab coat was leaning over a stretcher. The patient was wrapped in so much bandaging that he resembled a mummy from a horror movie. All that Franz could see of the patient were his impassive eyes and an area of blistered, blackened skin over his shoulder. He lay absolutely still as the doctor used a scalpel to dissect away layers of the burned skin.

Across the bed, a woman in a British-style nurse's uniform was peeling dressings from the man's upper arm, exposing more damaged flesh. With flaming red hair that spilled out from under her cap, a pale complexion and prominent freckles, the nurse made as much of an impression as her wrapped patient. She made fleeting eye contact with Franz, offering him a hint of a smile, before returning her attention to her work.

Franz's escorts bowed to the Japanese doctor and addressed him in a quiet, deferential voice. Without taking his eyes off the patient, the doctor grunted a few words in Japanese. The soldiers backed away, leaving Franz at the bedside.

"You speak English, I hope," the doctor said as he peeled away another fold of dead skin.

"I do, yes, sir." Franz bowed deeply at the waist.

"You are German."

"I am Austrian."

The man's shoulders rose and fell indifferently. "There is no Austria."

"Not anymore, no."

"You are a Jew. Your citizenship has been revoked." His accent sounded American. "So you are nothing."

"I believe I am considered a stateless refugee, sir."

"Exactly." The doctor snorted. "A nothing."

Sensing that silence was the best response, Franz lowered his eyes and watched as the Japanese doctor debrided more dead flesh. He couldn't help but admire the man's fluid and economical technique—he was clearly a gifted surgeon. The patient remained still throughout, but now his eyes, fixed on Franz's, lit up with a glimmer of curiosity. He appeared to be in no pain—all the nerve endings on his shoulder must have been burned away. Franz offered him a consoling smile.

The doctor straightened to face Franz. "All right, you have seen enough." The man was tall by Japanese standards, at least Franz's height. With bags under his eye, sun splotches on his cheeks and lines criss-crossing his brow, his gaunt face looked weathered. Franz would have estimated him to be somewhere between fifty and sixty years old, but he couldn't even be certain of that. The doctor turned the scalpel, blade outward, toward Franz in a vaguely threatening gesture. "Let's see if you are capable of finishing this." He snapped the fingers of his free hand at the nurse. "Find him gloves."

"Yes, Captain Suzuki," she replied, solving one mystery for Franz as she hurried over to the main desk.

Captain Suzuki glared at Franz. "I did not ask for your help, and I do not want it," he grumbled, waving the scalpel menacingly. "Am I clear?"

CHAPTER 8

Herschel had pestered Hannah relentlessly before she finally agreed to accompany him to Rabbi Hiltmann's "special meeting" after school at the synagogue. She knew how dimly her father viewed Zionism and, rather than try to explain that she was attending as a favour to a friend, Hannah had told her stepmother that she was going to the market. Sunny had been too preoccupied by the baby wriggling in her arms to even question it.

Fewer than half the seats inside the spacious auditorium of the Ohel Moishe Synagogue were filled. The ragtag audience consisted of zealous youths like Herschel, along with a few adult refugees, many of whom were elderly and seated alone. Uninspired, Hannah had begun to regret her decision to come when Rabbi Hiltmann rose to speak.

The rabbi stood silently at the bimah—the raised platform at the front of the synagogue, meant for Torah readings—for what felt like minutes, stroking his shaggy grey beard and staring out beyond the audience as though completely lost in thought. "What if God *sent* Hitler to us for a reason?" he finally asked of no one in particular. Although his tone was soothing, the effect was anything but. All around the room, heads snapped to attention. "I've heard people suggest that God might have allowed that *teiwl*, that *farseenisch*"—he used the Yiddish words for *devil* and *monster*—"to prosper as he has in order to test our faith. Perhaps He did." Hiltmann lapsed into another long pause. "But surely, after the past three thousand years, even God must be tiring of testing our faith. The razing of Solomon's glorious temple. The diasporas—our people expelled first from the Holy Lands and then later from England, France and Spain. And the pogroms—so many pogroms—with the lootings, the beatings and the slaughter." He sighed and then added rhetorically, "How much more can one people's faith be tested?"

The rabbi cast his gaze around the room, momentarily locking eyes with Hannah. Despite not being particularly tall or physically imposing, the grey-haired cleric commanded her attention. She felt as though he were speaking only to her. "What if Hitler and his Nazi henchmen represent not another in a long series of challenges but instead, as the English might say, a call to arms?"

Chaim Weissbaum, a pimply boy in the grade above Hannah raised his hand tentatively. "You mean God wants us to fight back, Rabbi?"

"Exactly, Chaim." Hiltmann nodded approvingly. "What if God is teaching us a lesson? A very painful lesson." He counted with his fingers. "The Egyptians, the Babylonians, the Romans, the Spanish and now the very worst of them all, the Nazis. How many more times will we abandon our homes to wander the face of the earth the moment some cruel king or self-anointed emperor takes issue with us?" He raised a hand skyward. "Perhaps God is telling us that enough is enough. To stop cowering. To stand up for ourselves. To accept no more diasporas." His voice didn't rise in volume or pitch yet was now inflamed with passion. "The Torah teaches us that we are his Treasured People. The sons and daughters of Israel." He paused again to scan the rapt faces in the room. "What if God is telling us that it is time to return home?"

The rabbi continued to speak—articulately and persuasively—without referencing any notes. He argued for the need for a modern Jewish homeland based on the biblical borders of ancient Judea, the lands east and west of the Jordan River once known as Eretz Yisrael. Although the themes were familiar enough, Hannah found his enthusiasm contagious. As the rabbi spoke, Hannah could picture the lands they would cultivate out of desert and the shining new cities they would build.

"We will, of course, try to find a peaceful resolution with the British," Hiltmann said. "We will appeal to their well-developed sense of fair play and justice." He shook his head gravely. "But we cannot wait indefinitely for them to allow us to return home. This is not merely a matter of convenience or even our Jewish birthright. No. It is our obligation—our *destiny*—to reclaim the land God has always intended for us."

* * *

As Hannah filed out of the synagogue alongside Herschel, she was the one who couldn't stop talking about the sermon. "The rabbi is absolutely right. What better time to act? How can we possibly wait for things to get worse?"

Herschel's face broke into a huge lopsided smile. "This is what I've been telling you, Hannah."

"But the rabbi tells it just a little better."

Herschel's laugh didn't fully conceal his wounded pride. Hannah reached for his hand, and the traces of hurt disappeared from his face. They walked hand in hand for several blocks, in shy, happy silence. Eventually, Herschel cleared his throat and said, "Your father, he's an influential man in the community."

"I've never really thought of Papa that way."

"People admire your father, Hannah. Zeyde says he is the best doctor in all of Shanghai."

"I have heard others say so too," she said with more than a touch of pride.

"If your father were to attend our meetings, Hannah. To support the cause—"

She shook her head. "He won't."

Herschel slowed and pulled her to a stop. "Why do you say that?"

"Papa has no time for Zionism. He thinks it's a hopeless fantasy. An idea that could be dangerous for the ghetto."

"Dangerous? How could a Jewish homeland be dangerous for us?"

"He told me that, back in Vienna, the Zionists used to incite anti-Semitism. The goys saw it as another example of Jews wanting more, a slap in the face to other Austrians, who had given them a home and citizenship. Papa worries that the Japanese might feel threatened by it too." She lowered her voice, even though no one could hear them. "You know how paranoid they can be."

Herschel reached out and took her other hand. She flinched, self-conscious about her left hand, but she didn't pull away. "You must convince him that it's not so."

"I can't, Herschel. It's hopeless."

"Like Rabbi Hiltmann says, if we cannot convince our own people, how can we possibly convince the British or anyone else that we deserve our own land?"

Hannah enjoyed the feel of his grip. She doubted anything she could say would sway her father's opinion, but she didn't want to disappoint Herschel. "I'll speak to Papa."

He flashed a grateful grin. "Good. That's very good."

They stood facing one another in the warm spring breeze, their hands intertwined. She wondered if he might lean in to kiss her—she hoped he might—but he just stood there. Finally, she broke the awkward silence. "I left a book at school. I have to stop there on the way home."

"I'll come too." He looked away. "If you want me to."

She let go with her left hand and pulled him along with her right. Even at their sauntering pace, they reached the Kadoorie School within a few minutes. The front door of the converted warehouse—the school had been originally funded by the Kadoorie family and other wealthy Jewish Shanghailanders—was locked, so they walked around the side toward the back door. As they were rounding the building, Hannah heard hissing and popping sounds, but it was Herschel who identified their source. "A radio," he whispered, slowing and pulling Hannah to a stop with him.

Suddenly, someone was blocking their path. Hannah would have recognized Avraham Perlmann—or "Avi," as everyone called him—from his swagger alone. She had always thought of the boy as a bully, but she still had a bit of a soft spot for him. As the shortest in the class, Avi seemed desperate to prove himself; Hannah empathized with his need to overcome a shortcoming.

Avi looked from Herschel to Hannah and back. "What are you two doing here?" he demanded. "You're not spying on us, are you?"

Herschel held up his palms. "No, Avi. We've only come to pick up a book."

Another of their classmates appeared behind Avi. "Easy, Avi," said Fritsch Herzberg, known by everyone as Freddy.

"They got no business here," Avi muttered. "They're just snooping."

Freddy clapped the shorter boy on the shoulder. "They're friends, remember?" He spoke English with his usual feigned American accent and in a style he seemed to have lifted directly from Hollywood films. "Hiya, Hersch." He turned to Hannah with a smile and a wink. "Good to see you, as always, Banana."

Hannah felt her heart speed up as a flush crawled over her face. She hated herself for responding to his charm, thinking of how completely she had fallen under Freddy's spell the year before. She had only snapped out of her crush after she was caught smuggling cigarettes into the ghetto for his father to sell. Since the terrible incident, which had resulted in her father's flogging, Freddy had hurt Hannah further by treating her with the kind of polite friendliness usually reserved for a distant relative or a meaningless acquaintance.

Now, though, Freddy eyed Hannah thoughtfully before he thumbed toward the grounds behind him. "Want to see something neat?" he asked her.

Herschel, whose command of English was minimal, turned to Hannah, confused. "Neat?"

"*Interessant*," Hannah translated into German.

"Why the hell would we show them?" Avi demanded.

"You won't be disappointed," Freddy said, ignoring Avi's protests as he turned back.

Herschel followed Freddy, who moved with the easy grace of an athlete. Hannah was reminded again of how dissimilar the two boys were. She followed them to a small clearing within the shrubs behind the school.

"Look at *that.*" Herschel pointed to a radio that was perched on an old blanket in the middle of the clearing.

Hannah had seen wirelesses in homes in the ghetto, but what distinguished this piece of equipment was its mouthpiece transmitter. It was one thing to listen to the banned Voice of America broadcasts but a far more serious offence to transmit over the radio. She knew that the Japanese would consider it tantamount to espionage, a crime that always ended in execution.

Avi jabbed a finger again in Herschel's face. "Not a damn soul, you understand me, Zunder? Not a damn soul."

Freddy pushed away Avi's hand. "Of course they're not going to tell anyone. They are part of this now. Aren't you?"

His tone sent shivers down Hannah's spine.

"Is it real, Freddy?" Herschel asked in awe. "Can you really transmit messages with it?"

Freddy nodded. "To about fifty miles away, give or take."

"Where did you get it, Freddy?" Herschel asked.

"It was lying around home," he said vaguely.

Hannah had heard rumours that the Herzbergs had recently been smuggling more than just cigarettes into the ghetto. Word was they were sneaking everything from kosher wine to typewriters past the guards at the ghetto checkpoints. The Herzbergs, like the Adlers, had been banned from leaving the ghetto after Freddy's father was caught fencing jewellery in Frenchtown. Hannah had no idea who their new couriers were, but she didn't doubt the rumours. After all, Freddy wore new clothes to school and, even more remarkably, always seemed to carry a lunch.

"What are you going to do with it?" Hannah asked.

"It's hard for me to slip out of the ghetto these days." Freddy chuckled. "But I've still got friends all over Shanghai."

"You mean you would use it like a telephone?" Herschel asked incredulously. "Isn't that dangerous?"

Avi snickered. "When was the last time you had any kind of reliable telephone service in this rotten town, Zunder?"

Ignoring Avi, Hannah turned to Freddy. "Is it really worth the risk?"

"Sure, why not?" Flashing another devil-may-care smile, he was the picture of teenaged bravado. "Besides, Banana, don't you think I'd make a dashing spy?"

CHAPTER 9

"*Ach*, you could drop Franz into the heart of a volcano, and he would make it out without so much as a singe." Ernst swirled a cigarette over his head to punctuate his point.

It was a game attempt to make light, but Sunny could see that his jocularity was forced. Since she had arrived, Ernst hadn't stopped smoking or pacing the cramped living room, brushing past the canvases that leaned against almost every square inch of the apartment's lower wall space.

In contrast, Simon Lehrer couldn't have been less animated. He stood at the lone dirt-streaked window, arms hanging limply at his sides and his gaze fixed on the street below. Sunny had first met the gregarious New Yorker before the war, when he was establishing the hospital for refugees. He had always seemed so carefree and youthful, someone who could find humour and joy in any situation. Even on her recent visits, he had been full of optimism at the prospect of a Japanese defeat and about his plans to whisk his family home to New York. But today he looked so different, as though the year of being a fugitive, kept apart from his wife and young son, had shrunk him, not only physically—his shoulders were now stooped and his face sunken, accentuating his hawk nose—but also in manner, which was unusually subdued.

"Well?" Ernst shook the cigarette demandingly at Sunny.

She inhaled the oil-paint fumes and cigarette smoke. "Well, what?"

"How are we going to bring Franz home?"

"Bring him home?" Sunny echoed in disbelief.

Ernst tossed his long hair away from his forehead. "We can't simply abandon him to some horrid little Japanese hospital in the middle of God knows where."

"What can we possibly do?" she said. "I don't know even know where they've taken him."

Simon turned away from the window. His gaze fell to the baby sleeping in Sunny's arms, and he mustered a small grin. Simon had been crestfallen when she arrived carrying Joey instead of his son, but he hadn't commented or complained. "Ghoya," he said.

"What about him?" Sunny asked.

"Ghoya sent Franz away. He could just as easily bring him back."

Sunny shook off the glimmer of hope. There was no substance to any of this talk. "Why would he do that?"

Simon shrugged. "If Ghoya thought he needed Franz back in the ghetto for some reason, then, believe me, the son of a bitch would bring him back. In a heartbeat."

Ernst nodded, motioning to Simon with his cigarette while addressing Sunny. "Is there any sense to this? What would motivate Ghoya?"

"Maybe some kind of medical emergency?" Simon suggested. "Something only Franz can fix?"

Sunny stared at her two friends. "What are you suggesting?"

Simon raised an eyebrow. "If Ghoya were to be seriously injured . . ."

"Natürlich!" Ernst clapped his hands. "Something requiring surgery. Something only Franz could repair."

Simon's eyes found Sunny's. Momentarily, she saw a violent intensity that was unusual for her gentle friend. "Franz did a bang-up job fixing you after that sailor stabbed you."

"Are you saying we should ambush Ghoya?" she asked in disbelief.

"Why not?" Simon said flatly.

"Impossible." Sunny shook her head vehemently. "Absolutely impossible."

Ernst sighed. "*Ja,* this might not be the most practical approach."

"We owe it to Franz to try something," Simon said.

They fell into silence. Simon turned back to the window. Ernst exhaled plumes of smoke as he studied the ceiling, lost in thought. Sunny gently rocked Joey, asleep in her lap.

"Don't forget," Simon spoke up, his back still turned to them. "We know where Ghoya eats lunch, right? Every day at that Café Aaronsohn. Like clockwork."

"Enough, Simon," Sunny sputtered. "We're not going to ambush the man!"

Simon glanced over his shoulder at her. "What if we poison him instead?"

"For what possible purpose?"

"None, I suppose." Simon paused. "Unless you could convince Ghoya that it was his gall bladder, or appendix, acting up."

Ernst patted his pockets, searching frantically for a fresh cigarette. "There must be such a poison, no?"

"There are some that would cause vomiting and cramping," Sunny said. A few possibilities came immediately to mind. "That's the easy part. But if he were to see another doctor—a Japanese one—they would never be fooled."

Simon glanced from Ernst to Sunny before turning his attention once again to the window.

Ernst laughed, clearly recognizing the impracticalities of the far-fetched scheme. "Back to the drawing board, then, is it?" he said.

As desperate as Sunny was to try anything to help her husband, poisoning Ghoya wasn't the answer. Still, she felt so overwhelmed by gratitude for her friends' support that tears began to roll down her cheeks.

Ernst laid a hand lightly on her shoulder. "We'll think of something. You'll see."

She reached up and squeezed his hand. "Thank you, Ernst. You too, Simon," she choked out as she wiped her eyes.

Simon craned his neck for a better view of the street.

"What is it, Simon?" she asked.

Ernst answered for his roommate. "Those Nazis must be passing," he sighed. "Baron von Puttkamer and his motley crew. Simon watches for them night and day. Like a dog at the window waiting for his master to return."

Simon paid no attention to the artist and instead consulted his wristwatch. "Three o'clock. Could practically set my watch by that creep."

"Leave them be, Simon," Ernst said. "They're merely overgrown children. Parading around in laughable uniforms with their ridiculous titles. Playing war while the real soldiers fight. The fools are as harmless as they are pointless."

"Harmless?" Simon spun from the window, his cheeks suddenly

blotchy. "Last Hanukkah—on Christmas Day!—when von Puttkamer and his cronies came within a hair's breadth of blowing up the synagogue and the hospital—was that harmless too?"

"And Joey," Sunny added.

"Yeah, Joey," Simon said. His former protegé, the baby's namesake, had died protecting the refugee hospital from the Nazi saboteurs. "They murdered the poor kid in cold blood."

Ernst held up his hands in surrender. "Perhaps not harmless. But most certainly pointless. Even they are not stupid enough to attack the ghetto again."

Simon resumed his watch at the window. "If you just got me a rifle, Ernst, I could do the rest."

"And by *the rest* you mean shoot up the street and kill no one but the odd stray dog or unfortunate coolie?"

"I know my way around a rifle," Simon said matter-of-factly. "I used to hunt squirrels on my uncle's farm in Upstate New York."

"The great American hunter, of course. I pity any goose-stepping squirrel who dares to enter our street." Ernst looked over at Sunny. "If he fires a single shot, every soldier in the vicinity will be here instantly."

Repositioning the baby under her arm, Sunny rose and joined Simon at the window. She wrapped an arm around his chest, feeling nothing but ribs. "It would be suicide, Simon."

"Maybe it would be worth it," Simon muttered.

She rubbed his back. "Not to Esther or Jakob, it wouldn't."

Simon stared out the window for a while longer before he turned to her, his face lighting up with the warmest smile she had seen from him in a while. He held his hands out to Joey. "Could I hold him, Sunny?"

* * *

The sun had disappeared behind a canopy of ominous grey clouds, making Germantown seem even more menacing than usual. Swastikas flapped from windowsills and flagpoles. Men marched about in uniforms of varying colours and styles, some wearing the distinctive brown jodhpurs and high black boots that Sunny had once found comical. Not anymore.

Most of the passersby ignored Sunny. The ones who acknowledged her did so with cold disdain or open sneers. As she hurried along the street, she kept her head down and Joey nestled against her chest. Aside from the uneasiness she felt in the hostile neighbourhood, she was also in a rush to get the baby home. He was squirming more now, and his plaintive cry told her that he was hungry. She prayed that Esther would be home and ready to feed him.

She rounded a corner and came to a jerking halt as two hands gripped her roughly by the shoulders. She looked up into the eyes of the man she had almost bumped into and froze, recognizing the brawny Korean who was Baron Jesco von Puttkamer's bodyguard.

"Watch out," the man snapped in English, squeezing her arms hard before letting go.

"Most solly, mister, most solly," Sunny said, falling into an accented pidgin English and averting her eyes.

"Clumsy Chink," the bodyguard grunted.

Sunny stared at her feet, desperately hoping he would lose interest. Realizing von Puttkamer had to be nearby, she involuntarily pictured him, tall and icily handsome with perfectly coiffed salt-and-pepper hair and intrusive eyes. She prayed he wouldn't recognize her. The last time she had seen von Puttkamer, she had been disguised as a street walker—heavily powdered and rouged, wearing a gaudy cheongsam—in order to deliver a written message from Franz, part of the fallout of the Nazi's failed Christmas Day synagogue bombing.

"Let me see her face, Yung Min," von Puttkamer said pleasantly.

Her stomach plummeted, but she pretended not to understand his German and kept her eyes fixed on the ground.

"Look at the baron," Yung Min snarled in English.

Sunny slowly raised her eyes. Von Puttkamer was behind his bodyguard, standing next to a middle-aged man she didn't recognize. Thin, with a pale and veiny face, the man wore a grey SS uniform; its ornately detailed emblems marked him as a high-ranking officer.

Yung Min glanced over his shoulder to von Puttkamer. "This is the one who came to your office last winter, Baron. The girl with the letter."

Von Puttkamer studied Sunny's face. "*Ach so*, it is you, isn't it, Fräulein?" he said pleasantly in German.

Sunny turned her upper body, moving Joey away from his line of sight. "My no savvy," she said in pidgin, continuing to play the part of an uneducated local.

"Yes, you are the one. I'm sure of it." Von Puttkamer's smile faltered. "You came with a letter from that doctor."

The SS officer went rigid beside him. "Not that miserable Jew who killed Hans?"

"Indeed," von Puttkamer said, motioning toward Sunny. "This one even brought me photographs of the brave lad lying in the snow with his throat slit."

Sunny's pulse hammered in her ears. Shaking her head wildly, she forced herself to maintain the act of a confused peasant. "My no savvy."

A thin smile returned to von Puttkamer's lips. "How is the good doctor, Fräulein?"

"I don't believe she speaks German, Baron," Yung Min said.

"Oh, I wouldn't be so convinced," von Puttkamer said, then switched to English. "Tell me, young lady, do you understand anything beyond that pidgin squawk?"

Sunny tilted her head from side to side. "My savvy little."

"Wonderful," von Puttkamer said, lazily running his gaze over her. She felt acutely self-conscious in her basic navy dress, as though she were standing naked in front of him. "You certainly are dressed differently from the last time I saw you."

She waved her free hand in front of her. "Solly, sir, my no savvy."

"Of course not." The baron sighed heavily. "Where are my manners?" He held a hand out to the scowling SS officer beside him. "Allow me to introduce Sturmbannführer Huber. Major Huber is the Gestapo chief here in Shanghai. He would be most interested in discussing poor Hans's fate with you and Dr. Adler."

"What are you saying to her?" Huber demanded in German.

"That you would like a word with Dr. Adler."

Huber scoffed. "More than just a word, let me tell you."

Von Puttkamer turned back to Sunny and spoke in English again. "Will you pass a message to the doctor for me?"

"I no talkee doctor no more," Sunny blurted. "He pay me. I catchee my baby. No more see doctor."

With surprising agility for a man of his size, von Puttkamer darted around Yung Min. He stopped inches away from Sunny, looming above her and blocking the view of the sky. The scent of his cologne filled her nostrils. When he spoke, his smile was gone. His eyes bored into her. "I think you are still in very close contact with Dr. Adler." He snorted at Joey. "I wouldn't be the least surprised if that mongrel baby of yours wasn't his as well."

Fighting back a shudder, Sunny shrugged as if all his insults were lost on her.

"You tell that doctor of yours that our business is not finished. Nowhere close," he shouted, spraying her face with spittle. "*Verstehen Sie?* You understand?"

CHAPTER 10

According to the clock on the far wall of the ward, the patient died at 5:06 a.m. Given the severity of the man's burns, the only surprise to Franz was how long he had survived. The man hadn't closed his eyes all night. They had remained open even in death, until Franz brushed them closed. Franz had never learned anything about the man: not his name, not his rank and certainly not how he had acquired his burns. Franz couldn't speak any Japanese beyond basic words such as *arigatō, kon'nichi wa* and *sayonara,* but it wouldn't have mattered if he could. The soldier had never uttered a word, even though he had remained alert until the end. At times, he had appeared curious about Franz's presence, but most of the time, he seemed simply resigned. Franz respected his dignified stoicism, but he had a more practical reason for wanting the patient to hang on, at least until six o'clock, when Captain Suzuki had promised to return. The only instruction the doctor had issued on his way out the door the night before was "Do not let any of them die overnight."

Aside from a baby-faced soldier on guard, Franz had been alone with the patients once the red-haired nurse, Helen Thompson, had gone to lie down at midnight. She had kindly offered to remain on the ward with Franz, but he saw no point in both of them staying up, since there was little for either to do but administer painkillers. Besides, Franz hadn't been told where, or even if, he had sleeping quarters of his own.

Earlier, he and Helen had chatted over cups of weak green tea. "The man with the burns," Franz had inquired. "When did he come?"

"Two days ago." Helen absentmindedly swept back her unruly red curls. "I don't know the first thing about him. Not even if he's a soldier or a sailor. His clothes were burned beyond recognition."

"The injuries are so extensive."

"Terrible. I was not expecting Captain Suzuki to do more than order painkillers." She lowered her voice, even though there was no risk of being overheard by anyone who understood English. "The heavy doses of morphine the captain sometimes orders—he must know that the patients will stop breathing once they have been administered."

"But he didn't order any for this patient?"

"Not in the usual dosage, no. Anyone can see the poor man doesn't stand a chance, but the captain insists on dressing changes and more and more debridement. As though we can somehow replace all that destroyed flesh."

Eager to change the subject, Franz said, "I once worked here at the Country Hospital."

"Oh? When was that?"

"From '38 to '41. Pardon me, Miss Thompson, but I do not remember meeting you here."

"It's Helen. And you didn't." Her smile was understanding, even amused. "I've only been here for a few weeks. I used to be a prisoner at Lunghwa Camp. I ran the infirmary there, such as it was. One day, two soldiers showed up out of the blue and plucked me from the camp without a word of explanation."

"Are you American?"

"Close." She smiled. "Canadian. From Toronto. My husband is an attaché. He works for the Foreign Service here in Shanghai. Or used to, anyway. So did my father."

Franz nodded. "Are there any other Western nurses at the Country Hospital?"

"Only one, as far as I know. Sister Margareta. She's Swiss."

"*Mein Gott!* Sister Margareta is still here?" Franz marvelled, remembering the stern old nurse in her white habit. "I thought she was well over a hundred when I came here five years ago."

"She's a hundred and twenty if she's a day." Helen laughed. "But I think even the Japanese are too frightened of her to let her go. And God is too afraid to take her."

Franz chuckled. "With good reason on both accounts."

"Besides, the Japanese nurses here aren't really trained as such. The girls have told me as much themselves. They are really only care aides."

"Are there any other Western doctors?"

Helen shook her head. "You are the first one I've encountered."

Franz still wasn't certain whether Ghoya had singled him out because of his ability or as a form of punishment. Perhaps it involved a degree of both. "Do you know why the Japanese chose you to work here?" he asked.

"Not because of my nursing skills," she said, but her laugh was easy. "Aside from the camp infirmary—and that hardly counts—I haven't worked as a nurse since I left Toronto over four years ago. I came to Shanghai to be the dutiful wife of a junior diplomat."

"So then . . ."

"I speak Japanese."

"Oh. Did you learn it here?"

Helen shook her head. "When I was twelve, my father was posted at the Canadian Embassy in Tokyo. We lived there for three years."

"That must have been something."

"Oh, I absolutely loved it. Everything about Japan. The food, the culture, and especially the people—so polite and kind. In all my time there, I don't remember anyone so much as raising his or her voice to me. Nowadays . . ." She sighed wistfully. "It's as though they were an entirely different race."

Almost without exception, all Franz had ever known of the Japanese was their warlike nature. But he had seen first-hand in Austria how a refined and cultured people could turn on their own compatriots seemingly overnight. He thought of a neighbour in Vienna, an older widow who had regularly shared fresh tomatoes from her garden with him and Hannah. After the Anschluss, she had only acknowledged them through anti-Semitic mutterings. And Hannah's cello teacher, who had once been so encouraging of her playing but later refused to "ever set foot inside a home polluted with Jews."

Keeping the thoughts to himself, he asked, "What do you know of Captain Suzuki?"

"Little more than you do. He's a talented surgeon, I can see that much. I think he must have trained in America."

"Why do you say that?"

"The way he speaks, and the expressions he uses. Once, when I dropped a retractor, the captain called me a 'dumb cluck.' I had to keep from laughing." Her smile faded. "But most of the time he treats me as if—" She paused to search for the words. "—I were a piece of equipment. Nothing more."

Franz cleared his throat and posed the question he had been desperate to ask. "Helen, do the Japanese let you go home after your shifts?"

She squinted at him. "Home, Dr. Adler?"

"I mean back to the camp where your family is staying."

"I am not in the same camp as my father."

"And your husband?"

"Not him either." Her affable facade showed its first cracks and she looked away. "Both my father and my husband were deemed political prisoners and transferred to Chapei Camp. I haven't seen them in over a year. I don't even know if . . ."

Embarrassed, Franz cleared his throat. "I apologize. I had no idea."

"Lunghwa Camp is surrounded by barbed wire and dogs. Whatever the Japanese call it—'Civic Assembly Centre' or other such doublespeak—it's still a prison. No, Dr. Adler, that camp is anything but home for me. I live here at the hospital now. I prefer it that way."

"I see."

Her expression softened, and she reached out to touch his sleeve. "I've never asked to go back. Maybe if you spoke to Captain Suzuki, he might allow you . . ." But her words lacked conviction, and their conversation soon petered out.

The thought of being trapped in the Country Hospital—with Sunny and Hannah so close and yet so far away, as if they were living at the North Pole—had hung over him like a pall for the rest of the night.

Franz was deciding if he should inform the young guard of the burn victim's death when Helen appeared on the ward in the morning, adjusting her cap and stifling a yawn. Franz motioned to the dead patient, but she didn't appear the least surprised. "How do you think the captain will take it?" he asked.

She frowned. "What else could he have expected?"

Franz didn't have to wait long to find out. Captain Suzuki marched onto the ward at twenty minutes before six with a soldier, a junior doctor and two Japanese nurses in tow. He wore a lab coat over a rumpled blue uniform, and his face was even more lined than it had been the previous day, as though he had been up all night too. Even before Franz had a chance to explain, the captain motioned impatiently to the burn victim. "When did he die?"

"Half an hour or so ago."

"Were you planning to just leave him there?"

"I . . . I didn't know the procedure—"

Suzuki brushed past Franz and stepped up to the bed. He stood there as motionless as the corpse, reminding Franz of the stoic fathers and husbands he had seen at the bedsides of lost loved ones back in Vienna. After a few moments, the captain spun away from the bed and hurled orders in Japanese to his cluster of subordinates. In seconds, the nurses had swaddled the body from head to toe in a sheet and the soldiers were whisking him off the ward. Within a minute, the bed was freshly made and awaiting its next patient.

The others followed Suzuki as he performed his rounds on the ward. He stopped to palpate abdomens and examine under dressings. He asked the odd question of Franz or Helen, but never once did he speak directly to the patients. As he left the last patient, he glanced at Helen. "Is the operating room prepared?" he asked in English.

Helen bowed her head. "Yes, Captain."

Suzuki turned again and headed off the ward. Uncertain whether to follow, Franz stood watching the others hurry after him, until Helen looked over her shoulder and beckoned him with a small wave.

They convened at the sink outside the operating room. No one spoke. After Suzuki had finished scrubbing, Franz washed his hands with a fresh bar of soap that he imagined could have been made to last a month at the refugee hospital. He donned the surgical gown and rubber gloves that one of the Japanese nurses held out for him. The ache from his broken rib was compounded by lack of sleep, and he braced his chest with his elbow as he followed Suzuki into the operating room. Inside, he felt the room spin for a few agonizing seconds, but the spell was mercifully short.

Franz recognized the man lying on the table as a patient from the ward. According to Helen, his leg had been badly crushed by the wheel of a truck. The mangled limb jutted out from a corner of the bed sheet. One glimpse at the mottled blue leg told Franz that his femur had been shattered and its blood supply compromised. The leg was clearly beyond salvage.

Without a word from Suzuki, the young Japanese doctor stepped up to the head of the bed. He mumbled a few words to the patient, covered his face with an anesthetic mask and began dripping ether onto it. The man was unconscious before the anesthetic's paint-thinner smell had even reached Franz's nostrils.

Suzuki held out a gloved hand to Helen, who passed him a scalpel. Standing beside him, Franz lifted a sponge off the surgical tray, preparing to dab at the incision that he was anticipating Suzuki would make. Instead, the captain thrust the scalpel handle-first into Franz's palm and stepped away from the bed, motioning impatiently at the patient.

As Franz slid into the vacated spot, he repositioned the scalpel between his index finger and thumb. With his other hand, he ran a gloved finger along the bumpy surface of the patient's thigh, which felt more like wood than tissue, searching for where the skin warmed from cool to body temperature. He finally located the spot, only a few inches below the hip. Franz considered seeking Suzuki's consent but, recognizing this as some kind of test, dug the scalpel deep into the tissue and began to slice around the thigh.

Suzuki watched in stony silence as Franz sutured the major blood vessels, sawed through the bone and finished stitching the wound shut over the stump where the patient's leg had been. The captain hadn't touched the patient or spoken a word during the half hour it took Franz to complete the procedure, and he made no comment afterward.

The nurses transferred the man to a stretcher while a soldier took away the black rubber bag holding the amputated limb. By the time Franz had scrubbed and changed gowns, another patient was lying on the table, anesthetized and prepared for surgery. The opening in the surgical drapes revealed a severe abdominal wound, from which poked a number of catgut sutures from a recent surgery.

Suzuki kept his arms folded across his chest as Helen extended the scalpel to Franz. He explored inside the belly with his other hand, finding multiple metallic fragments inside the wound. He operated more by feel than by sight, cutting away dead tissue, protecting vital organs and blood vessels, and plucking out more sharp pieces of shrapnel than he had ever removed from one person. All the while, Suzuki stood like a statue, offering neither advice nor assistance.

And so it went all morning long. Despite his anxiety over being separated from his family, the throb in his chest and his spiralling fatigue, by the fifth or sixth surgery, Franz realized that he was enjoying practising his craft again. He was reminded of a story he had read as a child about a concert pianist who stumbles across a perfectly tuned grand piano on the desert island where he has been marooned. Like the story's hero, for a while, Franz was able to lose himself in his passion.

He was standing at the sink for the eighth time that day, wondering why the captain was even bothering to scrub if he had no intention of operating, when Suzuki finally spoke. "You are competent enough," he grunted. "They were right about that much at least."

Franz was puzzled but just bowed his head and said, "Thank you, Captain."

"I merely stated a fact, nothing more." Suzuki turned away from the running water and locked eyes with Franz. "After today, you will assist me when it suits me and operate on your own when I say so."

"Thank you, Captain," Franz repeated to fill the awkward silence.

"Don't think for one moment that I need your assistance. I do not want you here." As Suzuki walked away, he added, "And, Dr. Adler, you will never have cause to thank me."

Back inside the operating room, Franz again felt twinges of light-headedness. He worked at a deliberately methodical pace on the next—and final, according to Helen—case of the morning. As he operated on a shrapnel-peppered arm, the dizziness returned in worsening waves. He worried his legs might buckle or his hands might slip and slice through some vital blood vessel or nerve.

The blunting of his technique wasn't lost on Suzuki, and Franz could feel the captain's critical gaze on him. But Franz managed to finish the procedure without incident, though he twice braced himself with a hand and thigh against the table.

It wasn't until the patient had been taken from the operating theatre and Franz was following Helen out that the room began to spin violently. The nausea came seemingly out of nowhere. He reached for any kind of support but found only air. The room tunnelled into blackness. He opened his mouth to tell Helen to turn the lights back on but no words emerged, and he felt himself toppling forward.

CHAPTER 11

I should be home, Sunny thought for the umpteenth time. Her palm was still bleeding where a shard of glass had cut her, but she warily reached her hand back into the wicker box. She dug another bottle free of the sticky mess of broken glass, powder and spilled tinctures.

After three days of posturing—including a threat to "blow the hospital up to the sky," as Ghoya had screamed at a nurse who had been in his office about an exit pass—the "King of the Jews" had allowed the refugee hospital to reopen. Earlier that morning, soldiers had returned the confiscated supplies, tossing the boxes onto the curb outside the hospital from a moving truck, breaking several bottles and spilling others. A couple of coolies had removed the boards from the front door, but many of the staff and patients were too afraid to return after the raid. Only three nurses and two doctors had reported back to work, including the old dermatologist, Dr. Goldman. Fewer than half the patients had moved back from the heim across the street. Two had already died at the hostel, largely from medical neglect. Even Frau Adelmann, still half paralyzed, had opted to stay in her flat rather than risk another run-in with the Japanese.

Sunny was too preoccupied with Franz's absence to worry about the soldiers returning. Five days had passed without a word from or about her husband. She missed him so much, she felt she might go out of her mind with worry if it weren't for Joey. The sight of her baby—even when he woke her at four in the morning crying with hunger—warmed her inside and gave her reason to persevere. She hated having to leave Joey with Esther to go to work these days. And it hurt to think that Esther, who was still nursing the baby, was more essential to Joey's contentment and survival than she was.

Feng Wei had visited only once since she had given birth more than a week ago. Sunny could still picture the girl hovering at the doorway, holding a basket of rice balls in one trembling hand and a candle in the other. Rather than stepping into the room, Feng Wei extended the gifts to Sunny from the threshold. She showed a small smile when Sunny lifted up the sleeping child to show her, but she frantically waved away an offer to hold the baby. "No, dear lady, not mine. Not mine!" Turning crimson, Feng Wei backed away from the door and fled down the corridor as soon as Sunny took the offerings.

Sunny would rather have stayed home with Joey, but she refused to break her promise to Franz. She would put in her time at the hospital, but as soon as she had finished sorting through the medicines and checking on her patients, she intended to rush back home to Joey, whom she now thought of as her son.

Sunny placed a bottle on the shelf and carefully extracted another from the box. She had to read the label: Ipecac. This was a medicine she had never administered. She remembered her father telling her he had once given her ipecac to induce vomiting when, as a toddler, she had drunk from a vial of her mother's perfume. She had no recollection of the incident. But the bottle reminded her of Simon's idea of poisoning Ghoya. As desperate as she was to see Franz, the scheme was absurd.

She finished unloading the bottles and the other supplies she could salvage and then headed out to make her rounds. There were only eight patients on the ward, where normally there would have been three times as many. She took temperatures, assessed wounds and changed dressings, but she refused to allow any of the patients—even Frau Klinger, who would have usually talked her ear off—to draw her into small talk.

At the last bed, Sunny found Herr Steinmann covered up to his neck with a blanket. Despite his welcoming smile, he looked far worse than he had the day before. His cheeks were sunken, and his skin was the colour of gunmetal. "Good day, Dr. Adler," Steinmann said in a weak but cheerful voice.

Sunny mustered a small grin. "How many times do I have to tell you? I am not a doctor, Herr Steinmann."

"Your husband feels differently."

She didn't want to think about Franz. "Are you having much pain?"

"Almost none."

Sunny realized that he was lying, but she also knew the hospital didn't have enough morphine to control his pain for much longer. "You will let us know if the pain becomes too severe?"

Steinmann chuckled softly. "I will let all of Shanghai know with my screams."

With his consent, Sunny lowered the blanket and lifted up his pyjama top to examine the surgical wound. She expected the infection to be much worse but was struck nonetheless by how far it had extended. The sutures were disintegrating and a loop of bowel protruded through his abdominal wall. Had Steinmann received proper post-operative care instead of being dragged across a dirty floor by the soldiers, perhaps the incision would have healed. It was too late now. They both knew it, but neither would admit it.

"Why the long face?" Steinmann asked. "It's coming along. You'll see. I'm one of those old men who is simply too ornery to die. Much to Herr Hitler's chagrin, no doubt."

She smiled but was silent.

"Where is the other Dr. Adler?" he asked.

Sunny hesitated. She hadn't told any of the patients about his arrest.

"Have the soldiers taken him?" Steinmann asked.

Sunny felt her eyes moistening and realized there was no point in trying to hide it. "I don't know where."

"Why did they arrest him?"

"To work as a surgeon for their army."

"Ah, but that's good." Steinmann lifted his hand up, but it dropped back to the bed before reaching her. "He's not a prisoner. He will be taken care of, then."

"What if they send him to the front?"

Steinmann frowned, but then dismissed her question with a shake of his head. "What good would an experienced surgeon be to them on the front lines? No, he must be in a hospital somewhere."

Out of the corner of her eye, she spotted Berta waving urgently from the nurse's desk. Sunny replaced Herr Steinmann's bandages and covered him back up. "I will check on you later," she promised as she headed for the nursing station.

At the desk, Berta spoke in a hush. "There's a priest at the door."

"A *priest*?"

"Not just any priest." Berta's lip curled slightly. "That awful Father Diego." The name rang a bell but Sunny couldn't place it. "The Spanish priest from the wireless. The one who admires General Franco so much. He's always so sympathetic to the Japanese and the Nazis on his program."

Sunny remembered. She had heard of the priest but had never listened to his weekly radio show, which was reputed to be more political than spiritual. "Why has he come?"

"He brought us a patient." Berta scowled. "A monk of some kind or other. To *this* hospital. Can you imagine?"

Sunny hurried down the hallway. At the front door stood a tall dark man in a black cassock with a white clerical collar. He was distinguished looking, Sunny thought, with his greying hair and deep dimples. The priest was propping up another man, who wore a brown robe with a rope tied at the waist. He kept an arm draped over the priest's shoulders as he hunched forward and clutched his other arm across his belly. His face was hidden by the dark hood.

Sunny had been raised Methodist—her mother had originally come to China as a missionary—but she had known enough Catholics to recognize the second man as a Franciscan monk. She turned to the priest. "Father, how can I help you and the Brother?"

The priest brought a hand to his chest and offered her a smile. "Ah, such a pleasure to make your acquaintance," he said in a fluid Spanish accent. "I am Father Diego. This is my colleague, Brother Dominic."

Dominic nodded without raising his head.

Sunny eyed the priest questioningly. A pained expression creased his features. "Dominic is not well. I fear he is suffering from intestinal colic or some such thing." He raised his hands. "Of course, my grasp of medicine is, frankly, medieval."

Dominic kept his head down and remained silent, but Sunny noticed him swaying slightly on his feet. "Father, you do realize this is a hospital for refugees." She paused and then added, "Refugee *Jews*."

"But a hospital nonetheless?" Diego arched an eyebrow. "In my experience, hospitals are typically as welcoming to the needy as are churches. Sometimes, regrettably, much more so."

"Our receptiveness is not the issue, Father. It's our resources, or lack of. I doubt we are capable of caring for Brother Dominic."

The priest's smile dimmed but didn't disappear. "I understood that surgeries are undertaken here. I had even heard that a very skilled Viennese surgeon worked at this institution."

"He no longer works here," Sunny said. "I am the only one capable of operating, and I'm a nurse."

Diego studied her. "You do operate, though?"

"I have, yes," Sunny said, being deliberately vague. She didn't like being evasive but, beyond her suspicion of the two strangers, she doubted the hospital had the capacity to offer them much help. "We have reopened only yesterday, Father. Our cupboards are nearly bare."

The priest adjusted his stance, shifting his weight onto one leg to better support his companion. He glanced at Dominic and then back to Sunny. "I understand. We may have to look elsewhere, but if my friend could just lie down for a moment or two."

Sunny noticed Dominic's legs trembling and, her medical instincts taking over, rushed to his other side. She wrapped an arm around an unexpectedly thick and padded chest. Under the smell of wool and sweat, she detected the odour of blood. Together, Diego and Sunny guided Dominic down the corridor toward the ward. With each step, Dominic seemed to lose more strength. By the time they reached the doorway, he was like a dead weight in their arms.

Nurse Miriam hurried over and helped place Dominic on the closest stretcher. As he hit the bed, the hood fell away from his face. Sunny didn't know what she had expected, but his appearance came as a surprise. He was young, twenty-five at the most. Fair-skinned and freckled, he had green eyes and sandy hair that was trimmed to a crew-cut. His pallor told Sunny that he must have lost blood—a lot of it, she suspected. Then she spotted brownish fluff poking through the neck of his robe, and she recognized it as the fur-lined collar of an aviator's jacket. She glanced skeptically at the priest. "Intestinal colic, Father?"

Diego formed a steeple with his palms. "Perhaps not," he said sheepishly.

"The pulse is rapid," Miriam called from the other side of the stretcher, her fingers clutching Dominic's wrist as she checked her watch. "A hundred forty per minute."

Sunny felt Dominic's pulse. Its faintness, more than its pace, alarmed her. She looked up and saw that his gaze was glassy. "What happened to you?" she demanded.

Dominic turned to the priest, seeking his approval. Diego nodded. "Flak," the young man rasped.

Sunny and Miriam shared a confused glance. Diego lowered his voice to a hush. "Anti-aircraft shrapnel," the priest said. "Brother Dominic—Lieutenant Lewis of the U.S. Navy, to be more precise—his plane was shot down. He parachuted to safety, but he has wounds from the flak."

A fugitive American pilot here at the Jewish hospital? Sunny's pulse hammered in her temples, but there was no time for questions. "I need to examine you, Broth—Lieutenant," Sunny said.

Without waiting for his consent, she yanked up his robe. Underneath, he was wearing a combat uniform—khakis and a bomber jacket. The jacket was torn and shredded, and much of the brown leather had turned black from blood. Sunny unzipped the jacket. A bloody rag was bunched up against his belly. She carefully moved it aside and pulled up his stained undershirt. Through the smears, Sunny spotted multiple wounds perforating the pale skin.

She rested a hand against his abdomen. Although she applied only the slightest of pressure, he grimaced in pain and his belly went as rigid as a board. Sunny made the decision even before her eyes found Diego's again. "I must operate. *Now.*"

CHAPTER 12

Do you need to sit, Franz?" Helen asked, closing the gap between them in seconds.

Franz tried to wave her off. "I'm fine, Helen."

While this was not exactly true, the attack had been relatively mild. He thought he had compensated well for the wobble in his step and was surprised Helen had even noticed. Then again, he had been aware of her vigilant eye on him all week, ever since he had fainted inside the operating room.

He could still picture the ceiling tiles revolving overhead and the room coning into a tunnel, followed by that sickening feeling of weightlessly falling. When the room had come into view again, Franz found himself lying on his back. He could feel something bony pressing into his mid-back and realized it was Helen's arm. She must have caught him as he fell because, aside from where her forearm pressed into his tender ribcage, he felt no other pain.

"Franz! Can you hear me, Franz?" Helen peppered him with questions.

Ignoring her, he craned his neck to scan the room. "Did he see me?" he croaked.

Helen grimaced. "Did *who* see you?"

"The captain."

"What does it matter? How are you—"

"It's all that matters!"

She shook her head. "I was the only one still in the room."

"Thank God," Franz said as he struggled to sit up.

"You shouldn't," Helen cautioned.

"It's passed, Helen. I'm all right."

His relief that Suzuki had not seen his collapse was enormous, but Helen wouldn't let it go so easily. To alleviate her worry, Franz concocted a story about suffering from petit mal and having experienced brief seizures ever since childhood. He refused to consider what might be the real cause of the attacks; he had too much else to face.

A week after the incident, Helen remained skeptical of Franz's explanation. Even now, following a spell that was little more than an aftershock, relative to an earthquake, she continued to hold on to his elbow as though she were propping up a stubborn old man who couldn't be trusted to support himself. "There's no harm in sitting down until you feel a little stronger," she said.

He shook free of her grip. "Thank you, Helen. I am fine. Honestly. And our patient is waiting."

"There are always patients waiting."

She had a point. He had no idea where they all came from, but the Country Hospital saw an endless stream of young casualties with bullet wounds, shattered bones and embedded shrapnel. Perhaps the Chinese guerillas in the countryside beyond Shanghai, who were reputed to be disorganized and prone to in fighting, had coalesced into a more effective force. Or maybe the wounded came from the faraway battlefields of Kwajalein, Rabaul and Imphal—exotic names that had meant nothing to Franz when he heard them on the illicit wireless broadcasts. Regardless, he was operating from morning to night.

Having evidently satisfied Suzuki on his first day operating, Franz had performed most of his surgeries since with little oversight and little assistance, save for the deferential, inexperienced Japanese aides who acted as scrub nurses. Helen occasionally assisted him, but only if Suzuki was not operating himself. Otherwise, the captain insisted on her presence during procedures, though she maintained that he hardly spoke to her and that "even a trained monkey" could meet the basic demands of being his assistant.

Franz didn't begrudge the long hours he spent in surgery. It was the only reprieve from his loneliness and relentless anxiety over his family. However, he found that fewer and fewer of the cases now challenged his skills enough to entirely occupy his focus. Inevitably, his thoughts would drift—he'd hear Hannah's joyous laughter or picture Sunny's serene smile—while his hands functioned automatically. He wondered how they were managing, especially with Sunny so intent on raising the neighbour's baby as her own—*their own*, he had to catch himself. He was still uncertain of how he felt about the idea, even beyond the impracticalities of adopting a baby in the middle of a war zone. In bleaker moments, Franz doubted he could go on without them. He could feel his will ebbing. He remembered his father in those horrible final days in Vienna, and how the proud man had finally just given in to his chronically weak lungs. Would his own drop attacks prove to be the equivalent of his father's asthma?

Helen's wry smile pulled him out of the miserable thoughts. "The Bible says it's a sin, you know?" she said.

Franz cocked his head. Helen didn't seem like a religious person, and he suspected she was being ironic. "*What* is a sin?"

"Pride."

Franz snorted a small laugh. "Pride is not my pressing concern."

"What is, then?"

"How sympathetic do you imagine Captain Suzuki would be to my condition?" he asked.

"Sympathetic?" Helen squinted. "You've had this condition since childhood, and you are still an excellent surgeon—the best I've ever seen. What difference would it make to the captain?"

"The captain never wanted me here," Franz pointed out. "Do you think he would tolerate me collapsing in the middle of surgery? That he would let me continue to operate if he knew I was having seizures?"

Helen bit her lip. "I suppose not, no." Then her eyes brightened. "If he didn't trust you to operate, maybe he would send you home. To Hannah and Sunny."

Franz had already considered this, but Suzuki had not struck him as an accommodating man. "Or maybe he would have me changing putrid dressings all day long, or perhaps send me somewhere even worse."

Helen considered this and nodded. "Right before one of these spells, do you get any kind of warning signs?"

"I usually feel light-headed for a few seconds before it becomes severe."

"All right, then," she said purposefully. "We will need some kind of signal between us."

"A signal?"

"So I can come to your assistance."

"Helen, that isn't necessary."

She arched an eyebrow. "Still nothing to do with pride?"

He sighed. "A tad, perhaps. But when—if—I have another spell, chances are you will not even be with me."

"I was there last week to catch you. And again today. How many other spells have there been?"

"Maybe one or two." He had actually experienced episodes every day for the past week. And he had passed out a second time too, but had fortunately fallen onto his own cot.

"Let's try this." She crossed her middle finger over her forefinger. "Just like when you were a kid covering up for some fib you told your parents."

He had never heard of this gesture—perhaps it was a Canadian custom—but he mimicked her hand position. "Like so?" he asked.

"Exactly." Her face broke into a smile that sent a flush across her cheeks.

Franz cleared his throat, feeling suddenly embarrassed. "The patient . . ."

"Is waiting, yes." She turned toward the sink.

By the time Franz had finished scrubbing, Helen had already entered the operating room. Holding his wet hands above his chest, he was about to go in too when he heard boots pounding along the corridor behind him. Glancing over his shoulder, he recoiled as he saw that the two approaching soldiers were wearing the white armbands of the Kempeitai. His heart sped even faster when he spotted Captain Suzuki following on their heels.

The Kempeitai men came to a snapping halt in front of him. The taller of the two glared at him venomously while the other one viewed him coolly, like a mover assessing a heavy chest of drawers that he would have to transport.

Suzuki spoke to the men in Japanese for almost a minute. All the while, Franz stood motionless, dripping hands held up like the victim of a robbery in a Hollywood film.

"You will go with them now, Dr. Alder," Suzuki finally announced.

"Go where, Captain?"

Suzuki shrugged. "Wherever they take you."

Feeling sweat beading across his brow, Franz dropped his hands to his sides. "Will I be returning?"

"It's not for me to say," Suzuki said impassively. "They brought you to me without consultation. They're taking you away in the same fashion."

* * *

The military vehicle, a spacious black Buick that smelled of hair tonic and talcum powder, hurtled eastward, toward the heart of Shanghai. Franz would have been elated to be heading in the direction of home, but the last time he taken a drive with the Kempeitai, they had taken him to Bridge House, the most feared address in all of Shanghai, because of Franz's suspected involvement in spreading rumours among the refugee community. During his daily interrogations at the Kempeitai headquarters, Franz had been drowned to the point of unconsciousness, and his arm had been broken in two places.

They drove through the International Settlement along Nanking Road, which had once been the retail heart of Shanghai: Asia's equivalent of Fifth Avenue or Savile Row. Most of the luxury department stores and specialty shops had long ago been boarded shut or converted to military offices and supply stations.

Franz's throat constricted as soon as the sedan turned onto the riverside Bund and headed across the Garden Bridge, over Soochow Creek, and into the Hongkew district. He buried his face in his hands, trying to compose himself and muster the strength it would take to walk through Bridge House's bronze doors and down its marble staircase, which led to the closest thing he could imagine to hell on earth.

When Franz finally pulled his hands from his face, he felt disoriented. The car had veered onto Broadway, the city's busiest—though hardly most glamorous—thoroughfare. They turned onto Ward Road, and as soon as he saw the ghetto checkpoint through the windshield, his chest welled in giddy anticipation.

The guard at the checkpoint waved the vehicle past. They had barely crossed into the ghetto when they came to a stop in front of a nondescript building at the corner. The smile slid from Franz's lips as the driver parked in front of the Bureau of Stateless Refugee Affairs. The Kempeitai men yanked Franz out of the car and shoved him down the path, aggravating the ache in his rib-cage. They dragged him into the building and past the startled exit-pass applicants who lined the narrow hallway.

Ghoya sat behind his desk, wearing one of his outdated double-breasted, wide-shouldered suit jackets. He didn't rise to greet Franz, just offered him a smile. "Ah, Dr. Adler, you have come back," he said, as though Franz himself had chosen to depart the ghetto for the Country Hospital.

Franz bowed at the waist. "I'm most pleased to be back."

Ghoya nodded from one Kempeitai man to the other. "Yes, yes." He laughed. "I saw to it myself that you had an official military police escort." He giggled. "Did you enjoy the company?"

Franz relaxed, assuming that the Kempeitai's presence must have been part of one of Ghoya's mind games. The little man continued to stare at him expectantly. "You are most welcome, Dr. Adler. Most welcome." Ghoya dismissed the Kempeitai men with a wave and then clasped his palms together, resting his chin on his fingers. "Much has happened since you left us. More smugglers, I am afraid. I cannot tolerate it. Not at all, no." He sighed. "I'm rather fond of Mrs. Cron too. She bakes me the most delicious babka."

Franz also had a soft spot for the spry woman who, though almost eighty years old, continued to volunteer every day in the kitchen of one of the heime. But he had trouble seeing the connection between smuggling and coffee cake. "Mrs. Cron?" he asked.

"Yes, yes," Ghoya said impatiently. "Two of her sons. They were the leaders of a smuggling ring. What choice did I have, I ask you? None. None at all."

Franz's heart sank. He knew both Felix and Isaac Cron personally. He was especially fond of Isaac, who was thoughtful and soft-spoken.

"They were grown men," Ghoya continued. "I couldn't be as lenient as I was with your daughter. Too soft, always too soft. No, no. I warned you all. Did I not?" Ghoya pulled his hands away from his chin and turned to look out the window behind him. "A firing squad, the day before yesterday. I am afraid we will have to leave the bodies there by the wall for a few more days. This smuggling nonsense. A lesson. Yes, it's a lesson my people simply must learn."

Franz was still absorbing this news when Ghoya spoke again abruptly. "I'm told you performed adequately for Dr. Suzuki."

"I hope so, Mr. Ghoya."

"Yes, yes. He says you are perfectly able. You will do just fine."

"You are sending me back to the Country Hospital?" Franz asked with alarm.

"Did I say that?" Ghoya demanded, looking around as if someone in the room might back him up. "Did I?"

"No, I just assumed . . ."

Ghoya eyed him coolly. "Go home, Dr. Adler. Yes, yes. To that mischievous daughter and your mixed-breed wife. Go home to them."

The elation resurged, though Franz remained wary. "Right now, Mr. Ghoya?"

"Why not?" Ghoya laughed. "Is there somewhere else you would rather be?"

"No. Thank you. Thank you." Franz was already backing toward the door as he bowed his exit.

"Oh, and Dr. Adler, I have reconsidered my position on the hospital. Yes, yes. I have decided that while you are still in Shanghai, I will allow you to work in that terrible little hospital."

Franz froze. "While I am still here?"

"Of course," Ghoya scoffed. "Did you not hear me earlier? You performed adequately. Captain Suzuki considers you ready."

"Ready for what, Mr. Ghoya?"

Ghoya laughed again. "You didn't think you would be staying in Shanghai, did you?"

CHAPTER 13

Sunny resisted the urge to run as she hurried home down Chusan Road. Father Diego matched her pace, but his head swivelled from side to side, taking in the busy street scene. "I had no idea," he marvelled.

"No idea of what, Father?" Sunny asked out of politeness more than interest.

"How industrious the Jews have been." He pointed to a sign that read PHARMACY in large block letters. "A pharmacy here in the ghetto? And look, a newspaper publisher."

"There are three Jewish newspapers: two are printed in German and one in Yiddish. And a football league and boxing team too." She sighed. "I don't imagine you would report any of that on your radio program."

Diego smiled. "No, probably not. It is unlikely to appeal to my listeners."

"Fascists?"

"For the most part, yes."

Sunny glanced around and then said in a low voice, "You are the voice of fascism on the wireless, and yet you shelter a wounded American?"

He arched an eyebrow. "And you, it seems, are the voice of the German Jews, yet you are neither."

The priest was right. Proud as Sunny was of her husband's tight-knit community, she still considered herself little more than a guest, a welcome outsider. She admired the people. She loved many of them. But it didn't help her understand them any better. They exhibited an almost boundless capacity for kindness and empathy, and yet they could be surprisingly petty. And the bickering! She had never heard anything like it. She hardly remembered having heard her father raise his voice, and certainly never in public. Yet it was unusual not to hear raised voices or cries of protest among any gathering of Jews, no matter how small. Sunny didn't trust the enigmatic priest enough to elaborate on her thoughts, so all she said was, "I'm also neither Chinese, nor Caucasian."

His face showed a trace of amusement. "Not everything is as it appears, Sunny."

So, you are *a spy, then.* "It must be dangerous," she said quietly.

"One has to be careful, yes."

Sunny thought of her own brush with espionage the previous year, when she had briefly operated as an agent for a local Resistance cell. It had begun innocuously enough after she had made a few discreet inquiries through a Chinese colleague whom she suspected of being connected to the Underground. But she soon came to regret the decision. She had envisioned herself treating wounded Resistance fighters or passing messages along the spy chain. Instead, she had been forced to spy on the only honourable Japanese officer she had ever known, ultimately helping to target him for assassination. She had narrowly escaped being caught by the Japanese. The other members of her cell were subsequently brutally tortured and publicly executed, their corpses left for days on public display as a warning to others.

Sunny didn't feel safe sharing any of this experience with Diego, so instead she said, "The Japanese could raid again at any time. The lieutenant cannot stay at our hospital much longer."

"Of course not." Diego slowed to a halt. "Please understand that we came to you only as a last resort."

"But you came nonetheless." Sunny stopped and turned to him, unable to suppress her anger any longer. "I hope you understand that you've exposed all of us to great risk."

Diego held up his hands penitently. "You have no idea how sorry I am."

"We don't need your sympathy, Father. Or your regret. What we need is for you to move the lieutenant out of our hospital."

"Without question." Diego nodded solemnly. "When is the soonest, medically speaking, he can be moved?"

Sunny considered the question. Lieutenant Donald Lewis was incredibly fortunate to be alive. In the operating room, Sunny had sliced him open from breast bone to pelvis, expecting the worst. Lewis's belly had been riddled with sharp fragments of flak, along with slivers of leather and fabric from his uniform. She found three pieces of metal less than an inch from his aorta, the largest artery in the body. His spleen had been penetrated by a twisted shard of metal, but the bleeding had been contained and, amazingly, his intestines and liver were uninjured. Wounds to those organs would have proven fatal. Sunny had to remove countless metal fragments, mop up the bleeding and tie off several small blood vessels in the process. Normally, she would have expected Lewis to remain in hospital for weeks, but the circumstances were far from normal. "He will need at least three days before he can even get up, let alone travel."

Diego took the news in stride. "Three days, then."

It was a ridiculous time frame, but Sunny appreciated that the risk of keeping Lewis at the hospital, where the Japanese might find him, was too great, not only for the hospital but for the lieutenant himself. "Where will you take him?" she asked.

"We will find a safe house for Dominic—" He chuckled at himself. "—*Donald* outside the city. To Free China in the west."

"Find?" Sunny gawked at him. "You don't have one yet?"

"Not yet, no. Not to worry, Sunny." Diego took her hand. "In three days, I will rid your hospital of both of us. This much, I swear to you."

Sunny didn't doubt the priest's sincerity as she pulled free of his warm grip. She thought again of the lieutenant, who had struck her as more like a frightened teenager than a combat pilot. "I have a friend. Perhaps she can help."

Diego's cheeks coloured. "Usually, I wouldn't dream of imposing. However, we are in the process of . . . restructuring our operation."

Sunny thought of the thirteen dead men from her own Resistance cell whose bodies she had seen on the busy street corner months before. They had been beaten almost beyond recognition and left hanging from scaffolding. She wondered bleakly if the word *restructuring* meant something similar had befallen his own operation.

"I will let you know if my friend can help," she said as she turned to leave him.

* * *

Sunny found Esther and Joey inside the flat where she had left them that morning, sitting on the tattered couch. She fought off the now familiar stirrings of maternal envy as she watched Joey nurse.

Hannah was lying on the floor, happily bouncing Jakob on her belly. As soon as she saw Sunny, Hannah hopped to her feet. "Sunny! Any word from Papa?"

"No." Sunny shook her head. "Nothing yet."

Hannah's face fell. "It's been a week."

"I am going to see Mr. Ghoya soon."

"That awful man would never help Papa," Hannah grumbled.

"Perhaps if I can convince Mr. Ghoya he had a good reason to bring your father home."

"Like what?" Hannah's voice cracked. "Ghoya has a heart of stone. He won't ever let Papa come home."

Esther raised an eyebrow. "What sort of reason?" she asked.

"I don't know yet." Sunny held Esther's gaze, a silent signal between them. "I'm still working on the details."

"Natürlich." Esther cleared her throat and changed the subject. "You haven't, by chance, visited Ernst—or Simon—today?"

"No, Essie, sorry. With the hospital reopening, I haven't had any time to spare." Sunny had been frantically busy, but she also knew that it was her fear of running into Baron von Puttkamer again that was keeping her from venturing back to Ernst's apartment.

"Not to worry. I am sure Ernst will drop by sooner or later with another letter." Esther forced a laugh. "You know his old joke of being as reliable the ancient Greek courier?"

"Yes, how does Ernst always say it?" Hannah chimed in. She raised one palm in the air and brought the other to her chest, mimicking the flamboyant artist's delivery. "Neither snow, nor rain, nor heat, nor Nazis, nor Japanese devils keeps this courageous courier from the swift completion of his appointed rounds."

The three of them shared a small laugh.

Something slammed into Sunny's legs, and she looked down to see Jakob hugging her knees and pulling at the hem of her dress. She leaned over and swept him up in her arms. Playful as ever, he giggled and swatted at her face, trying to engage her in a game of peekaboo. He cried in delight as Sunny dipped him low and then swung him up. "You're as energetic as ever, aren't you, Jakob?" she said.

Esther grinned. "He never stops, that little menace. Thank God he's a good sleeper."

Sunny carried him back over to his mother. "Perhaps, we could make a trade?"

"*Ja*, I think your little *Schätzchen* has had his fill for now." Blinking drowsily, Joey wriggled under the blanket as Esther passed him over to Sunny. Sunny lowered Jakob to the couch and took Joey out of Esther's arms. She hugged him tightly, pressing her cheek to his and greedily inhaling his scent. She could feel the calm rolling over her now, the world suddenly more bearable.

"Sunny?" Hannah's face creased with gravity. Even though she had inherited more of her mother's fair-skinned looks than her father's darker features, now her expression was pure Franz.

"What is it, Hannah?"

"Do you really think you can persuade Ghoya to bring Papa home?"

Sunny reached out with her free hand to stroke the girl's cheek. "I don't know, darling."

Hannah's mournful gaze only compounded Sunny's loneliness.

Breaking off the eye contact, Sunny stood up. "I must get going. I've promised to visit Jia-Li today."

"How is your friend coping?" Esther asked.

"She doesn't ever mention Charlie, but . . ." Sunny sighed. "She's not good. Not good at all."

"*Ach,* my heart aches for that one," Esther murmured. "I can't even imagine."

How could you not? Sunny wondered irritably. Esther had lost her first husband to a lynch mob and her second had been forced into hiding by the war. Sunny realized the other woman's comment came from a place of compassion. She had to remind herself that her frustration with Esther wasn't rational. But she just wanted to escape the flat with her baby. "I better go if I hope to be back before curfew."

* * *

Sunny arrived at the Comfort Home just before six o'clock. At the dinner hour, the brothel was relatively quiet. Once word of Joey's presence spread through the mansion, though, a stream of young women drifted into the sitting room to greet him. Sunny passed Joey from girl to girl; she knew many of them from her visits over the years. It was both heartwarming and tragic to see the girls light up in Joey's presence. Sunny wondered how many had once been in Feng Wei's position, forced to give up their babies. She was also saddened to see many new faces among the crowd, including two boys who looked as if they hadn't even reached puberty.

The group swarming Joey finally thinned and Jia-Li appeared. She wore a stylish black hat and a matching gilded cheongsam that showed her garter through a waist-high side slit. Holding a sleek cigarette holder, Jia-Li resembled a hypersexualized version of a Hollywood femme fatale. "Leave us, please," she announced to no one in particular. There was a rush for the door, and soon Sunny and Jia-Li were alone with the baby.

Jia-Li cocked her head as she studied Joey dispassionately. "So this is your temporary house guest, is it?"

Sunny held him out to her friend. "This is my son. Joey."

Jia-Li just kept staring vacantly. "So you did it? You've convinced Franz to keep him after all?"

Sunny tucked Joey against her chest. "They've taken him." Her voice cracked. "They've taken Franz, *bǎo bèi*."

Jia-Li's distant expression evaporated. She rushed over and swallowed Sunny and Joey in a hug. "Oh, *xiǎo hè*, no! Not Franz too," she cried. "When did this happen?"

"Almost a week ago now."

"A week?" Sunny saw the hurt flash across her friend's eyes, but Jia-Li didn't comment. "Those filthy devils. They will not rest until they've destroyed everything. And everyone."

The tears threatened to flow again. "I don't know what do, *bǎo bèi*," Sunny said.

"We must find him. That's all there is to it."

"Impossible."

"Nothing is impossible."

"This is." Sunny looked down at Joey and shook her head. "I already discussed it with Simon and Ernst. Simon had this harebrained idea, but in the end we laughed it off."

Jia-Li looked interested. "Tell me, Sister, about this idea."

"There's no point. It's absurd."

"Humour me."

Sunny sighed. "Simon suggested we poison Ghoya."

"Yes," Jia-Li cried, squeezing Sunny's shoulders. "Poison the rat. He deserves nothing less."

"Not to kill him, *bǎo bèi*!"

Jia-Li's face scrunched in confusion. "No?"

"Just to make Ghoya sick enough to believe that he needs surgery that only Franz could perform." Sunny shook her head. "It would never work."

Jia-Li squinted in concentration. "How can you know until you try?"

Sunny was troubled by the look in her best friend's eyes. Whenever Jia-Li seized upon an idea, good or bad, she was loathe to let go of it. Sunny began to regret having mentioned the scheme. "It's ridiculous," she said, hoping to discourage her friend's interest. "Besides, I don't know the first thing about poisoning anyone."

Jia-Li's face lit with a smile. "Ah, but *I* do."

"No, *bǎo bèi*. It would be suicide to even try."

"For you, perhaps. Not for me. I am more experienced and more cunning in such matters." Jia-Li touched her chest. "After all, I'm a consummate survivor. You have said so yourself."

"Listen to me, *bǎo bèi*," Sunny said, her concern rising. "Forget Simon's idea. It's not why I have come to see you. I do need your help, yes, but not for that."

"For what, then?"

Sunny lowered her voice. "There's an American pilot who was shot down . . ." As Sunny described the lieutenant's predicament, she could tell that her friend was only half listening. Clearly, Jia-Li's mind was elsewhere, thinking of poison.

CHAPTER 14

Café Aaronsohn smelled of boiled cabbage and fried meat, but Sunny's frayed nerves quashed her appetite. She sat at a corner table from which she could see the entire restaurant, as well as the street through the window. She held open a copy of the *Shanghai Jewish Chronicle* and pretended to read an article about the wedding of a couple who had been childhood sweethearts in Cologne and were reunited by chance fifteen years later, as peddler and customer at the Tong Shan street market. She had already read it twice.

Frau Aaronsohn buzzed up to the table and refilled Sunny's water glass. "Have you decided yet, Fräulein?" she asked anxiously.

"Yes, thank you," Sunny said. "I will have the kugel, please."

"*Wunderbar*. A good choice."

Sunny had tried only the noodle-and-potato casserole once before and had found the taste overwhelming, but it was the only dish on the menu that she could afford. Although too nervous to eat, she would look conspicuous without a meal in front of her. Besides, she suspected that if she didn't order soon, she would be forced to abandon the prime table.

The wall-mounted clock above the door read 12:42, but there was still no sign of Ghoya. Sunny had been assured that his routine was as predictable as the Swiss railway: he lunched every weekday at Café Aaronsohn at half past noon. Sunny felt more relieved than disappointed by his absence. Again, she chastised herself again for having ever let Jia-Li coerce her into proceeding with the scheme. *Why did I ever listen to her?* Sunny wondered for the umpteenth time. But the truth was she had felt cornered. Jia-Li was determined to act with or without Sunny's cooperation. She had even somehow enlisted the brothel's physician, Ping Lok—a shady character who had ended up as a doctor to the underworld after his gambling and opium addiction had destroyed his legitimate career—to be her backup accomplice. Sunny felt duty-bound to go along with this. She was the one who had planted the reckless idea in her friend's head.

But now, with Ghoya presumably not coming, it seemed moot—to Sunny's relief. Just as she was about to cancel her order, the door flew open and Ghoya burst in with two soldiers in tow. Without waiting to be seated, he bustled over to the only empty table and plunked himself down. The soldiers claimed the seats on either side of him. The conversations in the room dimmed to a hush and eyes all over the restaurant fell nervously to the floor. Ghoya glanced around contentedly, revelling in the attention. Palms damp, Sunny had to fight off a tremor in her hands as she angled her face away from his.

"Ah, Mrs. Aaronsohn, I'm simply famished, famished," Ghoya cried out across the room. "My lateness could not be avoided today. Such a lineup at my office. The demands of my people, they never end."

Frau Aaronsohn rushed over. "You slave for us, Mr. Ghoya," she said obsequiously. "We are forever grateful for your assistance."

"As well you should be." Ghoya laughed, patting her arm

condescendingly. "Now tell me what I should have for my sustenance today."

"The kugel is fresh and—"

"No, no. No more kugel. I had it yesterday. Who can eat the same thing every day?" Ghoya said. Sunny thought of how most of the Jews in the ghetto lived off a monotonous daily diet of rice and scraps. "What else is there?"

"Felix has made a delicious matzo ball soup."

"Yes, yes! Just like the chicken noodle soup. And bring it with the Jewish bread. How do you call it again?"

"Challah."

"Yes. Bring the challah right away. I'm famished, I tell you. Just famished."

"Straightaway, Mr. Ghoya." Frau Aaronsohn hurried away from the table.

Sunny buried her nose deeper into her newspaper and stole a glance out the window. She still hadn't caught sight of Jia-Li, but she assumed her friend was lurking somewhere outside. While Sunny's chest thumped harder with every passing moment, Ghoya continued to loudly and unilaterally chat with Frau Aaronsohn, opining on everything from the shortcomings of French food to the likelihood of the Americans seeking a truce in the Pacific.

This is madness, Sunny thought. All she would have to do to abort the operation was get up and leave the restaurant. But her legs had turned to rubber, and she felt glued to her seat. Just then, Sunny spotted Jia-Li in the window. Her head was turned from the café, but her form-fitting black dress was unmistakable. Out of the corner of her eye, Sunny saw Frau Aaronsohn heading toward Ghoya's table with a plate of bread. Then Sunny noticed movement outside. Her heart leapt into her throat. Long seconds passed, but no one entered the restaurant.

Ghoya devoured the bread, spraying flecks of crust as he chattered on to Frau Aaronsohn, even as she headed back to the kitchen. A minute or so later, she re-emerged carefully carrying a steaming bowl of soup.

It was then that Jia-Li marched into the café and headed straight for Frau Aaronsohn. "Miss, miss," she cried in English as she blocked the German woman's path. "I will need a table for four."

"*Ich spreche kein Englisch,*" Frau Aaronsohn replied.

"Four," Jia-Li repeated in English, holding up four fingers. She pantomimed a table and chairs, her hands flying over the bowl. "For four of us." She raised her voice and enunciated slowly, pretending that she thought it would somehow make her intent clearer. "We need a table right away. *Mach schnell!*"

A young Jewish man rose from a nearby table. He grinned awkwardly at Jia-Li. "I can help. To translate. I speak English relatively well."

"Please do," Jia-Li said in feigned exasperation. "I'm not getting anywhere with this one."

Protecting the bowl close to her chest, Frau Aaronsohn shouldered her way past Jia-Li. "In a moment, madam, please," she said in German, flustered. "Allow me first to serve this soup, please."

"She asks that you give her a—" the young man began to translate.

But Jia-Li cut him off. "Oh, forget it. It was a foolish idea to ever come here." She turned on her heels and stormed out the door, adjusting her hat as she exited.

Sunny had not seen Jia-Li slip anything into the soup, but the gesture with her hat was the signal that she had somehow managed to spike it. There was no turning back now. Sunny's back tensed in terror. *What have we done?*

Frau Aaronsohn muttered an apology to Ghoya as she lowered the bowl onto the table and placed a soup spoon beside it. Sunny's breath caught again as she watched Ghoya pick up the spoon and dip it into the soup. But rather than taking a spoonful, he dropped the utensil, letting it rest again the rim of the bowl. He rattled the empty bread plate beside him. "More challah, please, Frau Aaronsohn. It would be a shame to eat this soup without bread, surely?"

The woman nodded and turned for the kitchen.

Ghoya reached for the spoon again, but instead of eating, he used it to toy with a matzo ball.

Time crawled. New and old worries coalesced in Sunny's head. *How long will it take for him to become ill? How do I approach him? What if he sends me away?* And the worst thought of all: *What if he suspects me?*

Finally, Sunny saw Frau Aaronsohn carrying a fresh plate of bread to the table. She rested it beside Ghoya's bowl. Nodding, he lifted the spoon to his lips and slurped. "Perhaps a little salty," he pronounced. "But otherwise good. Yes, yes, it will do fine."

Ghoya was taking a second spoonful when the door flew open again. Sunny almost leapt out of her seat when she saw it was Franz filling the doorway. His eyes met hers for a fleeting, charged moment before he walked straight over to Ghoya's table. "Good day, Mr. Ghoya," he said. Sunny watched in shock.

"Dr. Adler?" Ghoya lowered his spoon and stared at Franz, clearly annoyed. "Can you not see I'm having my lunch? Am I not entitled to a minute or two of privacy? Is that so much to ask?"

Franz clasped his hands beneath his chin, as though praying.

"I only wanted to thank you again for letting me return home."

Why, Sunny wondered, was her husband ignoring her and behaving so oddly? But she was too scared to move.

"This is hardly the time, Dr. Adler," Ghoya grumbled.

But Franz persisted. "It was so magnanimous of you, Mr. Ghoya. A reflection of your strength and compassion as a leader."

Seeming placated, Ghoya jutted out his lower lip. "Obviously, yes. Still, this is not the time or place for it."

"I cannot tell you how grateful I am." Franz flung his arms apart, knocking the ceramic soup bowl off the table with the back of his hand. It shattered on the floor with a shriek, soup splattering everywhere.

Ghoya hopped up. "You clumsy fool!" He swung his open hand wildly, contacting Franz's cheek with a sharp crack. "Clumsy, clumsy fool!" He swung it a second time in a backhanded motion that slammed into Franz's lip, spraying blood and knocking him backwards.

The soldiers on either side of Ghoya leapt up. One drew a pistol from his belt and aimed it at Franz's head.

"No! Please, stop," Sunny cried as she jumped up from her seat.

But Frau Aaronsohn beat her to the table, waving her hands frantically. "It's all right, Mr. Ghoya," she cried. "An accident, nothing more. I will get you a fresh bowl straightaway."

CHAPTER 15

"Your mouth, Franz," Sunny said, running her forefinger along his swollen lower lip. "It's still bleeding."

Franz ran his tongue over the chipped tooth and licked away the salty blood. Despite everything, including the fact they were standing on a busy street corner, he couldn't help himself. He pulled Sunny close and pressed his lips to hers. Joy and relief bloomed inside his chest, fuelling his desire. He held her tightly and longed to be alone with her, to run his hands down her bare back and to feel their legs intertwined. "This morning I didn't know if I would ever see you again," he said between kisses. "God, I've missed you."

"You can't imagine." Her voice caught. "But you're home now."

Yes, but for how long? The jolt of reality stung worse than Ghoya's palm. He couldn't muster the courage to tell Sunny that his return was only temporary.

Sunny trailed kisses along his cheek and chin. "How did you know?" she asked.

"Know what, darling?"

"About the soup."

"As soon I got home, Essie told me what Jia-Li was planning. She was so worried about you."

"I didn't want to involve Essie. But she had to know, Franz. In case I was caught."

He nodded. "The moment I stepped into the restaurant, I could tell from your expression that Jia-Li must have already done it."

She kissed him along his neck. "Knocking his bowl onto the floor like that. So brave but so rash. He could have killed you."

"*Ach*, he's mainly bluster, that one."

She angled her head, her expression turning grave. "No, Franz. Don't ever underestimate him. Did you hear about the Cron brothers?"

Franz had been thinking of the two men as he stepped into the restaurant, his throat constricted with dread. But he just smiled and stroked her cheek. "The way Frau Aaronsohn calmed down Ghoya and practically disarmed those soldiers—she's my new hero."

"And you are *my* hero." She pointed across the street to the restaurant. "Still, it was so foolish what you did in there."

"I'm the foolish one?" He laughed. "Who dreamed up this crazy idea to poison Ghoya's soup? It would have never worked, you know."

"I knew it from the start! But once Jia-Li got the idea into her head, I couldn't dissuade her. I thought it would turn out even worse for her if I didn't go along with it." She kissed him again, her tongue tracing his upper lip. "Darling, you know I would've done anything to bring you home."

Franz couldn't bring himself to hurt Sunny with the truth about his return, the temporariness of it. "I know."

She reached for his hand. "Speaking of home, let's go now. You must see Joey."

"I saw him already," Franz said, careful to maintain the lightness in his tone. "With Esther."

Sunny angled her head, her eyes wary. "He's not going anywhere, Franz."

"I didn't say otherwise," Franz said, deciding that it wasn't the right time to argue the point.

Sunny's face lit up. "He's so gorgeous, you have no idea. Oh, and that little smile of his—it could melt the North Pole."

Despite his doubts, Franz had to laugh. His wife sounded more like a Jewish mother than a Chinese parent. Here, relatives considered it unlucky to gush openly over a child.

Sunny pulled him by the hand. "We had best leave before Ghoya finishes his lunch."

The clouds had cleared and the late April sun beat down on the street, hinting at the unforgiving heat that summer would soon bring. Kung Ping Road was its usual hub of activity and commerce. Franz and Sunny walked past the usual array of Jewish peddlers standing in front of their makeshift stalls, selling everything from used clothes to pieces of furniture. Franz even spotted a handsome art deco–style wireless that reminded him of the prized Aero radio he had kept in his living room in Vienna. Where, Franz wondered, did these refugees keep finding items to peddle? His family had run out of their resaleable belongings years ago.

As Franz and Sunny walked hand in hand along the busy street, people greeted them with smiles, waves and even "*Guten Tag, Herr Doktor.*" There were one or two disparaging glances but, as usual, Franz didn't know whether the reason was racism, envy or the disdain for hand-holding among Orthodox Jews.

Despite the community's diminished ranks—reduced by death, not emigration, as the refugees couldn't leave Shanghai—Franz had heard that the refugee population still numbered twenty thousand strong. There were far too many refugees for Franz to know them all, but he was surprised by how many he did recognize. He was acquainted with many in the community through the synagogue and the Refugee Council, and he recognized others as former patients or their family members. His sense of pride in how well his community had persevered was tempered by a bitter realization that any day he could again be ripped away from them.

Sunny turned to him with a frown. "Something is wrong, Franz?"

"Nothing. Just idle thoughts."

Sunny squeezed his hand. "Tell me."

"For so long, I'd thought of Shanghai as only a temporary refuge. A shelter of last resort."

"And now?"

"It's beginning to feel more like home."

Sunny yanked him to a stop and kissed him again. "Oh, Franz, you have no idea how much I love you."

"Actually, darling, I think I do."

"Shanghai isn't so bad, is it?" she murmured in his ear. "One day soon, when the war is over and the Japanese are gone, we could find a house like we had before."

He could see how desperately she wanted him to share in her dream, but Franz had difficulty imagining the city as a permanent home, even if they were to survive the war. Besides, Ghoya's words—"You didn't think you would be staying in Shanghai?"—hung over him. Concerned that she might pick up on his dark mood, he simply nodded and changed the subject. "Tell me, what else has happened since I've been gone?"

As they walked, Sunny updated Franz on the developments in the ghetto. Although he wasn't surprised to hear of poor Herr Steinmann's death, it still conjured memories of his own father's passing. Sunny went on to describe her confrontation with Baron von Puttkamer and Major Huber, and their threats of reprisal against him. Franz was particularly troubled to hear that von Puttkamer had recognized Sunny. Preoccupied with his worries, he was slow to notice how fidgety Sunny had become. He slowed to a stop. "Something is bothering you, isn't it?"

Looking away, she nodded.

"What is it?"

"I know I promised to never again get involved with espionage, but this time it wasn't my doing—"

Franz's neck tensed. "Oh no, Sunny, don't tell me. Please, God. You didn't get involved with the Underground again? Not after the last time. When your own cell turned on you—"

"No, not the Underground." She waved her hands frantically. "An American pilot. He had been shot down." She hurriedly told him about Father Diego and Lieutenant Lewis, and their dramatic appearance at the refugee hospital. "I'm so sorry, Franz. I didn't know what else to do."

As alarmed as he was at the thought of an American pilot hiding in their midst, Franz felt proud of her swift actions. He caressed her cheek. "What choice did you have, darling? I would have done the same."

Sunny smiled lackadaisically. "Maybe by tomorrow the lieutenant will be stable enough to move from the hospital."

"Move to where?"

"Perhaps the Comfort Home."

"Would Chih-Nii really allow it?"

"The basement hideaway is still in use from time to time. Jia-Li thinks Chih-Nii might be willing to help, yes.

Franz nodded. "What's he like, this pilot?"

"He's so young, Franz. Still looks like a boy. I can't believe he flies one of those giant bombers. It's as if—"

Sunny was interrupted by a man's voice coming from behind them. "Good day, Dr. Adler."

They turned to see Rabbi Hiltmann, in his black suit and hat, approaching. Despite a limp from an arthritic hip, he caught up to them quickly. Franz returned his handshake. "Rabbi, you remember my wife, Sunny?"

"How could I forget? After all, I married you to this lovely woman, did I not?" Hiltmann glanced at her with a paternal smile. "You too, Sunny, are always welcome in our *shul*. You understand that, of course."

Sunny nodded gratefully. "Perhaps one day, Rabbi."

Hiltmann turned back to Franz. "That daughter of yours has a good head on her shoulders. She has much to contribute to our discussions."

"Your discussions, Rabbi?" Franz asked.

"The meetings at the *shul*. Hannah and her friend, Herschel, attend regularly. The young lady is full of ideas. She deeply appreciates the urgent need for a homeland in Palestine."

Franz stiffened. He couldn't help feeling slightly betrayed. Hannah had never mentioned attending any Zionist gatherings.

"We are meeting again tomorrow, Dr. Adler," Hiltmann said. "It would be an honour if someone of your standing in the community were to join us. Besides, wouldn't it be wonderful to have multiple generations of Adlers in attendance?"

Franz shook his head. "I think not, Rabbi."

"Oh? May I be so bold as to ask why not?"

"I don't believe in Zionism."

"And why is that, Doctor?"

"I think it's a pipe dream. Worse than that, Rabbi, I think it's a contagion."

"A contagion?" Hiltmann raised a bushy eyebrow. "Like a disease, you mean?"

"In effect, yes," Franz said, knowing his words lacked tact. "One that serves to stir up anti-Semitism among the gentiles wherever it spreads. The same way a virus spreads a cough."

Sunny reached for his arm. "Franz," she cautioned.

But the rabbi appeared unperturbed by the rudeness. He stroked his beard thoughtfully. "So, if I understand you correctly, the issue is not that anti-Semitism flourishes everywhere we Jews live, but rather that talk of a Jewish homeland incites it?"

"I can't deny that we Jews seem to be resented wherever we go. But yes, I also believe that talk of Zionism only makes our situation worse."

"Ah." Hiltmann nodded slowly. "So it's best not to stir the pot? To always appease these goys who deign to allow to us live among them? To hide our heads in the sand and apologize for who and what we are?"

"I'm not saying that—"

"Because that turn-the-other-cheek strategy worked so well for us in Hitler's Germany?" The rabbi laughed bitterly. "How many times did I hear my learned friends and colleagues tell me that the Nazis would eventually lose interest if we didn't fight back, if we just ignored them?"

"This is China, not Germany," Franz said. "We are here as refugees at the whim of the Japanese conquerors."

"Forced into a ghetto."

"Perhaps, but at least it's not one of those terrible camps where they've imprisoned the British and Americans citizens. Or worse."

"For now," Hiltmann grunted.

"Exactly so," Franz said. "Our existence here is tenuous. What is the point of discussing a Jewish homeland on the other side of the world when we can't even cross the street without a pass? Why provoke the Japanese over absolutely nothing?"

Hiltmann leaned back as though he had been slapped. "You think of this as nothing?"

"Nothing that is real, anyway. Or has any chance of becoming real while the war goes on. Our life here is hard enough. Why should we risk making it any worse for this hopeless dream of a homeland?"

Hiltmann shook his head and sighed. "You know, Dr. Adler, I'm reminded of the words of another doctor I once knew. Dr. Mendelbaum. A wonderful, gentle man. A pediatrician and leading member of my congregation. In 1935, when the Nuremberg Laws were first passed, I remember him telling me, 'Well, at least it's over now.' 'What do you mean over?' I asked him. And he explained to me that since the Nazis had taken our rights and citizenship away, there was nothing worse they could do to us. I told him then what I tell you now: this is only the beginning." He paused and looked from Franz to Sunny. "They sent Dr. Mendelbaum to Dachau in 1938. He never came back."

Franz shook his head, embarrassed that he didn't feel more sympathy, but it was an outcome he had heard too many times. "Rabbi, what does any of it have to do with talk about a Jewish homeland?"

"Don't you see, Dr. Adler?" Hiltmann asked philosophically. "We must begin somewhere."

"Even here, in Shanghai?"

"In Shanghai, in Warsaw, in New York—even in Madagascar if there are any Jews there," Hiltmann said. "It begins with a movement. A belief. God has shown us He will not protect us unless we defend ourselves. Unless we Jews all over the world band together to stand up for ourselves—with our own army, if necessary—we will surely be wiped off this earth."

CHAPTER 16

Father Diego removed his clergyman's galero and wiped his brow with the back of his hand. "Already so muggy and not even May yet. I'm afraid we are destined for another punishingly humid summer."

"Not unlike my last twenty-nine summers here, Father." Sunny didn't mean to sound brusque, but she couldn't help herself. She hadn't requested the talkative priest's company on her walk home. Her thoughts were on her family, not on the priest or even the American pilot, whose continued presence at the hospital jeopardized the lives of everyone around him.

Diego offered another benevolent smile. One seemed to precede each new request of his. "Tomorrow morning, then?"

"Yes." Sunny sighed.

"Everything is arranged on the other end?"

"They are expecting the lieutenant at the Comfort Home. My friend has seen to it."

"You are convinced Donald is fit to travel?"

"Fit to travel?" She shook her head. "His wounds are improving, but you must remember he underwent major surgery and his blood counts will surely be low. He shouldn't get out of bed for at least another week." She paused. "I'm hopeful he will survive the journey."

Diego's smile faltered only for a moment. "With God's grace."

"I assume Donald will become 'Brother Dominic' again for the journey?"

"Why not?" Diego laughed. "From fighter pilot to Franciscan friar, it's the most natural of transformations."

"And how will you get him there?"

"We will leave as we came, in a rickshaw. This time, God willing, without all the blood."

Diego's attention was drawn to two patrolling soldiers who approached them from the other end of the block. As the men neared, the priest nodded congenially and greeted them with the words *yoi tsuitachi*—which even Sunny understood as Japanese for "good day." Without a trace of acknowledgement, the soldiers marched between Sunny and Diego, deliberately shouldering them off the sidewalk.

As she continued walking with Father Diego, Sunny's thoughts drifted back to her family. She was so relieved to have Franz back home. The unexpectedness of their reunion had only heightened their desire. They had stayed up the past three nights making urgent love as quietly as they could, a crib wedged beside the bed and the rest of the family asleep on the other side of the paper-thin walls. The intensity of Franz's embraces had stirred her own libido to new heights.

Sunny was also touched by Franz's new-found interest in Joey; he had even taken a few turns changing the boy's diapers. Yet, she still felt troubled by the way he interacted with him, and wished that he felt the same unconditional love for Joey that consumed her. But when she saw Franz holding the baby, she sensed in him a hint of reluctance, even resignation.

"Your movements are not restricted to the ghetto, are they, Sunny?" Diego asked, drawing her back to the present.

She glanced over to him with barely concealed irritation. "Pardon me, Father?"

"Unlike the refugees, you are free to come and go from the ghetto as you please. Correct?"

"No one, aside from the Japanese and a few other select nationalities—such as the Spanish—" she held his gaze pointedly—"is free in Shanghai."

Diego motioned over his shoulder toward the soldiers who had just passed. "Of course. All I meant to suggest is that you do not face the same scrutiny at the checkpoints as the other refugees."

"My husband and stepdaughter are refugees. I was born here."

"Yet in spite of your American heritage, you are not considered an Allied citizen?"

"I'm half American by blood only. My mother died when I was young. I've never carried an American passport. To the invaders, I'm just another Chinaman."

He eyed for her a moment. "No doubt you could pass for fully Chinese if need be."

Sunny stopped, as did the priest. "Why does any of this matter, Father?"

"I've been most impressed by your poise." Diego nodded to himself. "The way you have cared for Lieutenant Lewis, medically and . . . in managing his stay. Most admirable. You seem—what is the English word?—unflappable."

Sunny took his warm smile as a harbinger of a new, and potentially dangerous, request. "What is your point, Father?"

Diego put his hat back on and casually angled it forward, casting a slight shadow across his eyes. "Acquaintances of mine are seeking certain information."

"What sort of information?"

"Regarding ship movements in the harbour."

Sunny dropped her voice to a whisper. "Are you asking me to spy for you, Father?"

He pursed his lips. "I'm merely wondering if you would be willing to pay close attention to the ships in port and perhaps keep a record of their whereabouts."

Sunny realized that Diego's grammar had improved and his accent had lessened since their initial encounter. *Are you really Spanish? Or even a priest?* She could feel her pulse hammering in her temples as she struggled to keep her voice calm. "What is preventing you from making those same observations?"

He swept his hands up and down his chest, indicating his cassock. "I would be somewhat conspicuous at the docks."

"Even if you were to wear civilian clothing?"

"Have you been to the harbour lately? You do not see many Caucasians around. Even the Germans don't frequent the wharves." His eyes narrowed. "You, on the other hand . . ."

Sunny stole a glance over either shoulder and then shook her head vehemently. "No. Absolutely not! "

"I see," Diego said, his expression remaining tranquil. "Forgive me, Sunny, I had to at least inquire."

Something compelled Sunny to explain. "Last year, I stumbled into a situation . . . with the Underground. It ended in disaster. My whole family was in terrible danger."

"Very understandable." He nodded. "However, my acquaintances have no association whatsoever with the Resistance."

"The Americans?"

Diego shrugged. "It's of no consequence, really," he said pleasantly. "Especially since you will not be further involved."

"I cannot become involved, Father. I just can't. Do you understand?"

His voice changed, and he now seemed truly compassionate. "I've already asked more of you than I had a right to. And I am forever grateful for the assistance you have provided us."

His kindness only compounded her guilt. She was reminded of that horrible winter's day the previous year when she had stood by and watched, frozen with fear, as two Jewish teenagers were executed across the street from her by an impromptu firing squad. The plaintive looks in the boys' eyes were still burned into her consciousness.

Diego tilted his head. "What is it, my child?"

Sunny shook off the memory. It was the shame of her passivity then that had steered her toward the calamitous involvement with the Underground. She wasn't about to repeat the same mistake. Even if she were willing to break her promise to Franz and muster the nerve, there was no way she would risk Joey's future. She shook her head again. "I have a baby now, Father."

* * *

Even before Sunny opened the door, she could hear Ernst's animated voice. Stepping inside, she found Esther in the kitchen performing her daily ritual of hand-combing the rice and picking out maggots. Ernst sat on the couch holding Joey in one arm while

Jakob climbed across his knees. Sunny couldn't help but grin. It was one of the rare times she had seen the artist looking even remotely ill at ease.

"Ah, Sunny. Rescue me from these tiny terrors," Ernst cried. "They have no appreciation for a man's basic need for a smoke."

Sunny hurried over, kissed Ernst on the cheek and eased Joey out of his arm. Her baby stared up at her with placid eyes. She recognized the traces of a smile forming at the corners of his lips. Emotions welled and she pressed her face to his. "My beautiful, beautiful darling," she whispered into his cheek.

Ernst laughed. "Your beautiful, beautiful darling could use a fresh diaper."

Nodding, Sunny pulled out from behind the couch the basket in which she kept the clean cloths. "How are you, Ernst?"

Jakob climbed up into Ernst's lap. Ernst bounced him on one knee while he fished a cigarette out of his jacket pocket and lit it. "Better now," he said. "Much easier to cope with these parasites one at a time."

Sunny looked over her shoulder to Esther. "Where are Franz and Hannah, Essie?"

Esther let a handful of rice fall back into the pot. "They left together a few minutes ago for *shul,*" she said.

"The synagogue? On a Thursday?"

"That's what Hannah told me," Esther said weakly.

Sunny noticed that Esther's eyes were bloodshot and tear-crusted. "What is it, Essie?"

Esther wiped her hands and lifted a piece of paper off the countertop.

"From Simon?" Sunny asked.

Esther only nodded.

Sunny glanced over to Ernst, who rolled his eyes. "*Ach*, her husband is being dramatic, is all."

"He's not himself," Esther said.

"He will be fine, Essie. Simon has just been cooped up in the flat for too long." Ernst chuckled and exhaled a stream of smoke. "Exceptional as I am, I must admit, anyone might go a little crazy being stuck with me night and day. After all, genius comes at a cost."

Esther shook her head. "His letters used to make me laugh with tears. Now . . ." she sighed, "in one paragraph, he goes on and on about his plans for us in New York. As if the war is already won. And in the next, he talks about prowling around Germantown. It's such madness, I can't even tell you."

Sunny finished pinning the fresh diaper and lowered Joey's faded cotton gown. "He must feel so helpless, Essie. With you and Jakob so close and yet . . . Still, Simon is one of the most sensible men I've ever met."

"Does this sound sensible to you?" Esther lifted the letter and began to read. "'Sometimes they march right past me. These clown princes of Shanghai. The same ones would've happily collapsed the synagogue down on top of you and our Jakob. And to know they would try it again in a heartbeat. It's all I can do not to reach for the knife in my belt.'" She looked up from the page, wide-eyed. "Listen to him carry on—as if he were the hunter, not the prey."

"It's nothing but talk, Essie." Ernst set Jakob on the floor and rose to his feet. "I have heard the same thing a hundred times before."

Esther stepped over and took Ernst's hand in hers. "It's so dangerous for him to be out on the streets. He doesn't look like the rest of them. And if he spoke two words to them, they would recognize him straightaway for an American." Her voice cracked. "God help us if he were to ever run into that horrid von Puttkamer. You must talk some sense into him, Ernst."

"You think I encourage this idiocy?" He ran a hand through his dishevelled hair and sighed. "Beside, how could I stop him? He usually goes out when I'm not home."

"I will speak to him," Sunny said, her throat tightening at the prospect of venturing back into Germantown.

"Oh, thank you, Sunny. Thank you." Esther sniffled.

Ernst lit a fresh cigarette. "When it comes to von Puttkamer, Sunny, you should be more concerned about your own husband."

Sunny clutched Joey tighter. "What have you heard about him, Ernst?"

"Rumours, nothing more. The baron doesn't confide in me anymore."

"He doesn't suspect that you are the one who warned us about the bombing last winter?" Esther asked.

"No. Nothing like that." Ernst brushed the thought away. "I would be dead already if he did. No, based on a few of his charming remarks, I think he suspects I might not be up to the lofty Aryan standard of masculinity. In the baron's eyes, being a *Tunte*—a degenerate queen—might even be a worse crime than fraternizing with Jews."

"What about Franz?" Sunny pressed. "What did you hear?"

"You remember Gerhard?"

"The young man who followed von Puttkamer around the ghetto? The one with the sneer?"

"The same one who informed me of the baron's plans to bomb the synagogue, yes. He's not as bad as you imagine. In fact,

Gerhard still keeps me in the loop." Ernst smiled to himself. "I'm beginning to suspect that young Gerhard has no such issues with my . . . tendencies."

"What did Gerhard tell you?" Sunny demanded.

"That the baron was carrying on about Franz just yesterday."

"Carrying on?" Dread crawled up Sunny's spine. "What he did say precisely?"

Ernst sighed out a whorl of smoke. "Von Puttkamer blames Franz for the failed bombing. And for Hans's death." He looked away. "Apparently, the baron was talking of 'evening the score.'"

CHAPTER 17

Hannah could tell by Herschel's fidgeting that he was desperate to walk ahead of the adults, but she stuck determinedly by her father's side. A few weeks before, she would have felt self-conscious walking down a busy street with her father's arm draped over her shoulder. Not anymore. He had been home for four days, but Hannah couldn't shake the awful sense that he might be taken away again at any moment. And she intuited from her father's attentiveness—the way he always seemed to be watching her, ever since his return—that he shared in that fear.

"Is it true someone has a big birthday tomorrow?" Herschel's grandfather asked in his refined German, which carried only a remnant of a Polish accent.

"Not a big one, Herr Zunder," Hannah said. "Only fourteen."

"Surely they are all big at your age." Zunder laughed. "Only when you get to be ancient like me do they stop mattering." According to Herschel, his grandfather was over seventy but, with his admirable posture and spry gait, the man didn't strike Hannah as old at all.

Franz rubbed Hannah's shoulder affectionately. "Perhaps not for my daughter, but it's a very big one for me, Herr Zunder. I can't believe how quickly she is growing up."

"Will there be a party?" Zunder asked.

"Zeyde, please," Herschel said.

Zunder looked over to Franz, bewildered. "Tell me, how am I embarrassing the boy now? By simply asking if there will be a party for his girlfriend?"

"Zeyde," Herschel groaned, his face reddening instantly.

Hannah felt her own cheeks burning, but she enjoyed hearing the word. Neither she nor Herschel had yet referred to one another as boyfriend or girlfriend. She could sense her father's eyes on her now, but she was too embarrassed to look at him, or at Herschel, so she lowered her gaze to the ground.

"I don't know about a party, Herr Zunder," Franz said. "However, you and your family are more than welcome to join us for dinner tomorrow."

Pleased as Hannah was at the thought, she worried over what Esther could possibly prepare for them all. Lately, their suppers had consisted of rice and soggy green vegetables that were so flavourless they weren't even worth identifying. She stole a quick glance at Herschel, but he was still too mortified to look at her.

"We would be honoured to join your family, Dr. Adler," Zunder said. "Providing you will allow my Dora to bring dessert."

"Dessert?" Franz shook his head. "No. That would be asking far too much."

"No one should celebrate a birthday—certainly not one as important as the fourteenth—without one of Dora's linzer tortes."

"A linzer torte?" Franz repeated, impressed. "How could she possibly?"

"Felix Klingermann is an old friend of ours."

"Of the bakery Klingermann's?"

"Precisely," Zunder said. "For special occasions, Felix will always allow Dora to borrow a few supplies and use the oven."

Practically salivating at the prospect of the delicacy, Hannah fixed her father with her most persuasive smile.

"As long it will not cause you or your wife too much trouble, Herr Zunder," Franz finally said. "We would appreciate it greatly."

"It will cause me no trouble at all and, as for Dora, it's a labour of absolute love. So it is settled, then."

With Zunder setting a brisk pace, they reached Wayside Road and turned onto the busy thoroughfare. A Japanese transport truck coughed out a plume of blue smoke as it roared by. A long black Citroën, one of the rare automobiles without military markings, rolled slowly past them in the other direction.

They walked past the entrance to the Lyceum Theatre, which ran a revue in German and Yiddish four nights a week. Hannah had never been inside, but she'd heard Freddy Herzberg mimic the comedic acts so often that the building felt oddly familiar to her. Across the street, a pack of young bearded Hasidic Jews in long black coats and hats stood clustered outside a building that temporarily housed the Mir Yeshiva. Although the students kept to themselves, Hannah was familiar with the story, which had become legendary in the ghetto, of how the entire student body and faculty of the religious school had escaped from Lithuania through the Soviet Union and Japan, eventually ending up in Shanghai. Apparently, it was the only yeshiva in continental Europe to survive the war intact.

Zunder waved in the direction of the students. "Look, Herschel," he said. "Go tell your rabbi that we don't need to build a homeland in Palestine. We have one right here."

Hannah had never before heard Herr Zunder mention Rabbi

Hiltmann or Zionism, but Herschel had complained that his grandfather was no more supportive of the movement than her father was.

"It's not the same, Zeyde," Herschel said, his voice lacking its usual conviction.

"What's so different, boy? You have Jewish culture, education and religion. All on the same street."

"True, Herr Zunder." Franz pointed to the intersection ahead, which marked the perimeter of the ghetto. A soldier stood rigidly with a rifle across his chest. "But Jews can also be shot for crossing the very same street without a pass. That hardly seems like much of a homeland."

Hannah wondered if she had misheard or misunderstood her father. Zunder turned to Franz with a disappointed frown that wrinkled his face and made him look much older. "You too, Dr. Adler? You put stock into this Zionist fantasy?"

Franz showed Hannah a tiny wink. "I agree, Herr Zunder, that it might amount to little more than a fantasy. However, it doesn't mean the concept has no merit."

Hannah heard the hum of an engine and glanced over to see a black automobile turn the corner onto the road behind them. She couldn't tell if it was the same car that had passed them earlier, but her attention was drawn back to Herr Zunder, who sighed heavily. "The land of milk and honey, is it?" he said.

"It could be one day, Zeyde," Herschel said.

Zunder raised a hand skyward. "Rivers of gold and lakes of chocolate sound wonderful too, but are they really worth risking what little we have left?"

"I am not a Zionist, Herr Zunder," Franz said. "Up until the Anschluss, I lived a completely secular existence."

Zunder nodded approvingly. "So you were assimilated then."

"More than just assimilated; I had turned away from Judaism altogether."

"Did you convert to Christianity, Dr. Adler?"

"No, but back then I saw myself as many things—Austrian, Viennese and, of course, a surgeon—but a Jew?" Franz shook his head. "No, I disdained all religion, particularly my own."

"And who says you weren't right to?" Zunder said, anger seeping into his voice. "My own son, he found religion. He became active in the local Jewish Federation. And who do you think was among the very first people the Gestapo came looking for the day after Kristallnacht?"

"Zeyde," Herschel said.

Hannah realized that Herr Zunder was talking about Hershel's father. Seeing the hurt in the boy's eyes, she resisted the urge to wrap him in a hug.

Zunder smiled tenderly at his grandson. "Your parents are safe somewhere in the relocation camp, *Liebling*. We heard this from their old neighbours. I was merely pointing out to Dr. Adler that activism comes at a price."

"Perhaps," Franz said. "But I'm beginning to see that inaction carries a cost of its own."

Zunder nodded knowingly. "Ah, so the rabbi has got to you, has he? He is nothing if not . . ." Zunder's words tapered off as the black automobile's tires crunched to a halt beside them. The back doors flew open and four men wearing homburgs and trench coats despite the heat climbed out. Only one of them was Asian. He was tall and muscular, and his impassive face looked neither Japanese nor Chinese to Hannah. The fair-skinned young man beside him had angular Nordic features and might have been handsome had it not been for his scowl. The third man was older, about her father's age, with a weak chin and dark, glaring eyes. But it was sight of the last one to emerge that practically stopped Hannah's heart. She would never forget the day Baron von Puttkamer had come to her school—for no apparent reason other than to intimidate the students, parents and staff—and paraded around the classrooms like a sadistic landlord taking glee in hand-delivering eviction notices.

Herr Zunder grabbed for Herschel's shoulder, and they both stumbled back off the sidewalk. Franz pulled Hannah close to his side.

With a reptilian smile, von Puttkamer stepped toward them. "Ah, Herr Doktor, we have been looking all over for you."

"Why would you be looking for me, Baron?" Franz said.

Von Puttkamer's gaze drifted from Herschel to Hannah. Herschel's face was drained of colour. Hannah's mouth felt parched and her fingers trembled, but she maintained the eye contact until von Puttkamer turned back to her father. The baron held a hand toward the open car door. "I think this matter is best not discussed in front of the children," he said calmly.

Hannah felt her father's elbow gently guiding her behind him as he stood his ground. "Shall we make an appointment to meet, then?"

Von Puttkamer just smiled as though happily reminiscing. "There is a degree of urgency to our conversation."

"Papa," Hannah croaked, her voice thick with dread.

"I am not getting into that car," Franz said defiantly.

The man with the furious eyes shook his fist at Franz. "This is not an invitation, you *filthy* Jew," he growled. "You will come with us right now."

Von Puttkamer rested a hand on his colleague's arm and gently pushed it down. “Pardon Major Huber’s brusqueness.” He nodded to the two other men with him. “However, the major does have a point.”

Hannah clung to her father’s back, but he pushed her away as the two men moved forward. The Asian man stepped to one side of Franz, and the younger German, the other. A moment of agonizing silence followed. The men shared a glance and then grabbed Franz by the upper arms.

“Let go of me!” Franz exclaimed as he struggled wildly in their grip.

“Herschel, no,” Zunder cried from somewhere behind Hannah.

Suddenly, Herschel whizzed past her and launched himself at the tall Asian man, landing on his back. The man reacted with the speed of a cat. In one motion, he spun and flipped the boy hard onto the ground. Herschel landed with a loud moan, and before he could move, the man kicked him in the side.

Hannah screamed. She threw herself at the other man holding her father. She dug her teeth into his arm and bit down as hard as she could.

The man yelped and flung out his arm, knocking her backwards. “You kike bitch,” he bellowed. “I will kill you.”

Winded and terrified, Hannah lay on her back, her legs trembling uncontrollably. Then she noticed the soldier at the end of the block. He had turned toward the commotion. *“Tasukete!”* She screamed the Japanese word for help. “Please help us. *Tasukete!*”

The soldier ran toward them, raising his rifle as he approached.

Herschel rocked on the sidewalk, but everyone else stilled as the soldier neared. He swung the muzzle of his rifle from one person to the next, uncertain where to level it. He finally settled on the Asian man to the right of Franz.

Von Puttkamer took a step forward. "A misunderstanding. Nothing more. We are Germans, not Jews." He snapped his right arm in salute. "Heil Hitler."

The soldier pivoted, aiming his rifle at von Puttkamer's head while barking at him in Japanese.

The baron lifted up his other hand and took a step back. "All right. None of this is necessary." He nodded to the car behind him. "We will leave now."

"What do you mean, leave?" Huber growled through his clenched teeth. "What about this murdering Jew?"

"Next time," von Puttkamer said as he slowly backed away from the soldier and toward the car. "We will settle this next time."

CHAPTER 18

"I don't think I've ever seen a surgeon smile through an entire surgery," Franz remarked.

"How can you tell behind my mask?" Sunny chuckled.

"Your eyes, my darling, they're beaming."

Sunny tied another loop of catgut across the abdominal wound. Otto Berg had been so stoic about his ruptured appendix that his wife brought him to the hospital only after she had caught him surreptitiously vomiting in the alley. Sunny had already closed the incision effectively, but she had been taught that, when it came to surgical closure, redundancy was always safer, so she added one more stitch for good measure. Only once she had tied it off did she address her husband's observation. "There are few things more gratifying than a straightforward appendectomy, especially when performing it before my old teacher." She laughed. "You don't enjoy operating with your student anymore, Dr. Adler?"

"Very much so, but you're hardly my student. You are my colleague."

"When it comes to surgery, Herr Doktor, I will always be your student."

Franz nodded to the bucket that held the patient's excised

appendix, which resembled the blackened tip of a burned breakfast sausage. "In this case, the pupil might have exceeded her master. I think you could have removed Herr Berg's appendix in your sleep."

"You can stop with the flattery, Dr. Adler," Sunny said. "After all, I am a married woman."

Berta, who sat at the head of the bed performing the duties of anesthetist, sighed. "You two," she said with an amused shake of her head.

Sunny looked over at her husband. "Besides, I have every reason to smile. The hospital is operating again. We have anesthetic, at least for the time being. Donald will be discharged today. My husband is home. And best of all, our family—our *growing* family—is healthy and intact."

"A true blessing, *kayn ayn horeh*," Berta said, uttering the Yiddish expression that Esther also favoured, which Sunny understood to be the equivalent of *Don't jinx it*. "Although, as I heard it, it was a very close brush yesterday," Berta added.

Franz cleared his throat. "Well, yes, but Mr. Ghoya has allowed me to come home."

Berta shook her head. "No, not that awful man. I was speaking of—"

"That's all in the past, Frau Abeldt." Franz cut Berta off with a withering glance. "None of this is appropriate discussion for the operating theatre."

Sunny turned suspiciously to the head nurse, a squint replacing her smile. "What happened yesterday, Berta?"

Berta glanced over at Franz, her eyes fearful and confused. "I . . . I merely meant that it seems as though Dr. Adler returned just yesterday."

Sunny dropped the needle driver onto the surgical tray. She looked from Franz to Berta and back. "What is it? What really went on yesterday?"

Franz held her gaze for a moment and then, defeated, exhaled. "Not here, Sunny." He motioned to the patient, who had begun to stir on the table. "Berta, would you mind bandaging the wound if Sunny and I were to step out?"

"Of course, Dr. Adler." Her voice sounded still flustered. "I will take care of it. Go ahead, please."

Sunny followed Franz into the hallway, where they both paused to drop their gowns and masks into the laundry hamper before continuing on to the staff room. Franz closed the door behind them, isolating them in the cramped, stale-smelling room. "Yesterday, on Chusan Road, I was accosted by von Puttkamer and a few of his cronies."

Sunny clutched the back of a chair. "What do you mean 'accosted'?"

"They showed up out of the blue. Von Puttkamer said he needed to speak to me urgently." He went on to describe the standoff with the Nazis.

As shocked as Sunny felt, she also suspected that Franz was downplaying the details for her benefit. "So were it not for that Japanese soldier, you would already be dead by now?"

"Darling, that is perhaps a bit dramatic."

"What else do you think they had in mind for you?" she snapped. "Schnapps and schnitzel?"

"I still have the photographs from their attempted attack on the synagogue and the hospital. Von Puttkamer knows that if he were ever to try—"

She cut him off with a firm shake of her head. "You . . ." The words lodged in her throat. When she spoke again, her voice was hoarse and wounded. "You and Hannah weren't even planning to tell me about this?"

"I was, yes, eventually." Franz reached out to touch her shoulder, but she leaned back and shook off the contact. "With Hannah's birthday dinner, and the Zunders coming, I thought it best not to upset you right now."

"Oh, Franz, can you not see? It's so much more upsetting that you thought it was best to hide this from me."

His expression remained resolute. "What good could have come of telling you, Sunny? To make you worry over something else you have no control over?"

"It's about trust, Franz. We promised to share everything, good or bad. I learned that lesson last year with the Underground. I thought . . ."

He stared at her helplessly, and then his expression turned apologetic. "I should have told you." He reached for her hand. "I'm sorry, darling."

Sunny pulled away from his touch. "What about the next time?"

"If von Puttkamer comes back?"

"*When* he comes back."

Franz nodded. "As you can tell from Berta's loose lips, the rumours have already spread through the ghetto. This morning, a group of youths from the synagogue followed me to work. My own bodyguards, apparently."

She shook her head. "A gaggle of unarmed boys won't be able to protect you from them."

"I'll be more careful," he muttered.

"How, Franz? By hiding inside all day long, like Simon has to?"

"That might be a little extreme. We will think of something. Until then, I'll keep the boys from the synagogue close."

There was a knock at the door. Sunny opened it to find Father Diego standing beside Lieutenant Lewis, dressed again as Brother Dominic, except this time he wore the hood of his brown habit down. Although he looked slightly more robust than he had on the day of his arrival, his complexion was still wan, despite his enthusiastic grin. "I am checking out today, Sunny," he said in his flat Midwestern accent. "I wanted to stop by to thank you again. For saving my life and all."

"I only removed fragments of shrapnel," Sunny said. "Anyone with a scalpel and forceps could have done the same for you."

"Well, I for one echo the sentiment of my young Franciscan friend." Diego turned to Franz. "Your wife's humility is absolutely impenetrable. Does she ever take credit for anything?"

Franz shot her a cautious but tender glance. "Precious little, Father."

Ignoring the other two, Sunny summoned a smile for the lieutenant. "How do you feel on your feet, Donald?"

"Kind of like I just pulled my plane out of a barrel roll and a pitchback." The young pilot laughed self-consciously. "I can't really complain, though. A lot of the guys back in the squadron would kill to be in my shoes. After all, I'm on my way to live at a cathouse."

Diego cast Lewis a look that was more amused affection than disapproval. "You will not be living there, Donald. Only a temporary stopover."

"How much longer before you'll get Donald out of Shanghai, Father?" Sunny asked.

"Days. A week or two at the most."

Lewis grinned again. "I'm sure I can hold out there a week or two. As long as my wife doesn't find out. I think she'd almost prefer it if I were put in a Jap POW camp. Rosemary's got a real jealous streak."

"No doubt Rosemary would prefer most to have you home, and we will get you there," Father Diego promised.

"For as long as you stay in Shanghai, I can look after your wounds and dressings," Sunny said.

Lewis grimaced. "You're going to come to visit me at a brothel?"

Sunny laughed softly. "I know the Comfort Home well. My best friend works there."

The incredulity on the lieutenant's face intensified. "Your best friend is a . . . ?"

Sunny didn't flinch. "She is one of the most amazing people you will ever meet."

Diego grinned. "One does meet the most extraordinary people only in the most extraordinary of places."

"Yes, I suppose," Sunny said, then turned back to the pilot. "But Jia-Li has been through so much of late. She is not herself these days."

"What happened to her?" Lewis asked.

"That is a very long story," Sunny said as she turned for the door. "And it's time for us to leave."

"*Us?*" Franz folded his arms across his chest. "Sunny, you're not planning to go with them?"

"I have to speak to Jia-Li and Chih-Nii."

"But, darling, what if . . ."

"The lieutenant and I are discovered en route," Diego finished Franz's sentence.

"You're not coming with us. No way, no how." Lewis shook his head adamantly. "It's a terrible idea, Sunny. I would never fly wing to wing on a midday sortie into enemy territory."

* * *

In the end, they reached a compromise: Sunny rode in a separate rickshaw from Hongkew to Frenchtown. Lewis and Diego were already waiting in the Comfort Home's sumptuous sitting room. Chih-Nii stepped through the doorway in a shimmering black cheongsam with a pink fringe. Sunny couldn't help but be reminded of the dancing hippopotami in the Disney movie *Fantasia*, which she had seen only weeks before the attack on Pearl Harbor had cut Shanghai off from its supply of Hollywood films. But the expression on Chih-Nii's rouged face looked anything but amused. "You are certainly not the first two clergymen to darken the Comfort Home's doors," the madam announced. "I hope you are not both planning to stay."

Diego raised his hands. "I would be honoured to remain here, madam. To teach and to learn. But alas, my commitments elsewhere are manifold."

"I am not exactly sure what you could teach us, Father," Chih-Nii grunted.

"To welcome God into your heart, I would hope."

"I am not convinced God could afford my prices." Chih-Nii smiled thinly. "But I have little doubt there is much you could learn here." She turned to Sunny. "Ah, there's my exotic buttercup. The one who delivers me no end of complications. Why, Soon Yi, if I didn't love you so . . ."

"Our friend won't be staying long," Sunny said sheepishly, aware of the magnitude of the favour she was asking.

Chih-Nii interlocked her fingers. "A week or two at the most is what I have been promised."

"If that." The priest stepped forward. "I am Father Diego. It's a pleasure to make your acquaintance." Chih-Nii ignored his outstretched hand. Unperturbed, Diego indicated the lieutenant. "Allow me to introduce Brother Dominic."

Lewis bowed his head. "I am most grateful for your hospitality, ma'am."

Chih-Nii sized the lieutenant up with a calculating eye and then snorted. "My own brother would look more convincing as a man of the cloth. And he's addicted to the pipe."

Just then, Jia-Li coasted into the room, a cigarette holder dangling from her lips. "Ah, newcomers," she said in English. "Tell me, are you clients or fugitives—or perhaps both?"

"Careful," Chih-Nii snapped in Mandarin.

"I always am, Mama," Jia-Li replied airily as she drifted over to greet Sunny with a hug that left the scent of jasmine and tobacco in its wake. "Sister, I've missed you."

"Me too, *bǎo bèi*."

"Is it true? Franz is home with you?" Jia-Li giggled. "That ridiculous little tyrant really did release him? Even without sampling our special soup?"

"It's all true." Sunny was bursting to tell her best friend of Franz's run-in with the Nazis and how he had tried to hide it from her, but she realized now wasn't the time. "Jia-Li, this is Don—Brother Dominic."

Jia-Li floated over to Lewis and wrapped him in a quick hug. He winced in pain but then smiled shyly, appearing as rattled as most men were when first encountering Jia-Li. "Ah, our American pilot. A true war hero," she gushed in English as she released him. "Thank you, thank you."

"Shut your mouth," Chih-Nii snarled in Mandarin. "Ears are everywhere. Are you trying to get us killed?"

"Never, Mama." Jia-Li reached out to stroke the madam's face.

Chih-Nii batted her hand away. "Take them downstairs," she ordered.

"It would be my great honour." Jia-Li bowed theatrically and turned to lead them out of the room.

Sunny was about to follow Diego and Lewis out when Chih-Nii grabbed her by the elbow. "A quick word, little one?"

After the others had disappeared down the hallway, Chih-Nii interlocked her fingers and rested her arms across her protruding belly. "I am deeply concerned."

"The priest swears it will only be a matter of days—"

"That is an entirely separate concern." Chih-Nii cut her off with a terse wave. "I am speaking now of our mutual friend."

"You don't think Jia-Li is on the pipe again, do you?" Sunny asked. Despite Jia-Li's erratic behaviour, her pupils hadn't appeared constricted.

"Perhaps yes, perhaps no." Chih-Nii's shrug was difficult to read. "What I do know is that she is becoming reckless. Dangerously so."

"Like the way she was talking about the Brother's true identity?"

"In English too!" Chih-Nii shook her head, disgusted. "That is merely the tip of the iceberg."

"What else?"

"There was an incident."

The hairs on Sunny's neck bristled. "What sort of incident, Mama?"

Chih-Nii considered the question for a moment, then her lips twisted into a placating smile. "Ah, but that's all in the past now. Suffice it to say, I am no longer convinced we can trust our golden orchid or her judgment."

CHAPTER 19

June 9 1944

As Franz held Joey in his arms, he surveyed the people gathered on Ward Road. He couldn't remember the last time he had seen a Jewish crowd looking as jubilant. The news of the Allies' D-Day landings had spread from neighbour to neighbour. It was all anyone in the ghetto seemed to be discussing. People clustered around radios, hanging on every word from the banned Voice of America broadcasts, which described the beachheads the Americans, British and Canadians had secured in Normandy. Franz had never heard of any of these places, but it sounded to him as though every square inch of captured sand had come at a bloody cost. The reports reminded him of the gut-wrenching tales of slaughter that he had heard as a teenager in Vienna from traumatized veterans of the Great War.

The collective sense of optimism was contagious. Franz felt a lightness in his step that he hadn't experienced in ages. It had to do with more than just D-Day. Since returning home, the episodes of dizziness had subsided in frequency to one every few days and had become milder in nature. Moreover, a month had passed without a von Puttkamer sighting, though the young volunteers—many of whom came from the ranks of the Jewish boxing club—still shadowed him on the streets. Franz had even begun to wonder if Ghoya's threat about being dispatched from Shanghai had been nothing more than another one of his groundless threats. Despite Franz's wariness, hope was germinating.

Sunny pointed at a group of young Jewish women across the street. Their faces were pink and vibrant, and they talked animatedly, giggling among themselves while their children ran up and down the sidewalk chasing a soccer ball made of tightly wadded old newspapers and string. Another cluster of women stood at the far end of the block. Across from them, a group of teenagers from the school formed a small circle. Among them was Hannah, whose back was turned to them.

Sunny rolled her eyes good-naturedly. "The way people are carrying on, you would think that Berlin had already fallen."

Franz shrugged his shoulders as much as he could with Joey asleep in his arms. "Remember when Paris fell to the Nazis and England was teetering? It all seemed so hopeless then."

"Has it really changed that much?" Sunny asked. "The Germans still hold Paris and, aside from a few beaches in Normandy, the rest of France."

"True, but now Hitler's precious *Festung Europa*—Fortress Europe—has been breached. People have reason to celebrate. They deserve that much, Sunny."

She reached for his elbow and gave it an encouraging squeeze. "As do you."

"Even if Germany does eventually fall, there is still Japan," Franz pointed out. "Who knows how long they could hang on for?"

She offered him a small rueful smile. "Whether the Japanese admit it or not, the war is lost for them too. Everyone says so."

Franz chuckled. "By *everyone,* you mean a bunch of refugee gossips?"

"The radio announcers say so too," Sunny said. "How can one little island empire—no matter how ferocious or vicious—hold off the rest of the world? It's not possible, Franz."

"Let's hope not," he said.

Joey squirmed in Franz's arms and mewled. Franz repositioned the baby across his chest, gently swaying him to and fro. Joey found his fingers and began to suck noisily on them. He stared up contentedly at Franz.

"You see," Sunny cooed. "He loves you."

"Just because he stopped crying?"

"No, silly, the way he's looking at you. He knows you're his father."

The idea felt foreign to Franz, as though he were trying on someone else's clothes. Franz wanted to experience that same overwhelming connection to Joey as he had with Hannah in her first months—that sense that nothing else in the world mattered—but he still had too many doubts. "It's all happened so suddenly, Sunny."

She laughed. "That tends to happen with babies."

"You know what I mean, darling. I . . . we had no warning."

Her lips tightened. "We've discussed this, Franz."

"Discussed, yes," Franz said. "We haven't necessarily agreed."

Sunny stiffened. The last remnant of her smile vanished and her eyes creased into a squint. "So you're still not willing to accept him into our family?"

"It's not so much the issue . . . a matter of . . . accepting." Franz stumbled over the words.

"Then what is the matter?"

"I am not convinced our home is the best place for him—that we should keep him—under the current circumstances."

Sunny reached out and grabbed Joey out of Franz's arms, startling the baby and dropping his blanket in the process. Franz bent down to pick it up off the filthy sidewalk. He stood up and offered it to her, but she had already turned her back on him. "How can you talk this way?" she demanded.

"I am only trying to be realistic." He swirled a hand in the air. "This celebration, it's not real. Nothing has changed. We are still prisoners of war."

"Not forever, we won't be," she said as she hugged Joey ferociously.

"Perhaps. Until then, every day it's a struggle to find food. Even rice. And, if you're right about Japan's defeat, it will surely only get worse before the war ends. Perhaps much worse. Especially in the ghetto. They will not leave quietly."

"So you would have me just give Joey away, would you?" she asked, still facing away from him.

Franz reached for her shoulder but stopped himself, knowing she would only shrug it off. "Not forever. No, darling. I'm only suggesting we find him a safe home until our situation here stabilizes. Perhaps one of your cousins' families—the one who lives in Frenchtown, maybe—could take him in? Then when the Japanese are gone . . ."

Sunny spun back to face him, her eyes red and burning but her expression steadfast. She snatched the blanket from his hand and swaddled it around Joey. "So you have decided, then?" she asked calmly.

Franz shook his hands in frustration. "When have I ever had any say in the matter?"

"From the very first day."

He shook his head. "No, Sunny. This is exactly like when you joined the Underground."

"How can you say that, Franz? How can you compare *that* to adopting a child? Is that really how you see it?"

"Only in the sense that you made both decisions without involving me." And before he stopped himself, he blurted, "Remember how it turned out with the Underground."

Sunny's mouth fell open and her eyes clouded with hurt. She stared at him. "Joey is my son," she finally said. "I will never ever abandon him. If he has to leave our home, then so must I."

"When did I say you should abandon him? I am merely suggesting—"

Sunny pivoted and walked off without waiting for Franz to finish.

Franz stood helplessly on the street corner, watching his wife go, feeling acutely alone. A noise from behind him drew his attention. He glanced over his shoulder and noticed movement at the far end of the street. The crowd of people began to disperse. A number of them called out to their children, who dutifully abandoned their game to join their parents. Two soldiers made their way through the crowd. Ghoya walked between them.

Franz tasted acid. The blood drained from his cheeks. He wondered if he might swoon again, but his fear kept him upright. He glanced over and noticed that Hannah had broken free of her friends and was moving toward him protectively. He waved her off with a small, frantic hand gesture. She stopped where she was, her face taut with worry.

Ghoya's crazed grin was like a dagger to his chest. "Ah, Dr. Adler, we have been looking for you high and low," the little man declared as he and his entourage approached. "Yes, yes. High and low. You were not at the hospital or your home, only the other Jewess and her wild brat." He looked skyward in mock sympathy for Esther's plight. "I knew you couldn't be far. Not far at all."

Franz didn't reply, just lowered his chin and dropped his gaze to the pavement.

"The time has come, Dr. Adler," Ghoya announced.

Franz's limbs felt wooden. He didn't dare glance in his daughter's direction. "May I go home and put a bag together before I leave, sir?"

"I am not a savage. You will have plenty of time to say your goodbyes. You will not be leaving until the morning."

"Am I going back to the Country Hospital, sir?" Franz asked, daring to hope.

"The Country Hospital?" Ghoya echoed in surprise before turning to his subordinates and making a joke in Japanese that evoked only a cackle of his own. "No, no, no. Not the Country Hospital. I believe I was very clear with you in my office. Was I not? You will not be staying in Shanghai."

"May I ask where I will be sent?"

"Of course you may, Dr. Adler," Ghoya said, his tone friendly again. "Ichi-Go."

The word meant nothing to Franz. He couldn't help but steal a glimpse at Hannah, who stood frozen, appearing more crestfallen than frightened. "Where is Ichi-Go, sir?" he finally asked.

"Ichi-Go is not a place, Dr. Adler. No, no. Not a place at all."

Bewildered and almost beyond caring, Franz just stared blankly at Ghoya.

"Operation Ichi-Go is the future of the great imperial Empire of Japan. And with it, all of Asia."

II

CHAPTER 20

July 15, 1944

Franz swallowed more saliva as the truck lurched again on the twisty dirt road, dipping up and down over another massive pothole. He wondered whether they would be forced to stop to repair a tire, as they had done twice already in the past three or four hours.

His seemingly endless journey from Shanghai had included every conceivable means of transportation. He had been in transit for over a month, without knowing his final destination until only recently. It had begun with such urgency, when the soldiers whisked him from his home to a transport plane at an airstrip on the outskirts of the city. He had flown inside the fuselage of the freight craft, forced to sit on a wooden crate that might have contained anything from food to live ammunition. After the plane had landed hundreds of miles inland on a runway in the middle of nowhere, he had been carried by a rickety old barge along the Yangtze to Wuchang.

Franz had languished for over two weeks in the war-ravaged city, ordered to stay in a tiny, featureless room. Franz's only consistent contact in Wuchang had come in the form of a sullen Japanese private who spoke in broken English and was no more comprehensible than the pidgin-speaking peddlers in Shanghai. The private brought him meals twice a day, usually rice with some kind of dried fish smothered in a foul-smelling sauce. Franz had little appetite, and the salty taste turned his stomach, but he forced himself to choke down the food just so its smell wouldn't linger in the oppressively stuffy room, where sleep was next to impossible even without the stench.

From Wuchang, Franz had been taken southwest by train in a boxcar crammed with Chinese men, most dressed like the farmers Franz had seen in guidebook photographs of China's countryside. Franz was forced to disembark the train a few miles outside the devastated city of Changsha, which the Japanese had recently captured. He spent another few days hunkered down in a tent pitched among the extensive rubble of flattened houses and buildings. He couldn't help wondering how many civilians had been inside their homes when the bombs had fallen.

While in Changsha, Franz took his orders from a Japanese lieutenant who had been schooled in Cambridge before the war. He spoke highbrow English that made him sound like one of the elite pre-war Shanghailanders. Franz had no interest in talking to the man, but the officer seemed pleased to have someone to impress with his command of the King's English. The lieutenant explained that Operation Ichi-Go meant, in English, Operation Number One. He took great pride in informing Franz that it was the largest operation to date in the Pacific war, and how, with its "inevitable success," it would not only unite the Japanese empire from Manchuria to Indochina but also rid it of the airbases from which American bombers had been harassing the Japanese homeland.

On Franz's final day in Changsha, the lieutenant announced that he was being dispatched to a field hospital somewhere near

Hengyang. Franz had never heard of the city, but according to the lieutenant, its capture was one of the key objectives in Operation Ichi-Go, somehow related to a vital railway intersection and the "gateway to Southern China." Franz wasn't interested in the lieutenant's jingoistic chatter, and it only depressed him further to learn that the offensive was gaining ground and the Japanese were apparently on the verge of conquering Eastern China.

The lieutenant drove Franz out of the city to a waiting convoy of trucks and other military vehicles. Without a word of goodbye, Franz climbed into the back of a troop transport. None of the other young infantrymen aboard appeared to understand English, or German. Their response to Franz—a round-eyed stranger in an ill-fitting khaki uniform, devoid of any insignia—was similar to that of the other soldiers he had encountered along the way. At first, they regarded him with curiosity or hostility or a combination of both. Inevitably, they lost interest and treated him as if he didn't exist. Franz noticed that they hardly even spoke among themselves. Eventually, he began to feel pity for some of them. Several looked to still be teenagers and seemed as miserable as he was to be heading to the front lines. He realized that, regardless of the colour of the uniform, these young soldiers were pawns in the war as much as he was, potentially sacrificing everything to try to sate the ambitions and greed of their masters.

They inched along the road for two agonizing days, though Franz considered *road* to be a generous description for the windy, bombed-out route that abruptly alternated from paved to dirt and back. They often had to stop for the soldiers to clear debris or to assemble makeshift wooden plank-bridges to cover the most gaping of the artillery craters. Franz's constant loneliness was punctuated only by the moments of terror when the truck traversed one of the rickety, mortar-damaged bridges that dotted the road.

Franz had trouble remembering how many days had passed since he had been torn from his family, but his memory of the final minutes with them was as acute as ever and, at times, he wished he could forget. Hannah had not stopped crying. He hadn't seen her as tearful since she had been eight years old, trembling in his arms in the electrified darkness of Kristallnacht. Esther was so upset that Jakob had to throw a tantrum just to get her attention. But Sunny's response had devastated him the most. Tears coursed down her cheeks as she whispered hollow words of encouragement and promises of a speedy reunion. All the while, she cradled Joey almost protectively in her arms. Franz didn't even mention their earlier dispute as he kissed her goodbye, tasting the salt of her tears. What could he have possibly said to make it all right again?

The rumble of an explosion somewhere in the distance jerked Franz out of the memory. Over the growl of the truck's engine, he heard a few more booms echoing. When the truck crunched to a halt, he knew they had reached their destination even before he looked out back and spotted the tents.

Franz followed the soldiers as they climbed out of the truck. The sun was still high in the sky, but the weather lacked the ferocity of a Shanghai summer. He stood in a clearing cut out of the dense bushes and low-lying surrounding trees. Tents were laid out in organized rows that could have covered two or three square city blocks. The soldiers dispersed in various directions, leaving Franz alone on a dirt path. Two men trotted noisily past him carrying a stretcher draped with a sheet bearing a sizable blood stain.

"You were supposed to be here last week," a familiar voice snapped.

Franz turned to see Captain Suzuki standing across from him in a waist-length lab coat, his arms crossed in annoyance. Franz bowed his head respectfully. "Good day, Captain Suzuki."

"They promised me you would be here last week," Suzuki grumbled without returning the bow, "when the wounded were piling up as high as sandbags during a flood."

Franz motioned to the troop transport behind him. "I only just arrived."

Suzuki eyed him coldly. "There is no rest here." He turned and headed down the path. "Ever!"

Franz hurried after him. They passed more orderlies shuttling patients in and out of tents on stretchers. The dirt roads between tents were too narrow for trucks or troop transports to navigate, but the occasional open-air military vehicle—the "Japanese jeeps," as the boxy cars were known in Shanghai—would rattle past occasionally, forcing them to stand off to the side. Every so often, Franz heard the rumbles of distant explosions coming from somewhere beyond the treeline.

As they walked past *A*-shaped and square tents of various sizes, Suzuki grunted descriptions such as "supplies," "mess hall," "convalescence tent" and "barracks." Then he turned abruptly off the path and strode toward the largest of the square tents. Franz followed him through the flap opening into what appeared to be a mobile operating theatre. White-clad men bustled about, shuttling patients and moving equipment. Three stretchers loaded with wounded men were lined up in front of an area separated by canvas walls, which Franz assumed was the operating room.

Suzuki walked over to a sink in the corner, where a rubber pipe snaked up to a tank mounted high above it. He hung his lab coat on a nail, donned a surgical mask and cap and then scrubbed at the sink. Before he had even turned around, a male nurse was waiting with a sterile gown and gloves at the ready. The nurse offered Franz a cap and mask and showed him to the sink.

Once gowned, Franz followed Suzuki into the walled-off operating room. The wooden floorboards creaked with each step he took toward the operating table, where a patient was waiting. Franz couldn't help but be impressed by the mobile setup, better equipped as it was than the operating room at the refugee hospital. It was bright with overhead light from two operating lamps positioned above the gurney. A full surgical tray stood by the table. Four other men were present, all of them masked and gowned. Despite the buzz of activity, no one spoke, and the room was as quiet as a monastery.

The scrub nurse faced away from Franz, sorting surgical utensils on the tray. It wasn't until she turned and he saw the red curls poking out from beneath her cap that he recognized her for Helen Thompson. She said nothing, but her eyes softened with a welcoming smile. For a fleeting moment, Franz experienced a sense of relief.

Suzuki snapped a few orders in Japanese to the man at the head of the bed, who held the anesthesia mask and ether. Franz viewed the patient. The young man's expression was taut with pain and fear as the anesthetic mask was lowered over his face. His exposed right arm was swollen, deformed at the forearm and missing its hand altogether, ending instead in a bloody stump of bandages. The only question in Franz's mind was how far above the elbow they would have to amputate. Suzuki solved that mystery by painting the patient's shoulder with iodine. Once it was cleaned and draped, Suzuki brought scalpel to skin and, without even testing if the patient was still responsive, sliced fluidly through the flesh across the curve of the shoulder.

They worked in silence for several minutes. After the major blood vessels and nerves had been tied off and Suzuki had removed the upper arm from the shoulder socket, he remarked, "Sometimes we see as many injuries from weaponry malfunction as we do from enemy fire."

"How so, Captain?" Franz asked.

Suzuki nodded to the patient. "I am told a grenade detonated in his hand just as he was throwing it."

Franz cringed at the thought. "What horrible luck."

"On the contrary." Suzuki sliced through the centre of the last tendon that was holding the arm attached. "He is a very fortunate man."

"This man?" Franz blurted as he pulled the arm free of the man's body.

"He gets to go home," Suzuki said.

"Without his arm."

"To parents who will see their son again. Maybe to a wife who has cried herself to sleep most nights since he left." Suzuki ran a suture through the exposed muscle. "So few of them will," he said almost under his breath.

Helen eyed Franz quizzically as she handed him a pair of scissors, but neither commented. Suzuki's cheeks flushed slightly, and he cleared his throat. "You will finish this case, Dr. Adler. And the others to follow."

"Yes, Captain," Franz said.

"This is not the Country Hospital." Suzuki dropped the needle driver holding the stitch onto the tray. "Stop the bleeding. Remove as much shrapnel as possible. Amputate when limbs are beyond simple salvage." He shook his finger at him. "But no heroic surgeries, Dr. Adler. You will not be doing anyone—least of all yourself—any favours. Am I clear?"

"Yes, Captain."

Suzuki nodded to Helen. "If you have any doubts, Mrs. Thompson can advise." With that, he turned and walked out of the operating room.

Franz finished suturing the wound, leaving the shoulder so smoothly contoured that it resembled the armless torso of an ancient Grecian statue. By the time he had scrubbed at the sink again and changed into fresh gloves, the next patient was already on the table and the anesthetist was dripping ether onto the facemask.

Helen acted as Franz's translator. Franz was desperate to ask Helen more about the field hospital and the battles raging around it, but he kept the questions to himself, unsure if any of the other assistants understood English.

The patients kept coming. Franz removed three legs, plucked out pounds of bullets and shrapnel and tied so many stitches that he lost count. He allowed two patients—one of whom was missing a fist-sized section of his skull, and another whose lung had been compressed by a chest full of blood—to die while still under anesthesia. He bleakly wondered how many of the young men who had ridden with him in the troop transport would end up on this table with comparable wounds, if they even made it to the hospital.

All day long, the operating table kept filling with new casualties. Franz was almost surprised when, late in the evening, the orderlies removed a patient from the table without replacing him with another. His neck and shoulders ached. He had fought off three or four bouts of dizziness. But he walked out of the operating room feeling slightly more alive than he had when he had entered.

He stood with Helen outside the tent in the warm evening, her silhouette illuminated only by the glow from the light inside. She extracted a pack of cigarettes from her pocket and, after he waved off her offer, lit one for herself. "I wasn't expecting to see you so soon, Franz," she said. "Or, to be honest, ever again."

"Likewise. But, I must say, you are a welcome sight." He cleared his throat. "How long have you been here?"

"Two weeks."

"And how are you coping?"

She looked at him and chuckled, answering only with an exhalation of smoke.

A series of booms rang out louder than any previous ones. Startled, Helen tensed for a moment before her shoulders relaxed. Franz glanced in the direction of the sound. The trees glowed and then vanished back into darkness.

"We're near the front, are we?" Franz asked.

"Not that near." Helen shrugged. "You get used to it. Besides, those are Japanese bombers. It's not them you need to fear."

"What, then?"

"The Chinese and American planes."

"They would bomb a hospital?"

"If they get the chance." She took another long drag on her cigarette. "Hard to blame them, all things considered."

Ahead of them in the distance, the dirt was lit by the jiggling headlamps of an approaching truck. Franz saw other sets of lights following behind the first. Helen sighed. "It's going be another long night."

"More wounded?"

"It's non-stop."

Another, closer, set of headlights lit the road from the opposite direction. Helen and Franz took a step back off the road, but the approaching jeep slowed to a stop in front of them. Helen stiffened and dropped her cigarette, stamping it out surreptitiously.

The driver hopped out and opened the vehicle's back door. Captain Suzuki stepped down, followed by another man. The latter was dressed in an officer's uniform and walked with a pronounced limp, leaning heavily on the cane in his right hand.

Helen bowed deeply at the waist and remained bent over as the men approached. Sensing her anxiety, Franz mimicked her pose. Suzuki said something to her in Japanese and, as soon as she straightened, Franz did so too.

The ranking officer stared at Franz for a penetrating moment. His lean face was cast in shadow, but Franz sensed that he was younger than Suzuki. When the officer finally opened his mouth, he was surprisingly soft-spoken. Suzuki translated his words into English. "Major Okada—our unit's commandant—wishes to welcome you. And to thank you for your efforts to mend our brave casualties."

Franz bowed again.

This time, Okada nodded very slightly in return. He spoke again to Suzuki in a conversational tone before turning and limping back to the car without so much as a glance at the others. Suzuki's eyes drifted from Franz to Helen, and then he turned and followed after Okada without translating his last few remarks.

The jeep drove off, leaving them in the near darkness. Franz turned to Helen. "What did Major Okada say just now?"

Helen shook her head, her gaze on the departing taillights. "Major Okada said that he expects you to work very hard and perform well while here."

Franz eyed her, but she didn't meet his stare. "And if I don't?"

"The major." She paused. Fear crept into her tone. "Franz, you must be so careful around that one."

CHAPTER 21

The midday sun's pounding heat and blinding glare were so relentless that Sunny was regretting her decision to venture out. She steered the rusted pram's stiff wheels toward Broadway, hoping to catch a breeze coming off the Whangpoo. Despite having drawn the canopy over the pram, she worried that Jakob and Joey would overheat inside it. She stopped to check on them again. They were still both fast asleep, so she picked up her pace and hurried along the dockside.

The port was as busy as ever. Japanese naval craft competed with merchant ships and even junks and sampans for berths and harbour space. One ship towered above the others, though. Sunny identified the craft as the cruiser *Idzumo* from its three smokestacks. She hadn't seen the ship in port for at least a year. She thought back to how, only hours after the attack on Pearl Harbor, the *Idzumo* had chased down and mercilessly sunk the British gunship HMS *Peterel.* This had marked the beginning of the Pacific War in Asia. The graphic accounts of the *Idzumo*'s machine gunners mowing down British sailors as they bobbed helplessly in the water ran through the Shanghailander community like an electric current, setting a terrifying precedent for what the previously protected Europeans could expect from the invaders. The brutality came as no surprise to Sunny. She had witnessed so much worse, including the rape of children and the murder of her own father. The Japanese had taken everyone who had meant the most to her: her father, her amah and now her husband.

Oh, Franz, what have they done with you? A month had passed since she had last laid eyes on him. The memory of their inadequate goodbye plagued her. There were so many things she wished she had told him.

Sunny had been to every hospital in the city, hoping against reason that she would find him. Her first stop had been the Country Hospital. It had taken three attempts just to get through the doors of her former workplace. In the end, she and Jia-Li had had to pose as flower girls delivering bouquets to the wounded soldiers. But they hadn't found Franz or anyone who fit the description of a Japanese-speaking Canadian nurse or an American-trained Japanese surgeon. Their next stops, the Shanghai General and two naval hospitals, proved equally fruitless. Franz wasn't in Shanghai.

The sight of two soldiers patrolling on the other side of the street sent her into a silent rage. *Where have you savages taken him?* She had never known such hatred. It scared her, but it was also liberating and helped tamp down the grief.

Sunny pushed the pram toward Garden Bridge—the iconic double truss bridge that spanned Soochow Creek. She had to bend her knees and push from her calves just to manoeuvre the pram's uncooperative wheels onto the walkway. As she wheeled it, her gaze drifted out to the harbour again and she began to mentally sort the vessels, focusing on the warships.

She knew more about identifying naval craft than most civilians. Her father had been a consummate anglophile with a fascination with the Royal Navy. In the summertime, he would sometimes take her down to the Public Garden or the Bund. There, he had taught her to identify the different classes of warships in the harbour from the size and shape of their hulls and turrets. Aside from the *Idzumo*, Sunny counted three destroyers in port. She also spotted four riverboats and three patrol boats. She noted the subtle differences in their shapes and markings, which made even the riverboats distinguishable from one another.

Sunny came to the end of the bridge's walkway and quickly looked about. No one, not even the cluster of sailors standing on the nearby corner, paid her any attention. *Just a mother walking her children along the riverfront*. How easy it would be to make this a routine.

As she passed the sailors—close enough to pick up the odour of their sweat—her blood boiled again. She had to bite her tongue to stop herself from screaming, *What right do you have to take everything from us?*

* * *

Sunny's anger melted into limp fear as she wheeled the pram onto the streets of Germantown. She checked that her scarf was secured tightly around her head, and hid as much of her face as possible. She kept her eyes to the ground and quickened her pace as she headed for Ernst's flat.

At the corner of his apartment block, she stole a glance up the street. Her heart stopped when she spotted three dark uniforms approaching. For a horrified moment, she thought the older man leading the group might be the odious Major Huber. But she calmed slightly when she realized he was just some other self-important Nazi. She lowered her eyes again and continued on toward the building, forcing herself not to run.

At Ernst's door, she had to knock three times and identify herself in the quietest voice possible before the door opened a crack and then swung wider. Simon reached for the pram and pulled it into the apartment, closing the door as soon as Sunny had cleared the threshold.

Simon bent down and eased the sleepy Jakob out of the pram. "Oh, there's my little fella. Jakey." He kissed the toddler repeatedly until the boy squirmed so violently that Simon had to set him on the floor.

Jakob tottered over to Sunny and grabbed her leg while staring up suspiciously at the bearded man. Simon crouched down to his level and rubbed the scruff on his cheeks. "Buddy, it's me. Your daddy. Papa." And then he even added the Yiddish that Esther often used: "*Tate*."

Jakob didn't budge. He tugged at Sunny's leg and said, "Up. Up."

"Teaches me for being too lazy to shave." Simon laughed, undeterred by his son's guardedness. He covered his face with his hands. "Where did Daddy go?" He flipped his hands open like shutters and cried, "Peekaboo. Here he is." After a few rounds of this, Jakob let go of Sunny's legs. Soon he was giggling. And then he raced over to Simon and grabbed at his hands, trying to pull them away from his face. Eventually, the two fell into a playful wrestle, with Jakob crawling on top of his father's chest.

Sunny was relieved to see Simon in a gregarious mood, but as she watched the display of paternal love, she couldn't help longing for Franz. After a few more minutes of wrestling, Simon stood and swept Jakob up in an arm. "Don't suppose I could interest you in a cookie?" he asked.

Jakob tugged at the collar of his father's stained shirt, pleading. Simon carried him to the kitchenette and took a tin down from a shelf. Jakob's eyes went wide as he clumsily thrust his hand inside and extracted a shortbread.

"Sorry, buddy. Uncle Ernst's cookies aren't very fresh." Simon released Jakob back to the floor, where he sat happily gnawing on the tough cookie. Simon rushed over to Sunny and wrapped her in a bony hug, scratching her face with his whiskers. "Ah, Sunny. Bringing my little guy to me—I can't thank you enough. I just can't. You have no idea."

Stepping back, Sunny indicated the pram where Joey was still sleeping. "I do, actually."

Simon leaned over to peek inside. "Ah, look at this guy. He's adorable. He and Jake are going to be such great pals. That poor ghetto won't know what hit them."

"Soon," she agreed with a small laugh. "Where's Ernst?"

Simon straightened, his smile fading. With his face thinner than ever, his nose appeared even more prominent against his sunken cheekbones. "He told me he was going to the market. To look for more art supplies."

She cocked her head. "You think he might be somewhere else?"

"I wonder if he's out with that Gerhard again." Simon frowned. "Ernst spends a lot of time with that one."

"He has been alone for a long time now."

"Maybe so, but why does he have to choose a Nazi?"

"Gerhard was the one who tipped Ernst off about the Christmas Day bomb plot."

"A Nazi is a Nazi," Simon snorted. He gently laid a hand on her shoulder, and when he spoke, his tone had softened. "Have you had any word about Franz?"

Sunny shook her head, swallowing. "He could be anywhere. Even in the middle of some battlefield."

"They took him for his medical skills, remember?" Simon reassured her with deliberate optimism. "They wouldn't risk putting their top surgeon at the front lines or anything so moronic." Sunny nodded emptily. "He's coming back, Sunny. I know it in my bones."

She didn't comment, but that didn't deter Simon. His face lit up with fresh enthusiasm. "You should think about coming with us."

"Oh, where are you going?"

"*We* are going to the Bronx. All of us. Where else?" He laughed. "I know the perfect spot. In Highbridge. The cutest brownstone. We could each have a floor. The boys could wreak havoc in the neighbourhood. We'd find you jobs at Lincoln Hospital or somewhere. We'd all get season tickets for the Yankees, of course. And don't worry," he added with a laugh. "The place is as Jewish as the ghetto, so you'd feel right at home."

"And how are we going to get to New York?" Sunny scoffed. "On a Japanese battleship?"

"It's only a matter of time now, Sunny. And not much, at that. The Allies are sweeping through Europe. The Pacific won't be far behind." He nodded in the direction of Jakob and Joey. "Time to start planning for these kids' future—ours too—after the war."

As inviting as the idea was, Sunny was desperate not to succumb to false hope again. So she reached into the back of the pram and pulled out Esther's letter.

Simon's eyes brightened as he took the envelope from her. "How is she?" he asked.

"As good as she can be without you."

"It kills me to be away from Essie." His face reddened. "I'm sorry, Sunny. Oh God, what an idiot I am. I don't need to tell you, of all people, that."

"It's all right, Simon."

He looked over to Jakob, whose face was smeared with wet cookie crumbs, before turning his attention back to the envelope. "Go ahead," Sunny encouraged. "Read it."

Simon tore it open. He was chuckling as he began reading, but the laughter soon turned to sighs. By the time he finished, he was shaking his head.

"What did Essie say?" Sunny asked, intuiting Simon's unease.

"That she won't write me anymore if I keep leaving the apartment." He cleared his throat. "She won't even let you bring Jakob to see me if she hears I have."

"She's only trying to protect you, Simon."

"From what? My own sanity?" He rolled his eyes. "I've been cooped up in this walk-up for a year with nothing but that crazy painter for company. Sometimes, I forget what it's like to breathe anything but oil-paint fumes and smoke. Every once in a while, I have to get out and stretch my legs."

"And what if the Nazis spot you?"

"How? None of them have a clue who I am."

"You don't look like them, Simon. And you certainly don't sound like them. Even I can hear your accent when you speak German."

Simon pointed toward the window. "I'm always careful out there."

"I am too," Sunny said. "But I still ran straight into von Puttkamer."

"If I happen to, trust me, it will be worse for him."

She stiffened. "What does that mean?"

"It would be so easy, Sunny."

She lowered her voice. "To kill him?"

He just nodded.

Sunny exhaled. "Even if you could get your hands on a gun . . ."

"I don't need a gun."

"Then how?"

Simon shrugged. "I would have surprise on my side. That, and the long butcher knife I always carry with me."

The calmness in his eyes concerned Sunny as much as his words. "Stop this nonsense. You're a husband, a father, a provider, a nurturer—not an assassin. It's not in you, Simon."

"You might be surprised."

"Not this way. No. It would never work. Jakob would lose his father, and Essie her husband. Is that what you want for them?"

He tipped his head from side to side. "If it meant they were free of von Puttkamer?"

"There are countless other Nazis to take his place. Some worse than him. You know it as well as I do."

"Von Puttkamer is the one with the schemes. The one who tried to blow up the synagogue and the hospital. The one who tried to abduct Franz in plain daylight." Simon paused. "Maybe the others would think twice if they saw what became of him."

"It will never work," she repeated.

Simon pulled Jakob to his chest and hugged him tightly. He looked back up at Sunny with plaintive eyes. "After everything they've done to us, Sunny? Don't you ever just want to fight back?"

CHAPTER 22

There was no rest at the field hospital. Franz's first seven days had blended into a blur of exhaustion. In some ways, he felt as though he had been reliving the same day: wakened by a bugle blast at four thirty, performing rounds and changing dressings on patients for an hour or two, followed by twelve or more hours of operating—sometimes as the only surgeon, other times as Suzuki's assistant—and then more post-operative care. He didn't return to his tent until well after midnight. Franz ate his meals with the lowest-ranking soldiers, and only if he could find time to get to the canteen between duties. Aside from the people who worked in the operating tent, the others at the camp treated him like a ghost; he half suspected he could walk naked down its pathways without anyone noticing.

The work taxed Franz more than anything he had ever experienced, even more than his busiest days as a surgical intern at the Allgemeines Krankenhaus, the general hospital in Vienna. His fractured rib had healed to the point of painlessness, but his knees and back ached from all the time he spent on his feet. And alarmingly, the bouts of dizziness had recurred. He had almost collapsed twice, and he had started to keep track of the nearest available support posts he might prop himself up against in case of sudden light-headedness.

As Franz now stood beside the operating table waiting for the next battle victim to be carried in, he noted that Captain Suzuki's mood was particularly sour. Then again, it had been a grizzly day, even by the field hospital's standards. It felt to Franz as though most patients who reached the table left with one less limb than they'd had on arrival. Worse, some patients were beyond salvaging.

The orderlies carried in a stretcher bearing an unconscious man, his eyes open but rolled back in their sockets. His hands were draped across his belly, and it took Franz a moment to realize that the man had been holding in his own intestines. Before the orderlies could transfer the patient onto the operating table, Suzuki shouted in Japanese and snapped his fingers wildly at them. Their heads bowed, the two orderlies hurriedly carried the doomed man out of the room.

Suzuki glowered at Franz. "Banzai charges."

"Excuse me, Captain?" Franz said.

"Why we are seeing such carnage today. Banzai charges."

"Is that some kind of weapon?" Franz asked.

Suzuki snorted in disgust. "I suppose it's best described as a military tactic. But not a particularly good one."

Franz shook his head in bewilderment, feeling the room spin a little as he did so.

"*Tenno Heika Banzai!*" Suzuki said. "Or, 'Long live the Emperor!' What the soldiers cry as they launch a wave of human assault against the enemy line. In olden days, when guns or bows and arrows took time to reload, it made some degree of strategic sense to storm the enemy with swords drawn. Less so now when they are charging with sabres at men who point machine guns back at them."

"Oh, that's awful," Helen piped up.

"*Awful* loses its meaning in times of war, Mrs. Thompson. But the banzai . . ." Suzuki shook his head. "Those are wasteful."

Franz only nodded. The last five years had numbed his capacity to be shocked at the extent of human stupidity, cruelty and waste.

The orderlies returned, carrying a new patient. This man's entire upper body was covered in a sheet and, for a confused moment, Franz wondered if they had brought in a corpse. But then he spotted movement under the sheet and recognized the acrid smell of burned flesh.

The sheet fell away as the patient was transferred onto the operating room table. His face was blistered and distorted beyond recognition. The man's clothes were blackened and singed, and every exposed inch of skin on his arms and torso were burned as badly as his neck and face. One of his eyes was swollen completely shut, and the other opened little more than a slit, revealing a pale brown eye that moved watchfully around the room.

Franz glanced over to Suzuki, assuming he would chase the orderlies back out along with the patient. But instead, Suzuki stepped up the table and spoke to the man in a calm voice. The man answered so hoarsely that Suzuki had to put an ear to his mouth to understand him. After a short conversation, Suzuki turned to the anesthetist and nodded for him to put the patient to sleep.

Franz turned to Suzuki with a quizzical expression. "What happened to him?"

"The truck he was driving flipped over. He was trapped inside. The engine, it caught fire."

"I see. But, Captain, his injuries . . ."

"We will debride the blisters," Suzuki snapped. "Only then can we know whether the skin might heal."

Franz nodded, catching Helen's skeptical eye across the table.

They worked in silence, removing layers of blisters and destroyed flesh from both sides of the patient's body. Suzuki must know how hopeless the man's condition was, Franz thought, but he carried on as if it were routine surgery. After the operation was finished and the man was wrapped in bandages—the only gap an opening for his one working eye—Suzuki announced that he was leaving Franz to finish the rest of the cases.

With Helen's assistance, Franz operated on several more casualties. None of the others was burned but their wounds were horrific, and Franz doubted that even half of them would survive to see the next morning.

After the day's last surgery had been cleared from the operating room, Franz joined Helen out in front of the tent, where they had stood on his first night at the camp. The tip of her cigarette radiated in the fading twilight. "Do they provide you with cigarettes?" Franz asked.

"Not officially," Helen said. "The captain gives me his supply."

"That's generous of him."

"Not really. He has no interest in them. He calls it a 'filthy habit.'" She coughed into her hand again and then laughed. "I suppose he might be right too."

"When did you take it up?"

"In Shanghai. Shortly after my husband left."

"Left?"

"When they took Michael to the internment camp." It was first time Franz had heard Helen mention her husband by name. She hardly spoke of him at all. "I was never much of a knitter."

"A knitter? I do not understand, Helen."

"The smoking. I needed something to do with these." She wiggled her fingers. "Idle hands and all."

"Ah."

They stood quietly together before Helen asked, "Your daughter, Hannah. How old is she?"

Franz felt a slight pang in his chest. "Fourteen."

"Practically a young woman."

"She can be so grown up at times, yes. After all, she has experienced more . . . change than some people see in a lifetime." He paused, remembering how Hannah had clung close to his side in the days after he had been allowed to return home from the Country Hospital. "And yet, other times, I still see the child in her."

"Sounds like a teenager." Helen chuckled. "I remember what that was like."

Franz smiled to himself. "I am too old to remember any of that."

"I knew about change back then too. My family moved to Tokyo just before my thirteenth birthday. Come to think of it, I am an only child, just like your Hannah."

"Yes, well, Hannah might not be an only child anymore."

Helen angled her head. "What could that possibly mean?"

"Sunny, she—*we* have adopted a child. It was all rather unexpected." Franz went on to tell her about Joey's sudden appearance in their lives.

Helen must have sensed his reticence about the adoption. "You didn't want another child?" she asked.

"I would do anything for Sunny."

She inhaled again from her cigarette before dropping the stub to the ground. "You don't sound like the most exhilarated of new fathers."

"How can I possibly be?" He shook his head. "I'm a prisoner here. Held at the front lines. I doubt I will ever see my wife or daughter again, let alone this baby. How will she be able to feed another mouth while living inside that miserable ghetto?"

Helen turned away. The silhouetted outline of her shoulder began to bob up and down gently and Franz heard soft sobs. He stepped closer. "Helen, I am so sorry. Don't listen to my doom and gloom. I'm exhausted, you understand."

She held up a hand to stop his approach. "It's not that," she said.

"No?"

"Michael and I, we were going to have children." She sniffled. "And then he left . . . he just left."

Hands dangling uselessly by his side, Franz felt tongue-tied, at a complete loss for words. By the time he stupidly blurted "So the Japanese didn't intern your husband?" Helen had already disappeared back into the tent.

* * *

An hour passed before Franz caught up to Helen inside the convalescence tent that passed for a surgical ward. Ten full beds ringed its perimeter. Helen's eyes were dry, and she even mustered a collegial smile for Franz, but her demeanour made it plain that she had no interest in continuing their discussion.

With Helen translating for Franz and the patients, they moved from bed to bed, adjusting dressings and examining sutures, looking for signs of infection or gangrene. Franz was struck again by the patients' stoicism. Despite their massive wounds, broken bones and missing limbs, he didn't hear a single peep or groan of pain. Even their expressions were remarkably calm, ranging from impassive to deferential. It wasn't until Franz reached the third-to-last bed that he encountered an exception.

The skinny patient wore thick, round glasses and looked more like a shop clerk than a solider. Franz had earlier removed two bullets from his back. One had been lodged only a fraction of an inch from his spinal cord. The young man was sweating, and his head swung from side to side as though he was expecting someone to sneak up on him. Franz assumed he was suffering from post-operative delirium, possibly even hallucinating. He ran the back of his hand across the patient's forehead but detected no fever to suggest an infection.

Helen laid a hand on the boy's arm and spoke to him in Japanese. The man shook his head frantically as he answered. Helen turned to Franz. "I don't believe he's delirious, Franz," she said. "He knows where he is."

"Is he in pain?"

"He says not."

"What is it, then?"

"He just keeps repeating that he had to turn back. He had dropped his glasses and he couldn't see."

"What does he mean 'had to turn back'?"

She shook her head. "I have no idea."

The room began to swim around Franz, and he instinctively spread his legs wider and reached for the nearby intravenous pole to steady himself. He pretended to study the IV bottle until the light-headedness passed a few seconds later.

If Helen had noticed the episode, she didn't acknowledge it. "Maybe the poor man is reacting to the morphine?" she asked.

"Perhaps." It was possible. Some medications, especially narcotics, were notorious for causing behavioural side effects. "Let's hold off the painkiller for a while."

The patient in the next bed was trembling under his covers too, but his shaking came from fever, not anxiety. He had lost one leg just below his knee, and as soon as Franz pulled back the dressing, he appreciated how badly infected the wound already was. Franz saw from Helen's eyes that she also recognized the gravity of the situation. "We will start him on sulpha drugs, of course, but he's going to lose the rest of the leg," he said. "There is no doubt."

Helen explained this to the patient, who nodded as calmly as if he had just been told that he was going to need to change his socks.

They moved on to the last bed in the tent, where the badly burned man lay wrapped like a mummy. Franz was surprised to see him alive, let alone breathing comfortably and staring up attentively with his one exposed eye. Helen spoke to him in gentle tones, and he replied in a croak. "He claims not to be in any pain," she told Franz.

"The fire must have burned away his nerve endings. Fortunately."

She nodded. "Should I remove any of his dressings?"

"There's no point, Helen."

The flap to the tent folded open noisily. Two young officers walked inside, followed by Major Okada. None of them acknowledged Franz or Helen, but the two officers fell behind Okada as he limped over to the bed at which Franz had begun his rounds. The major spoke briefly to the patient in his soft voice before moving on to the next bed, leaning heavily on his cane and dragging his right foot behind him as he went.

Franz had seen Okada only twice since the first night at the camp, and only from a distance. The major was young, perhaps in his mid-thirties, with sharp features—more aristocratic than handsome—and a bearing that commanded deference despite his hushed voice. Okada moved from bed to bed, spending no more than a minute with each patient.

Franz noticed that the scrawny, bespectacled patient grew more restless as Okada's entourage made its way closer. When the major reached his bed, he simply stared down at the agitated soldier. Finally, the major spoke to him in his usual quiet tone. The patient shook his head adamantly and answered in a fearful voice. Franz glanced over to Helen, hoping for an explanation, but she was riveted by the conversation.

"*Okubyōmono*," Okada said, deliberately enunciating each syllable.

The man responded with a flood of panicky words.

"*Okubyōmono*," Okada repeated, raising his voice slightly.

"What does that mean?" Franz whispered to Helen.

"Coward," she said softly without taking her eyes off them. "The major is accusing the boy of running away from the banzai attack."

Again, the soldier tried to argue his case. The major cut him off with a shriek. "*Okubyōmono!*" In one motion, the major hoisted his walking stick and swung it down, the carved wooden handle smashing into the side of the patient's head.

Screaming in surprise and pain, the man tossed his arms up to protect his face. Okada swung again, cracking the cane's handle into the man's nose. Franz heard the repulsive crunching of bones breaking as blood sprayed from the patient's face and his glasses flew off his head.

"Are you out of your mind?" Franz cried in English. "This man just had surgery!"

He began to move forward, but Helen grabbed him by the arm and shifted to block his path. "Leave it," she whispered frantically.

Even though the patient was now lying limp and motionless, Okada again cocked the cane over his head. Franz wriggled free of Helen's grip and took two steps toward the bed. The rush of dizziness came out of nowhere. The room darkened and went black even before his head met the ground.

CHAPTER 23

I shouldn't have come.

Curiosity, Hannah reminded herself. It was the only reason she had accepted Freddy's unexpected invitation to meet. But it wasn't curiosity that was making her chest flutter as she walked along the uneven sidewalk. The guilt gnawed deeper with each step she took toward the schoolyard. She felt rotten enough for not having told Herschel, but it was even worse imagining how disappointed her father would be if he knew. After Franz had been flogged for Hannah's crime of smuggling cigarettes into the ghetto for Freddy's family, she had vowed to never again associate with the dangerous boy.

Oh, Papa. A lump formed in Hannah's throat, and she worried she might break into tears again. Papa had always been there, the only parent she had ever known. Before now, the longest she had ever been apart from her father was one week, but now he had been gone for over a month already. A pall had descended on their home. It was killing Sunny. Even Esther was struggling. Without his steadying presence, the two women bickered as never before. What Hannah wouldn't have given to hear his calm voice or to see his understated smile.

I can't do this, Hannah thought. Just as she was turning away from the school grounds, a voice called to her. "Banana! Over here."

Hannah looked over her shoulder to see Freddy Herzberg standing at the side of the building, beckoning her with a friendly wave. She hesitated. "Come on," he encouraged in English, the only language he ever seemed to speak despite his German upbringing. "Avi isn't here. It's only us. And I am just about to do it."

Swallowing back her guilt, Hannah headed over to Freddy, pulling her sleeve down over her left hand. Only Freddy could ever evoke such self-consciousness in her, and she resented him as much as herself for the feeling. She followed him around the back of the school to the clearing in the shrubs, where the transmitter rested on a blanket, quietly hissing static.

"Why here?" Hannah asked him in a conspiratorial whisper. "Why not somewhere inside? Would that not be safer?"

Freddy swirled a hand around. "This is perfect. The place is abandoned over the summer. Besides, no interference. No tall buildings, walls or other radio antennae to block the signal."

Hannah nodded. "So the sound is clearer?"

"That, and the signal travels a lot further."

"How far does it go?"

Freddy shrugged. "Depending on the weather, up to fifty miles. But today, it only has to reach Frenchtown."

"Why?"

He pulled a pack of cigarettes out of his pocket and extended it to her. She declined the offer, and he tucked them back into his pocket without lighting one. "I have a friend in Frenchtown."

"A friend of the family's, I suppose?"

"Matter of fact, yes." Freddy grinned widely. "I've missed that spunkiness, Banana."

Her heart beat quicker, but she hid it behind a roll of her eyes. "Have you found another girl to be your lackey?"

Unperturbed, Freddy shook his head. "We don't do that anymore. My pop promised your pop. Remember?"

"I do," she lied. Her father had never spoken of the incident after his flogging. Sunny had once told Hannah how Franz had confronted Freddy's father after her arrest, but even Sunny didn't know the specifics of their run-in, certainly nothing about a promise between the two men. "So how do you get your cigarettes into the ghetto?"

Freddy winked. "Some mysteries are best left unsolved."

Hannah turned again. "I think I should go."

Just as she was ducking her head beneath a branch, Freddy said, "Coolies."

"What about them?" Hannah asked.

"The coolies don't need passes to get in or out of the ghetto. No one inspects their rickshaws." He laughed. "They blow in and out like the wind."

"I don't know whether or not to believe you," Hannah said without turning back to him.

"*Verzeih, bitte,*" Freddy said, surprising Hannah with German and with the contrition in his tone. "I really am sorry for the suffering we—I—caused you. And your father. If I had known someone was going to get hurt . . ."

"You would have done it anyway."

"No, I wouldn't have. I swear, Hannah."

She wavered before heading back to him. "How does it work?"

"The radio?" He laughed.

"The business. With your friend in Frenchtown."

"Oh, we agree on a time. He calls me. I tell him how much we need. And presto—a day or two later, the rickshaw shows up."

She dropped her voice to a near whisper again. "What if the Japanese catch you?"

"Ah." He brushed the idea away with a backhanded sweep. "I'm too slick for them. Besides, we are always careful."

Nothing that Hannah had seen or heard so far supported the claim, but she was too intrigued to argue. Freddy stepped closer to her. "Is Herschel your boyfriend now?" he asked.

"No—well, yes." Her cheeks heated. "Herschel is a good friend and a good person."

Freddy tilted his head, amused. "But is he your *boyfriend*?"

"I suppose he is, yes."

Still smiling, Freddy laid a hand on her upper arm and squeezed it, launching a jolt of electricity through her. "Then he's a very lucky guy." He stared into her eyes. A voice in Hannah's head told her to turn and run, but she felt paralyzed. Herschel's touch—even his sweet clumsy kisses—never brought the same rush of adrenalin that Freddy's could.

A loud hiss of static broke the spell. "Tango, tango, are you there?" a disembodied voice asked.

Freddy pivoted and, in one motion, dropped to his knees. He grabbed the mouthpiece off the radio. "Go ahead, Foxhole."

"How many?" the hollow voice asked.

"Forty cartons, twenty bottles," Freddy said.

"When?"

"Tuesday."

"Okay."

Freddy switched off the dial. The speaker popped loudly, and then the static vanished as the radio shut down. He looked over to Hannah with another wink. "The key is to keep it short. The Japs, they know how to triangulate a radio transmission."

CHAPTER 24

Sunny buried her face in the collar of her dress, trying to shield her mouth and nose from the plume of black smoke. It didn't work. The taste of the coal dust made her cough, but she kept fanning the briquettes, hoping to keep them alight. The traditional Shanghainese stove resembled an upside-down flowerpot and was burning the only fuel available in the ghetto: briquettes recycled from burned coal and compacted river mud. Lighting the maddeningly inefficient briquettes used to be Franz's duty, one of the few situations that could cause him to lose his temper. How she wished he were here now, tending the stove and muttering curses in German.

Behind her, Ernst and Esther sat side by side on the couch. Cigarette in hand, Ernst chatted away non-stop, while Esther nursed Joey under a blanket that covered her to her shoulders.

"*Ach,* this little one gets a little heavier with each meal, Sunny," Esther said.

"Because you provide so well for him," Sunny said.

"I'm just his bottle. Nothing more. You are his mother." Esther smiled encouragingly. "That is what matters most in his world."

Sunny's cheeks flushed. She fanned the coals even harder, relieved to hear Ernst change the subject. "Are we not two short of a full house? Where have Hannah and Jakob gone?"

"Hannah has taken him to get hot water," Esther said.

Ernst rubbed his hands together. "Ah, what are we cooking? Perhaps I can stay for lunch after all."

"Bed bugs," Esther said.

"Bed bugs?" Ernst groaned in disgust. "Honestly, I'm more of a Wiener schnitzel man."

"We don't eat them, Ernst. We douse the mattresses and railings in hot water. The heat chases out the bed bugs. Our feet finish the job." Esther sighed. "Jakob loves it. He thinks it's all one big game."

"Can you imagine, Essie, if I had told you ten years ago in Vienna that this was to be our fate?" Ernst sighed. "Steaming out bed bugs in some Chinese hovel?"

"We are still alive," Esther pointed out.

"Am I supposed to assume that's preferable?"

"I think so." Esther laughed, still beaming from her husband's latest letter. "Simon swears he's not going out anymore." She looked hopefully to Ernst for confirmation. "Correct?"

"Not that I have witnessed. Of course, sometimes I'm gone much of the day."

"Does he talk about ambushing von Puttkamer or any of the others?"

"Not to me, no. All I get is more of his infernal prattle about those Bronx Bombers of his. I tell you this: he has turned me into a Boston Red Sox enthusiast. And I have no idea who or what those even are."

"Thank God!" Esther laughed happily.

"Besides, Essie," Ernst said, assuming a gossipy tone. "Your husband is apparently not the only one with designs on assassinating Nazis."

"Ernst, don't even joke," Esther admonished.

Sunny raised her head and looked over to Ernst. "Has something happened?"

"Not here. In Berlin—well, in Rastenburg, to be specific. They tried to kill him. Hitler himself."

Esther's eyes went wide and she slapped her hand to her mouth. "Who did?"

"His own officers. There was a bomb."

"And?" Esther said, holding her breath.

Ernst rolled his eyes. "Of course he survived. With only minor injuries. You can't kill an artist as talentless as that one. The gods of mediocrity will not allow it. They're rounding up the conspirators all over Berlin."

"Of all people to survive a bombing," Esther groaned. She fumbled under the blanket and Joey emerged smacking his lips contentedly.

Sunny stepped over to ease him out of Esther's arms. Joey looked up at her with a little grin that lightened her worries. She cradled him against her neck, enjoying the warmth of his cheek against hers as she burped him.

"And Franz?" Ernst asked. "Have you heard any news, Sunny?"

"No," Esther answered for her.

"You still have no idea where they've taken him?" Ernst persisted.

Sunny shook her head. "I plan to go see Ghoya."

"Not to poison his soup again, I hope."

Sunny shook her head. "That wasn't my idea, Ernst. You know that."

Esther looked over to Sunny with a discouraging frown. "It won't help to ask for anything from that monster."

"Do I not owe it to Franz to try?" Sunny asked as she bobbed Joey up and down, lightly tapping his back. "If you didn't know where Simon was—*how* he was—is there anything you wouldn't do to find out?"

Esther opened her mouth to speak but instead just nodded.

Sunny hankered for fresh air. Joey would need to nap soon, and a stroll in the pram would help him get to sleep. Sunny realized she was destined to end up back on Broadway, heading toward the Garden Bridge, as she had for the past three days. She could still picture the configuration of the Japanese vessels in the harbour from yesterday's walk, but they would have changed positions overnight: the ships moved constantly, never mooring in one spot for too long.

A series of light, rapid knocks drew Sunny's attention.

"Are you expecting someone?" Esther whispered to her.

When the door rattled softly again, Sunny could tell from the tentative sound that it wasn't the authorities. She opened the door to find a Chinese boy, no more than thirteen or fourteen years old, standing at the threshold. He looked vaguely familiar and, for a horrible moment, she wondered if he could be a relative of Feng Wei's come to reclaim Joey. But then she recognized him as one of the young boys she had met in the sitting room at the Comfort Home.

"Mama beckons you," the boy said in Shanghainese without greeting.

"Why? What does Chih-Nii want?"

"Your help."

"My help? With what?"

"There has been an incident," the boy said, turning to leave.

* * *

The rickshaw driver dropped Sunny and the boy, who had been no more forthcoming during the ride, outside the Comfort Home. Ushi was waiting at the curb. The colossal guard whisked her down the garden pathway and through the mansion's entrance. Rather than escorting her to the sitting room, he led her up the curved staircase to the second floor, where Sunny had never been, and down the hall to the third bedroom on the right. He knocked four times and then the door opened a crack. Sunny had to turn sideways to slip through the opening, Chih-Nii pulling the door closed as soon as she had entered the room.

Sunny's chest was drumming even before she saw the naked man sprawled on the four-poster bed. He lay on his back, head turned sharply to the right, a sheet twisted around his legs up to his upper thighs. Everything above that was exposed.

"He was still alive when I sent for you, buttercup," Chih-Nii said in dull voice.

Sunny glanced at the madam, who still stood by the door with arms folded. Her gaze fell back to the body on the bed, a middle-aged man with a small paunch. "Who is he?" Sunny asked.

"A client."

"I assumed as much."

"Of Jia-Li's."

Sunny too had surmised that. "What happened to him?"

"Some kind of heart condition, apparently." Chih-Nii sounded skeptical.

"You said he was still alive when you found him."

Chih-Nii brought her fingers to her neck. "He still had a heartbeat, but he wasn't breathing."

Sunny moved closer to the bed. The man stared placidly out the window as if lost in a daydream. She knew he was dead, but she went through the motions of running the back of her hand over his still warm brow and feeling his neck and chest for any sign of life. Her breath caught in her throat when she noticed the trace of blood at the crook of his elbow. She pretended to check his pulse there as she rubbed away a small scab.

"And?" Chih-Nii demanded.

Sunny swallowed. "Even a pathologist couldn't tell what he died of just by looking at him."

Chih-Nii smiled as if letting Sunny in on a private joke, but the expression didn't last. "This could cause us no end of grief," she groaned.

"Has no one ever died at the Comfort Home before?"

"It happens," Chih-Nii said. "Hearts have been known to give out in the throes of passion."

"So what's different about this man?"

"He was an important man. A major." Chih-Nii pointed to the bundle of clothes that lay carefully folded on the chaise longue in the corner. Two white armbands rested on top of the pile. "In the Kempeitai."

The officer's death was certain to draw the full scrutiny of the dreaded military police. Sunny didn't want to consider what could happen if they suspected that his death wasn't of natural causes.

Chih-Nii locked eyes with Sunny. "This is not the first."

"Of Jia-Li's clients?"

Chih-Nii nodded gravely. "About two months ago. Another officer. He barely survived."

"May I speak with her, Mama?"

Chih-Nii hesitated and then motioned toward the door. Sunny followed the madam out of the room, down the stairs and into the office. Then Chih-Nii stepped out of the room and closed the door behind her, leaving Sunny alone with her friend.

Jia-Li sat behind Chih-Nii's mahogany desk wearing a black silk nightgown, her hair pulled back in a band. She doodled on a piece of paper as Sunny sat down across from her. Sunny glanced at her drawing: a bouquet of flowers, probably peonies, her friend's favourite. Jia-Li looked up with a faintly amused smile. "I am more than a little jealous of your friend, *xiǎo hè*."

"Which friend?"

"Ernst. An artist of his skill. To create something from nothing. What a gift that must be."

Sunny reached across the desk and laid her hand on top of Jia-Li's. "Are you all right, *bǎo bèi*?"

"Always. Why shouldn't I be?"

Despite her carefree words, Sunny noticed the slight tremor in her friend's hand. "Your client. The major."

"Ah, the poor man." Jia-Li shrugged. "It can't be helped."

"We both know it's not so."

"Not to be indelicate, Sister, but I had worried about the major in bed." Her gaze returned to the sketch on the desk. "His level of exertion. Many of them are . . . exuberant with me. But this one, with his grunting and gasping. And the sweating! As if he had just run up the side of a mountain. I imagine his heart just wasn't up to the challenge."

"His heart wasn't the issue."

"How can you be sure?"

"Because he didn't die of natural causes."

Jia-Li looked up, her eyes steely. "Who dies of natural causes in a snake pit?"

"I saw the needle mark at his elbow. Heroin."

Jia-Li smiled. "You must be confused. Where would the major have got his hands on opium's brighter and bolder little sister?"

Sunny squeezed Jia-Li's hand so tightly that her fingers ached. "You can't continue this. It's suicide, *bǎo bèi*."

"No, *xiǎo hè*." Jia-Li's smile vanished. She stared at Sunny, her gaze unwavering. "It's their karma. And my duty. Nothing else."

CHAPTER 25

The glare was blinding. The throb between Franz's ears intensified. It took him a moment to make out the upside-down face of Captain Suzuki hovering above him. The familiar scent of iodine drifted to Franz's nose and he finally gained his bearings. He was shocked to find himself lying on the operating table where he had spent most of the last week working. He reached up toward the source of the pain on his scalp but a hand grabbed his arm before he could touch his head.

"Hold still," Suzuki barked as the hand gently guided Franz's arm back to his side. "Your skull is not broken."

"That is . . . good," Franz rasped.

The hand squeezed his arm reassuringly before letting go. "How do you feel, Dr. Adler?" Helen asked just as her face came into view.

"A slight headache but otherwise fine, thank you." He decided not to mention his intense nausea and vertigo. "How did I get here?"

"Like every other patient," Suzuki grunted. "You were carried in on a stretcher."

"I must have fainted."

"I think so, yes," Helen said.

"Medical students, certainly, but I can think of few trained doctors who faint at the sight of blood," Suzuki said.

The image of the crazed major beating the patient over the head with the handle of his cane came back to Franz. "The circumstances were not entirely usual," he said.

"What is usual anymore?" Suzuki asked rhetorically.

Franz felt a pinch and then saw a thread of catgut slither across his nose. "How many stitches?" he asked.

"Nine so far," Suzuki said. "You will require several more. The laceration is deep. I must close it in layers."

Franz saw double, two sets of side-by-side scissors' teeth as Helen cut the suture right above his nose. Suzuki leaned away from the light, and Franz had to close his eyes against the painful glare. "Is the boy . . . ?"

Suzuki shook his head once. "The private should never have turned back during the charge."

"He went back to pick up his eyeglasses," Franz said.

"Glasses are of little use when one is charging a tommy gun."

Arguing further was as senseless as the fighting itself, but Franz wanted to keep Suzuki distracted, so he said, "The major, his limp?"

"What about it?" Suzuki asked.

"A battle wound?"

"Hmm," Suzuki said as he ran another stitch. "I am told it happened in the Philippines. His pelvis was shattered and the sciatic nerve destroyed."

"So now he is forced to command a field hospital? Behind the front lines?"

"Major Okada is a decorated war hero. He has been deployed all over the Pacific. This assignment . . ."

"Is humiliating for him?" Helen suggested.

"Your words, Mrs. Thompson, not mine," Suzuki said. "However, I do not believe Major Okada is accustomed to overseeing medical personnel."

"Or the wounded," Helen added pointedly.

"True," Suzuki agreed.

"And you, Captain?" Franz asked as he felt another poke from the suture needle.

"I am a surgeon, not a commander."

"Were you in the army before the war?"

"Before the war, I was in San Francisco."

Franz started to lift his head but the tug of a stitch held him back. "Hold still," Suzuki snapped.

"How . . . how did you possibly end up here?" Franz asked.

Suzuki went quiet. Then he laughed in a low rumble. "This question from an Austrian Jew who works in a Japanese field hospital in the middle of China?"

Franz laughed too. "I suppose it cannot be any stranger than my journey."

Suzuki ran in three or four more stitches before he spoke again. "A wedding," he finally said.

"A wedding?" Franz asked.

"My son was getting married. In Nagasaki, where his wife's family lives. My wife and I came back to attend the wedding."

"And the war broke out?"

"Japan has been at war with China for over ten years." Suzuki sighed. "But while we were in Nagasaki, Pearl Harbor was bombed. America declared war."

"So you enlisted?"

"I was bound by duty," Suzuki said, his inflection suggesting it should have been obvious to Franz.

"Did your son enlist as well?"

A sharp poke made Franz wince and he felt the needle deflect off his skull. "Enough chitchat," Suzuki snarled. "This is not a bridge club."

Suzuki sewed the last of the stitches in cold silence, then dropped the utensils onto a tray. The worst of Franz's giddiness had passed, and he started to push himself upright. Helen's arm slipped behind his back and helped raise him up to sitting. His head pounded, but he willed himself to remain upright while the room spun around him.

Suzuki eyes narrowed. "What good are you to me, Dr. Adler?"

Taken aback, Franz said, "I . . . I work as hard as I can, Captain."

"What will happen the next time?" Suzuki pressed. "When you pass out into an open wound, halfway through surgery? Who will take care of the patient? And who will save you?"

"As I said, Captain, it was an exceptional circumstance. I was not expecting—"

"What kind of fool do you take me for?" Suzuki scoffed.

"I don't understand."

"I cannot count all the times I have seen you near the point of collapse. That first day at the Country Hospital, you would have smashed your head open then too, had Mrs. Thompson not been there to catch you."

Franz looked over to Helen, the surprise on her face evident. "You saw that, Captain Suzuki?" he asked.

"I was willing to turn a blind eye." Suzuki shook his head. "No more. I cannot put our patients in jeopardy."

"As a child, I used to have epilepsy," Franz hurriedly launched into the lie. "When I become overly fatigued, sometimes I have these epileptic drop attacks—"

"Nonsense," Suzuki snapped.

Helen glanced over to Franz, her eyes questioning, but she said nothing.

"This is obviously syncope, not epilepsy," the captain continued. "Drop attacks from the collapse of the circulatory system."

Franz's stomach tightened as he again visualized Okada's attack on the private, and wondered if it was his standard response to any failure in the line of duty. "Are you going to inform the major?"

Instead of answering, Suzuki said, "Lie down."

Franz complied, relieved to be reclining again. Suzuki readied his stethoscope, then slipped a blood pressure cuff around Franz's upper arm and inflated it. After measuring Franz's pressure, he instructed Franz to sit up again. He took further readings with Franz sitting and then standing. The captain pulled his stethoscope from his ears. "Orthostatic hypotension," he pronounced. "Your systolic blood pressure drops by twenty-five millimetres when you shift from lying to sitting and another fifteen when you stand up. Are you not terribly dizzy each time you rise?"

"Sometimes, yes," Franz said, feeling stupid for having never considered the diagnosis.

"How long has this been going on?" Suzuki asked.

"The last six months or so."

"Is it always so persistent? Or does it come and go?"

Franz considered. "It comes and goes. When I was travelling here from Shanghai, when I was not performing surgery—standing on my feet for such long periods—the episodes almost disappeared."

Suzuki frowned. "What were they feeding you on the journey?"

Franz thought back to the unpalatable meals. "They often brought me dried salty fish, sometimes twice a day. I do not know the name for it, but the smell was terrible."

"Kusaya," Suzuki said, nodding to himself. "Yes, indeed. It is made with brine and loaded with salt. That must be it."

Franz flushed with relief and embarrassment. "Are you suggesting that I might simply be suffering from salt deficiency?"

"For your sake, it had better be the cause." Suzuki turned away. "I will instruct the cook. You will start back on kusaya twice per day." He marched out of the operating room without another word.

Helen stood over the tray preparing bandages. "You lied to me about your drop attacks?" she asked almost casually.

"I'm sorry, Helen. I was embarrassed—and afraid. I had no idea what was going on. It was easier to bury my head in the sand."

"Is that so?"

"I haven't told anyone. I feel like such an imbecile. After all, I am supposed to be a doctor."

She looked over and eyed him for a cool moment before a smile crept onto her face. "Yes, but only a surgeon."

Franz chuckled. "Not much of a doctor, I grant you."

"Sit down," Helen said.

As Helen gently cleaned blood away from his hair, Franz remarked, "The captain behaved oddly when I asked about his son, didn't you think?" She nodded. "Has he ever mentioned him to you?"

"In all the months I've known Captain Suzuki, this is the only time I've ever heard him discuss his family. In English or Japanese."

"And Major Okada?" Franz said, lowering his voice. "What he did to that man in the tent."

Helen stiffened slightly. "I warned you about the major."

"Have there been other incidents?"

"I have only heard rumours. But I have seen it in his eyes. The fanaticism. I knew he was dangerous."

"We live in the golden age for fanatics, as my friend Ernst would tell you."

Helen finished cleaning the wound and gently swept his hair down over his forehead. She lifted a roll of white bandage and began to wind the cloth around his head.

"Is this really necessary?" Franz groaned. "I will look even more foolish than how I already feel."

"I don't tell you where or how to make your incisions, doctor. You need to trust me with the bandaging."

Franz sat as still as he could while Helen continued to wind the wrap. She softly hummed a tune that was unfamiliar to Franz, but he sensed a trace of hurt in her otherwise placid expression. "Helen, I'm sorry."

"For what?" she asked.

"For upsetting you earlier." He coughed into his fist. "About your husband."

She laughed softly. "How could you have possibly known?"

"It wasn't considerate of me to carry on about my troubles as though you had none of your own."

Her face softened with an understanding smile. "You never have to apologize for worrying over your family."

"Still . . ."

Helen nodded. "You know, I was the one who convinced Michael to move to Shanghai."

"He was reluctant?"

"It was 1938. Michael thought it foolhardy to accept a posting in Asia when the Japanese were sabre-rattling." She sighed. "I wanted to be nearer to my father. And I convinced Michael that they would never dare touch British interests in the Far East."

"I thought the very same when I first arrived here," Franz said. "That was also in 1938. In December."

"That was not the only thing I was wrong about." Helen closed her eyes and looked down. "I never dreamed that Michael would run off with Marjorie Wilson either. After all, she and her husband, Hamish, were our best friends in Shanghai."

"Oh, Helen, I'm so sorry," he mumbled, self-conscious at his useless words.

"Michael didn't even tell me to my face." Head still lowered, Helen only shrugged. "One day, I came home to find this rambling letter. He was already gone. It was so typical of him, all regret and rationalization. As best I can tell, it was somehow my fault that he had run off with another woman. Maybe it was? I am such a fool."

"He's the fool."

"Thank you," she murmured. "I suppose I should have left Shanghai right then and there. Gone home to Toronto."

"You still could have?"

"Yes, this was October of '41. I had even booked passage on a ship leaving for Singapore and onward to Vancouver."

"Why didn't you leave?"

She looked back up at him, her eyes misting over. "I just couldn't go home. No, not like that. With my marriage failed and my tail between my legs. I was so ashamed."

"You did nothing wrong."

Helen reached up and adjusted the bandage on Franz's head, tucking it carefully behind his ears. "Yes, I did. I chose the wrong man," she finally said, allowing her fingers to linger on his earlobes.

CHAPTER 26

The late morning sun blazed down hotter than a furnace on Sunny and the others in the unshaded queue. She had already been lined up outside the Bureau of Stateless Refugee Affairs for over an hour but had yet to reach the building's entrance. She was thankful she had opted to leave Joey at home with Esther.

Sunny picked up on a few curious glances from the refugees around her, all of whom had come to apply for exit passes. A number of people recognized her from the hospital or ghetto, and they greeted her with friendly words and smiles. She overheard murmured complaints about the heat and the slow-moving queue, but in typical Jewish fashion, no one tried to shove or butt in line.

When Sunny had first moved to the ghetto, she was struck by the adherence to orderliness and protocol among the Jewish refugees. It was so different from local Chinese culture, in which it was acceptable for people to elbow their way to a destination. She had once remarked on this to Franz, who pointed out that the Jews' tendency toward compliance had made it easier for the Nazis to marginalize and persecute them.

Sunny's chest ached again at the thought of Franz. She had known so much loss over the past few years—her father, her amah, the first Joey and so many other friends—but she hadn't known she was capable of missing anyone as intensely as she did her husband. She had begun to dread sleep because it was heart-wrenching to wake up from her dreams to discover that he was still absent.

To distract herself, she focused instead on her best friend. Fortunately for Jia-Li and everyone else at the Comfort Home, the Kempeitai men were more concerned with getting their dead comrade clothed and far away from the brothel than with determining the cause of his demise. Still, Sunny had little faith that her best friend wouldn't try to overdose another customer. Chih-Nii had sworn she wouldn't let Jia-Li work until she was convinced the girl was in a proper state of mind, but of that Sunny was skeptical. The madam was a businesswoman for whom money would always come first.

Sunny finally reached the front of the line and Ghoya's office. She was sweating from more than just the muggy weather when he beckoned her in a shrill, "Next!"

Ghoya was scribbling on a piece of paper as Sunny approached his desk. Looking up at her, he did a double take. "What is the meaning of this?" He slammed his pen down on the desk. "The lineup is for refugees only."

Sunny bowed deeply. "Mr. Ghoya, I am Sunny Adler, Dr. Adler's wife."

Ghoya squinted at her and recognition crept onto his face. He leaned back in his chair, smirking. "Yes, yes. I remember now. He married one of you, didn't he?"

"Yes, sir," Sunny said uncertainly.

Ghoya drummed his fingers on the desk. "If you have come about the sister-in-law, my answer is still no. No passes for anyone in your family. That is final. Absolutely final."

"No, Mr. Ghoya. I have come about my husband."

"Oh?" Ghoya angled his head. "What about Dr. Adler?"

"I was hoping you could tell me where he went."

Ghoya grinned madly. "Where he went? He went precisely where I sent him."

"Where is that, sir?"

"I can't tell you that," he scoffed.

"Please, Mr. Ghoya. I realize I am asking a lot, but it would give me and my family such peace of mind to know where my husband is."

Ghoya hopped to his feet. "No, no, no. Don't you see? I cannot tell you that because I do not know where he is."

Her breath caught in her throat. "Has something happened to him?" she croaked.

"No. Although perhaps." He laughed grimly. "In war, anything can happen."

"I do not understand, Mr. Ghoya." Sunny couldn't keep the whimper from her voice. "Please, sir."

"Ichi-Go, woman," he cried.

Fighting back tears, she held out her hands in incomprehension.

"The greatest military operation in the history of Asia," Ghoya trumpeted. "Our troops are moving westward as we speak, uniting the north and south of China in one glorious march. Your husband works in one of the field hospitals. They move with the rest of the divisions. He could be anywhere from Wuchang to Hengyang right now."

Sunny swallowed. "Is he safe?"

"Safer than our brave men on the front line." Ghoya shrugged. "The field hospitals are protected."

She had no idea what that meant, but she took a modicum of solace in his casual words. "Oh, I see."

Ghoya stepped around his desk and approached her. He allowed his eyes to wander up and down her body, ogling her unabashedly. Although he didn't lay a hand on her, Sunny felt violated. Fighting the urge to flee, she mustered a meek smile.

"It must be difficult for you without your husband," Ghoya said clumsily. "Very difficult indeed."

"At times, yes," she said hoarsely. "It can be lonely."

"I am an important man. Yes, yes." He swept his arms through the air. "Not only in the Designated Area but in all of Shanghai. I know people. I know people all over China!"

From this close, she could smell his cologne. "I am sure you do."

"What if I could find Dr. Adler for you?" Ghoya arched an eyebrow. "Perhaps send him a letter. Or perhaps . . ."

Warding off nausea, Sunny leaned in closer to Ghoya until their heads were almost touching. "Or perhaps what, Mr. Ghoya?"

"Perhaps I could even inquire whether his military service is still required? Perhaps I could see about bringing Dr. Adler back to Shanghai?"

"Oh, Mr. Ghoya," Sunny breathed, feeling the tears well. "You have no idea. No idea."

He eyed her lasciviously. "And if I went to such trouble for you, what could I expect in return?"

Subduing the tremble in her hands, she reached out and touched the back of his wrist. "My eternal gratitude," she said in the huskiest voice she could muster.

Smiling, Ghoya watched her caress the back of his hand. Suddenly, his eyes darkened. He jerked his hand from hers and slapped her cheek. Before she could even react to the sting, he slapped her backhanded across the other cheek. "Your kind is all the same," he cried. "All the same! All the same!"

Sunny backpedalled a few steps. "I . . . I don't understand."

"You miserable half-breed, you whore," he shrieked. "I would never touch you. Never, never. Get out of my office! Go, go!"

Sunny wheeled and rushed for the door.

"If I ever see you again . . ." Ghoya's threat followed her down the hallway as she desperately shouldered past the others still waiting in line.

Sunny had made it only a few steps out onto the street before she vomited, against the side of the building. The shame was worse than the burning in her cheeks or even the fear. She had just acted in the moment, without even thinking it through, but she was overcome by remorse over what she might have done to try to secure Franz's release.

She wiped her mouth and hurried away, desperate to put distance between herself and Ghoya's office. Without even thinking about her destination, she found herself on Broadway again. She stared out at the harbour, mentally noting the Japanese ships and their positions, glad for the distraction. Even before she had turned away from the water, she had made up her mind.

* * *

Sunny had often admired the twin spires of St. Ignatius Cathedral in the heart of Frenchtown, but she had never set foot inside the church before. Were she not so upset, she might have stopped to appreciate the stately arches above the nave or the light that filtered through the imposing stained-glass windows. Instead, Sunny headed straight for a nun who was rising from her prayers and asked after Father Diego.

The diminutive nun led her through a door behind the altar and down a hallway to a door at the far end. She knocked once and Father Diego answered. His face quickly broke into a welcoming smile and Sunny thought he might hug her, but he just clasped his hands together. "What a wonderful surprise," he cried. "Come, please sit."

Closing the door behind Sunny, the priest led her to the desk inside the small, tidy office, sitting down across from her. "What happened to you, Sunny?" he asked with concern.

She reached up and touched her still-stinging cheek. "In the heat, sometimes I get a rash."

Diego's eyes narrowed skeptically. "The heat, is it?"

"Yes, Father."

He accepted the lie with another wide grin. "You will be pleased to hear that Brother Dominic made it home safely."

"Oh, that is good news."

"How are you, Sunny?" Diego asked. "And Dr. Adler and rest of the family? Everyone is well, I trust."

Instead of answering, Sunny dug a hand into her pocket and pulled out a crumpled piece of paper. She smoothed the page that she had sketched just before arriving, then slid it across the desk to him. Squinting, he studied it carefully. "A map?" he asked.

She nodded. "Of the harbour."

He pointed to the various *x*s on the page. "These marks, what do the characters and numbers below them mean?"

"The digits before the first character are numbers that I have given to the different Japanese naval craft." She pointed to one that read *12R3*. "As an example, I have called this ship number twelve. I will never use twelve for any other ship but this particular one."

"And the letter *R*?"

"It stands for cruiser. Each of the letters represents a type of ship. For example, *T* stands for frigate, *B* for riverboat, *R* for cruiser and so on."

"What about the last number—three?"

"That represents the number of days that particular cruiser has been in port."

Diego studied the map in silence for several seconds and then looked back up at Sunny, the smile returning to his face. "I am most impressed, Sunny," he said. "Most impressed."

"I walk my son in his pram past the port every day. No one ever notices us."

"Even when you draw maps?"

Sunny shook her head adamantly. "I draw them later. From memory."

"Clever."

"Will it be helpful to your . . . people?"

"It would have been, yes, but I am afraid we've had another setback." Diego sighed.

"How so, Father?"

"The Japanese triangulated the signal of our radioman. May the Heavenly Father bless his soul." Diego made the sign of the cross on his chest. "We have no way of transmitting this information to the people who would need it."

"What about a courier? One of the local coolies, perhaps?"

Diego exhaled heavily. "Our people are situated well outside Shanghai. Even if a runner could make it to them, by the time this reconnaissance reached them, it might already be obsolete."

"So it's of no use to you?"

"Not until we have another radioman. No."

Sunny felt utterly defeated and deflated. The mortification from her run-in with Ghoya washed back over her. She wanted to crawl under a rock. She wished the ground would swallow her up. *What was the point of any of it?*

CHAPTER 27

The explosions weren't much louder, but Franz couldn't remember having felt the ground shake under his feet before. He couldn't see anything beyond the early dawn light sifting through the trees, but he knew the fighting must have moved closer to the field hospital.

He checked his watch and saw that it was nearly five o'clock. He was accustomed to ignoring hunger pangs, but he craved an espresso. In Vienna, a stiff shot of coffee used to get him through the longest days of surgery. Each day at the field hospital seemed to bring more wounded men with even worse injuries than the soldiers preceding them. Franz sometimes lost himself in the work; technically, it was among the most challenging of his surgical career. With unlimited supplies of equipment, anesthetic and other medications, he could perform more complex operations in this tent in the middle of a war zone than he could have inside the refugee hospital. But he would have given his right arm to be back in Shanghai.

Franz wondered if Sunny had managed to keep the hospital open and operational. No one was more capable than she, but how could she run a hospital while raising a baby on her own? Well, not entirely alone; he had no doubt that Esther was helping. Hannah too. Over the past year, his daughter had outgrown her rebellious, early adolescent stage and matured into the person he had hoped and expected she would become. He was pleased that she had found Herschel, the kind of boy who would always put her first. Perhaps they would marry one day? It broke Franz's heart to think that no matter whom she wed, he would probably not be there to witness it.

Shaking off the despondent thoughts, Franz ducked into the convalescence tent to perform his rounds. The bed where the bespectacled private had lain was now empty. The badly burned patient from the day before was still alive, and Franz was surprised to see Captain Suzuki sitting at his bedside. Suzuki, who rarely spoke to his post-operative patients, appeared to be huddled in conversation with the man.

Franz bowed a greeting to the captain and got a nod in response. The always-deep circles under Suzuki's eyes were dark as coal. "Did they bring you kusaya this morning?" he demanded.

"I would have preferred eggs and sausages, but yes they did, thank you."

"Do you remember what I told you on the subject of gratitude?"

"That you will never give me reason to thank you."

"Precisely," Suzuki said. "Any spells today?"

"Not so far, no," Franz answered honestly.

"The day is just beginning," Suzuki grunted.

Franz turned to the patient. His partly open eyes were glassy and unfocused, his breathing choppy. At one point, the man stopped breathing for several seconds before he gasped a loud inhalation.

"He has only a few minutes left," Suzuki said.

Not certain whether to leave or stay, Franz stood watching the patient's stuttering respirations. Finally, he asked, "Do you know this man, Captain?"

"I met him only yesterday."

"I see."

Suzuki was quiet for a few moments. "I imagine dying of burns is one of the most ghastly ways to go."

Franz remembered the day he first met Suzuki at the Country Hospital, and the special attention the captain had given to a badly burned patient there. "Do you believe there is a good way to die, Captain?"

"Quickly. Honourably." Suzuki pointed to the patient. "Not like this. Having your body burned and then waiting for death to catch up. No one deserves that."

Franz sensed something more to it, but he didn't ask. Instead he said, "Shall I check on the other patients?"

"No need. I rose early this morning. I have already attended to them." Suzuki sighed. "You should go to the operating room."

"Are we expecting another day of heavy casualties?"

Suzuki responded with a grim chuckle. Another boom echoed outside and the ground shifted slightly. "The combat seems to have moved closer to us, sir," Franz said.

"I can't imagine how that is possible," Suzuki said wryly. "That would involve a retreat. And the Imperial Japanese Army moves in only one direction. Forward."

* * *

The field hospital was overwhelmed by the slew of casualties that rolled in throughout the morning. There were too many wounded men to manage them all in the operating room. The tent overflowed with soldiers wrapped in blood-soaked dressings. Some lay quietly on stretchers, others writhed and moaned on the bare ground, their suffering palpable. They began to triage patients outside the tent. Franz pulled dislocated shoulders and hips into their joints, and reset broken bones without the benefit of an X-ray or, at times, even a stretcher.

At one point, Suzuki pulled Franz aside. "From now on, we will take only the most straightforward injuries into the operating room."

Franz pointed to a man whose eyes were clenched shut as he clutched a grave open abdominal wound. "What about the others?" he asked.

"The nurses will dress those with larger wounds. If they survive, we will operate later." The captain locked eyes with Franz. "Anyone with a weak pulse or low blood pressure receives a very generous dose of painkillers. Do you understand?"

"Enough to stop their breathing?"

"Enough to keep them comfortable!"

Franz lost track of the time and of the patients. He doubted he had ever sutured as many wounds or reset so many bones in a day. Finally, in the early evening, Suzuki announced that the team had to take a break so soldiers could wash away the blood and debris that were contaminating the operating room.

Franz stepped outside the tent to stretch his back. It occurred to him that, although his neck ached and his hands were stiff and fatigued, he had not experienced any light-headedness since rising. Perhaps Suzuki's diagnosis and treatment were accurate, he thought. But what difference would it make in the long term?

Franz saw the collection of trucks and other vehicles that had transported the casualties to the camp. Across the way, he spotted Helen leaning against a tent post, smoking a cigarette. As he joined her in the waning twilight, she offered a tired smile. "Just when you imagined it couldn't get any worse," she said.

"Sometimes it seems as if it can only get worse."

"I suppose." Helen tucked a red curl behind her ear. "You performed miracles today."

"You too. But it feels as though we're only stalling the inevitable."

"For you or them?"

Franz smiled. "All of us."

"For what it's worth, I was impressed."

Franz smiled in gratitude. "The man with the extensive burns . . ."

Helen took a long drag from her cigarette. "He died."

Franz nodded. "I found the captain sitting at his bedside this morning. I think he might have been consoling him."

She frowned. "He does pay special attention to burn victims."

"I wonder why. Perhaps there is some—"

She cocked her head and held up a hand to interrupt. "Do you hear that?"

He listened carefully until he picked up on the low hum.

She pointed southward. "Over there, Franz. Planes."

Squinting in the low light, he saw three planes flying from the south in tight formation. They appeared to be heading west. Their pitch was lower than the familiar whine of the Japanese Zeroes, and their shapes didn't fit any of the aircraft Franz had seen patrolling overhead. He glanced over to Helen, whose eyes were fixed on the sky. "Those aren't Japanese," he said.

"No," she agreed.

The planes' wings tilted, and they banked toward the field hospital. The hum rose to a roar as the fighters descended. Shouts went up throughout the camp. People sprang into action. Franz grabbed Helen by the wrist and yanked her around the side of the tent. He dropped to his knees and pulled her to the ground beside him under the cover of a canvas overhang. He hovered close enough to feel her breath against his cheek.

The rat-a-tat-tat of aerial gunfire filled the air. The road where Franz had just been standing sprayed puffs of dirt as the shells exploded. The thunder of engines was deafening as the planes zoomed overhead. Franz sighted a pair of predatory eyes and a mouth full of jagged teeth painted across the nose of one of the planes. Stars and stripes were tattooed along its fuselage.

Helen covered her head and screamed as the supply tent across from them rattled and then collapsed under the strafing. Heart thudding in his ears, Franz threw himself on top of her, shielding her body with his.

Glass shattered as the nearby trucks were hit by a barrage of gunfire. Helen squirmed beneath him. "Don't move," Franz cried.

The planes flew past the camp, but he kept her pinned beneath him. He watched the planes bank again and turn back. As they strafed the camp a second time, he could hear the whiz of bullets around them. The ground a few feet away erupted in more sprays. Helen trembled violently beneath him.

Franz braced himself for another pass, but this time the din of the engines faded. He looked up and saw the planes retreating southward. Soldiers scattered all around, but Franz didn't release Helen until he was convinced that the planes wouldn't return. Finally, he rose to his feet and helped Helen up.

She continued shaking as she leaned against him. He supported her with an arm across her shoulders. "We could have died, Franz," she murmured.

"I think they were targeting the vehicles."

"Was it the Americans?"

"American planes, at least," Franz said. "The Flying Tigers. But I've heard they've trained Chinese pilots to fly them too."

"Why would they attack a hospital?"

"Maybe they can't tell what it is from the sky."

"Or maybe they just don't care."

Her shivering subsided, but Franz heard sniffling and saw that she was crying. "They are not coming back, Helen."

"Maybe not now, but they will," she sobbed. "You've been right all along, Franz."

"About?"

"We are never going to make it out of here."

"Don't say that."

"It's true."

"Helen, you're in shock."

She leaned her head in close to his. "I've never seen things more clearly."

He rubbed her shoulder. "It will get better. You will see."

She touched his other hand lightly. "You saved my life."

"Not at all."

She left her still trembling fingers on his hand. "I think I would go out of my mind if you weren't here with me."

Even in the weak light, Franz recognized the look in her reddened eyes. "It's important to have friends, especially at such vulnerable times," he said.

Helen leaned forward and pressed her moist lips against his. Franz let his mouth linger on hers, overwhelmed by the intimacy and warmth. Then reality showered over him like ice water. He jerked his face from hers and stumbled back a few steps. "I . . . I . . ." Words deserted him.

CHAPTER 28

Where is Hannah?" Sunny asked.

"I believe she has gone out with Herschel," Esther replied.

Hannah hadn't intended to eavesdrop on her aunt and stepmother. She almost spoke up from where she lay on her bed in the loft, but she felt awkward announcing herself in mid-conversation. She was supposed to have gone out with Herschel, but she still couldn't bring herself to face him. Nothing more had happened with Freddy aside from that one electrical touch, but her feelings alone were betrayal enough.

"So that awful Ghoya won't tell you where he has sent Franz?" Esther continued.

"He never will, either," Sunny said dejectedly.

"We just have to wait a little longer, then."

"Waiting is the one thing I cannot do."

"What choice do you have?"

Sunny didn't answer right away. "I went to see Father Diego."

"Oh, Sunny." Esther's voice dropped so low that Hannah had trouble hearing her. "What would Franz say?"

"How can I possibly know? He's been gone almost six weeks. Who knows what's happened to him in that time?" Sunny's voice rose in anguish. "Or if he's even alive."

"*Bays di tsung!*" Esther said in Yiddish and then repeated herself in German. "Bite your tongue. You can't ever think such things."

"Why not?"

"It only tempts fate."

"You Jews are as superstitious as the Chinese," Sunny scoffed. "Besides, what more can possibly go wrong?"

"Joey!"

A moment of agonizing silence came next. Even Hannah held her breath.

"If you were to be caught spying," Esther continued unapologetically, "you would never see him again. Is that fair to your son? And how could I possibly manage two babies on my own?"

"When did I ask you to?"

"You don't need to ask, Sunny," Esther cried. "You should know that. We are family."

"How can I just do nothing, after all they've done to us?" Sunny said. "To Yang. To Charlie. To Simon. And now to Franz. There's nothing I wouldn't do to get him back. Absolutely nothing." She hesitated. "I . . . I told Ghoya as much. Do you understand?"

Hannah didn't fully appreciate Sunny's insinuation, but she inferred from Esther's long pause that her aunt must have. "Of course I understand. He's your husband."

"Oh, Essie." Sunny's voice cracked. "It was a disaster. I'm so ashamed."

"You were only trying to help Franz."

"And yet I think I made it even worse."

"I am sure that's not so," Esther said. "Sunny, if you were to become a spy, it wouldn't help to bring Franz home or to change anything, except for the worse."

Sunny's voice became firmer. "If there was one less Japanese ship in the harbour because of the intelligence I supplied, or if my efforts helped shorten this war by one second, then surely it would be worthwhile."

"Not to your family. Certainly not to Franz. Or to Joey."

"Besides, it doesn't matter," Sunny said. "There's nothing I can do to help the Allies anyway."

"What do you mean?"

"My reconnaissance is useless. Father Diego told me as much. His radioman was arrested, and without a transmitter to relay the information, they can't pass it on in time to the people who would need it."

"Good," Esther said. "It's settled, then. You see? This is fate."

Before Hannah had even thought it through, she blurted, "I know someone with a radio, Sunny."

"Hannah?" Sunny called up to her. "You have been in your room this whole time?"

Hannah got to her feet and hurried down the ladder. Esther was sitting on the couch with her knitting needles and yarn dropped in her lap. Jakob played with his wooden blocks on the floor at her feet. Sunny was cradling Joey in her arms. Both women stared at Hannah in obvious alarm. "How much have you heard?" Sunny demanded.

"All of it," Hannah admitted.

"Hannah-*chen*," Esther said, sounding more disappointed than cross. "You know better."

Hannah lowered her head. "I was going to say something, but I'd already heard more than I should have."

Sunny squinted at her. "What were you saying about a radio?"

"I know someone who has one," Hannah said. "I am sure he would be willing to help."

"Who?"

Hannah looked away again. "Freddy Herzberg."

"Hannah," Esther cried. "You are not still in contact with *that* boy?"

"We're in the same class," Hannah said.

"Yes, but how do you know that he has a radio transmitter?"

This time Hannah met her aunt's eyes. "He showed it to me."

Esther grimaced. "Oh, Hannah. After what happened last year? After what he put your father through?"

"It's different now. Freddy has changed."

"People like him don't change," Esther said.

Sunny shook her head adamantly. "Regardless, children cannot be involved in this."

"We are not children," Hannah said evenly, trying to not come across as too defensive. "I'm fourteen and he's a year older than me."

"And he will never see sixteen if he gets mixed up in this nonsense," Esther said.

"Your aunt is right," Sunny agreed.

Hannah felt something hard on her leg and looked down to see Jakob pressing a block into her thigh. He grinned impishly. "Block, Anna, block," he said. He still couldn't pronounce the *H*.

"Soon, Jakob." Hannah turned to Sunny. "What if Freddy were to lend you his radio?"

"No. This is madness," Esther insisted.

But Hannah could see that Sunny was wavering. "Let me talk to Freddy, at least," she said. She was certain she could somehow make them see things her way.

* * *

Hannah didn't even try to fool herself into thinking that her excitement had anything to do with espionage or even helping her stepmother. The truth was that she wanted to see Freddy again.

She found him kicking a paper ball back and forth with his friend, Avi Perlmann, on busy Kung Ping Road, where the two boys often loitered. She was elated by the enthusiastic smile with which Freddy greeted her. Avi was not so welcoming. "What do you want, Adler?"

Ignoring Avi, Hannah said to Freddy, "I need to speak with you."

"So talk," Avi said.

"In private." Hannah glanced at the shorter boy. "Go away, Avi."

Avi's shoulders stiffened and his nostrils flared. "No one tells me what to do. Especially not some girl who—"

Before Avi could complete the insult, Freddy shoved him backwards. "You heard her, Avi. Scram. Get lost."

Avi stumbled back a step or two. He glared at them before he spun on his heels and stomped away.

"He'll get over it," Freddy said with another broad smile. "It's nice to see you again so soon, Banana."

Fighting off a blush, Hannah said, "Can we talk somewhere more private?"

Freddy led her to a lane a few blocks away. Despite being lined with houses on both sides, it was devoid of pedestrians or other traffic. Hannah spoke in a whisper as she hurriedly described the situation, without mentioning Sunny by name. Then she told him of their need for a radio transmitter.

Freddy eyed her with awe. "You mean we'd actually get to guide the American bombers?"

"Not 'we,' Freddy." She shook her head. "They would only borrow your radio for a few hours. You would never even meet them."

Freddy squared his shoulders. “Uh-uh. No way. I promised Pop I would never let it out of my sight.”

“So you won’t do it, then?”

“I’ll do better. I’ll send the messages myself.”

Hannah shook her head. “They refuse to involve us in this. They say it’s too risky for kids.”

He raised an eyebrow. “Kids?”

“Not teenagers either.”

Unruffled, Freddy pursed his lips. Hannah could practically see the wheels turning in his head. “Surely they are going to send the intelligence in some kind of code? Like they do in the spy films.”

“I guess so, yes.”

“Then it’s no more risk than what I’m taking right now.”

“How so?”

“All right, say the Japs do triangulate my signal. It would be gobbledygook to them. They wouldn’t be able to tell if I was ordering cigarettes from Frenchtown or sending ship coordinates to the Americans.” He laughed. “Or, for that matter, playing rummy with a pal.”

Hannah saw his point, but she doubted Sunny would be swayed. “They will never agree to it, Freddy.”

He shrugged. “Then they won’t have a radio to use, will they?”

CHAPTER 29

The priest appeared so natural holding Joey in the crook of his elbow and rocking him back and forth—*more comfortable than Franz has ever seemed with the baby in his arms,* Sunny thought sadly. "Such a little treasure," Diego gushed. "Were my life not dedicated to the Church, I would have a brood of my own."

"Is your life really dedicated to the Church, Father?" Sunny asked.

Diego cocked his head, curious but not troubled. "I like to think so. Why do you ask?"

"Your connection with Brother Dominic and the . . . others. It was so unexpected. I wondered if you are everything else that you appear to be, Father."

"Ah, I see." Diego laughed. "Yes, I am very much a man of the cloth. I am even Spanish. From Seville."

Sunny lowered her voice. "How does a Spanish priest get involved in espionage in Shanghai?"

He glanced over her head, as if to assure himself that the door was shut. "Purely by accident, let me assure you."

"I have never heard of an accidental spy."

Diego laughed again. Joey cooed happily. "Have you heard of a city called Badajoz?"

Sunny shook her head.

"Of course you would not have," Diego said. "It's a small provincial city—hardly more than a town—in the west of Spain. Near the border of Portugal. My first seven years in the priesthood were spent in the United States, in Chicago. Badajoz was my first diocese on Spanish soil. I was pleased to be going home, though I had no idea that I was returning at the worst of times."

"The Spanish Civil War?" Sunny asked.

"Yes. It was the summer of 1936. And Badajoz was one of the first cities to fall to the Nationalists." Diego sighed heavily. "The fighting was fierce, but the Republicans never stood a chance. The city was overrun in a matter of days. To be honest, at the time, I was pleased."

"Pleased?"

"I was apolitical. The Nationalists claimed to defend the Church, but I didn't pretend to understand the issues. It hurt me to see Spaniard killing Spaniard. I simply wanted it to be over. When the fighting ended, I assumed all would return to normal."

"It never does," Sunny said, thinking of her own city.

"Very true." Diego tickled Joey's chin until the baby smiled for him. "Such a treasure," he repeated before turning back to Sunny. "One hot and muggy Friday morning in Badajoz—it was August—a young girl burst into the church in the middle of mass. Anjelita was her name. Such a beautiful girl, from such a lovely family. Both parents were teachers." He sighed. "Anjelita—she was perhaps nine or ten years old—was hysterical. She sputtered something about her mother and father having been taken away, but she was too upset to make much sense. She led me by the hand to the town's central bullring." He closed his eyes, reliving the incident. "I knew there was trouble when I saw the phalanx of soldiers surrounding the building. And the silence—such a haunting silence from inside. I will never forget it as long as I live." He opened his eyes. "Of course, the soldiers refused to allow me to enter. I had to bluff my way in by telling them that I had been sent by the bishop at the request of their commander."

Sunny waited silently, hanging on the priest's every word, while dreading the story's outcome.

"To be honest, I was never as much of an aficionado as I should have been. Seville is, after all, home to the world's greatest bullfighters. My father, now there was a true aficionado. He would often take me to bullfights when I was young. I found it so sad to watch the bulls taunted and weakened by the *banderilleros* and picadors. Sometimes, I would cry during the *estocada*—the matador's fatal thrust. I even once saw a matador gored. I was terribly frightened." He shrugged. "My father, I imagine he was embarrassed. Or perhaps he knew I didn't have the stomach for it. Either way, he stopped taking me to the bullring."

Diego pinched the bridge of his nose. "Of course, nothing I had ever seen inside or outside a bullring prepared me for this particular summer morning. You see, the Nationalists, they had led the prisoners into the ring at dawn. Men and women, unionists, socialists, teachers, intellectuals—almost all of them civilians. I had no idea who they all were or what they had been accused of." He drew a circle in the air with his free hand. "The commanders had set up a ring of machine gunners where the spectators normally stood for the bullfights. From what I understand, the soldiers didn't stop firing until their cartridges were all spent." He closed his eyes again. "By the time I arrived, bodies were everywhere.

They covered most of the ground, like a bloody human carpet. I spent the morning moving from one person to the next, praying the Requiem Aeternam for their souls. One woman who had been shot in the belly, she cried out to me. I made the mistake of calling to one of the soldiers for help. That poor woman . . ." He crossed himself. "I stumbled across Anjelita's parents near the centre of the ring. They were lying together on their backs, her head turned to his, their fingers intertwined."

Sunny had heard grislier stories than Diego's—blood curdling reports of child rape and live mutilations from massacres in places such as Nanking and Changjiao—but something in the priest's account moved her deeply. "I'm so sorry, Father."

"It was a long time ago. And I witnessed other atrocities—the Republicans were no saints either—in the years that followed. But my view of the Nationalists—of all fascists—was forged that morning in Badajoz."

"And your radio show, Father?"

Diego grinned coyly. "My radio persona is my cover, as they say in the Hollywood films."

"Were you sent to Shanghai to spy?"

Diego held up his hand. "Pardon me, Sunny. I have already said far too much."

"It's all right, Father," she reassured.

He studied her, appearing far sadder and more vulnerable—older even—than ever before. "I have tremendous faith in you. I would put my life in your hands, my child."

"It's all right, Father. You don't have to tell me anything."

"It feels good to tell someone. My own confessor." The smile returned to his lips. "In truth, my career in espionage began here through a chance encounter."

"With whom?"

"An American who attended our church. I thought he was simply another of the many foreign businessmen in the city."

"But he was a spy?"

Diego nodded. "I believe he worked for American military intelligence in some way, but he was vague about his precise role. Regardless, months before Pearl Harbor, he predicted the Japanese aggression and the fall of the colonies in Asia, including Shanghai. He correctly suspected that I, being Spanish and a priest, would have more freedom than most. He asked me if I would be willing to be his 'eyes and ears' in Shanghai."

"But the risk, Father."

"It was an easy decision, really. I had already seen and heard enough from the Japanese to know they were no different from the fascists in Europe." He grunted in disgust. "I was already on the wireless with my spiritual program, of course. The American, he was the one who suggested I become more political—more sympathetic toward the Axis powers—that in fact it would be prudent for me to appear so. And, as with everything else, the American was correct. I have been above suspicion thus far."

"Doesn't it concern you that you might be influencing your listeners? Generating sympathy for the Axis?"

Diego chuckled and shook his head. "At first it did, Sunny. Very much so. I have since come to realize that people's minds were made up long ago. I am not recruiting anyone to the cause. The insightful ones can see through my message." He shook his head. "The others—the sympathizers—they hear what they want to hear. Meantime, it permits me to do a modicum of good."

"So you run the American spy ring in Shanghai?"

"Hardly," Diego cried. "What I do is—what do they say?—small potatoes. We shelter a few downed pilots. And, before my radioman was arrested, we reported what we could observe from in and around the city. That is the very modest extent of my cloak-and-dagger activities. I swear to you."

Joey squirmed, and Sunny held out her arms. Diego passed the baby across his desk to her. Joey continued to fuss until Sunny found him his thumb to suck on. "It's about the radio that I've come today," she said.

"Then I am afraid you have wasted a trip." Diego held up his hands helplessly. "It will be a few more weeks before our new transmitter arrives."

"I know someone with access to one."

"A radio?" Diego leaned forward. "That he will loan us?"

Sunny felt unease bubbling in her stomach. "He's willing to help, but he will not loan it to you."

"I do not understand."

"My stepdaughter has a friend." Without mentioning his name, Sunny told Diego about Freddy's offer to transmit her surveillance records of the harbour.

"How can we involve a boy of that age?" Diego shook his head. "The risk . . ."

Despite her misgivings, Sunny persisted. "Apparently, he uses the transmitter once or twice a week anyway. He insists there would no more risk in relaying our messages than there would be in playing radio games with his friend in Frenchtown."

Diego leaned back in his chair, considering the suggestion. "The Japanese would have no way of knowing to whom he was sending messages, would they?"

"No. And the boy claims that if a transmission is brief enough, it's almost impossible to triangulate its source."

The priest eyed her silently, lost in thought. Finally, he said, "It will only be temporary. A matter of a week or two, hopefully, until our own radio arrives."

"And we would always keep an arm's-length distance from the boy," she said. "I learned that much from my experience with the Underground. People must be kept separate in case someone is captured. He will never know who we are. And I will never share his identity with you."

"Then how would you get the reconnaissance information to the boy?"

"I will secure a drop box of some sort."

"Yes, I see." Diego formed a steeple with his hands and gazed upward. "Can we, in good conscience, proceed with this?"

Sunny didn't know if he was asking her or God, but she answered anyway. "We might not have any other choice."

* * *

By the time Sunny reached the Comfort Home, Joey was fussing inconsolably. Even a bottle of weak sugary tea didn't appease him. Apparently, Joey wasn't the only one out of sorts. When Sunny arrived, Jia-Li relayed a message through Ushi that she was refusing to see anyone, even her oldest friend.

Sunny insisted on waiting. After an hour, just as Joey finally settled back to sleep, Ushi returned and beckoned her to follow him. He led her downstairs and into the wine cellar. Sunny had to sidle through a secret passageway hidden behind a false wall in the cellar to reach the basement hideaway. It consisted of a common room with bedrooms behind it.

Despite the late afternoon hour, Jia-Li was in pyjamas. She sat on a couch, an unlit cigarette dangling from her lips. Her usual jasmine fragrance was absent, replaced by the stale smell of unwashed hair. Her pale face was free of makeup and her lustrous hair was tied in a messy bun. Her cheekbones were even more prominent than usual. "You have lost weight, *bǎo bèi*," Sunny observed.

"I hear that happens to prisoners," Jia-Li snorted.

"Mama moved you down here for your own safety."

Jia-Li laughed bitterly. "Chih-Nii moved me here for the same reason she does everything. Her own convenience."

"Not so. We are all so worried about you, *bǎo bèi*."

"Your worry is misplaced. And unwanted."

Sunny turned Joey toward her friend, but Jia-Li wouldn't look up at either of them. "He's growing so fast, Sister. He won't be easy to carry much longer. Would you like to hold him?"

"No," she murmured.

Sunny sat down beside Jia-Li and reached for her friend's hand. Jia-Li didn't pull away, but her fingers lay limp in Sunny's. "I need to ask a favour of you, Sister."

Jia-Li chuckled. "You want help from a prisoner?"

"I just need to hear something from you, *bǎo bèi*. Something that will give me peace of mind."

"What is it?"

Sunny squeezed Jia-Li's hand tighter. "If something were to happen to me, I need to know that you will look after Joey."

Jia-Li's head snapped up. "Why would something happen to you?"

"This is Shanghai. You know as well as I do, anything can happen here."

Jia-Li stiffened. "Stop it, *xiǎo hè*. You can't fool me. Why are you asking me this now?"

"Esther would help, of course," Sunny said, avoiding the question. "But if Franz and I are both gone, Joey cannot stay in the ghetto. Esther couldn't cope with two babies on her own. Perhaps your mother could help? Or one of the cousins, they—"

Jia-Li yanked her hand free of Sunny's and stood up. She pointed the cigarette accusingly. "Tell me, *xiǎo hè*—you are not involved with the Resistance again?"

Sunny shook her head.

Jia-Li's face creased in suspicion. "Who, then?"

"Do you remember Father Diego?"

Jia-Li frowned. "The one who brought us the pilot?"

"He works for the Americans." Sunny went on to describe her last conversation with him.

As Sunny was talking, Jia-Li reached out and eased Joey out of Sunny's arms and into her own. Cradling the sleeping baby, Jia-Li shook her head. "You can't do this. I forbid it."

"I have to, *bǎo bèi*."

"Anyone can spy on the port," Jia-Li said. "You are the only one who can take care of this one."

"I need to hear you promise me," Sunny said.

Jia-Li sniffed Joey's head. "I love the scent of babies. They smell of innocence."

"Promise me," Sunny persisted.

"I can't. I won't." Jia-Li shook her head. "I will do something better. If you convince Chih-Nii to free me from this dungeon, I will go to the port and spy on the ships myself. Happily."

"What do you know about Japanese ships?"

"They have no business in our harbour, I know that much. Besides, how hard can it be to tell them apart?"

"I know you, Sister. You couldn't tell a battleship from a sampan."

"So I will learn."

"Never." Sunny laughed. "And as for drawing a map from memory, there is no one with a worse sense of direction than you. Remember when we were young, how you would get lost on our own street?"

Jia-Li smiled for the first time. "It was a winding road."

Sunny rested her hand on her friend's shoulder. She stared intently into Jia-Li's eyes. "I have to do this. For my father, for Yang and especially for Franz."

Jia-Li's only response was to hold Joey's face against her neck, but Sunny could see that her friend was wavering. Her hand tightened to a grip on Jia-Li's shoulder. "Promise me you will be there for your godson."

Jia-Li's eyes widened, simultaneously moved and surprised. "My godson?"

"Of course."

Jia-Li smiled again. "Yes, all right."

Sunny hid her relief behind a stern expression. "That means no more funny business with soldiers or Kempeitai or anyone else who comes through the Comfort Home. You understand, *bǎo bèi*?"

Jia-Li kissed Joey on the top of his head. "Yes, *xiǎo hè*. I promise."

CHAPTER 30

Despite the sense of foreboding that hung over the camp in the wake of the air raid, the planes did not return. Casualties, however, rolled into the operating room all night long. Usually, Franz spent his days operating on the wounded men who had come from the front, but this time he recognized several of the victims. Seven men had died during the raid, and three more did not survive surgery, including the only one his four tentmates who spoke passable English. They couldn't stem the bleeding from the man's hemorrhaging pulmonary vein, which had been shredded by a large-calibre bullet that perforated his chest from back to front.

Despite such horrors, Franz was thankful for the distraction of work. He wouldn't have slept anyway. He had avoided eye contact with Helen throughout the surgery, but his turbulent thoughts kept cycling back to their kiss. He couldn't deny his complicity in the moment or the comfort he had found, easily imagining Helen's lips to be Sunny's. He doubted he would ever see his wife again, and he craved physical comfort. He worried that he wouldn't be able to trust his self-restraint a second time.

At just after five o'clock that morning, the last of the wounded—a man whose femur had been shattered by a bullet—was carried out of the operating room on a stretcher, a bulky dressing where his right leg had once been.

"Come with me," Suzuki said as he stripped off his gloves and operating gown.

Franz followed him out into the stippled light of dawn. They passed the bullet-riddled, windowless wrecks of the destroyed troop transports. The dirt road had been torn up by the barrage of bullets, as if tilled with a hoe. Soldiers were busy all around the camp repairing tents and replacing those that had collapsed from the gunfire.

They entered the row of tents that formed the officers' residences. Suzuki led him into one at the end of the row. The spacious tent was sparsely furnished with a cot, a plywood wardrobe and a wooden desk that had two folding chairs on either side of it. A tea set was waiting on top, steam escaping from its pot. Suzuki poured two cups of the green tea, its floral bouquet familiar to Franz's nose. It was the only flavour the Japanese ever seemed to serve.

Franz studied the only other object on the desk, a framed photograph of the captain with his wife and son. Wearing a dark civilian suit, Suzuki stood unsmiling but proud between a skinny young man in a similar suit and a woman in a patterned kimono. In the backdrop, a grand suspension bridge arched over a sparkling body of water.

"My family and I had just driven over the Golden Gate Bridge for the first time," Suzuki said. "It was taken two days after the bridge opened. Late in the spring of 1937."

"I remember reading about it in Vienna," Franz said as he sipped his tea. "It's the longest bridge in the world, is it not?"

Suzuki nodded. "The longest span of any bridge ever built. Over a mile long. It's truly a marvel."

"Did you enjoy your time in America?"

"My time in America? You ask me as though I were there as a tourist." Suzuki chuckled humourlessly. "I only came back to Japan to attend my son's wedding. America was our home until December 7, 1941."

Franz empathized with the captain. He knew what it meant to have his country ripped out from underneath him. "Austria was mine until March 12, 1938."

"The day of the Nazi occupation?"

"The Anschluss, yes."

Suzuki sipped his tea in silence. "In San Francisco, I trained under Dr. Leo Eloesser. Perhaps you have heard of him?"

Franz shook his head.

"Dr. Eloesser is a pioneer in the field of thoracic surgery, an extremely capable surgeon. He is also famous in California as a humanitarian and a patron of the arts. He is close friends with the Mexican painters Diego Rivera and Frida Kahlo."

"Is Dr. Eloesser Jewish?"

Suzuki nodded. "I worked with several Jewish doctors at the San Francisco General. I considered some of them friends. In America, I was never aware of the anti-Semitism that seems to flourish in Europe."

"It wasn't always the case in Europe either. Particularly not in Vienna. It was such a cultured and tolerant city when I was young. Jews like Sigmund Freud and Arnold Schoenberg were the toast of the town."

"What happened?"

"What always happens to us." Franz sighed. "Times turned bad and someone blamed the Jews. It has happened time and again throughout history, from the famines in Egypt to the Black Death and now the Depression. Jews have always been the world's scapegoats. But never more so than under the Nazis."

"Why do you think that is?"

"Many reasons, I suppose. We have always been a quiet and easily identifiable community. And Jews have often succeeded professionally and financially. We attract resentment like flowers draw bees." Franz thought of one of Rabbi Hiltmann's themes. "But perhaps most importantly, it's because we Jews don't have a real home. We are a minority—perpetual guests and outsiders—anywhere we live. Without a national identity or an army to protect us."

Suzuki considered this. "Are you suggesting that if the Jews were to have their own nation, anti-Semitism would end?"

"Anti-Semitism has thrived for five thousand years, Captain. It probably always will. But if the Jews were to have their own homeland, it at least might provide us with a sanctuary from the Hitlers of this world."

Suzuki frowned. "And how will you ever achieve this homeland? Who will give you the land, or the freedom?"

"We will probably have to fight for it."

"More war. More suffering for your people." Suzuki grunted a laugh. "Will it be worth it?"

Franz rubbed his tired eyes. "I don't really know what anything is worth anymore."

"You are not alone," Suzuki muttered.

Franz put down his cup and asked the question that had been on his mind ever since the planes struck. "Will you relocate the camp, Captain?"

"That is Major Okada's decision to make." His tone was skeptical.

"What is the point of bringing injured men to a hospital that is the target of enemy crossfire?"

"It is not my decision," Suzuki reiterated.

"Helen and I were outside when the planes came," Franz said. "We heard the whistle of the bullets. Helen was . . . traumatized."

Suzuki gazed forlornly into his cup. "That is unfortunate."

"The planes will return, Captain."

"I imagine so, yes."

Franz stared at Suzuki, desperate to crack his stoic fatalism. "Surely you must have influence with the major?"

Suzuki grunted another bitter laugh. "Aside from the Emperor himself, I do not know of anyone who has influence with Major Okada."

* * *

Franz was nauseated and wobbly with fatigue by the late afternoon. He realized how prophetic Suzuki's words had been: there never was any rest at the field hospital. The day after the air raid, trucks rolled into the camp with fresh casualties from the field. Franz couldn't remember how long he had been awake, but it must have been at least thirty-six hours. He sutured wounds and reset broken bones, explosions pounding and heavy artillery fire drumming steadily in the background. Rumour around the camp was that the Kuomintang army of Chiang Kai-Shek had sent reinforcements to Hengyang for a massive counterattack.

Just as alarmingly, Franz's dizziness had returned. Twice so far that day he had had to find an excuse to sit down during surgery. After the day's last casualty had been removed from the table, Franz was heading out of the room when his legs turned to rubber and buckled. Just as he was bracing himself for the fall, a pair of arms enveloped his waist and eased him to the ground and onto his back.

Helen knelt down beside him, her face creased with concern. "Franz, can you hear me? Are you all right?"

He glanced around, relieved to see they were alone in the room. "Yes. Thank you."

She squinted. "The episodes have come back?"

Embarrassed, Franz looked away. "I have not eaten today."

"You must, Franz. You heard what the captain told you."

"I was . . . preoccupied."

She slid her arm out from under his back. "I will go find you some of that salty fish."

Before she could stand up, Franz reached for her wrist. "Helen, last night . . ."

It was her turn to look away. "We don't need to discuss it."

Franz hung on to her arm. "Please."

"I was in shock," she said. "I acted without thinking. I am so sorry."

"There is no need to be sorry."

"You are married." Her voice cracked.

He released her arm. "These are far from normal times."

"That doesn't excuse what I did."

"What *we* did."

She hovered beside him but continued to avoid his gaze. "After my marriage—after my husband left me—I was angry, of course. With Michael. But the person I blamed most was Marjorie. She was supposed to have been my friend."

"You have never even met Sunny." He realized how meaningless the words sounded as soon they left his mouth.

"And yet I feel as if I know her. I am certain I would like her."

"I have no doubt the two of you would get on well."

"You think so?" Helen laughed. "I'm not so sure she wouldn't see straight through me, the way I should have with Marjorie." She stood up and hurried toward the tent's flap. "Don't get up. I will bring some kusaya."

Franz pushed himself up to sitting, fighting off the lightheadedness. "Helen . . ."

She glanced over her shoulder at him, her cheeks flushed. "Yes?"

His tongue felt thick, and once again he couldn't summon the right words. "Thank you for . . . catching me."

After Helen had left, Franz got to his feet and took a few cautious steps to test his balance. Feeling steadier, he headed out of the tent without waiting for her to return. He wanted to escape his mortification and, he conceded to himself, further temptation. Helen's vulnerability only made her that much more attractive. And he felt as confused as he was ashamed by the feelings.

Lost in thought, Franz found himself back on the path toward the officers' quarters. He slowed when he spotted Captain Suzuki conversing with another man behind the row of tents. His companion's back was turned, but Franz recognized Major Okada from the cane in his right hand alone.

Franz was about to turn away when he heard the major's raised voice. "*Okubyōmono*," he screamed.

Franz shuddered, recognizing the Japanese word for *coward*—the term Okada had repeatedly hurled at the poor private before the savage beating.

But Suzuki only bowed his head in calm resignation. Okada raised his cane above his head. Franz froze, resisting the urge to yell a warning to the captain.

"*Okubyōmono*," the major cried again as he swung the cane.

Suzuki didn't flinch as the handle whizzed through the air and struck the top of his scalp. He looked up momentarily in Franz's direction before his legs gave way and he crumpled to the ground.

CHAPTER 31

Hannah stepped out of her building to find Herschel Zunder sitting at the curb in the blazing midday sun. He looked up at her with an expression that was somewhere between hopeful and lost. "*Guten Tag*, Hannah," he said, rising to his feet.

She instinctively tucked the envelope she was carrying further into the waistband of her skirt as she approached. "Hi, Herschel. I didn't realize you were coming over today."

"I wasn't. I didn't mean to surprise you. It's just that Rabbi Hiltmann has called another meeting at the *shul*, and I was hoping..."

"For today?"

"Yes, in about an hour." He looked down at his feet. "I thought maybe we could go there together."

"Oh, Hersch, I would have liked to, yes. But I promised my stepmother I would run a few errands."

"I see." He continued to study the ground. "Will you be seeing Freddy again?"

Hannah hesitated. "Not straightaway, no," she said, appreciating how unconvincing her words must have sounded.

Herschel squared his shoulders and looked back up at her. "All right, then. I'd better not keep you any longer."

Hannah spotted the hurt behind his brave expression, and she felt her cheeks flushing. "Let's plan to go to the rabbi's next meeting together," she said in a cheerful tone that she knew came off as forced. "I would like that."

"Yes, all right," Herschel said as he turned to walk away. "Goodbye, Hannah."

"Herschel," she called after him.

"Yes?" he said without looking back at her.

"I'm sorry." Then she hurried to add, "That I couldn't go with you today."

He nodded without slowing his pace. Her heart sank watching him walk away, but as soon he rounded the corner, she headed in the opposite direction, toward the school.

Hannah was usually impervious to Shanghai's punishing summers—Ernst teased her that she must be part cold-blooded to thrive in such heat—but today the sweat was dripping off her brow by the time she neared her destination. The envelope tucked in her skirt reminded her of the sheer terror she had felt the previous year while waiting at the ghetto's entry checkpoint, her coat lined with illicit packages of cigarettes for Freddy. But with the fear came exhilaration. And this time, she was doing something important. And, of course, it gave her an excuse to see Freddy again.

Freddy was grinning from ear to ear when Hannah reached the clearing behind the school. She noticed that his pants were at least two inches too short for him, which confused her—usually he was the most fashionable boy in the ghetto. But she didn't want to embarrass him, so made no comment.

"Hiya, Banana," Freddy cried. "You ready to help win this war?"

"Sh, Freddy," she cautioned, but she couldn't keep the smile off her lips.

"There's no one ever here in the summer." He shrugged nonchalantly. "Guess we might have to find a new spot when school starts again in September, huh?"

"It won't matter then. They will only need our help for a week or two."

He chuckled confidently. "We'll see about that."

"This isn't a game, Freddy," she said, trying to inject a gravity that she didn't feel into the conversation.

"Doesn't mean we can't enjoy ourselves." He reached out and stroked her upper arm. "We're spies now, Banana!"

A warm tingle spread across her chest. "Not really."

"Yeah, this is real espionage stuff. Just like in the movies."

"But this isn't make-believe. We could get arrested or . . ."

Still, Hannah was sorry when he pulled his hand from her arm. "You got the list?" he asked.

She glanced furtively from side to side before extracting the envelope from her waist. Freddy snatched it out of her hand. "I better go set up the radio," he said.

She shook her head. "That's not the list they want you to transmit."

He tore open the envelope and read from the slip of paper. "What's this?"

"The address of the drop box."

"Drop box? I don't get it."

"They say it's too risky for me to carry the actual list." Hannah pointed to the piece of paper. "That's the location where you are to pick it up from each time. You'll find it buried under four white stones arranged in a row."

"Smart. A drop box. Yes." He grinned again and showed the page to Hannah. "I know this place."

She waved it away, having promised Sunny that she would never try to find out the location. "Don't tell me."

He shook the paper at her. "Come on, Banana, aren't you a little curious?"

After a brief hesitation, she took it from his hand. Written there was the address of a quiet alleyway, directly across from the school.

"So the list is waiting there?" he asked.

She nodded.

He stuck the paper into his mouth, chewing it into a wad that he eventually spat into the bushes beside him. "Can't be too careful, right?" he said with another smile. "Stay here. I'll go get it."

"I'm not supposed to be here when you transmit."

"Makes sense. Probably for the best." He jutted out his lower lip. "Too bad, though. Would have been nice to have you by my side for our first real mission."

"I can't, Freddy."

"It's okay," he said matter-of-factly. "I'm sure I can tell you about it later."

Hannah could feel her guilt mounting. She had already lied to Herschel and broken one promise to Sunny. The voice in her head told to turn and run, but she was desperately intrigued. And she was thrilled by the conspiratorial intimacy. "So long as no one comes around, I guess I could wait a few minutes."

"That's the spirit."

As soon as Freddy trotted off, Hannah began to have second thoughts. It was foolish to defy Sunny. She paced the clearing, her nerves frayed. Every sound startled her, even the rustle of the leaves in the wind. Her pulse thudded in her ears, and she half expected Ghoya and his men to appear at any second.

In a few minutes—which to Sunny felt more like a few hours—Freddy came racing around the side of the school, his face damp with sweat.

"Found it," he announced as he marched past her and disappeared into a clump of bushes. He emerged seconds later with a blanket tucked under one arm, his body tilted sideways under the weight of the black sack that he carried by a strap over the shoulder of his other arm. After he spread the blanket on the ground, he carefully set the sack on top of it and extracted the body of the radio transmitter. He uncoiled a loop of copper wire and ran it along the ground to a nearby tree.

"Where did your father get the transmitter?" Hannah asked in a whisper while Freddy continued to assemble it.

"One of our neighbours, Herr Silbermann, used to be a radio engineer in Munich. He brought with him two sets that he made over there." Freddy laughed. "Herr Silbermann loves his cigarettes. Besides, Pop paid him top dollar for this one. Everyone wins."

Sunny heard the whine of brakes out on the street. Her legs tensed and her back stiffened. "How much longer, Freddy?" she demanded.

"Relax, Banana. No one's looking for us." He stopped to admire his work before pulling a sheet of paper from his pocket and unfolding it. "I just have to tune into the right frequency."

Hannah anxiously watched as Freddy dropped to his knees and fiddled with the dials on the front of the machine. A red light glowed and the speaker began to spit static. Freddy lifted the microphone to his mouth and read from the page. "Alpha echo foxtrot. Alpha echo foxtrot."

Hannah held her breath, but the speaker only hissed static in response. Freddy adjusted more dials and repeated the greeting.

After a few seconds of dead air, a tinny voice replied, "Alpha echo foxtrot, go ahead, delta bravo victor."

With a glance at his wristwatch, Freddy raised the sheet in his hand. He began to read off a series of alpha-numeric code in a slow, calm voice, but Hannah noticed a tremble in his hand. Her heart pounded, and her eyes darted around, on the lookout for unexpected movement.

Finally, Freddy lowered the page and said, "Confirm, alpha echo foxtrot."

"Confirmed," the ghostly voice echoed.

Freddy switched off the dial. The static disappeared and the bulb's glow faded. He checked his watch again. "Under a minute," he announced, hopping to his feet.

"It's done? Already?"

He grabbed her by the shoulders and danced her around in a circle. "Under a minute, Hannah. Can you believe it?"

"Like real spies." She laughed, giddy with relief and elation.

Suddenly, Freddy held her still. Before Hannah even realized what was happening, his lips were on hers.

No, Freddy, this is wrong.

But she couldn't help herself from responding to the kiss. Her face heated as his tongue darted between her lips. Then she felt his hand gently squeezing her breast through her blouse. The prickly warmth spread all the way down to her toes.

CHAPTER 32

Is it fair to say the tables have turned?" Suzuki asked.

"Literally, Captain." Franz chuckled as he ran another suture through the gaping wound on Suzuki's scalp. The cane's blow fortunately hadn't fractured the captain's skull. It had been less than forty-eight hours since Franz had lain on the same operating table while Suzuki stitched his head closed. "However, I doubt salty fish will solve your problems."

"Unlikely."

Franz cut the suture and rethreaded the needle. "Thank you, Captain," he said.

Suzuki sighed. "I do not wish to have this conversation again, Dr. Adler."

But Franz persisted. "For speaking to the major about relocating the field hospital."

Suzuki craned his neck to look up at him. "What makes you think this had anything to do with that?"

"I am assuming, Captain."

Suzuki only grunted as he relaxed his head on the table.

"Is it safe to assume that we will not be moving camp?" Franz asked.

"It is."

"And if the enemy planes return?"

"Then they return, Dr. Adler."

"And then more lives will be lost."

Suzuki laughed grimly. "How does that possibly matter anymore?"

The captain was right. It had stopped mattering long ago. Franz ran another stitch through the scalp wound, the rhythm of the surgical procedure his only reprieve from the misery he felt.

"We are not all blind, Dr. Adler," Suzuki said.

"Excuse me, Captain?"

"Many Japanese, perhaps most of us, realize the war is already lost. And has been for a long time. Some people refuse to recognize or acknowledge this truth. Others . . ." Suzuki sighed. "To them, it doesn't matter."

"Martyrs?"

"They consider themselves traditionalists. Like the samurai of old, who found honour in death through hara-kiri preferable to surrender."

"People like Major Okada?"

He hesitated. "Yes."

"But not you, Captain?"

"As a doctor, such waste of life is contrary to my teaching."

"Mine too, Captain."

Franz ran a few more stitches in silence. Suzuki had refused anesthetic and, as Franz had expected, didn't show a flicker of discomfort.

"You asked me once about my attention to burn victims," Suzuki offered.

"Yes," Franz said, confused.

"I was not entirely truthful with you, Dr. Adler."

"How so?"

"Have you heard of Guadalcanal?"

"Yes." Franz had heard of the island on Voice of America broadcasts. "It's in the Solomon Islands, is it not?"

"I was stationed at Guadalcanal for three months before I learned that my son, Ichiro, was on the same island."

"He was in the army too?"

"Ichiro was a medical student at the University of California. An American citizen. His friends there used to call him 'Ike.' He was never supposed to enlist. But after I went off to war, Ichiro badgered my brother, who worked for the High Command in Tokyo. My brother found a way in for my son, as a medic."

Franz ran in another stitch, waiting for Suzuki to continue.

"His commanding officer told me Ichiro was an able medic. Very able. The squadron felt as though they had their own physician. Ichiro, he never did anything in half measure." Suzuki sighed. "By January of 1943, the Americans had secured much of the island, but the fighting had reached a stalemate. On January 15, Ichiro was in a bunker at the front, attending to the wounded. It was the same day the Marines introduced a new weapon to the war in the Pacific." He lapsed into silence.

"Which weapon?" Franz finally prompted.

"The flamethrower."

Franz wished he hadn't asked.

"They incinerated the bunker," Suzuki continued. "They told me Ichiro was on fire as he ran twenty yards across the beach to the jungle."

Franz pictured the skinny boy from the photo on Suzuki's desk.

"Ichiro . . . his flesh might have been destroyed, but not his spirit." Suzuki closed his eyes momentarily before continuing. "He was still alive when I reached the field hospital five days later. The doctor there—a wise country man from the south—told me he had never seen anyone fight death with such ferocity. Only the skin on Ichiro's feet had been spared. He looked as if he had been dipped by the heels into a vat of boiling oil. But his eyes, they were as bright as ever."

"He sounds incredibly brave."

Suzuki grunted. "Ichiro was determined to make it home. To say goodbye to his wife and his mother."

Franz thought of the two burn victims Suzuki had worked to keep alive in spite of their hopeless prognoses. Now it made sense. *He must have been trying to give them the same opportunity.*

Suzuki looked away. "I imagine Ichiro might have made it home had the Marines not overrun the field hospital."

Franz swallowed the lump in his throat. "I am so sorry for your loss, Captain."

Suzuki smiled wistfully. "Ichiro, he made me very proud."

* * *

Franz was alone in his tent. His three remaining tentmates were all still on duty. Despite his exhaustion, he couldn't get to sleep and just kept tossing and turning on the narrow mattress. After hearing Suzuki's story, he couldn't stop thinking of his own family. What could be worse than losing a child? He would rather run across a beach engulfed in flames himself than have anything terrible befall Hannah.

A soft rap at the tent's flap pulled him from the troubled thoughts. He rose to his feet to find Helen at the entrance. "People are saying that Major Okada attacked the captain," she said in lieu of a greeting.

"Yes. Twenty stitches to his scalp, but he is all right now," Franz said. "Come inside, please."

Helen hesitated before following him. "Why did the major attack him?"

"The captain didn't say." Franz misled her with the truth, unable to admit to Helen that Okada had no intention of moving the camp out of harm's way. She eyed him suspiciously. Franz patted the cot beside him. "Please, have a seat."

Helen smoothed the blanket at the end of the bed and sat down. She crossed her legs and brushed nervously at something Franz couldn't see on the hem of her skirt.

He folded his arms self-consciously. "I wish I had tea to offer you."

"No matter. I'm sick of green tea. I miss my orange pekoe." She smiled as she patted the mattress beside her. "You shouldn't be standing after the episode earlier."

"I'm feeling better, Helen." Franz sat down at the far end of the cot. "How are you?"

"I keep scouring the horizon for airplanes." She offered a tired smile. "It's no longer relaxing to go outside for a smoke."

"Please, go ahead."

Her cheeks reddened. "I don't smoke inside. Michael disapproved of it, and now it's ingrained in me."

Franz tried to look anywhere but into her jade-green eyes. "I am not an advocate of smoking either. But, if I may say so, your husband strikes me as a fool."

Her face flushed deeper. "You're sweet. And terribly kind."

Her lips appeared so inviting. The distance between them seemed like nothing. Franz resisted the urge to move closer.

"I am not going to make it home, Franz." Helen's voice quivered.

"Don't say that."

Her eyes misted. "I've never been more certain of anything."

He laid his hand on top of hers and squeezed it. "You've been traumatized, Helen. You can't know that. None of us can."

She stared down at their hands. "I can't help the way I feel about you." She sniffled softly and then eased her hand away from his. "But none of it makes this right, Franz."

Franz hung his head and looked at his open hand as if it had betrayed him. "Of course not."

They sat together in charged silence for several seconds until a commotion from outside broke the moment. The tent flap burst open and a soldier ducked into the tent. His eyes darted around, and then he called out in Japanese. The flap rustled again and Major Okada stepped inside, dragging his damaged leg behind him. He slowly took in the surroundings before his frigid eyes found Franz's. Helen immediately bowed her head but, shocked by the intrusion, Franz met his stare.

Okada spoke in his usual soft voice, but the soldier with him translated his words into English with the tone of a police interrogator. "Is it common for you to entertain women in your tent?" he demanded.

Franz glanced over to Helen, whose chin was still touching her chest. "This is the first time Miss Thompson has ever been here."

The soldier translated for Okada, who squinted skeptically. He murmured another question. The soldier promptly translated. "The major wishes to know where you two were during the raid yesterday."

Helen said nothing, so Franz responded for them. "We were outside the surgical tent. We had to dodge for cover. The bullets flew right past our heads."

The soldier conveyed Franz's answer to the major. "Who else saw you?" Okada asked through the translator.

"I have no idea." Franz picked up on the menace behind Okada's blank stare. "We were lucky to survive."

The major scowled, unconvinced, and turned angrily on Helen. "You are American," he accused through the translator.

"No, Miss Thompson is Canadian." Franz tapped his own chest. "And I am Austrian."

Okada's lip curled and he sneered silently at Franz. Finally, he said a few words. "You are all worthless and untrustworthy. No better than the Chinese," the translator snarled.

"We have been working day and night to mend the Imperial Army's injured," Franz said, desperate to appease Okada.

Okada lifted his cane, tapping the shaft against his palm. "The airplanes never attacked us before you came here," the translator accused.

"We almost died too, Major," Franz said.

Okada slapped his cane loudly, then stopped suddenly. "So you say."

"We were brought here to help with the wounded, Major Okada," Franz pleaded. "We are healers. That is all we know."

Okada slowly levelled his cane at Franz like a sword. Franz's breath caught. He involuntarily leaned back, resisting the urge to protect his head with his hands. Okada drew circles in the air in front of Franz's face, continuing to speak in a low voice. Before the soldier could translate, Helen jumped up and stepped between them. Okada jabbed his cane into the centre of her chest, but she didn't back down. She addressed him in Japanese in a strong clear voice.

Okada's look of surprise gave way to another vicious scowl. He raised his cane above his head, poised to strike.

"No, don't," Franz said as he began to push himself to his feet.

But Helen waved him off. She met Okada's threatening glare and spoke to him again in a calm voice.

The cane hovered over her for several tense seconds. Finally, the major lowered its tip to the ground and spun away, hobbling out of the tent without saying another word.

"What did you say to him, Helen?" Franz demanded as soon as he was gone.

"The truth."

"Which is?"

"That you and I did nothing wrong." She smiled, but her eyes clouded with a defeated hopelessness that Franz had never before seen in her. "And that only a coward strikes the helpless."

CHAPTER 33

Even the shade from the trees lining the pathway in the Public Garden offered no reprieve from the heat and humidity. Sunny could feel her damp cotton dress clinging to her, but she was too focused on the harbour to pay much attention.

That's 15R2, she thought as she studied the blackened hull of the battered cruiser, which listed heavily to the portside. Another cruiser—she had designated it 22R4—was still upright, but smoke wafted off its badly damaged stern. She presumed that the gunboat 19B2, now nowhere to be seen, must have already sunk to the bottom of the Whangpoo.

Sunny had woken at dawn to the distant rumbling of explosions. She heard the whine of Japanese Zeroes overhead as they raced to confront the enemy planes. She knew that it must be the Americans bombing the harbour, but whether the raid was successful—that she didn't know until she and Ernst reached the Public Garden, Jakob and Joey in tow.

As Sunny stared out at the carnage—the result of her reconnaissance—she didn't feel elated or even as excited as she had expected to. Instead, her emotions were unsettled and darker. Their intensity troubled her.

"Boats! Boats!" Jakob cried from where he sat perched on Ernst's shoulders.

"Well, yes, they certainly used to be," Ernst said with a chuckle. He looked over to Sunny. "Apparently, someone does listen to the radio."

Sunny pointed to 4R5, her code for the *Idzumo*, the prize of the Shanghai fleet. It stood unmolested exactly where she had reported it to be moored. "They didn't sink her."

"There's always the next time."

"Maybe. Maybe not. The Japanese might sail it somewhere safer."

Ernst glanced to either side, then said in a quiet voice, "You do realize the Japanese will be watching very closely from now on."

"The American pilots must be aware of that."

"I meant you, Sunny. They will be—" Before Ernst could elaborate, Jakob bounced up and down on his shoulders as though riding a hobbyhorse. "Enough of that, Jakob. Despite this noble mane, I'm no Lipizzaner stallion. Time to play on the ground." He plucked the boy off his shoulders and lowered him to the pathway. "No swimming in the river, though. Tempting as it may seem in this ungodly heat, that filthy water would kill you quicker than one of Sunny's guided torpedoes." The boy picked up a stick and dug at the dirt with it. Ernst turned back to Sunny. "The Japanese aren't fools. They will be watching the port for spies."

Sunny gently rocked the pram even though Joey was already asleep. "Anyone who works near the harbour could be a spy. You really think they would be looking at a mother and her children?"

"Not specifically, no. But I suspect they will scrutinize anybody and everybody."

"We'll be all right," Sunny said with more confidence than she felt.

Ernst dug a cigarette from his pocket and lit it. "Just be careful. After all, it will take some doing to replace you." He winked. "Where in that miserable ghetto am I supposed to find another gorgeous, half-breed femme fatale?"

Sunny chuckled. "And you, Ernst?"

"What about me?"

"You live among Nazis. If they were to ever learn who you are . . ."

He blew out a stream of smoke. "*Ach*, they're far too blinded by their own self-importance to ever concern themselves with who *I* am."

"And Gerhard?"

Ernst pulled the cigarette from his lips and eyed her suspiciously. "What about him?"

"I understand you are spending a great deal of time with him."

"So what? He's interested in my art. Besides, I have nothing but time on my hands."

"I'm not saying—"

"Do you have any idea what it's like to be cooped up night and day with Simon? It's almost enough to send anyone head-first out the window."

Sunny touched his arm. "Is it safe to spend so much time with the boy?"

"Gerhard is not a boy," Ernst said defensively, pulling away from her touch. "He's twenty years old."

"But is he not one of them?"

Ernst shook his head. "May I remind you that, if not for Gerhard, your precious hospital and the synagogue would be nothing but a pile of rubble? How many Jews did he save last Christmas by tipping us off to von Puttkamer's plot?"

"It's not Gerhard. I worry about you." She mustered a grin. "After all, do you have any idea how hard it would be for me to find another artistic genius with your flair for melodramatics?"

He pursed his lips, fighting back a smile. "Impossible, I grant you."

"You are being discreet though, right?"

He rolled his eyes. "Discretion comes second nature to people like me, Sunny."

"Good."

Jakob dropped the branch he had been playing with and tugged at Ernst's pant leg. "Up! Up!"

"Of course, your highness." Ernst bent over and lifted Jakob back onto his shoulders. He turned to Sunny, his expression downcast. "It's been over a year since I saw Shan."

"I know."

"I will probably never see him again. It doesn't make it right, of course, but I would understand if he were to . . ."

Sunny stroked Ernst's arm again, and this time he didn't pull away. "I have no doubt."

Ernst hopped up and down, bouncing Jakob on his shoulders. The boy giggled uproariously. Ernst glanced to Sunny. "I didn't mean what I said about Simon. He's a good man. A rash fool, but a good man still."

"I know."

"He's in a bad way right now," Ernst muttered.

"What is wrong?"

Ernst looked uncharacteristically sheepish. "I promised I wouldn't say anything."

"About what?"

"I shouldn't . . ."

"Tell me, Ernst. Please. For Essie."

He hesitated. "Simon, he couldn't go through with it."

"Through with what?" It suddenly hit Sunny, and she squeezed Ernst's arm hard enough to make him flinch. "Not von Puttkamer?"

* * *

Sunny hadn't intended to accompany Ernst home, but she felt compelled to see Simon. Even with a scarf tied around her head and walking elbow in elbow with Ernst, she felt horribly exposed on the streets of Germantown. But they made it to Ernst's flat without incident, save for Joey waking up inconsolably cranky from his nap.

Ernst hadn't exaggerated. She had never seen Simon looking worse. His cheeks and chin were covered in patchy stubble, and his eyes were more sunken than ever. Even the presence of Jakob didn't elicit his usual optimism. Simon sat on the couch clinging to his son until Jakob eventually wriggled free of the embrace and refused to climb back onto his father's lap.

Joey fussed from heat and hunger, calming only after Sunny offered him a bottle of sugary water. She sat down beside Simon, holding the bottle while rocking Joey on her knee. Ernst stood at the window with his back to the room.

"What happened, Simon?" Sunny asked.

Simon's eyes were fixed on his son, who was playing on the floor with pieces of a wood easel. "I froze."

"Tell me, Simon," Sunny encouraged.

"I ran right into the son of a bitch," Simon said. "And he was alone too."

"Just von Puttkamer? No bodyguard?"

"Just the two of us. No entourage. Hardly anyone on the street."

"And?"

"He walked right past me. Even gave me one of those sharp nods only the aristocratic Krauts can pull off. So close I could smell the bastard's aftershave. I could feel the knife handle under my jacket. It would have been so easy."

"But you promised Essie."

He shrugged. "I wasn't out looking for him. I just ran into him. Alone. Maybe a once-in-a-lifetime break."

"What did you do?"

"I stood there," he grunted. "Stiff as a statue."

"Who wouldn't?" Sunny said.

"Then the damnedest thing happened." Simon's shoulders sagged further. "Von Puttkamer stopped, Sunny. Not three yards in front of me. Lighting a cigarette. There couldn't have been a better time. His back to me, his hands busy with the cig, no one there to protect him . . . And what did I do?"

"You came to your senses, apparently."

"I just stood there trembling like a child."

"You are not an assassin," Sunny insisted. "There's no shame in that."

"The man who plotted to kill my family? Probably is still planning to."

"You're not an assassin," she repeated.

But Simon wasn't listening. "If I were just a little stronger, a little braver, I could've done everyone in the ghetto such a favour."

Sunny had heard enough. "Stop it, Simon!"

Simon stared in surprise. Even Ernst did a double take.

"Enough of this self-pity," Sunny snapped. "You had no business going out in the first place. You were risking Ernst's life. After all he's done for you." She threw her hands up in the air. "And as for the people in the ghetto?"

Simon stiffened. "What about them?"

"Tell me what would have happened if the Nazis had caught you before or after your attempt on von Puttkamer? Would that make your wife and child somehow safer?"

"Probably not," Simon conceded.

Sunny shook her head in disbelief. "Even if they hadn't caught you, for them to even suspect that a Jew had come into their neighbourhood to kill one of their own . . . You think that would persuade the rest of the Nazis to leave the ghetto be?"

Simon hung his head in defeat.

"So you've proven you're not a cold-blooded killer. So what? The world is overrun with those." Her tone softened. "The best way—the only way—you can help your wife and son right now is to stay inside and keep your head down until you can all be together again."

CHAPTER 34

The ground still shook every so often from explosions and heavy artillery fire. Occasionally, the wind changed directions, bringing the sulphurous stench of gun smoke into the camp. But there was no other indication that the fighting had moved any closer to the field hospital in the week since the air raid.

Inside the operating room, new faces had replaced those of the staff members who had been killed. All evidence of the attack—the collapsed tents and wrecked trucks—was gone, either removed or repaired. But the relatively calm week had been no more comforting to Franz than a lull in an electrical storm. He sensed that the others were on edge too, but Helen had told him that no one else in the camp would dare discuss it for fear of inciting Major Okada's wrath.

Franz now stood across from Captain Suzuki, assisting him on the last scheduled surgery of the day. It had been the lightest day at the camp that Franz could remember. It was only four o'clock, and they would have already finished had the case not been so technically challenging. The heavyset Japanese officer on the operating table had four separate bullet wounds in his belly. Miraculously, he had not sustained any significant injury to his vital organs or major blood vessels, but extracting the bullets from the layers of fat and bowel was proving to be a tedious exercise.

Suzuki carefully removed the long forceps from the gaping wound that ran the extent of the patient's abdomen. The metallic teeth emerged clasping the fourth bullet, its nose crumpled from the impact against the man's spinal bones. Suzuki dropped the slug into a metal pail and exhaled with satisfaction as it clanked noisily against the bottom. "I have done the taxing work," Suzuki said. "You may now close the wound, Dr. Adler."

"Yes, Captain," Franz said.

Suzuki raised an eyebrow. "And the spells, Dr. Adler? Have they improved?"

"Yes, sir," Franz said, being mindful not to thank him again. "Your diagnosis was most accurate. The dizziness has gone away since I began to regularly eat that kus . . . kus . . ."

"Ku-sa-ya." Suzuki accentuated each syllable. "There are those who consider it a delicacy."

"I am not among them." Franz realized he had probably not eaten something as nutritious in years, but at times he still struggled to choke down the salty fish.

Suzuki stepped back from the table and pulled off his gloves. "As long as it keeps you off the floor."

Franz decided to capitalize on the rare instance of casual conversation. "Captain, how long would a field hospital such as ours stay in the same spot?"

"It depends."

"On what?"

Suzuki grimaced, as though the answer were obvious. "On the progress of the campaign—Ichi-Go—of course."

"Have you heard any word?"

Suzuki rubbed his chin. "We were told that that the Imperial Army had breached the defensive perimeter outside Hengyang. And that the Chinese were in full retreat."

Franz would have never before imagined that word of a Japanese victory could improve his spirits. "Surely that is good news, Captain. Someone told me that Hengyang was the strategic key to Ichi-Go."

"I would interpret the reports of our victories with caution, Dr. Adler. In Guadalcanal, the radio announcer was boasting of how we had bravely repelled the American forces at the same time as we were abandoning the island." Suzuki sighed. "Even if the reports are accurate, there will soon be a new strategy."

"What would that mean for us?"

"In all likelihood, they would move the field hospital forward to support the new front line."

"Move us forward?" Franz couldn't hide his disappointment.

Suzuki's eyelids crinkled, his expression verging on sympathetic. "Dr. Adler, if you are wondering whether they will send you home, I can save you the trouble. The answer is no."

The words hit Franz harder than a blow from Okada's cane. Franz had begun to hope that if he survived long enough to see the campaign at Hengyang end, the Japanese might let him return to Shanghai. He was desperate to see Sunny again, to make things right with her over the baby and everything else, including his conflicted feelings for Helen. He lay in bed at night fantasizing about a reunion with his family, picturing the delight and surprise on Sunny's and Hannah's faces as he burst through the door.

Anxious for a distraction, Franz raised the suturing needle. Just as he was preparing it with fresh thread, he picked up on a muffled sound from outside. The room quieted. Even the anesthetist lifted the ether mask from the patient's face and glanced upward.

The rumbling intensified. Franz's veins turned to ice. He dropped the needle on the table and turned to Suzuki. "Where is Helen?"

"I believe she went to change dressings," Suzuki said.

"In the recovery tent?"

Suzuki nodded solemnly.

Franz wheeled and raced for the doorway still wearing his mask, gloves and gown.

Outside, soldiers were scattering along the pathway in both directions. Franz heard the sound of trucks being hurriedly started. He looked up and spotted planes overhead, six of them in tight formation, descending relentlessly on the camp.

"Franz! Franz!" Helen called to him over the roar of the aircraft.

His eyes darted over to where she stood in front of the recovery tent, about thirty feet away. He ripped off his surgical mask. "Stay where you are, Helen," he shouted.

"What?" Helen began to move toward him.

"Cover," he screamed as he pantomimed, covering his head with his arms. "Take cover!"

The planes swooped down like huge, hungry hawks. Franz pointed wildly at the tent's overhang beside her. After an agonizing moment for Franz, Helen dove beneath it.

Just as the planes' wings began to spit fire, Franz lunged to his right and rolled up against the side of the operating tent. Bullets whizzed past him, several thudding into the tent's canvas just above him. Dirt danced up off the pathway. Three soldiers fell to the ground before they could even raise their rifles. Glass shattered.

Franz heard the whoosh of another tent collapsing. He pressed himself as tightly as he could against the tent.

The planes thundered directly overhead, casting ominous shadows over the camp. Franz lifted his head and looked over to Helen. Her head popped out from behind the edge of the tent.

"Stay down," he cried. "They're coming back!"

Helen hesitated before jerking her head back down. Franz glanced over his shoulder to see the planes banking steeply back toward the camp. He braced himself for another terrifying pass. The staccato thumping of gunfire exploded all around him, and the dirt path came to life from the hail of bullets.

As soon as the shadows had passed over again, Franz poked his head up in search of Helen, but he couldn't see her. He held his breath, his eyes scanning frantically until he spotted her in her hiding place. Relief gave way to fear as he saw her shoulders rising and realized that she was climbing to her feet.

"No, Helen!" He motioned urgently to the ground. "Stay down! They're coming back!"

But Helen stood up. Above her, he could see the planes bank in another tight circle and turn back yet again toward the camp. Dread mushroomed inside his chest. "*Down, Helen!*" he screamed. "Get down!"

But instead, she took off running down the pathway toward him. "Franz," she cried.

The planes were upon her in seconds, their wings sparking with gunfire. Franz watched in horror as the sprays of dirt chased her down the trail.

Helen made it to within ten feet of him when she was struck. Her head jerked back before she keeled forward to the ground, unable to even break her fall with her hands.

As the shadow of the last plane flashed overhead, Franz leapt to his feet and raced out to her. He grabbed her wrists and dragged her frantically toward the cover of the operating tent. She was no more responsive than a sack of salt.

As soon as he pulled her beneath the overhang, he rolled her onto her back. Blood had turned her hair a dark shade of red. Her wide green eyes stared past him at the empty sky. He placed two fingers on her neck in search of a pulse, but even before his hand met her cool skin, he knew he would find none.

As the planes swooped overhead again, he held her ruined head in his hands and rocked her back and forth, indifferent to the gunfire around him.

"I'm sorry, Helen. I'm so sorry," Franz said as he stared into her lifeless eyes. "You, of all people, deserved to go home."

CHAPTER 35

Joey sat on Hannah's lap, captivated by the old wooden rattle in his hand. Only a few flecks of paint remained on its smooth, worn surface. Sunny sat across from them, sewing up a tear in a cloth diaper.

Hannah's gaze drifted up to a framed black-and-white photograph on the wall above her stepmother's head. It depicted the *longtang* a few blocks away. The building still housed several families, including a classmate and her relatives, despite its roof having partially collapsed years before during a Japanese bombing. "Remember how Papa used to love to photograph those old buildings?"

Sunny glanced over her shoulder at the photograph. "It's true. The grander buildings, like the ones on the Bund, never interested him much. Only the decrepit ones. He always said they had the most character."

Hannah nodded. "I think Papa found beauty in things that were often overlooked."

Sunny dropped the diaper into her lap and brought a hand to her eyes. She sniffled a few times and then began to quietly sob.

Hannah knew her stepmother missed Franz as much as she

did, but she couldn't remember ever having seen Sunny cry before. "Did I say something?"

Still covering her eyes, Sunny shook her head. "Did you notice that we are talking about your father in the past tense?"

"I didn't mean it like that, Sunny. It's just that he hasn't been able to use his camera in so long."

"He couldn't find any film for it, not even on the black market," she choked out. "His only hobby." Sunny wiped her eyes with the back of her wrist. "I'm sorry, Hannah. I don't know what has got into me."

"Sometimes, I burst into tears just thinking about him," said Hannah.

Joey jerked the rattle up to his face. Hannah giggled at her baby brother's adorable clumsiness and hugged him tighter. These days, despite her father's absence, laughter came more easily to Hannah. There had been two further clandestine visits alone with Freddy behind the school. The last time, the kissing had continued for ages and only stopped when his hand had slid up between her thighs. She had jumped back from the bold touch, more out of surprise than outrage. Hannah doubted she would pull away as quickly the next time, not after the thrilling warmth she had felt at his fleeting touch. But she was conflicted over more than just the daring caresses or their vexed history. There was also Herschel to consider. She still didn't know how she was going to break it off with the sweet boy. Meanwhile, she had kept inventing excuses to avoid him.

"Sunny, did you have many boyfriends before Papa?" Hannah asked.

Sunny looked over to her, eyes dry but still reddened. "Not too many, no."

"Oh." Hannah rested her chin lightly against the top of Joey's head.

"Why do you ask? Is everything all right with you and Herschel?"

"It's . . . fine."

Sunny frowned. "That doesn't sound fine."

"What if . . . what if I'm not sure about us?"

"You are only fourteen," Sunny said. "You shouldn't be sure about anything."

"But what if I don't . . ." Hannah sighed. "Feel the same way about him?"

"You're no longer smitten?"

"No." Hannah swallowed. "I don't think so, but how can I be sure?"

"You just know. With your father, sometimes I get butterflies at just the sound of his voice." Sunny cleared her throat. "The kindest thing you can do for Herschel is to be honest with him. If he's not the one, you need to tell him so."

Hannah didn't say anything as she began to gently bounce Joey. She knew her stepmother was right, but the thought of that conversation filled her with dread. She wished there were a way out that didn't involve hurting Herschel.

Sunny squinted at her. "This doesn't have to do with Freddy, does it?"

Hannah hesitated. She knew it was already too late when she said, "Not really, no."

"Oh, Hannah," Sunny groaned. "Not after what that boy put you and your father through last year."

"He's changed, Sunny."

Sunny shook her head vigorously. "Believe me, Freddy is not to be trusted."

Hannah straightened. "Look how much he is doing to help us. He is risking so much for us."

"He's very brave, I agree." Sunny nodded. "But do not ever mistake courage for kindness or decency."

"You don't know him the way I do," Hannah said.

"Believe me, in some ways, I know him better than you do." Sunny viewed her solemnly. "And your father? What would he have to say?"

"I probably will never find out, will I?" Hannah blurted, regretting the words even before she saw the hurt flash across Sunny's face.

* * *

Hannah was still racked with guilt as she entered the clearing behind the school. Today, even Freddy's hungry kisses couldn't distract her from her troubles. "What's the matter, Banana?" he asked, pulling back from her lips and holding her by the shoulders.

"I don't think I should be here."

"Sure you should." He winked. "We're partners in crime."

His words only heightened her unease. Oblivious to her angst, Freddy glanced at his watch and said, "It's almost time." He knelt down beside the transmitter, which was already set up on the blanket, its copper antenna snaking over to a nearby tree.

Hannah noticed that Freddy was again wearing clothes that were too small for him, the hems of his pants not even clearing his ankles. This time, she couldn't hold back her curiosity. "Freddy, have you grown recently?"

He frowned in confusion and then, understanding, broke into laughter. "Nah, I'm just trying to look a little younger."

"Why would you want to look younger?" But the answer came to her with a sudden chill. "It's in case they catch you, isn't it?"

"Never hurts to be careful." His reckless grin didn't match his words.

Suddenly, the gravity of everything—the potential consequences of their espionage, her duplicity with Herschel and her father's absence—enveloped her like a cloud of smoke. "I'd better go, Freddy."

Distracted, Freddy turned a knob, causing the transmitter's light to glow red again. The speaker popped and crackled. "It's time." He reached inside his shirt and unfolded the coded page. He lifted the microphone. "Alpha echo foxtrot. Alpha echo foxtrot."

After several seconds—which, to Hannah, felt much longer than the previous time they had transmitted—a reedy voice replied, "Alpha echo foxtrot, go ahead, delta bravo victor."

In his usual steady voice, Freddy read off the list of digits and characters. He lowered the page and said, "Confirm, alpha echo foxtrot."

The speaker hissed, but no words came through.

"Confirm, alpha echo foxtrot," Freddy repeated.

Nothing.

Just as Freddy was reaching to switch off the dial, they heard the voice again. "Not confirmed, delta bravo—" The reception cut in and out. "Repeat. Please repeat."

Alarmed, Hannah looked at him. "It will take too long, Freddy."

He raised the page and listed off the codes again, his tone still even but his cadence quicker. "Confirm, alpha echo foxtrot."

The speaker hissed furiously before the voice returned, "Not con—" The words cut in and out. "Not confirmed, delta bravo victor. Repeat."

Hannah couldn't control the shuffle in her feet as she waved frantically at Freddy. "Off! Turn it off!"

He glanced at her, his expression unusually anxious. "One last time. I swear." He held the microphone to his mouth and spat out the list, his voice no longer composed.

Finished, he switched off the radio. "Confirmed, delta bravo victor," the other voice said just as the red light dimmed and the speaker went dead.

Hannah brought a hand to her mouth. "That was too long, surely."

Freddy jumped to his feet and frantically gathered up the copper wire. "Get out of here, Hannah!"

She hesitated. "I can wait for—"

"Go," he cried.

She turned and rushed for the street.

Before she reached the side of the building, Freddy shouted, "Stop, Hannah!"

She too had heard the roar of an engine, followed by the heavy squeal of brakes. She froze, then spun back to face Freddy. His eyes were as wide as saucers. The copper coil fell from his hand. He chopped his hand wildly toward the foliage behind the school. "The bushes!"

Hannah dashed across the clearing and threw herself into the shrubs. Branches scraped at her face and exposed arms. She kept struggling forward, pushing herself as far into the bushes as she could. She dropped to the ground, squeezing herself between branches and trying to keep her breath quiet.

Hannah heard guttural shouts in Japanese. She looked all around for a sign of Freddy, but all she could see were tree roots. The yelling grew louder. She tried to ward off the encroaching panic, but it was no use. *The bushes are the first place they will look for us.*

Then she heard Freddy's voice, loud and clear. "I was only fooling around. I have this buddy in Frenchtown. He and I play on—"

He was cut off midsentence by the sound of his own high-pitched moan.

CHAPTER 36

Franz's gaze kept drifting down to the red stain on his gown. The blood wasn't Helen's, but it still reminded him of her death. *Why did you run, Helen?* he thought for the umpteenth time.

Franz couldn't focus on anything beyond the memory of holding her limp body in his arms. Distracted, he reached out with his scissors and began to chew through the base of his patient's spleen.

"Not yet, Dr. Adler," Suzuki cried as his hand clamped down on Franz's arm.

But it was too late. He had cut through the splenic artery and it was spurting blood like a ruptured hose. Suzuki plunged his hand into the open wound and grabbed for a pair of clamps with the other. Blood pooled up his wrists as he attempted to stop the hemorrhaging.

Franz stood and stared, dumbfounded by his glaring error. He had just cut through a major artery before it was tied off. Even a medical student would have known better.

Finally, the blood stopped dripping out of the wound. "Sponge, please, Dr. Adler," Suzuki said with a look that was a mix of relief and incredulity.

Franz started to help mop up the excess blood.

Suzuki glanced at the anesthetist, who placed two fingers on the patient's neck and then said something in Japanese. Franz inferred from his tone and his nod that the patient was still alive.

"I'm sorry, Captain," Franz said. Usually, he would have been mortified by such a mistake, which was as bad as any he had ever committed inside the operating room, but he was too devastated by Helen's death to consider much else.

"You are distracted," Suzuki said as he ran more sutures deep inside the wound. "It is understandable."

They finished the surgery in silence. After the patient had been removed from the table, Franz automatically headed to the sink to scrub for the next. He had no idea how many more casualties from the air raid would pass through the operating room, but it didn't matter. It would be another sleepless night, whether or not he worked through it.

"I need your assistance, Dr. Adler," Suzuki said from behind him.

"I will be scrubbed soon."

"Not here," Suzuki said.

Franz dropped his damp hands to his sides and turned to face Suzuki.

"Come with me," the captain said.

Outside, the skies were clear but the bitter odour of gun smoke still hung in the air. As Franz followed Suzuki down the pathway, he couldn't help but glance down at the place where Helen had fallen. Two narrow boot skids marked the spot, but soon even those would be erased and there would be nothing left to commemorate her passing.

Suzuki led Franz toward the convalescence tent, which overflowed outside with recovering men, many covered in thick bandaging. Three more trucks had been destroyed by enemy planes, but one troop transport stood with its engine idling and a ramp leading into the back of it. A young lieutenant met them outside the tent with a sharp salute for Suzuki. The two officers spoke for a short while. The tent's flap rustled and Major Okada hobbled out, leaning heavily on his cane but moving with fierce determination.

Franz bowed his head deeply as Okada joined them. The major ignored Franz altogether, but his eyes shot daggers at Suzuki. When he finally spoke, his voice was as soft as ever. Suzuki hardly said a word in response. Finally, Okada raised his cane and shook it skyward before swinging it out toward Franz. Rather than fear, Franz felt only a storm of anger and hatred. *You are just another bully in a world drowning in them.* He even considered snatching the weapon out of Okada's hand, despite the consequences, but he just squared his shoulders and said, "You should have moved the camp, Major. This is your fault. Her death is on your head."

The major's eyes darted to Suzuki for a translation. The captain lowered his chin to his chest and mumbled a few sentences.

Okada turned back to Franz with a malicious scowl. The butt of the cane came to a stop right between Franz's eyes. After several seconds, Okada let it fall to the ground. He wheeled and limped away without another word.

Franz looked over to Suzuki. "What did you tell him?"

"Enough."

"You didn't translate what I said, did you?"

Suzuki rubbed his temples. "I cannot cope with one more casualty tonight. Besides, I still need your help." He ducked through the tent's flap opening.

Inside, every bed was full, and several men lay on the ground. Although Franz had grown to expect it, he was still struck by the stoicism of the wounded Japanese. Not one uttered so much as a groan, despite their grave injuries.

Suzuki motioned toward a soldier who lay on a wooden stretcher, covered by a blanket up to his chest. The youth looked to be barely in his teens, but his colour was better than most of the others, and Franz saw no obvious wounds or dressings. "Help me lift him," Suzuki instructed as he raised one end of the stretcher.

Franz took the other end and lifted it easily, the soldier was so light. They manoeuvered through the maze of bodies on the ground. At one point, Franz stumbled and the stretcher wobbled from side to side. The boy raised his arms to try to stabilize himself, and Franz saw that his legs remained motionless.

"A spinal injury?" Franz asked as soon as they were outside.

Suzuki nodded. "A shattered thoracic vertebra. He is paralyzed from the base of his chest down."

"What can we do for him here?" Franz asked.

"Nothing, which is why we are sending him home." Suzuki pushed Franz and the stretcher in the direction of the waiting truck.

Franz walked backwards up the ramp. Inside the truck were other stretchers, loaded onto the built-in benches. A soldier took the stretcher from Franz and steered the patient into an open slot. Franz followed Suzuki back to the convalescence tent. He wasn't surprised when the captain headed directly for a burn victim in the far corner. Together they carried this man out to the truck too. The soldier had to make room to squeeze the stretcher in between the others.

"Surely the truck is full, Captain," Franz said.

"There is room for one more," Suzuki said.

Franz started back toward the tent, but Suzuki caught his arm as he passed. "No. No more casualties, Dr. Adler."

"Who, then?"

Suzuki released his arm. "You."

"Me?" Franz was stunned. "I do not follow."

Suzuki squinted. "These men are ill. They require an escort."

Franz fought off a glimmer of hope. "An escort to where?"

"The truck will transport you to Changsha. From there, you will be flown to Shanghai."

"Shanghai?" Franz almost choked on the word.

Suzuki shrugged. "It's the only place with hospitals equipped to care for these men."

Franz was almost afraid to ask. "And afterward? Will I be sent back here?"

"I do not want to ever see you here again." Suzuki showed him a tired smile. "You very nearly killed my previous patient. That kind of assistance, I can do without."

Franz felt the ground swaying beneath him, but he knew that his low blood pressure wasn't to blame. "You are letting me go home, Captain?"

Suzuki shook his head. "I am dispatching you as a medical escort. What happens to you once you get back to Shanghai is none of my concern."

Franz's chest felt as though it might burst as he turned away. "I will go get my bag."

Suzuki grabbed him by the wrist. "The truck is ready. You will go now."

"It will take me but a minute."

"You will go now," Suzuki repeated as he squeezed Franz's wrist tightly.

Franz suddenly understood. "You haven't told Major Okada, have you?"

Suzuki let go of Franz. "I am a captain in the Imperial Army. I am capable of issuing my own orders."

"You will be in trouble with him, Captain."

"Either you get in that truck immediately, or I will dispatch you in the next one heading out to the front line. This much I know, Dr. Adler. You are not welcome at this camp for a moment longer."

Franz bowed deeply. "Thank you, Captain."

This time, Suzuki didn't admonish him for his gratitude. Instead, he said, "My one regret is not having sent Mrs. Thompson away when I had the opportunity. It was most selfish of me."

"Helen respected you, sir."

Suzuki only grunted. At a loss for words, Franz held out his hand to shake Suzuki's. But the captain turned away with just a curt nod. He called out to the nearby lieutenant, uttering a series of orders.

Franz climbed into the back of the truck. The soldier managing the stretchers eyed Franz as if he were a feral cat seeking refuge in a hold, but he said nothing. The door slammed shut behind them. Franz squeezed himself onto the hard seat between two stretchers. Emotions raged inside him. As heartbroken as he was over Helen's death, he couldn't believe that he might be going home to Sunny and Hannah.

The truck's engine continued to idle. Franz looked out the window as the driver and the lieutenant stood talking. He wanted to scream at the driver to just climb into the truck and get moving, to get him away from this place.

Just then, Major Okada reappeared at the end of the road. Franz's heart leapt into his throat as Okada made directly for the truck. Franz leaned back, trying to make himself invisible. "Not now," he mumbled under his breath in German. "Not when I'm so close."

Suzuki stepped into the road in front of Okada. He snapped his fingers at the driver and barked at him in Japanese. The man spun and headed for the truck. Franz held his breath. Suzuki met Okada and his entourage, blocking their path. Okada lifted his cane and shook it at the truck, but Suzuki stood his ground.

The truck clunked into gear and jerked forward. Franz covered his face and muttered a prayer for the truck to keep moving. Eventually, the camp disappeared from sight behind them.

CHAPTER 37

The front door whooshed open, startling Sunny. She glanced down at Joey, asleep in her arms, before she looked over to the doorway. She had expected to see Esther and Jakob but instead found Hannah standing there. "Hannah, you scared me half to death. And Joey is still—"

The frantic look on her stepdaughter's face stopped Sunny midsentence. Hannah rushed over to her. "It's Freddy," she cried.

"Oh, Hannah, what happened?" Sunny's worry soared as she spotted the leaves tangled in Hannah's dishevelled hair. "What has that boy done to you?"

"Nothing," Hannah cried as she knelt down in front of her. "They've arrested him! The Japanese!"

Sunny went cold. "While he was using the transmitter?" she whispered.

Hannah nodded, fighting back tears. "He'd just finished broadcasting."

"Oh, God, you were there too?" Sunny gasped.

"The reception was no good," Hannah sputtered. "The transmission kept dropping. I told Freddy to stop, but he kept repeating it. It took too long. The signal seekers, they drive around the city—"

Sunny grabbed Hannah's shoulder. "What happened to Freddy?"

"We were in the clearing behind the school. The truck—it appeared out of thin air. The soldiers were everywhere. *Sie waren überall.*" In her distress, Hannah lapsed into German. "Freddy told me to hide in the bushes. I thought he was going to follow me."

"So where did he go?"

"I think he just stayed and waited for them."

Sunny released Hannah's wrist. "Why would he do that?"

"To protect me. Don't you see?" Hannah sobbed. "They would have searched the bushes and found me too."

Sunny hurried to bundle Joey up in his blanket. The baby's eyes opened and his face puckered into the beginnings of a cry. Ignoring his whimpers, Sunny jumped to her feet and pointed at the loft. "Go get your bag, Hannah. Throw what you can into it. Nothing too heavy. We must leave straightaway."

"Leave? But we have nowhere to go."

"We must get out of here. *Now*," Sunny cried. "The Kempeitai—they will come for us."

"Freddy doesn't know you're involved," Hannah said. "Besides, he would never turn me in. Never."

"They will make him talk. Trust me, Hannah." Sunny had an unwelcome flashback to the day a year before when she had stumbled across the men from her Underground cell dangling from the scaffold on the street corner. Some had been tortured beyond recognition.

How could I have put children in the path of such danger? Sunny felt nauseated with guilt. "Freddy will talk eventually," she mumbled. "Anyone would."

"We must help him," Hannah pleaded.

Sunny would have walked straight into Bridge House and

turned herself in if she thought it would make a difference. But she knew better. "Darling, no one can help Freddy now." She looked down at her fussing baby, unable to face Hannah's plaintive eyes. "All we can do is save ourselves."

Hannah sniffled. "And what about Esther and Jakob? We can't just leave them."

"Of course not." Snapping out of her self-recrimination, Sunny focused on their escape plan. "I will pack a bag for each of them. We will catch them on the street before they return home."

"And go where?"

Sunny hadn't thought that far ahead, but it occurred to her that there was only one choice. "The Comfort Home."

Hannah's mouth fell open. "The brothel? We can take the children there?"

"It is more than that, Hannah. There is a hideaway in the basement. We'll be safe there."

"How will Esther get out of the ghetto without a pass?"

"I don't know." Sunny wanted to scream in frustration. "There must be another family who can take in her and Jakob? How about the rabbi? Surely he must know someone who can help. Yes, we will take her to the synagogue."

Hannah nodded distractedly. "What will they do to Freddy?"

Sunny again pictured her Resistance colleagues, their faces beaten, their bodies broken and their fingers snapped like twigs underfoot. Forcing the image from her head, she grabbed Hannah by the shoulders. "There is no time for that, *Liebchen*. Go get your bag!"

Hannah shook free of Sunny's grip. She stared defiantly at her stepmother and then, tears streaming down her cheeks, she headed for the loft.

Despite Joey's howls of complaint, Sunny lowered him to the floor, then started pawing through Esther's drawers. She packed some clothes into two canvas bags, one for each family. Reluctantly, she decided to leave behind their boots and winter coats—their bulk would be conspicuous.

Hannah was waiting for her at the door. Her eyes were clear, but she avoided Sunny's gaze. "I am so sorry, Hannah. This is my fault. All of it."

Hannah sniffed a few times. "We knew the risks."

"How could you possibly know?" Sunny held out her hands. "You are only—"

The knock silenced her. Hannah backed slowly away from the door, as though it might be booby-trapped. Sunny was calmed by the gentle rap—it didn't sound like that of the soldiers—but her hand trembled nevertheless as she turned the knob.

Freddy stood at the threshold. His shirt was ripped, his upper lip bloodied and his right eyelid bruised and swollen half shut. But his smile was as bright as ever as he stepped into the room.

"Freddy," Hannah cried, throwing herself into his arms.

"Hiya, Banana," he said, dancing her around in circles.

Hannah planted her lips on his and kissed him ferociously. Embarrassed, Sunny turned her head away, but she couldn't suppress her laugh of relief.

The teenagers finally separated long enough to speak. "How is this *nes*—this miracle—possible?" Hannah demanded.

Freddy chuckled. "I'm way too smart for those yellow devils." He glanced over to Sunny with an apologetic wave. "No offence, ma'am. I was talking about the Japs, of course."

"We use the same term in Shanghainese," Sunny said with another laugh.

Hannah shook him playfully by the shoulders. "But how, Freddy? How did you get free of them?"

"Simple. I cried."

Hannah scrunched her face. "You cried?"

Freddy stared at her, then his lower lip quivered and he sniffled. Soon tears welled and dripped down his cheeks. "I was only playing, sir," he whimpered theatrically, his voice cracking like a boy going through early puberty. "My friend and I talk on the radio. We pretend we are broadcasters. Like Edward Murrow or . . . or Tokyo Rose."

"You're so clever, Freddy," Hannah said.

Freddy's voice dropped to its normal timbre and the tears dried up. "Not bad, huh?"

"And they believed you?" Sunny asked.

"Not right away, no." He touched his black eye. "But lucky for me, one of them spoke English."

"So how did you convince them?"

"I radioed Sergei. In Little Russia."

Sunny shook her head. "Sergei? Who is he?"

"We buy our cigarettes from his family," Freddy said. "He's the fellow I place our orders with."

"How did you know you could reach him today?" Sunny asked.

"He was waiting."

"Why?"

Freddy touched his temple. "Sergei and I had this backup plan all arranged. If the Japs were to catch me, I'd call him and we'd pretend that we were just fooling around with the radio. Like a couple of kids playing with a new toy. Sergei caught on right away. He was totally convincing."

"Not as convincing as you, I bet," Hannah said proudly.

Freddy rolled his eyes. "The stupid Japs mocked me. They called me a little girl and made fun of me for crying."

"But you got the last laugh, Freddy." Hannah embraced him fiercely again. "You're so clever."

Sunny could have hugged the boy too. "I have to agree with Hannah. You performed like a master spy."

"Maybe so," he snorted. "But the Japs confiscated the radio. Papa is going to be miffed."

"A small price to pay, all things considered," Sunny said.

Freddy frowned. "How are we going to make the next broadcast to the Americans? Can you get me a new transmitter?"

"No," Sunny said.

"No matter," Freddy said. "We can probably get our neighbour, Herr Silbermann, to build us a new one."

Sunny shook her head vehemently. "Absolutely not, Freddy. Never again."

Freddy appeared taken aback. "We can't just stop now."

"We can and we will," Sunny said. "No more broadcasts. No more spying. We will never be so lucky twice."

CHAPTER 38

The truck rumbled along Great Western Road, passing mansions that had once housed the wealthiest and most influential Shanghailanders, the families who had run the city prior to the Japanese invasion. Franz could see how the properties had fallen into disrepair—their lawns yellowed and their gardens overgrown—but never had he been happier to see the familiar buildings. He would have loved to have his camera with him; there was something noble about the houses' weathered dilapidation.

Up until now, Franz had refused to really believe he would ever get here. Even after the truck had left the field hospital at Hengyang and the plane had taken off from the airstrip outside Changsha, he had not completely trusted that he was going home. Not until he caught sight of the city's outskirts did he let the possibility into his heart. With every block they travelled toward the ghetto, his elation rose.

Franz was so distracted that he had to be reminded by the orderly to check on the patients inside the truck. Miraculously, none had died en route. But it was only a matter of time for the extensively burned soldier. Franz could feel the man's raging fever even through the gauze wrapping his forehead. He had slipped into a coma, and his breathing was growing shallower by the minute. Franz worried that if the man died in transport, the Japanese might blame him—or worse, divert the truck before reaching Shanghai. He was desperate to keep him alive during the last few miles to the Country Hospital, which he understood was their destination.

Franz manoeuvered between the stretchers through the cramped, airless truck. He reached the burn victim's stretcher just as the man took a final, gasping breath.

The orderly turned around at the sound. In hopes of buying time, Franz laid a hand on the man's shoulder and spoke to him in German, as though comforting him through his distress. The orderly watched them quizzically for a few seconds before turning back to another patient, whose bandages he was busy adjusting.

Franz continued to speak to the dead man in conversational German. He plugged his stethoscope into his ears and pretended to listen to his chest. As he pulled out his eartips, he asked the motionless man, "How will the Major Okada punish the captain for letting me go?" *No doubt the cane,* Franz thought sadly.

After a few more minutes of feigned examination, Franz felt the truck turning. He looked out and saw the grand facade of the Country Hospital. He called out to the orderly and, as soon as he had the man's attention, closed his eyes and shook his head gravely. The orderly merely shrugged in acknowledgement of the patient's death.

The truck came to a stop and the rear door opened. As Franz stepped into the punishing heat, he was almost disoriented by the blinding sunlight. Soldiers and nurses milled around the troop transport, unloading stretchers but paying no attention to him.

Searching for an authority figure, he followed one of the stretchers along the walkway and into the hospital's grand foyer.

For a moment, Franz's elation gave way to sadness as he realized that this was the place he had first met Helen. Without her warmth and kindness, he doubted he could have survived the last few months.

"Dr. Adler, Dr. Adler," a voice called.

Franz's blood went cold at the sound of the shrill voice. He turned to see Ghoya marching toward him from the other side of the foyer, two guards in tow. "I have been waiting for you, Dr. Adler. Yes, I have." Ghoya extended his arms as he neared. "To personally welcome you home."

"Thank you," Franz said, bewildered.

"No, thank you, Dr. Adler." Ghoya cackled. "For your most dedicated service to the Imperial Army."

"I was only doing my job."

"Like a good soldier." Ghoya clapped Franz on the shoulder. "Yes, yes!"

Ghoya's friendly manner made Franz even more uneasy. "May I ask what you intend next for me, sir?"

"What to do with you indeed." Ghoya fished into his suit pocket and extracted an envelope. He made a show of pulling out the letter inside and slowly unfolding it. "Captain Suzuki wrote me about you."

"Captain Suzuki is a fine surgeon," Franz mumbled.

"He says the same of you. A most capable surgeon. Those were his very words." Ghoya paused and the smile slipped from his face. "Or, at least, that you used to be a capable surgeon." He stared at Franz as though the implication was obvious.

Franz shook his head in confusion. "Pardon me, sir?"

Ghoya studied the letter intently. "Ah, here it is. Allow me to translate. The captain says you started to make terrible errors in the operating room. That you were collapsing during surgery. That he could no longer rely on your assistance." His eyes scanned the letter again. "That you suffered from—what is the expression?—'combat fatigue.' Yes, yes." He snorted. "Combat fatigue."

Franz could feel sweat beading on his forehead. *Suzuki must have written the letter in an attempt to prevent me from being sent back to the field.* But had the strategy backfired, he wondered?

Ghoya raised an eyebrow and then gave Franz the once-over. "Fatigue, is it? Hmm. Your eyes are not bloodshot. I don't see any circles beneath them. You do not look so tired to me. Not so tired at all."

"The days were long. There was no rest at—"

Ghoya silenced Franz with a slap to his cheek. "You embarrassed me, Adler. I promised them a competent surgeon." He shook the letter at Franz. "And what do you do? You surrender to combat fatigue like a pimply-faced teenager."

Face stinging, Franz felt a trickle of blood run across his jaw, but he didn't even bother to wipe it away.

Ghoya balled up the letter and tossed it onto the marble floor. "What to do with you?" His tone calmed. "It is a problem. Yes, it is."

"I am terribly sorry, Mr. Ghoya." Franz bowed his head. "There are no excuses for my behaviour. The last thing I intended was to embarrass you."

"After all I have done for you and your people." Ghoya heaved a sigh. "Embarrass me you did."

"It will not happen again, sir."

"Of course it will not!"

Franz lowered his chin to his chest, expecting to be slapped again. But he wasn't.

"Fortunately for you, I am a very forgiving person." Ghoya folded his arms. "Perhaps I could find it in my heart to give you a second chance."

"A second chance?"

"Not at Captain Suzuki's hospital, of course. He would never have you back. But the Imperial Army is advancing swiftly across the continent. There are still many wounded. Many field hospitals to man."

Franz's pulse drummed in his temples. *Not now. Please. Not when I'm this close to home.*

"But how can I trust you to go back into the field?" Ghoya scoffed. "You might show more of the same weakness and cowardice." He looked to his expressionless escorts and asked them, "How would that possibly help the great Imperial Army? And how would it reflect on me?"

"It wouldn't help at all, sir," Franz replied.

Ghoya only snorted and then changed the subject. "Your woman, she came to see me."

"My wife did? Sunny?"

"Yes, yes." Ghoya grinned maliciously. "A most interesting visit. Most interesting indeed."

Franz could feel his shoulders tensing. "How so, Mr. Ghoya?"

"She tried to persuade me to bring you back to Shanghai." He raised an eyebrow suggestively. "Yes, yes. She was most eager to persuade me."

Not trusting what might come out of his mouth, Franz kept his eyes on his feet and mumbled, "I see."

"Your woman, she was prepared to do anything to persuade me. *Anything*, you understand?"

Franz clenched his fist surreptitiously against his leg. "That does not sound like Sunny," he said through clenched teeth.

"Oh, Dr. Adler, people surprise you when their backs are against the wall." Ghoya howled with laughter. "Against the wall. Yes, yes. Even your own wife."

Franz could feel his face heating and more blood trickling down his cheek. He wanted to claw at the little man's eyes and tear his protuberant ears off his head, but he just dug his nails into his palm and swallowed back his rage.

"Not to worry, Dr. Adler. Not to worry." Ghoya patted him on the shoulder as though they were old chums. Franz couldn't help flinching. "I am the King of the Jews. I would never succumb to such base temptation. Never!"

Franz's hand relaxed. "Yes, of course."

"What to do with you, indeed." Ghoya turned for the entrance. "Ride with me back to the Designated Area. I have no doubt I will find some use for you there."

* * *

Ghoya chatted non-stop during the twenty-minute drive to the ghetto. Franz was so eager to see his family that he barely heard the prattle. Ghoya alternated between complaining about the ingratitude of the refugees and congratulating himself on how smoothly the ghetto ran under his watch.

Franz was overjoyed when the car rattled across the Garden Bridge and onto Broadway. The thoroughfare bustled with the usual sights: clusters of sailors and soldiers, coolies lugging heavy loads on their backs and shoulders, street merchants hawking their wares and the "wild pheasants"—the young dockside prostitutes—selling their bodies under the midday sun. Franz felt as if he had been away forever and, paradoxically, as though he had never left.

The car whizzed past the checkpoint and pulled up to Ghoya's office, where a lineup of refugees already snaked around the side of the building. "Look how far you have put me behind, Dr. Adler," Ghoya said jovially. "My work for my people, it never ends."

"I am sorry, sir," Franz said. "It was most kind of you to offer me a ride."

Ghoya flicked his hand toward the door, which the driver was opening for them. "I have seen more than enough of you for one day. Go, go."

Franz didn't hesitate. As he was climbing out of the car, he heard Ghoya's high-pitched voice following him. "We will speak again soon. Yes, yes, soon. Until then, take a bath. You stink."

As soon as his feet hit the sidewalk, Franz broke into a run. He had just rounded the corner onto Muirhead Road when he spotted Sunny on the other side of the street. Breathless, he watched as his wife, keeping her head down, pushed the pram purposefully ahead of her.

He raised his arm and sniffed at his shirt, self-conscious. But he couldn't wait any longer. He darted across the street. It wasn't until he was a few strides away that Sunny looked up and saw him. The pram jerked to a halt. Her mouth fell open and the colour drained from her cheeks.

"Oh, darling." The words caught in his throat.

"It can't be," Sunny sputtered. "I'm dreaming, surely."

"No." He rushed over and wrapped her in his arms, squeezing her so tight that he could feel her ribs pressing into his. He clung to her, afraid that she might somehow slip away if he loosened his grip.

They rocked silently on the street for a minute or two before Sunny wriggled free of his embrace. "I have so much to tell you, Franz."

"I do too." Franz suddenly realized what he needed to do, what he should have done months before. He crouched down and peeked beneath the canopy that shaded Joey from the sunlight. He gently lifted up the baby, tucking him under his right arm with a slight awkwardness. He looked up at his wife. "First, though, tell me about our son."

The smile lit up Sunny's face, and her eyes brimmed with tears. She couldn't have looked more beautiful.

III

CHAPTER 39

April 30, 1945

As Franz stripped off his surgical gown and gloves, he felt as if he had been thrust back into the field hospital. He thought again of Captain Suzuki. He had never heard what had become of the man who had saved his life, but he hated to consider what Okada might have had in store for the honourable captain.

Little had changed in the eight months since Franz had returned to Shanghai and yet, in a way, everything was different. The Allies were winning the war; it was only a matter of time. According to the Voice of America broadcasts, Berlin was on the verge of falling to the Soviets. The Americans had landed on Japanese soil and were island-hopping their way to Tokyo. An air of inevitability had hung over Shanghai all winter long, like a poorly kept secret that people politely pretended not to have heard.

The Japanese, however, continued to behave as if nothing had changed. Ghoya rationed out passes and reigned over the refugees as unpredictably as ever. He had still not found “a use” for Franz, as he kept putting it, but it didn't stop the little man from harassing him. Meanwhile, the Kempeitai hounded the ghetto, raiding homes even more often than before, in search of subversives.

They had torn up Franz's flat twice in the past two months alone. During the last raid, they had confiscated an electric fan, along with a bag of rice that one of the smirking soldiers had claimed "looked suspicious."

The signal-locating trucks constantly roamed the streets, seeking out any and every spy transmission. They reminded Franz how lucky his family had been. He still had flashes of anger with both Sunny and Hannah over their recklessness. At night, he sometimes awoke in a sweat from a recurring nightmare of having returned home, only to learn of their grisly executions. The only person Franz didn't really blame was Freddy. He was actually grateful to the teenager for his bravery, so much so that Franz had not forbidden Hannah from continuing to see him, though he would have preferred that she had stuck with Herschel. Franz could never shake his suspicion that Freddy was a con man and, like his father, was not to be fully trusted.

At home, there were no secrets between him and Sunny. After she had confessed to spying at the harbour, Franz had volunteered the truth about Helen and their kiss. He was relieved, though a bit puzzled, by Sunny's forgiveness, wondering why it hadn't bothered her more. His guilt aside, he still missed Helen. At times, he wondered what might have happened between them if not for that deadly air raid.

Despite everything, life was better and more fulfilling than Franz would have ever dared to dream during those long days at the field hospital. His family was together. Most nights, there was food on the table, if only rice and vegetables. Half a teaspoon of salt dissolved in water, which he choked down once a day, was enough to keep his drop attacks away. And, most significantly, he had a baby son.

For the first few months after his return, Franz had had to feign an attachment to Joey. But over the fall and winter, the child had found his way into Franz's heart. Joey was nothing like his cousin, Jakob. The older boy was a force of nature: inquisitive, fearless and playfully destructive. Joey was as timid as his cousin was adventurous. He was quick to startle, and when he cried, it was more of a whimper than a demand. Joey had been walking since he was nine months old, though he did so by tentatively holding on to furniture or people's hands. He hadn't spoken a word yet, but there was something in his intelligent gaze and bashful smile that Franz found irresistible. Perhaps it was Sunny's response to the toddler that had been most affecting. Franz had never known his wife to be more contented. In retrospect, Franz regretted having ever questioned whether keeping Joey was best for the family; now he could see that the family wouldn't have been complete without him.

But most others in the ghetto had not been as lucky as the Adlers over the past year. Many refugees, especially the very young and the elderly, had died of malnutrition during the winter. A brief outbreak of cholera in the early spring had claimed a number of children. Yet, somehow, the refugee hospital had survived. The Russian Jewish community had made good on its promise to provide funding and support. Supplies had been as intermittent as the old building's heat and running water, but the past month had been particularly fruitful on the black market. The shady characters who sold Franz medical necessities, inevitably stolen from other hospitals in the region, had been flush with anesthetic, catgut and even antimalarial drugs and sulpha antibiotics. Franz couldn't remember the last the time the hospital had been so well stocked. As a result, he and Sunny had been busy operating again, removing stone-riddled gall bladders and repairing bothersome hernias.

As Franz walked down the hospital's corridor, a commotion on the ward pulled him from his introspection. He heard raised voices before he even stepped inside. "You can't bring that filthy beast in here," Berta cried. "This is a hospital."

"There's nothing filthy about him," Franz heard Ernst reply. "Besides, you think Kaiser Wilhelm wants to be here? Around all these sick people and their germs?"

Franz walked in to see Ernst standing near the head nurse with his arms folded in indignation, while his newly acquired gibbon monkey, which he called Kaiser Wilhelm, perched on his shoulder. The monkey kept one arm wrapped around Ernst's neck while he pointed a long finger at Berta and hooted. Most of the patients were watching in fascinated silence.

Franz had to bite back a smile. "It's all right, Berta. Come on, Ernst, let's get the animal away from the patients."

"That is fine with me, but I do believe the woman works here," Ernst deadpanned.

"Dr. Adler!" Berta exclaimed. "This is simply too much."

Hiding his laughter behind his hand, Franz admonished his friend. "That's enough, Ernst."

"All right, we'll go." Ernst made a small theatrical bow. "My apologies, madam. Kaiser Wilhelm's as well."

After Franz had led Ernst and the monkey into the staff room, he said, "I've been meaning to ask you. That old neighbour who left you the monkey. Why did he name him after the Kaiser?"

"I am not entirely sure if he meant it out of respect or disdain. Probably the latter. These old Nazis still harbour such resentment over how the Great War ended and what was sacrificed at Versailles."

"Why did he leave him to you anyway?"

"Herr Schmidt was a widower with no real friends. Even the other Nazis didn't like him. I didn't either. Insufferable old blowhard. But I always liked Kaiser Wilhelm."

"Enough to keep him?"

The monkey hopped up and down on Ernst's shoulder, seemingly aware that they were discussing him. "Absolutely," Ernst said. "He's better company and smarter than most people I know. Besides, we're good for one another. I bring him bananas, and he brings me a certain air of respectability and gentility."

"Nonsense." Franz laughed. "He just makes you seem even more eccentric. If that's even possible."

"Kaiser Wilhelm and I will not dignify that remark with a response," Ernst said with a mischievous grin. As though on cue, the animal's lips also formed a smile.

"And your other roommate?" Franz asked. "What does he think of the monkey?"

"They get along well enough. Simon has finally found someone willing to listen to him carry on about all that baseball nonsense. The poor, dear monkey." Ernst reached up and stroked his pet on the chest. "However, I do wonder if Simon might soon fly the coop, to use one of his awful Americanisms."

"Is he talking about leaving again?"

"You know how homesick he is to be with Essie and Jakob. More so than ever. And with the war winding down, he's convinced no one will notice if he sneaks back into the ghetto."

"Then he's a fool," Franz grunted. "The Japanese are more on guard than ever."

"You talk to him, then. He won't listen to me."

"You know I can't leave the ghetto. Perhaps Sunny can talk

some sense into him." Franz shut the door behind them. "There's something else I have been meaning to discuss with you."

Ernst sighed. "I recognized that tone. What is it now?"

"Von Puttkamer and Major Huber."

"What about them?"

"Are you still in touch with them?"

Ernst shook his head. "Remember? The baron shuns me now. Considers me a degenerate." He paused. "Come to think of it, so do I. But I don't view it in the same negative light as the baron."

"And your friend Gerhard?"

Ernst squinted. "What does any of this have to with Gerhard?"

Franz sympathized with his friend. Ernst's defensiveness was an understandable necessity. "I was wondering if von Puttkamer still confides in Gerhard at all."

"*Ach,* I see." Ernst craned his neck to look up at his monkey, who had begun to groom the artist's untamed hair. "I don't believe so. Apparently, von Puttkamer and his ilk have become increasingly secretive as the Third Reich implodes around them. Why do you ask?"

Despite the relative privacy of the staff room, Franz spoke in a hush. "They've been spotted in the ghetto recently."

"Doing what?"

"I'm not sure, but I doubt they came to do anything constructive." Franz paused. "I suspect they might be following me."

"Again?"

Franz nodded. "There was a black sedan. I've seen it two or three times parked near our home and the hospital. I could never tell who was inside, but it strikes me as too much of a coincidence."

"Another kidnapping attempt?"

"Perhaps."

"Be careful of von Puttkamer, Franz. There are few things more dangerous in this world than a wounded bull." Ernst snapped his fingers. "What happened to those bodyguards of yours? The Jewish youths?"

The last time Franz had spotted the black car, parked around the corner from his apartment, he'd considered seeking help but felt too embarrassed to ask. "I don't want to alarm Sunny."

"Sunny doesn't know?" Ernst rolled his eyes and laughed. "Actually, you might have found the only thing more dangerous than a wounded bull—a wife kept in the dark!"

"She has enough to worry over. In the meantime, is there anyone you might be able to speak to . . ."

"Ouch! Not so rough." Ernst yanked the monkey's paw away from the clump of hair he was grasping. The animal hooted. "All right, Franz. The kaiser and I will make a few discreet inquiries. See if we can find anything out. I might be a pariah in Germantown, but he is one remarkably well-connected monkey."

Franz laughed. "Thank you."

"They say Berlin will fall any day. To the Russians, no less." Ernst reached up and stroked his pet's back. "The end of Nazi Germany? Of Hitler himself? Who would have dreamed it possible a few short years ago?"

It struck Franz too as surreal. But for him, like the other Jews in the ghetto, the news was tempered by the flood of first-hand accounts emerging from the death camps liberated by the Allies, unimaginable stories featuring walking skeletons and corpses piled like stacks of logs. "I will believe it when I see the hammer and sickle flying over the Reichstag."

"The Reichstag? Göring and his cronies burned that down eons ago." Ernst dug in his pocket, pulled out a piece of dried fruit and held it up to his pet, who snatched it from Ernst.

Franz chuckled. "You and that monkey—it actually makes a certain degree of sense."

"So what will you do after the war, Franz?"

"I cannot think that far ahead."

"With the Soviets already in Berlin?"

"Victory in Europe is inevitable. No question. But who knows how long the Japanese will fight on? It could be years."

Ernst shook his head. "Never. Not when the whole world turns its attention to one island nation. I wouldn't be at all surprised if Stalin joins in on the fun. Mark my words, it will be months at the most before Shanghai is liberated."

"Shanghai free? Could you imagine?"

"And then what?" Ernst asked. "You would continue to run a hospital for refugees here?"

"Sunny wants us to stay."

"And you?"

Franz weighed his answer carefully. "Shanghai has been wonderful to me, to us. But I cannot imagine raising the children here after the war."

"You would go back to Vienna?"

"Never," Franz said. "For all I care, Vienna can fall into the Danube. I will never again set foot on Austrian or German soil."

"So where does that leave you?" Ernst asked. "England? America?"

Franz eyed the monkey, who stared back at him as if listening for his answer. "I have been considering somewhere else altogether."

"Palestine."

Franz shrugged noncommittally.

"That reminds me." Ernst reached into his pocket again. Franz was expecting to see a pack of cigarettes emerge, but instead it was an envelope. "For you. From Simon."

Franz reached for it. "Not for Essie?" he asked.

"Today, I have the profound honour of being your mailman."

Franz tore open the envelope, extracted the letter and began to read.

Dear Franz,

I can't believe how long it has been since I last saw you. More than two years now. I miss shooting the breeze with you over coffee. Although the jury is still out on that gut-wrenching Austrian stuff you love so much. Seems to me it could pass for crude oil.

I'll never forget the moment you and your family stepped ashore in Shanghai. Of course, I mainly had eyes for Essie, but your expression has stuck with me too. I saw so many refugees arrive in those days. Almost without fail, their faces were clouded with bewilderment, fear and despair. Not yours. You looked so damned stoic, with that effortless dignity and poise of yours. On the other hand, you hardly said a word, so I half-wondered if you were mute! I thought to myself, Now here is a classy Old World guy, someone who is going to make a difference to this community. And how right I was. I'm so proud of what you and Sunny have accomplished with the slapdash shell of a hospital I started.

As you know all too well, these days I don't get to see much of anyone except Ernst. And grateful as I am to him for taking me in and protecting me and all, well, I don't have to tell you, he isn't the easiest fellow to live with. Sometimes it feels like I have two roommates: Ernst and his gigantic ego. Three, if you count that wild monkey. At least they keep me entertained most of the time. Besides, whenever I get fed up, I just have to talk baseball and that shuts him up pretty quick.

Franz, I know it's not official, but the Japs are finished. Done. The Americans just have to dot the i's and cross the t's on this war. It's time for us to plan for the future, my friend. Not only for us and our gorgeous brides, but for the little tykes too. We both know that our future isn't here in Shanghai.

Essie tells me that you're seriously considering Palestine. This, from the guy whose cheeks used to pale at the mention of Zionism? It's an admirable idea, and no doubt Rabbi Hiltmann is selling it as hard as my dad used to push oak dining tables on his customers. And maybe if it were just you and Sunny, it would be the right thing to do. But, Franz, you have your family to consider. You can't just stick Hannah and baby Joey in the middle of some disputed desert. It's not the place for them. I'll tell you where is, though. New York. Not only do we have the world's best ball team, but we have one of the best hospitals, right there in the Bronx. Lincoln Hospital. Imagine it, a first-rate facility for an ace surgeon like you. I even have a great brownstone already picked out for us all. Plenty of space.

Essie and I would love nothing more to have the family all together. The States would offer so many terrific opportunities for Hannah and Joey. It would be good for Sunny and you too. Very good. I know this in my heart. I want you—no, I need you—to seriously think about this, Franz.

Forever your pal,

Simon

CHAPTER 40

Sunny hadn't expected to see Father Diego again, let alone to bump into him at the Comfort Home. The last time she had seen the priest was after Freddy's arrest, when she had found him at his church. Diego had listened sympathetically enough as Sunny described Freddy's close brush with the authorities, but he had then tried to talk her out of quitting her surveillance of the harbour, promising there would be no further need to involve the teenagers. Sunny had bolted from his office even before he finished his pitch, vowing to herself that she was done with Diego and his schemes forever.

The priest now greeted her warmly, as if they were meeting outside the church after a service rather than on the steps of a brothel. "You look marvellous, Sunny. And the *nene*." Diego pinched Joey's cheek. "Look how the little one has grown. Not a baby at all."

Despite the nature of their previous encounter, Sunny was genuinely pleased to run into the charming priest. "It's hard to believe he's already a toddler." With a flush of pride, she set Joey down and let him walk. He held on cautiously to her finger for support.

"You will be running soon, little one," Diego encouraged. "And then none of us will be able to keep up." He knelt down and extended his arms to Joey but, as Sunny expected, the boy skittered behind her leg, whimpering to be lifted. Sunny picked him up again.

Diego laughed. "I don't blame you, Joey. I remember being scared of priests when I was little. All those old men in their long black dresses, my brothers and I used to joke." He straightened up. "It's good to see you looking so well, Sunny."

"You too, Father," she said and meant it. Even in his black cassock, Diego struck her as handsome and debonair, as though he were a Hollywood matinée idol only playing the role of a cleric. "How are things with you?" she asked.

"All is well, thank God. The church is still standing. Our congregation is thinner, sadly, but as devoted as ever. The only complaint I have is that it is becoming harder and harder to find good news about the Axis powers to share with the followers of my wireless program."

Sunny smiled. "I wish I could say I was sorry to hear that."

Diego laughed. "Frankly, it's a pleasant dilemma for me."

She lowered her voice. "And your secular work?"

"I still dabble here and there."

She nodded toward the door. "Is that what brings you to the Comfort Home?"

He smiled noncommittally. "God's work knows no boundaries or barriers."

Sunny checked behind her. "Is it safe for you to be seen here?"

"No one looks at me twice, especially not the Japanese. The men around here are far more concerned about being recognized themselves. Besides, I'm not the first man of the cloth to visit the

Comfort Home. And I will certainly not be the last." He nodded knowingly. "However, I try to make it clear that I have come only out of spiritual obligation and not as a client. And you, Sunny? Have you come to see your friend Jia-Li?"

"I—we," she said, glancing at Joey, "try to visit at least once a week. It's harder for her to come to me."

"Such an engaging, intelligent woman. Her spirits seem brighter than when we first met and yet . . ."

"Yet what, Father?"

"She still seems very much a tortured soul."

And always will be, Sunny silently concurred. Joey squirmed in her arms. She looked down at him and smiled. Franz was right, the boy could do no wrong in her eyes. "I better get him inside. He's impatient to see his auntie." She extended her hand to Diego. "It's lovely to see you again, Father."

Diego took her hand but held on without shaking it. "Tell me, Sunny. Do you still live in the same building?"

"Yes, why?"

It was Diego's turn to lower his voice. "Are you familiar with the transmitter in Hongkew? The one just outside the ghetto?"

Sunny eyed him with suspicion. "Yes, of course. Why do you ask?"

"The Japanese, they use the transmitter to communicate with their armies throughout China and their ships all over the Pacific. It's very powerful."

She shook her head adamantly. "No, Father. I cannot. Don't even ask me. I will never get involved again. Never."

"You miss my point, Sunny." Diego pointed overhead at the cloudless blue sky. "The transmitter, it's very likely to be a target."

"Target? You mean for the Americans bombers?"

"Precisely."

Sunny's shoulders tightened with foreboding. "What do you know, Father? Tell me, please."

"Not much. Except that targeted bombing is extremely difficult, if not impossible, in residential areas. Which is precisely why the Japanese situated the transmitter where they did."

"So the Americans plan to bomb the ghetto too?"

"I am saying that *if* they do target the transmitter, it is very possible that some of the bombs could stray and land in the surrounding neighbourhoods. Secondary damage is almost inevitable in such instances."

Secondary damage. Her stomach plummeted. She thought back to the days of the first invasion of Shanghai—and how she had watched in horror from the safety of the International Settlement while, across Soochow Creek, buildings in Hongkew crumpled like tents in a windstorm. She held Joey a little closer. "What can we possibly do to prevent bombs from falling on us?"

Diego squeezed her hand once before releasing it. "You can be vigilant. If you hear the planes overhead . . ."

"We cannot outrun bombs."

"No, but you can escape your building. You can find shelter as soon as the air-raid siren sounds."

Sunny laughed bitterly. "That is the running joke in the ghetto. That the air-raid sirens don't sound until the enemy planes are directly overhead."

Diego smiled, patient as ever with her. "Then watch for the planes. Listen for their engines. They need to have visual sighting, so they will strike only in daylight. All I'm advising, Sunny, is to be prepared. For the rest, God will watch over you."

* * *

Sunny was still contemplating Diego's warning as she sat in the drawing room waiting for Jia-Li. At her feet, Joey played with a rattle. She was convinced that the sly priest knew more than he was letting on, but what difference did it make? Even if she was told the exact day and time of an airstrike, where could they possibly hide within the confines of the ghetto?

Joey stopped shaking the rattle every so often and stared at it as though it were about to do something magical, though he never seemed disappointed when it didn't. Unlike Jakob, who needed constant stimulation, Joey could amuse himself for hours with a single toy. Sunny would have happily watched her son all day, but a few minutes later, Jia-Li breezed into the room. She wore a black silk gown tied loosely at the waist. Her hair was pulled back in a bun, her lips were painted ruby red and her face was heavily powdered. She looked almost Japanese—which, Sunny supposed, was the intent.

After almost three months of "captivity," as Jia-Li described her stay in the basement hideaway, Chih-Nii had allowed her favourite and, not coincidentally, most in-demand girl to return to the living quarters upstairs. Clearly, Jia-Li had begun to work again, though she had never said as much, and Sunny had never asked.

"Who's my handsome fella?" Jia-Li cooed at Joey.

Rather than withdrawing, as he did with most adults, Joey tentatively raised his arms to Jia-Li. He was never shy with her. Franz had once joked that her effect on men knew no age limits, but Sunny knew there was more to it. Jia-Li had become smitten with Joey. Almost every toy he possessed had been a gift from her. She doted on Joey, taking up her role as his godmother and protector with gusto. Sunny suspected it was the only thing that had kept her from further risky behaviour, like poisoning more of her clients.

Jia-Li swept Joey up and spun him in circles. He giggled softly as she dipped him up and down. Then she stopped and pressed her lips to his head. "I could eat this one up, Sister." She leaned over and kissed Sunny on both cheeks. Her fragrance made Sunny think of cinnamon and peaches.

"He is rather cute, isn't he?" Sunny said.

"Rather, I should say." Jia-Li mimicked a highbrow English accent, just as they'd used to mock stuffy Shanghailanders in their childhood.

Jia-Li lowered Joey to the ground and sat down beside Sunny. She took Sunny's hand in hers and held on to it so lightly that their skin barely touched. "Tell me, what is the news from the outside world, *xiǎo hè*?" she asked. "And no war news. I hear more than my fill of that. Tell me about you and the family. Or any juicy gossip will do just fine."

"Little to tell, thankfully, *bǎo bèi*." Sunny nodded toward Joey. "When I'm not at the hospital, this one keeps me busy."

"Hmm." Jia-Li pulled out a pack of her favourite Russian cigarettes and a lighter from her pocket. She went through the motions of offering one to Sunny but didn't even wait for her friend to say no before lighting up her own cigarette. "All is otherwise well at home?"

"Busy." Sunny chuckled. "Little Jakob is an adorable terror. A real handful for poor Esther. For all of us, really."

Jia-Li bit her lip. "And Simon?"

"Ernst is still sheltering him in Germantown. Over two years now."

Jia-Li laughed airily. "Could you imagine those two together day and night? Like Frick and Frack!"

"There's three of them now. Ernst has a monkey."

"A *monkey*! What does Ernst need a monkey for?" Jia-Li rolled her eyes. "He practically is one himself."

Sunny clutched Jia-Li's wrist. "Oh, Sister, I meant to tell you. Hannah is so grateful for the birthday present you sent her."

"She likes the scent?"

"Loves it. She wears it all the time. She can't stop talking about it."

"It was nothing. Mama will let the Comfort Home run out of water before we ever run out of fragrance."

"Fifteen years old, *bǎo bèi*. Hard to believe. Hannah was such a little girl when I first met her. Now she's almost a woman." Sunny sighed. "She is still dating that Freddy boy, though."

Jia-Li raised an eyebrow. "You don't approve?"

"He could charm a lion from his kill, that one. But I don't trust him at all. Neither does Franz."

Jia-Li blew out a ring of smoke that floated lazily skyward. "I've known a boy or two like that myself. It rarely ends well with those types."

Sunny knew it was true. Jia-Li's first boyfriend had got her hooked on opium and led her into the life of prostitution before abandoning her at roughly the same age Hannah was now. "There's another sweet boy, Herschel, who still calls after Hannah. He won't give up. It breaks my heart to see him suffer so. But Hannah only has eyes for Freddy."

"Typical," Jia-Li huffed her disapproval. "And Franz? How is the dashing doctor?"

"He's fine." Sunny couldn't fight back the grin. "Franz is such a wonderful father. After all, he raised Hannah single-handedly. But you should see him with Joey. So caring, so loving, so . . . so paternal."

"Ah, *xiăo hè*, where did you find a man like that? Some people have all the luck." She said it laughingly, without a trace of jealousy.

"And you, *băo bèi*? What is new?"

Jia-Li puffed out another smoke ring. "That is the beauty of the Comfort Home. Every day is exactly like the previous one."

Sunny didn't believe that her friend felt as nonchalant as she sounded, but she didn't press the point. Instead, she asked, "You saw Father Diego?"

"I did," Jia-Li said. "A dangerously charming man, that one. Such a waste that he's a priest."

"Sometimes, I still wonder if he really is."

Jia-Li laughed. "Oh, I'm certain he is."

"How can you tell?"

"The way he listens," Jia-Li said. "With his whole being. He invites confession."

"I suppose so. Yes."

Jia-Li looked away. "I told him, *xiăo hè*," she said quietly. "All about Charlie."

Sunny couldn't remember the last time she had heard her friend mention her husband's name. Any time Sunny had tried to talk about him, Jia-Li had clammed up or immediately changed the subject. "Everything?"

"Everything. Nothing." Jia-Li swallowed. "Only that each day without him is worse than the one before."

Sunny leaned forward and touched her forehead to Jia-Li's. "I cannot even imagine, Sister."

They sat together quietly. Then, as if a spell had broken, Jia-Li pulled away and took another drag from her cigarette. Charlie's memory vanished. "Priest or not, he doesn't come here on Church business," Jia-Li said. "Chih-Nii helps him out from time to time. Stashes a few more of his airmen in the hideaway. But he pays for the favour. After all, nothing is ever free with Mama. Not even patriotism."

"How much more of that business can there be left?" Sunny asked. "People say the war will end soon."

"People say all kinds of things. It doesn't make them true. Besides, the war hasn't been bad for Mama's business. And she will no doubt capitalize on peacetime too."

"And you?"

"I don't think much will change in my life either, except perhaps I'll see different uniforms crumpled at the foot of my bed."

Saddened by the thought, Sunny stroked Jia-Li's arm. "It would be the perfect time for you to get out of here, *bǎo bèi*. To forget this life and to come live with us. To be a dedicated auntie for Joey. That wouldn't be so bad, would it?"

"It sounds like bliss," Jia-Li said with a faraway smile. "And where would we all live together?"

Sunny shook her head. "When the war ends, it will be the end of the ghetto too. We will find somewhere bigger and better." She paused. "Of course, I still have to convince Franz that we should stay in Shanghai."

"Where does he want to go? America?"

"Simon wants us to go to America with him and Esther. To live in the Bronx, wherever that is."

"And Franz?"

"He's not certain. But he doesn't want to stay here."

"America, then? Or perhaps Australia? Even Canada?"

"I suppose. He's even talking about Palestine."

"*Palestine?*" Jia-Li gaped at her. "What would possess him to go there, of all places?"

"There's a rabbi in the ghetto who is most vocal about creating a Jewish state in Palestine. He's very persuasive. Franz has become intrigued."

"What, then? You just move the refugee hospital from here to Jerusalem?"

"Who knows what will happen to us, let alone the hospital."

Jia-Li scooped Joey up, perching him on her knee. "You can't just up and drag Joey away to some awful desert." She affected her English accent again. "I simply will not have it."

"I don't want to go either. I hear the British won't even allow any more Jewish settlers into Palestine. Apparently, the local Arab population is hostile. It could amount to leaving one war zone for another." Sunny shook her head. "Besides, you and I are both rooted here as deeply as the poplars and elms of Frenchtown."

CHAPTER 41

The bedroom was already muggy, and the calendar had only just flipped over to May. Franz suspected that the stifling heat of another Shanghai summer wasn't far away.

Sunny stirred beside him and stretched. "Is he still asleep?" she asked, her whisper evolving into a yawn.

Her leg was draped over his, so Franz had to stretch his neck to see Joey in the crib at the foot of the bed. The child kept so quiet that Franz wasn't certain. "I think so, yes."

Sunny ran her fingers lightly across Franz's chest. "It's such a lovely treat when he sleeps in."

Franz kissed the top of her head, drinking in the soapy fragrance of her lustrous hair. He wondered how she always smelled so fresh when they only had the luxury of a proper bath once or twice a month. "If only we could sleep in." Franz sighed.

Her hand rested delicately on his lower belly, two fingers digging tantalizingly below the string of his pyjama bottoms. "Why can't we?"

"We have surgery. Frau Ingelmann. She and her two hernias are waiting for us."

Sunny's hand slipped deeper into his pyjamas. "Her hernias have been waiting four years. What is another hour?"

Franz felt himself hardening at Sunny's touch. Frau Ingelmann would have to wait. He reached out and gently stroked her thigh, running his hand up under the thin fabric of her nightgown until it reached the warmth between her legs. She moaned quietly at his light caress. Pulling her nightgown up, she rolled on top of him. Effortlessly, she slid his pyjamas down. With one thrust, he was inside her.

After they had made love a second time, they lay sweating in each other's arms, giggling at their early morning exuberance. Sunny ran her hand through Franz's damp hair. "Mmm," he murmured. "Your fingertips feel wonderful."

She continued to massage his scalp gently. "Franz, I have been meaning to tell you. I ran into Father Diego yesterday."

His lifted his head up and away from her hand. "The spy? Where would you see him?"

"I bumped into him outside the Comfort Home while I was visiting Jia-Li."

"What did he want?"

"Nothing," she said, her tone slightly defensive. "But he went to pains to warn me about the air raids."

Franz wrapped the sheet across their chests. "What about them?"

As Sunny explained how the transmitter—and the ghetto by proximity—would be a target for the American planes, Franz's thoughts drifted back to the field hospital. With a sickening lump in the pit of his stomach, he pictured Helen keeling forward in mid-stride.

"Could you imagine, Sunny? If we were to survive the war, only to die at the hands of our liberators?"

"Father Diego says we have to remain vigilant."

"Vigilance won't defuse a bomb."

"No, but we need to be prepared. We cannot wait for the useless air sirens to sound. We have to head for the shelters as soon as we hear the first sounds of the planes."

He exhaled heavily. "Do you really trust those shallow bomb shelters the Japanese have dug?"

She pointed at the ceiling. "More than I trust the walls and roof of this decrepit building."

"Yes, I suppose so."

Arms intertwined, they lapsed into an intimate silence. Franz thought of the meeting he had arranged for today with Rabbi Hiltmann. He knew the rabbi wanted a commitment about Palestine. He turned his head to Sunny and saw that she was staring back at him. "Darling, if we do survive until we are liberated . . ."

"Yes?" she said.

"We will need a fresh start."

"You mean in Palestine, don't you?"

"There could be opportunities for us both there. To work side by side as surgeons."

"After the war, I will be a nurse again, not a surgeon. And I will be happy for it. Besides, there will be peace and security right here in Shanghai."

"We can't know that for certain. After all, the countryside is full of Communist rebels."

"That is the countryside. Not the city. Oh, Franz, how can we take Joey and Hannah away from their home and toss them right back into harm's way?"

"Darling." He reached for her cheek. "There are thousands of others like us already over there. Pioneers. You can't simply assume we will be putting anyone in harm's way."

She jerked her face away from his hand and sat up, her legs hanging over the side of the bed, her back to him. "Can you assume that we won't be?"

* * *

"Did you hear about the crematoria?" Rabbi Hiltmann demanded as soon as Franz reached him. The older man stood at the front of the Ohel Moishe Synagogue polishing the wooden bimah, the platform from which he read from the Torah, with a yellow rag. "The ones at the camp they called Auschwitz?"

The Adlers had never kept a wireless in their flat. Lately, Franz even avoided listening to broadcasts on the radios that their friends and colleagues hid inside their homes. He didn't want to hear any more about the extermination camps. His chest ached at the thought of all the friends and neighbours he'd left behind in Vienna. How many of them had ended up in those crematoria? "I've heard some rumours, yes."

"*Rumours?* Rumours are what you hear about the door-to-door salesman and the neighbour's wife. These are truths. Unimaginable, unbearably awful truths. Attested to by soldiers, newsmen and survivors, those poor souls who were lucky enough—or perhaps not, after what they have seen—to outlast their tormentors."

Franz nodded contritely. "It was a poor choice of words," he said, hoping to steer Hiltmann away from the subject.

"There were five crematoria in Auschwitz alone. I am told they were capable of burning five thousand bodies a day." Hiltmann scrubbed hard at an imaginary blemish on the polished wood. "More than a million people every year. Incinerated in one camp alone."

The magnitude of the murder was beyond Franz's comprehension.

"And the children's shoes?" Hiltmann attacked the bimah again with his rag. "Warehouses full of shoes. Can you imagine all those children? The monsters, they kept the shoes. Why? To give away to the Aryan boys and girls? Or maybe to keep as some kind of deranged trophy?"

Franz thought of the adorable Friedmann twins, Sarah and Rosa, who had lived in his building in Vienna. They had been such good friends of Hannah's. Franz had tried to talk their father into bringing his family to Shanghai, but Herr Friedmann was determined "to wait out the Nazis." Franz wondered if the twins' shoes were somewhere in those piles. But he just said, "The Nazis will be done soon. Everyone says so. Then the Allies will be able to bring those responsible to justice."

"Justice? *Justice?* How will justice help the millions who died in the gas chambers? What good will it be to all those children?"

Franz dropped his chin to his chest. "Nothing can help them."

"You are wrong, Dr. Adler." Hiltmann shook his rag angrily at Franz. "There is one, and only one, thing that will help all those lost souls."

"What is that, Rabbi?"

"If something good were to come from their deaths."

"You honestly believe that?"

"In my heart and soul." Hiltmann nodded slowly. "It is our duty as survivors to create a place where their memory will be preserved and honoured. Where their remaining family members—what few there might be left—can live and prosper."

"In Palestine?"

"In Eretz Yisrael!"

Franz's faith wasn't strong enough to believe that anything could help the dead, but the living were a different story. "A haven for Jews the world over."

"Exactly." Hiltmann shook his rag like it was a flag. "So you will come with us, then?"

Franz paused, remembering his conversation with Sunny. "I'm considering it, Rabbi."

"Good, Dr. Adler. We will need skilled doctors—surgeons, no less—most of all."

"My wife is more skeptical."

"Why? What would be stopping her?"

"There's my daughter. And we have a new baby to—"

"Hannah and the baby are the most important of all. Far more important than you or me. We have a whole generation of Jews to replace." Hiltmann stared at him intently. "You must make Sunny see this."

"Make her see?" Franz uttered a half-hearted laugh. "You don't know my wife like I do, Rabbi. Besides, Sunny has never left China."

"Then it's time she did."

"She worries about the children."

The rabbi stared at him unsympathetically. "Are you familiar with the old Yiddish proverb 'Better to die upright than to live on your knees'?"

"I've heard it before, yes."

"Well, the Nazis have proven that we Jews can no longer live on our knees, even if we try to."

An excited voice interrupted them. "Rabbi! Rabbi!" A bearded young man waved his arms as he rushed down the aisle toward them.

"What is it, Saul?" Hiltmann asked, annoyed.

“He’s dead, Rabbi,” Saul cried.

“Who is dead?”

“Hitler!”

Franz’s head swam as if he were about to relive one of his drop attacks, but his legs held firm.

Hiltmann rested a hand on the bimah. “Are you certain, boy?”

“Yes,” Saul cried. “The Nazis announced it themselves.”

“How?” The rabbi demanded. “How did that *farseenisch* die?”

“They haven’t said,” Saul said happily. “Only that he is dead and Berlin has fallen.”

Franz felt a lightness in his chest and a tingling in his fingers and toes. “Have the Nazis surrendered?” he asked.

Saul shook his head. “They have a new chancellor. Some admiral named Dönitz.”

Franz struggled to absorb the news. “Hitler is really gone?”

“Yes.” Saul laughed. “Everyone is saying so on the wireless. Even the Germans.”

Hiltmann pulled his hand from the bimah. “*Danken got*,” he finally said in Yiddish. “May they dump his body in an unmarked grave beneath a mountain of shoes.”

* * *

Franz wandered down Ward Road at dusk, lost in a fog of emotion. Hitler was dead. Berlin had fallen. But the Japanese were fighting on, and the ghetto might be bombed at any time by the Americans. And what about the millions of Jews who had been murdered in that one camp alone?

Franz hadn't even noticed the sedan rumbling along behind him until he rounded a corner and it turned to follow him. Looking over his shoulder, he froze as he recognized the car he had seen earlier, parked outside the apartment and also the hospital. Suddenly it came to a stop, tires crunching, and the back door flew open. Franz glanced around him. He would have called for help but, aside from a coolie resting against his rickshaw at the end of the block, the side street was empty.

His pulse pounded in his ears as he considered dashing for Muirhead Road. A pair of boots had already emerged from the car. Franz doubted he could outrun them all, but nevertheless he turned and raced into the narrow alleyway behind him. Looking back over his shoulder to see whether the men were following, he did not see the wall that seemed to come out of nowhere. Slamming into it, Franz toppled backwards to the ground. Before he could regain his bearings, a huge hand wrapped around his arm and hoisted him to his feet. Franz caught a whiff of soy as he looked up into the face of von Puttkamer's Korean bodyguard.

The tall man spun Franz around effortlessly and dragged him back toward the sedan, which was now blocking the lane's entrance. Franz was still gasping as he was shoved through the back door of the sedan and fell into the empty seat across from von Puttkamer.

"Ah, Dr. Adler," the baron said pleasantly as the door slammed shut. "We have much to discuss."

CHAPTER 42

Sunny slung the sack of rice over her shoulder while Hannah pushed the pram beside her, navigating Chusan Road's crowded sidewalk. Hannah enjoyed steering her baby brother in his carriage, even though its wheels often stuck and it had a tendency to veer to the right. Joey never seemed to notice the bumpy ride. He still wasn't talking, but as he sat in the pram, his keen eyes drank in the commotion around him.

Wednesdays were among the busiest days at the Tong Shan market, with street dentists and barbers competing for space with noisy merchants and smelly outdoor kitchens. The screams from one Chinese man, whose dentist braced himself against the chair while struggling to extract a tooth, followed them all the way down the block. Hannah noticed that the Jewish businesses—the pharmacy, the kosher bakery, the two restaurants and three cafés—appeared busier than ever. Little Vienna had developed a reputation beyond the ghetto, and it wasn't uncommon to see gentiles from the International Settlement among the locals, and to hear Russian, Finnish and French on the street.

After they had crossed the road and stepped into a quieter block, Hannah finally asked the question that had been on her mind all day: "Is Papa going to force us to leave, Sunny?"

Sunny cocked her head. "Force us to leave? Does that sound like your father?"

"You know what I mean," Hannah said, trying not to sound petulant. "Are we going to have to go to Palestine?"

"Nothing has been decided."

"Do you agree with him? That Palestine will be best for us?"

Sunny bit her lip, wavering. "Shanghai is the only home I've ever known."

"Then Papa shouldn't make you go."

Sunny stopped. "I thought you were keen on Zionism, Hannah. Remember? You and Herschel were the ones who persuaded your father to go to the meetings in the first place."

Hannah couldn't bring herself to tell Sunny the truth, so instead she said, "I was young and naive back then."

Sunny laughed. "And now you're old and worldly, are you?"

Hannah feigned insult. "Maybe it has only been a year, Sunny, but I've grown up a lot in that time."

"Yes, you have," Sunny agreed. "So why has growing up changed your mind about Palestine?"

Feeling her face flush, Hannah was desperate to sound convincing. "The rabbi and the others, they romanticize the whole idea. The garden of milk and honey, and all that. The truth is, Palestine is one big desert, full of hostile locals. Even the British don't want any more Jews to go there."

"Ah, I see. So this has nothing to do with Freddy, then?"

"Not at all," Hannah said, realizing she sounded defensive. "Well, Freddy's family has no plans to go. I would miss him, of course. But I don't want to leave Shanghai either. It's my home too."

An understanding smile crossed Sunny's face. "Your father and I are still discussing it, Hannah. Nothing is decided. I do share your concerns. And we will, of course, include you in the decision. I promise."

Hannah slowed to a stop almost involuntarily. As her stepmother continued down the street, Hannah called to her, "Sunny."

She looked over her shoulder. "Yes?"

Hannah couldn't hold it inside any longer. "I can't leave Freddy. I just can't."

Sunny turned back to Hannah, slipping an arm over her shoulders. "I know that's how it feels now—"

"It's not how it feels *now*," Hannah muttered miserably. "It's how it is. I love him. I would die without him."

"I know, darling." Sunny smiled again. "You are barely fifteen. Feelings change with time."

"No," Hannah cried. "These never will."

"If that is true, then it doesn't matter where you end up," Sunny said. "You will eventually find each other."

"Not if I am two continents away. On the far side of the world. How can we be together then?"

Sunny squeezed her shoulders tighter. "It will all work out, Hannah. I am telling you."

"Please, Sunny," Hannah implored. "Don't let Papa take us away."

Sunny was contemplative. "All right," she finally said. "I will talk to your father. That is all I can do."

Hannah realized it guaranteed nothing, but she felt somehow reassured. She was about to thank Sunny when she heard the shouting. As soon as they turned onto Tong Shan Road, they ran into the crowd gathering outside a grocery store. Chinese and Europeans formed a semicircle on the sidewalk. Hannah had to stand on tiptoe and peer between the shoulders and heads to spot the source of the din.

A Chinese man was kneeling on the sidewalk, his hands tied behind his back. He was flanked by two Japanese soldiers while a third man, who wore an officer's uniform with a sword clipped to his belt, stood directly in front of him. The officer was shouting at the man in Japanese. Hannah understood a smattering of Japanese, but the only word she picked up now was *dorobō* (thief) which the officer repeated three times.

Sunny grabbed Hannah by the arm and began to pull her away. "Come, let's get out of here, Hannah."

Hannah shared her stepmother's unease. She sensed that the accused man would end up in front of one of the impromptu firing squads, which had become so common that pedestrians sidestepped the bodies as though circumnavigating lampposts. She was about to turn away when the officer unsheathed his sword.

Before she could avert her eyes, the officer raised the sword and swung down viciously with both hands. She gasped as the blade sliced partway through the kneeling man's neck just below his jaw. A fountain of blood sprayed up and the spectators nearest to him jumped back. The officer struggled to free the blade. As soon as he did, the accused man's head flopped to the side and he toppled forward.

* * *

School was closed for the week and Hannah wasn't supposed to see Freddy until the next morning, but she needed to talk about what she had just seen. Only he would understand. So she ran the five blocks over to his family's flat, but Freddy wasn't there and his mother didn't know where he had gone.

Hannah headed toward the school, hoping to find Freddy somewhere along the way. She didn't see him, but she ran into Avi a block from the school. "Hello, Hannah Banana," he said in a mocking tone that made Freddy's affectionate nickname sound somehow hurtful. Avi had always been jealous of the time and attention she had taken away from his friendship with Freddy. At first, she had tried to win Avi over, but the harder she tried, the more unfriendly he had become. Eventually, she had given up.

"Where is Freddy?" Hannah asked in lieu of a greeting.

"What's the big emergency?" Avi sneered.

"Just tell me where he is."

"Yeah, sure. No problem." His smile bore a hint of a challenge. "I just saw him behind the school."

Sunny's stomach plummeted. "He's not using the transmitter again, is he?"

Avi's unpleasant smile only widened. "Not sure. Why don't you go ask him?"

Without another word, Hannah raced off for the school. She rounded the corner with her heart in her throat, expecting to see the radio set up to transmit. But the clearing was deserted. She was about to turn around when she heard noises coming from somewhere in the bushes. Reluctantly, she moved toward the sound. As soon as she reached the edge of the clearing, she spotted two pairs of intertwined legs. A girl was lying on the same blanket that Freddy had used with the radio, but Hannah couldn't see her clearly. But she could see all of Freddy. He was on top of the girl, his trousers down around his knees.

Hannah didn't even realize she had cried out until she heard her own voice in her ears. "Oh, Freddy!"

Freddy's head swivelled toward her, his face red from both exhaustion and embarrassment.

All the old hurts and insecurities came flooding back to Hannah. She tucked her vulnerable left hand behind her back.

"Hannah, wait," Freddy called.

The tears were flowing before she had even pivoted and dashed away.

CHAPTER 43

Franz sat in the backseat across from von Puttkamer and his impassive bodyguard. The silent driver was the only other occupant of the vehicle, which reeked of leather polish and cologne. Von Puttkamer leaned calmly back in his seat, resting his head against the window as though settling in for a long train ride.

Having finally caught his breath, Franz willed his voice to be strong. "Where are you taking me?"

"Not to worry, Dr. Adler. We are only going for a scenic drive. To give us a chance to chat." Von Puttkamer's smile and amicable tone were even more unsettling than his words. "You will pardon me if I confess that this is not one of my favourite neighbourhoods."

"I'm not permitted to leave the ghetto without a pass," Franz said.

"No one will know you have gone."

The words turned Franz's blood to ice. "Believe me, Baron, several people will notice."

Von Puttkamer shrugged. "It can't be helped."

Franz glanced out the window and saw the Ward Road checkpoint fly past. He had not left the ghetto since returning from the field hospital eight months earlier. He stole a quick glance at the door handle. He couldn't tell if it was locked, but it almost didn't matter.

To reach it, he would have to climb over the baron's bodyguard.

"Your Führer is dead," Franz said.

"Yes, I am still in shock over it," von Puttkamer said in a casual tone that belied his words. "All men die. Even the great ones."

"They say it will only be a matter of days until Germany surrenders."

"I agree. The war is lost. There is no point in arguing that."

"Then what is this all about? Why have you kidnapped me?"

"*Kidnapped* is such an ugly word." Von Puttkamer tsked. "I prefer the term *shanghaied.* It's both local and exotic. And so much more colourful, wouldn't you agree?"

Franz forced his breathing to slow. "What do you want with me?"

Von Puttkamer sat up straighter and the smile slid from his lips. "The war may be over, but business goes on. Accounts must be settled."

Franz tensed. "What accounts do you have to settle? *You* were the one who tried to bomb *us*."

Von Puttkamer's eyes darkened. "And you slit Hans's throat. He was hardly more than a boy."

"I didn't slit his throat. Besides, that 'boy' was trying to blow up the synagogue and everyone inside it."

Von Puttkamer stared long and hard at Franz. Time seemed to come to a stop. Finally, the baron relaxed back in his seat again. "Hans was only following orders," he said evenly. "As was I."

"You had orders to blow up the ghetto?"

"It certainly wasn't my idea."

Franz knew the baron was lying, but his breathing calmed and his shoulders relaxed. It occurred to Franz that von Puttkamer might not have abducted him out of vengeance. Perhaps the baron was looking to protect himself after Germany's collapse, even if it meant negotiating with a Jew. How rapidly the world was changing.

"No, the orders came from Major Huber," von Puttkamer continued. "Chief of Gestapo in Shanghai. I believe the major's orders came directly from Berlin. From Himmler himself, apparently." Von Puttkamer leaned closer to Franz, as though about to divulge a secret. "You know, in Berlin, they have never forgotten about those of you who escaped to Shanghai."

"*Escaped?*" Franz felt his anger building, like lava under pressure. "Is that what they call it? As if we were all hardened criminals?"

"Emigrated, then? It's merely semantics, Dr. Adler." Von Puttkamer dismissed the idea with a small wave. "You're missing my point. I was simply—"

"Let me tell you about my 'escape,' Baron."

Von Puttkamer shook his head. "That is not necessary—"

"The day after the storm troopers lynched my brother, Adolf Eichmann himself warned me that I had two weeks to get out of Austria or I would be sent to a concentration camp." Franz glared into von Puttkamer's evasive eyes. "You do know about the camps, Baron, don't you?"

Von Puttkamer brushed him away with another sweep of his hand. "I have heard a few unsubstantiated stories. After all, the victors get to rewrite history as they so choose. It's one of the spoils of triumph."

"Unsubstantiated?" Franz echoed hoarsely.

"I understand propaganda, Dr. Adler. At times, the publicity war is fiercer than the fighting on the front lines. One doesn't know who or what to believe anymore."

"Are you suggesting that the Allies made up these camps, then?"

"I'm not suggesting the Jews didn't suffer in Europe. Everyone suffers in wartime. War makes civilized people do uncivilized things. But I happen to know the Allies' accounts are grossly exaggerated."

"This is not your wireless propaganda." Franz's fury overpowered his fear about his safety. "This is the terrible truth. Death camps with millions of victims, including women and children. My daughter and I would have surely been among the dead had we not 'escaped' to Shanghai."

The Korean bodyguard leaned forward in his seat, but the baron restrained him with his arm. "It's all right, Yung Min. The doctor feels the need to vent."

"And you, Baron," Franz continued. "You would have undoubtedly pulled the trigger or released the gas or done whatever other monstrous thing you were ordered to do, had you been stationed in Poland instead of Shanghai."

"You are wrong, Dr. Adler," von Puttkamer replied calmly. "I am a patriotic man, yes. And I believe the Führer was a great man who did great things for our nation. However, I've always considered his opinion to have been a little extreme regarding the Jews. The Bolsheviks, absolutely. They represent a great threat to the entire world and need to be eliminated. Not so with the Jews."

Franz couldn't believe what he was hearing. "*Ach*, I see. We Jews should consider you a friend, then?"

Von Puttkamer snorted. "I won't deny that I find your race to be self-centred and obsessed with wealth and status. But the Jews were not the only flawed creatures in the Reich. Besides, now is the time for reconciliation, not blame, among all Germans."

"I was never German," Franz grumbled. "I am Austrian. Or I was, until you Nazis stripped me of my citizenship. You can keep it too."

Von Puttkamer folded his arms. "All right, Dr. Adler, you have spoken your piece. Enough self-righteous prattle. We need to discuss the practicalities of our future here in Shanghai."

"Our future?" Franz blurted. "Your future involves a prison cell or a firing squad."

Von Puttkamer turned to Yung Min. "You see? This is what happens when I try to reason with these people."

Franz peered out the window and recognized the bases of the art deco buildings that lined Bubbling Well Road. They would soon reach Germantown, and there might not be any turning back then. "Stop the car," he demanded. "I am getting out."

"You will get out when I say so."

"I will get out now."

Von Puttkamer uncrossed his arms. "I came to speak with you in good faith. To put our differences aside." He sighed heavily. "The way you talk, Adler, it makes me wonder what the point of it is. If I allow you to return to that miserable ghetto, you will only instigate and stir divisiveness and unrest among the rest of the rabble." He glanced over to the bodyguard. "Perhaps it would be best for everyone if you were not to return."

Recognizing that his tirade was falling on deaf ears, and increasingly aware of the danger he was in, Franz changed his tack. "It would be a mistake not to release me, Baron."

"Oh? Why is that?"

"Do you think I'm the only person in the ghetto who knows about the bombing plot? Or who has heard your radio program? Do you believe the others will feel any differently than I do?"

"Only time will tell," von Puttkamer said.

"I am a well-known member of the refugee community."

"So what?"

"I have told several people about how I've seen your car parked in front of my home and the hospital over the past weeks. If I were to go missing, the others would immediately assume you were responsible."

"And what proof would they have?"

Franz scoured his brain for a convincing response. "What will the American soldiers think when they roll into Shanghai? Perhaps some of them will have seen the camps in Europe. Do you honestly think they will require much proof to believe that it was a Nazi who abducted the ghetto's most prominent Jewish doctor?"

Von Puttkamer glanced uncertainly to Yung Min before turning back to Franz. "Say I release you. What do you intend to do?"

"Go home to my family."

Von Puttkamer's eyes narrowed and he motioned to himself and Yung Min. "I meant about us."

Franz held the baron's gaze. "I don't care what becomes of you—I swear to God, I don't—as long as I never have to lay eyes on you again."

Von Puttkamer slumped back in his seat. He suddenly looked older, smaller, than he had before. Finally, he swivelled his head toward the driver and shouted, "Pull over and let this worthless Jew out! I cannot tolerate another second in his presence."

CHAPTER 44

Sunny stood next to Esther in the cramped little space that passed for their kitchen. The two boys sat on the floor, each playing with one of Joey's toys. All the while, Hannah's sniffles and sobs drifted down to them from the small loft above.

"I will go talk to her again," Esther said.

Sunny squeezed Esther's wrist once before letting go. "I think she needs to be alone right now, Essie."

Esther shook her head in disbelief. "So upset over possibly moving to Palestine? We don't even know when or even if this will ever happen. There must be something more, surely?"

"Hannah says not."

"Should we go find Freddy? He's not my favourite by any means, but he always seems to know how to cheer her up."

"I think she needs to be alone," Sunny repeated.

Esther sighed. "It breaks my heart to see her suffer like this."

"Mine too."

"She has always been more than a niece to me," Esther said. "Before Jakob, I never thought I would have one of my own. Hannah never knew her mother. I liked to think . . ." She cleared her throat. "Of course, you are here for her now. Everything is completely different."

Sunny gazed into Esther's compassionate eyes. "You are the closest to a mother that Hannah has ever known. That hasn't changed. It never will."

Esther nodded gratefully. "Ironically, in Vienna, it was my Karl who was so involved with religion. Franz was nothing like his brother in that regard." She sighed. "He was suspicious of the Zionists. He viewed them as nothing but troublemakers."

"Even when I first met him here, he was the same. Something has changed in him."

"Regardless, Franz has taken it too far." Esther shook her head disapprovingly. "Of course, America I would understand. To come with us to New York. To keep the family together. But Palestine? With a baby? And a wife and daughter who do not even want to go? It's madness."

"It's very important to him." Sunny again found herself in the strange role of defending her husband's views even though they differed from her own.

"Family is the most important," Esther declared. "Even the Torah says so."

Sunny stroked her arm. "We Chinese always say the same."

Another paroxysm of sobs could be heard coming from the loft.

"I can't bear it, Sunny," Esther said, turning to the ladder that led to the loft. "I must at least try to talk to her."

This time, Sunny didn't try to stop Esther.

Sunny watched her son move the wooden blocks around on the floor. When Jakob reached out and grabbed one right out of Joey's hand, Joey just picked up another, unbothered. She smiled to herself at how much her son's temperament reminded her of her father's unflappable manner.

There was a knock at the door. Jakob sprang to his feet and ran over to answer it before Sunny had time to stop him. On the other side stood the young male prostitute whom Chih-Nii had sent to Sunny a year before.

Sunny's stomach plummeted. "It's Jia-Li again, isn't it?" she demanded.

The boy simply turned and beckoned her to follow.

* * *

The rickshaw ride was a blur of worry and awful imaginings. The boy hadn't told Sunny anything other than that there had been "another incident."

Inside the Comfort Home, girls and clients milled about as usual, but Sunny picked up on the charged air even before Chih-Nii arrived. The madam silently slipped her elbow into the crook of Sunny's arm and swept her up the circular staircase.

"How bad is it, Mama?" Sunny asked, fearing the answer.

"Bad, buttercup," Chih-Nii replied in a monotone. "Very bad."

Upstairs, two towering guards in matching black suits stood shoulder to shoulder blocking the entrance to the landing. They parted only briefly to allow Sunny and Chih-Nii to pass.

Sunny smelled the blood as soon as they stepped into the bedroom, but she couldn't see any. Jia-Li was lying on the room's four-poster bed, covered up to her neck by a flower-patterned quilt. Her face was devoid of colour, and she stared vacantly at Sunny as a young woman dabbed at her forehead with a damp washcloth. Ushi stood tucked into the corner of the room, looking like an overgrown child being disciplined at school.

Sunny rushed over to her friend, and the woman with the cloth skittered away. Only when Sunny reached the bedside did she notice the middle-aged man collapsed on the floor beyond it. He was wearing a Kempeitai officer's uniform. His eyes were rolled back in their sockets, and a knife protruded from his abdomen. Blood had turned most of his khaki shirt reddish brown. A revolver lay on the floor only inches from his body.

"What has happened, *bǎo bèi*?" Sunny demanded, yanking back the quilt.

The right side of Jia-Li's white corset was soaked red. It took a moment for Sunny to see the bullet's entry wound just above her breast.

"I wasn't going to break my promise to you." Jia-Li's voice was ragged and breathless. "You must believe me, Sister."

"Of course I believe you." Sunny's fingers looked for the pulse at her friend's right elbow. It was alarmingly rapid and faint. She looked over her shoulder at Chih-Nii, who stood as still as a marble Buddha at the foot of the bed. "Get some men and a stretcher," Sunny cried. "We need to get her to the hospital straightaway."

Jia-Li fumbled a hand out. Her fingers felt like icicles on Sunny's arm. "No hospital," she moaned. "I don't want to leave here."

"We have to take you to the operating room," Sunny cried. "We must stop the bleeding and repair your chest."

Jia-Li ignored her. "The devil, he kept telling me about the 'Chinks' he had killed," she breathed heavily. "How he loved to capture guerilla fighters. How he kept them alive for days and days, even after he'd cut off their arms and legs. How easily he could make them beg for death—without giving it to them." She stopped to pant for air.

"You must conserve your energy," Sunny implored.

But Jia-Li didn't listen. "It excited him, *xiăo hè*. I could see the stiffness in his pants as he told me about those brave patriots he tortured. I couldn't stop thinking of Charlie. What this devil would've done to my Charlie if he'd got his hands him on. I couldn't take it, *xiăo hè*. I just couldn't listen to another word."

"Oh, Sister," Sunny breathed, touching her forehead to Jia-Li's frigid cheek. "And the knife?"

"Ushi gave it to me. To protect myself from dangerous clients." Jia-Li's breathing grew even more laboured. "I keep it under the mattress. I didn't even realize I was reaching for it. I was thinking only of Charlie."

"Please, save your strength," Sunny pleaded. "We can discuss it all later. Right now we have to get you to the hospital. Franz will be able to fix you. I know he will."

Jia-Li's breath was cool on Sunny's cheek. "It doesn't hurt, Sister," she reassured quietly. "Only cold. And numb. So very numb. Just like how it used to be on the pipe. Floating above the room again. I always loved that feeling, *xiăo hè*. It feels like escape."

Sunny knew her best friend was in severe shock. Without immediate surgery, she would either suffocate on the blood accumulating in her chest or die from the hemorrhage. Sunny lifted her head away from Jia-Li's and glanced over to Chih-Nii. "Where are the men with the stretcher?" she screamed.

"No one is coming," Chih-Nii replied calmly.

"Are you crazy?"

"Don't you see, Soon Yi?" Chih-Nii said, her voice cracking for the first time. "Even if the hospital could help my beautiful orchid, the Japanese would only come for her. For all of us. There is no escape."

"Mama is right," Jia-Li said weakly. "Besides, I don't want to leave my bed, *xiǎo hè*. I just want to be with Charlie again."

Sunny felt the tears dampening her cheeks before she even realized she was crying. "Please, Sister, you can't leave me."

Jia-Li reached up tremulously and wiped the moisture from Sunny's cheek. "I will never leave you, Sister," she said. "But stay here with me now, *xiǎo hè*. That is all I need."

CHAPTER 45

May 31, 1945

By the time Franz reached the Kadoorie School, his shirt was drenched in sweat. He knew the mugginess only heralded the first of many approaching summer heat waves.

In the past, Franz had often walked his daughter to and from school, but months had passed since he had last stood out front waiting for the school bell to ring. The work at the hospital had been more intense than ever and, besides, he knew Hannah preferred the company of her friends these days. But he promised himself now that he would resume the school routine with his daughter and do the same for Joey once the boy reached school age.

While Franz waited, he reflected on the surreal happenings of the past month. Germany's surrender had come and gone with surprisingly little fanfare in the ghetto. The sheer scale of the mass murder of European Jews, which was becoming more widely known now, overshadowed any joy the refugees could take in the Nazis' defeat. The Japanese occupation prevented people from learning the specifics of what had happened to family and friends left behind in Europe, but Franz, like almost every other refugee, assumed the worst. No one could have been left untouched by the genocide. The question on most people's minds was whether any of their loved ones had survived.

It struck Franz as ironic that the level of anxiety among the Jewish refugees had actually risen in the wake of Germany's surrender. The threat of starvation had become even more acute since local farming and food distribution networks had been disrupted by the American bombing and Chinese ground advances. Stories of kamikaze pilots sacrificing their lives to attack American ships only fuelled the belief in the ghetto that the Japanese would never surrender. And if they planned to fight to the last man, then wouldn't they be certain to take the refugees down with them?

Reports of empty barges spotted on the Whangpoo River had ignited a rumour that the Kempeitai were about to invoke a plan—apparently first suggested three years earlier by visiting SS officials—to load the Jews onto empty ships and incinerate them upriver. Panic seized the ghetto. Franz was summoned to an emergency meeting of the Refugee Council. No one presented any evidence to support the rumour, but people were worried because Ghoya had refused to refute it. Franz tried to convince the others that such behaviour was typical of Ghoya, but his reassurances fell on deaf ears. The night after the meeting, several families stole out of the ghetto after curfew, attempting to disappear among the masses living in Frenchtown and the International Settlement. All of them were caught and viciously punished. Franz, who had tended to several of the victims, had not been surprised by the severity of the men's injuries, but he found the sight of women beaten to the point of unrecognizability deeply unsettling.

It wasn't an isolated episode either. As the Japanese sensed impending defeat, they behaved increasingly erratically. A few days before, a group of drunken soldiers had savagely attacked several elderly Hasidic Jews, seemingly for sport, killing two of them and maiming three others. Ghoya had blamed the old men for "inciting the soldiers."

All the while, American bombers and fighter planes passed overhead with increasing frequency. Sometimes they flew low enough to buzz the ghetto. Many of the Chinese and even a few brazen refugees would stand on the rooftops to cheer on the planes, waving flags and shouting out their support. The planes inevitably targeted ships in the harbour or buildings outside the city, but Franz kept his word to Sunny. At the first sign of the bombers, he would head for the shelter nearest to the hospital, often finding himself alone inside as others went about their business without paying any attention to the planes overhead.

The pall hanging over the ghetto was magnified at home. Hannah had become withdrawn and sullen. Esther blamed Franz. She had confronted him the week before with uncharacteristic ire. "How can you be so selfish, Franz?" Esther cried, her cheeks flushed. "To force this . . . this Zionist fantasy on your family. Your daughter is heartbroken and your wife is in despair. Is this what you want for them?"

The guilt was eating at Franz. He had tried to talk to Hannah after Esther's scolding, but his daughter refused to engage in discussion. Meanwhile, Sunny was lost in mourning.

Chih-Nii had spared no expense on Jia-Li's funeral, turning it into a spectacle for seemingly all of Shanghai to take part in. No one knew how Chih-Nii had deflected the blame for the Kempeitai officer's murder away from the Comfort Home, but Franz suspected considerable sums of money and other favours must have been involved. Regardless, the madam had held a three-day wake at the Comfort Home, with Jia-Li's casket ensconced in a mountain of white irises. On the day of the burial, the funeral procession wound its way through Frenchtown, led by the haunting tones of a traditional Chinese band. It wasn't until they reached the cemetery that Sunny finally broke down. Kneeling at the graveside and lighting the joss paper, she suddenly toppled forward, her soft sobs evolving into something much more anguished. To see Sunny, usually the epitome of composure and poise, weeping and clawing at the loose dirt beside the grave, broke Franz's heart. She hadn't shed another tear since the funeral, but sadness cloaked her like a cape.

The ringing school bell pulled Franz out of the memory. Students streamed out of the decrepit building, which still looked to him more like an old warehouse than a school. He spotted Freddy's tall figure among the pack of students and assumed that the girl with him was Hannah, but as soon as Franz glimpsed her dark hair, he realized that she wasn't his daughter. Freddy caught his eye and flashed him an awkward grin before veering off in the opposite direction.

Hannah emerged a minute or two later. Herschel Zunder stuck close by her side, but her gaze was fixed on the ground. "Hannah," Franz called to her.

She turned to Herschel and spoke to him briefly. The boy nodded before walking off.

"What are you doing here, Papa?" Hannah asked as soon as she reached him.

Franz hugged her, but she was stiff in his arms. "Do I need a reason? I used to walk you home all the time."

"I'm not a child anymore."

Franz might have teased her about her age but, reading her

fragile mood, he held his tongue. "I saw Freddy leaving a little earlier," he said.

Hannah only shrugged.

"Is something the matter between you two?"

"We are fine." She turned and began to walk.

Not that long ago, Franz would hold hands with Hannah on their way home. She would talk non-stop, sharing news from class: quizzes she had excelled on, plays she planned to audition for and new friends she had made or, occasionally, lost. But now she kept her distance from him and didn't say a word, forcing Franz to fill the void with small talk.

Once they reached Ward Road, Franz finally stopped and turned to her. "Listen, Hannah-*chen*, nothing is decided."

"Decided?"

"About Palestine. We don't know when Shanghai will be liberated. And once it has been, we don't know when or even if we will be able to leave."

Hannah only nodded, her eyes as despondent as ever.

"It hurts me to see you so unhappy." He cleared his throat. "I would never do anything to make you suffer. I want only the best for you, Hannah. You must know this."

"I do, Papa," she said quietly.

"When you were a very small child, I took such comfort in knowing we lived in the most enlightened and peaceful city in the world. That you would always be safe. But surely, if this terrible war has shown us nothing else, it has shown that we Jews will never be safe outside our own homeland." He paused, waiting for her response, but none came. "Believe me, *Liebchen*, I am not so keen on moving to a strange land in the Middle East that might be even hotter than Shanghai. But you were the one who used to tell me how badly they would need people like us—doctors, students, families and so on—to build this new country."

"I know."

Franz hung his head, his chest heavy. "Hannah, I will not force you to go. And we will never leave here without you. So, when and if the time comes, if you still feel—"

"I want to go, Papa," she said nonchalantly.

Franz couldn't hide his surprise. "You want to go?" he echoed.

"Yes. I want our family to move to Palestine."

"But . . . but Esther said that you were so upset."

Hannah sniffled. "It's not that." Her voice cracked.

Franz slid an arm around her shoulders. "What has happened, Hannah-*chen*?"

"It's Freddy." She buried her face in his chest.

Franz couldn't believe his own obtuseness. Even after seeing the boy on the steps with another girl, he hadn't put it together until now. "He has hurt you? *Again?*"

She just nodded into his chest and continued to weep quietly.

Franz rocked Hannah in his arms, listening to her sobs. His heart ached for her while his thoughts turned dark. *Never again will I allow that boy anywhere near you. Never.*

* * *

An hour later, Franz was back on the hospital ward. As he reset a cast on the arm of an elderly Hasidic Jew, his mind was miles away, fuming over Freddy.

"Don't you look official, Herr Professor Doktor," a voice said from somewhere behind him.

Franz turned to see Ernst, cigarette dangling from his lips and pet monkey straddling the back of his neck.

"Sir, the monkey," Miriam called frantically to him from across the ward.

"Is doing fine, Nurse," Ernst said. "However, we both thank you for your concern."

"No, sir, it's . . . it's not proper. The germs . . ."

"Kaiser Wilhelm has a strong constitution," Ernst said. "I am quite certain he will not catch anything here."

Franz stifled a laugh as he stripped off his gloves. He hurried over to Ernst and guided him off the ward and away from the flustered nurse.

They sat together at the table inside the staff room while Kaiser Wilhelm scurried about and climbed the furniture as though looking for something he had lost. "What brings you to the hospital?" Franz asked.

"People are disappearing from Germantown right, left and centre," Ernst said.

"Which people?"

"Your friend, the baron, to begin with."

"He's gone?"

"Yes, along with Major Huber and several others. Gerhard tells me they're trying to reach South America. To catch a boat to Argentina, of all places."

"I hope his ship sinks." Franz snorted.

"I will not miss the arrogant sod." Ernst blew out a stream of smoke. "I will, however, miss Simon. Well, eventually, anyway. Right now I am appreciating the blissful quiet."

"What does that mean, 'miss Simon'?" Franz sat up straighter. "Where did he go?"

Ernst crinkled his nose. "You must have seen him by now, surely?"

"Where would I see him?" Franz asked, on edge again. "You know I'm not allowed to leave the ghetto."

Ernst grimaced. "But Simon is *here*. In the ghetto."

"Since when?"

"Yesterday. When he left the flat."

"Unless he's already been arrested," Franz breathed. "I told you it would be foolish for him to try to leave."

"You think I encouraged this?" Ernst groaned. "I've spent most of the past year trying to talk him out of it."

Franz thought of the torturous week he and Simon had spent in the basement of Bridge House. *Oh, Simon, what have you done?*

* * *

Franz sidled down the narrow corridor to Ghoya's office, bypassing the long queue of dejected refugees and hearing only a few half-hearted protests as he cut in line.

Ghoya sat behind his desk lecturing the middle-aged woman who stood in front of him. Spotting Franz at the door, he broke into a smirk. "Ah, Dr. Adler," he said as though he had been expecting him. He turned back to the woman and dispatched her with a flick of his wrist. "Not today, Frau Silberstein. No pass for you. Go, go."

The woman shot Franz a scornful glance as she trudged past him.

Franz bowed deeply. “Thank you for seeing me, Mr. Ghoya.”

“It has been too long, Dr. Adler.” Ghoya placed his hands behind his head and leaned back in his seat. His amused smile suggested that he was in a good mood, but Franz knew how quickly that could change. “How is the family? Your disobedient daughter? Your charming wife? They are all well?”

Ghoya’s friendliness only compounded Franz’s unease. “Yes, thank you, sir.”

“Ah, good, yes. Tell me, Dr. Adler. You must have heard the rumours?”

“Which rumours, sir?”

“The barges!” Ghoya pulled his hands from his head and leaned forward in his chair. “The burning barges. It’s almost all you Jews are talking about these days.”

“I did hear some talk, yes.”

“Is this why you have burst into my office?” Ghoya demanded. “To find out if they are true?”

Franz carefully considered his response. He had come about Simon, not about the rumours, but he was acutely aware of the risk he was running. If Simon had not been arrested, the last thing he wanted was to tip off Ghoya to his friend’s presence in the ghetto. “Are they true, Mr. Ghoya?”

“You Jews, you worry so.” Ghoya clasped his hands together theatrically. “Worrying and fussing all the time like a bunch of old women. Yes, yes. Just like a bunch of gossiping old women.”

Franz forced a laugh. “We are a race of worriers, it is true. But this rumour is significant.”

Ghoya’s face puckered into an ugly frown. “This is war,

Dr. Adler. Who knows what to believe anymore?" he said, echoing what von Puttkamer had said to Franz.

"Yet you are the King of the Jews, sir," Franz gently probed.

"Yes, yes, I am. So what?"

"Surely, if anyone were to know, it would be you."

Ghoya stared up at the ceiling with a rare expression of introspection. "What is a king without his kingdom?"

"Are you saying that there are no plans—"

Ghoya hopped to his feet and cut Franz off with a wild wave of his arm. "There are those who say that the Imperial Army will lose this war. And soon too. Do you think this is possible, Dr. Adler?"

"I . . . I . . ." Franz stuttered, afraid there could be no right answer.

"Rumours, rumours, rumours." Ghoya cried, pointing at Franz as though he were personally responsible for all of them. "We are drowning in them."

"It seems so."

"We will never lose this war!" Ghoya answered his own question. "Our will is too strong. Our honour too great. The Emperor himself says that defeat is not an option."

"No."

Ghoya dropped his arms to his side and his tone calmed. "Shanghai . . . Shanghai is a different beast," he conceded. "As in Burma and the Philippines, our Imperial Army might have to withdraw. Yes, yes. A strategic withdrawal is very possible here."

Franz wondered hopefully if Ghoya might be sharing official military plans but quickly dismissed it as more likely just the musings of the man's erratic mind.

"I will stay here, regardless," Ghoya continued. "Yes, yes, I will stay with my people."

"Even if the army withdraws?"

Ghoya held out his open palms. "What kind of king abandons his people?"

Franz struggled to keep the disbelief from his face. "Very brave, sir."

"You understand, Dr. Adler?" Ghoya continued. "Honour above all else. My people, they will admire me for it."

Your people will lynch you for it, Franz thought. But he decided to try to capitalize on Ghoya's magnanimous mood. "As you say, sir, Shanghai is awash in rumours of late. I have heard another interesting one just today."

"More rumours?" Ghoya cackled. "You Jews. Nothing but a bunch of gossiping old women."

"Very true, yes." Franz feigned a chuckle. "I heard the military police might have apprehended a Jew who slipped into the ghetto."

"What did you just say?" Ghoya's eyes darkened and he took a step closer.

Franz silently cursed himself. Not only had the Japanese probably already arrested Simon, but he might have just made himself appear guilty by association.

"*The ghetto?*" Ghoya said in a shrill voice. "Is that what you called it?"

"Pardon me, sir. I meant to say the Designated Area. I am terribly sorry." Franz bowed his head while keeping one eye on Ghoya in case he was preparing to strike him.

But Ghoya had already moved on. "Jews sneaking *into* the Designated Area? Nonsense. Absolute nonsense. Would a mouse sneak into a mousetrap?"

CHAPTER 46

Joey was more than content to absorb the bustle around him from inside his pram, but Esther had to keep a tight hold on Jakob's hand. Any time he got free, he would disappear among the throngs of people milling along Tong Shan Road. The last time Jakob had escaped, it had taken Sunny and Esther fifteen panicky minutes to locate him. They found him only when Sunny overheard his distinctive giggle drifting out of the back of a Chinese teashop, where he sat on the old proprietor's lap, sharing her dumpling.

"I was a curious child like you, Jakob," Sunny said to the oblivious boy. "And Jia-Li was worse than me. There was no end to the trouble we would get ourselves into in our neighbourhood."

Esther reached out and touched the back of Sunny's hand. "You must miss her so."

Now Sunny wished she hadn't mentioned her friend. Discussing Jia-Li again now would only dredge up more memories and sink Sunny right back into the depth of her grief. "I do miss her. Terribly. I miss them all. Yang, Charlie, Joey and, of course, my father. Still, I'm luckier than most." She forced a smile. "I have my husband, my son and Hannah. And you and Jakob, of course. My family."

"Family, yes. We are fortunate that way, aren't we?" Esther matched her smile, but there was a touch of melancholy in her tone. She and Simon had been separated for so long.

"Speaking of family," Sunny said, "Franz is planning to talk to Hannah today."

"I hope he has more success than I've had." Esther shook her head. "I am worried about her."

"She's not herself, is she? Perhaps something happened with Freddy?" Sunny suggested. "He hasn't come around in a long time. And Hannah never mentions him anymore."

"That boy . . ." Esther sighed. "We have a saying in Yiddish. *A volf farlit zayne hor, ober nit zayn natur*."

"A wolf and its hair . . ." Sunny tried unsuccessfully to translate.

"A wolf can lose its hair, but not change its nature."

"Like the English expression: A leopard can't change its spots."

"Precisely," Esther said. "But who can know what is going on inside the girl's head? I wish she would just tell us what—"

Sunny heard a rumble and felt the telltale vibrations under her feet. She held up her hand to silence Esther. "Do you hear it, Essie?"

Esther studied the clear blue sky, but there was nothing to see. After a moment, she nodded. "The planes."

Sunny grabbed Esther's free arm. "Hurry! Around the corner. The shelter."

Over a howl of protest from Jakob, Esther swept her child up in her arms and jogged ahead. Sunny shoved the pram's stiff wheels forward, weaving through the crowd on the sidewalk, which was indifferent to the approaching planes. It wasn't until they reached the shallow bomb shelter—dug out of the side of the road and reinforced with haphazard piles of sandbags—that the air-raid sirens finally began to sound. Jakob squealed with delight at the cacophony. He pointed up at the bombers and fighter planes in formation overhead. "Big planes, Mama! Big planes!"

Only a handful of others joined them in the pit, which was a mere six or seven feet below ground level and no more spacious than the inside of a trolley bus. The local Chinese rarely bothered to use the shelters. From where Sunny crouched, she could see the legs and feet of pedestrians on the exposed sidewalk, watching the planes as though they were just aerial entertainment. Distant blasts thundered and echoed as bombs detonated somewhere outside the city. Sunny wondered if the bombers were again targeting the oil refineries in Pootung, on the other side of the river.

"They continue to spare the city," Esther pointed out as the booms quieted.

"So far," Sunny agreed. Almost everyone in the ghetto, including her own family, assumed that the Allied bombers were friendly and would never pose a threat to the refugees. But Sunny was still mindful of Father Diego's warning that the transmitter in Hongkew would eventually become a target.

They waited another few minutes until the planes had passed and their engines had completely died away before climbing out of the shelter and heading back to the street market. Sunny had wanted to shop for food with Esther, as she was increasingly worried about the lack of produce in her son's diet. Lately, Joey had been living almost off rice alone. But as they moved from stall to stall, she was horrified at the outrageous prices of fruit and vegetables.

Esther was examining blackened bananas at a grocer's stall when Jakob yelled, "Papa! Papa! Papa!" He pulled free of Esther and darted into the crowd.

"Jakob, wait!" Esther dropped the fruit and dashed forward, shouldering her way through the swarm of people.

Sunny steered the pram after Esther. As soon as she had passed the fruit stall, she spotted Jakob. The boy had jumped into a man's arms and was straddling his chest, obscuring the man's face.

"Simon?" Sunny ventured.

It was him. "Sunny!" he cried.

Esther by this time had doubled back, and upon seeing Simon, she slapped a hand to her mouth. "It can't be," she whispered, stumbling back a step. "*Mein Gott!*"

"Oh, gorgeous, you have no idea." Simon lowered Jakob and rushed over to her. Throwing his arms around her, he spun her in a full circle before putting her down. He took her head in his hands and kissed her face repeatedly.

Esther was still in shock. "How is this possible?"

Before Simon could explain, Sunny grabbed him by the arm and jerked him away. "*Not here,*" she insisted, aware of how exposed they were in the market. She shepherded them all down a nearby laneway.

Sunny had never seen Simon looking thinner or more haggard, but something else had changed about him. Then it dawned on her: the spark in his eyes was back. "Two years, Essie," he cried. "I couldn't keep away from you any longer. Another day and I swear I would've gone completely bonkers."

Esther sniffled. "Darling, the Japanese . . ."

Simon laughed. "They don't care. I waltzed right past the soldiers at the ghetto checkpoint."

Esther stroked the stubble on his bony cheek. "Are you certain, my darling? How can you be sure no one noticed?"

"I could have been waving the Stars and Stripes and whistling

'Dixie' and they wouldn't have looked twice at me." He howled with laughter, sounding for the first time in ages like the gleeful Simon of old. "What kind of maniac would sneak *into* the ghetto? Why didn't I think of that two years ago?"

Sunny didn't share his relief. "What about Ghoya and his men? They raid our flat routinely."

"Ghoya has no idea who I am. And besides, I won't be staying with you, anyway. I would never put you and Jake at such risk."

"You are not leaving?" Esther murmured as she clasped his face in her hands.

"Never again." He kissed her. "I'll stay right here in the ghetto. Just not with you."

"Where will you stay, then?"

"You remember the Lessners? Otto and Hedwig?"

Esther stared at him blankly.

"They arrived late in '39," he continued. "A funny old couple from Munich. No kids. Penniless. We set them up in the heim for a few months. I found Otto a job repairing typewriters. You must remember, Essie."

"I think so." Esther frowned. "There were so many you helped in those days, darling. I can't keep them all straight."

"The Lessners found their own flat in Hongkew. They set up in the ghetto long before there even was a ghetto."

Esther clapped her hands. "*Ach*, the Lessners. They are the ones who used to finish each other's sentences."

"That's them." Simon chuckled. "They always gave me way too much credit for helping them out of their jam. Told me they could never repay me. Well, soon as I got here, I headed straight over there and put their words to the test."

"And?" Esther asked.

"Poor Hedwig died last year from a stroke. But Otto welcomed me with open arms. I think he's pretty lonely without her. He says I can stay as long as I want to."

Esther cried with delight as she leaned forward to kiss Simon again. "Perhaps you can finish his sentences."

"So long as he allows me to be near you, I will start and finish every one of them. He'll never have to open his mouth again." His voice cracked. "Oh, baby, I can't believe I'm home."

CHAPTER 47

July 17, 1945

Ernst and Franz walked down Ward Road along with scores of other pedestrians. "Next time I flee a country, I will choose somewhere more hospitable—like perhaps the Congo," Ernst grumbled as he fanned himself with a rolled-up newspaper.

Franz wiped the sweat from his brow for the second time in less than a minute. The summer had been hotter and muggier than any of the previous five he had spent in Shanghai. The nights were even more unbearable. Even with fans and wet towels, sleep was nearly impossible.

Ernst motioned to the monkey perched on his shoulder. "Even Kaiser Wilhelm—who is from the tropics—has had enough of this weather."

But the monkey looked contented enough as he held onto Ernst's neck while busily grooming himself. Other animals hadn't fared as well through the recent heat wave. Every morning, the carcasses of dogs, cats and rodents could be seen scattered up and down the alleyways. More corpses—human, this time—lined the sidewalks. Most were coolies who had expired from heat stroke, but not all were adults. Franz was always sad to see the abandoned wicker baskets and burlaps sacks containing dead children who could have been Joey's age or even younger.

Ernst adjusted the pack he was carrying. The legs of an easel poked out the top. "You're finally ready to paint again, are you?" Franz asked.

Ernst shrugged. "I finally have some peace and quiet, with Simon gone."

Franz chuckled. "You miss him, though, don't you?"

"Absolutely. The same way I might miss a kidney stone."

"I don't believe it."

"Well, I suppose he was better company than the Communists in the village where I was forced to stay that one year. Of course, even the most rabid Marxist among them paled in their passion compared with Simon and his baseball." Ernst reached up and stroked the monkey's chest. "How is he coping?"

"Well. Very well." Franz nodded. "He's put on a little weight. Sunny says he's a new man since being reunited with Esther and Jakob."

"Is he still living with that old widower?"

"Herr Lessner, yes. He sees Esther and Jakob every day, but they never meet at our flat. They're careful."

Ernst nodded approvingly. "Essie deserves a little happiness."

Franz thought the same was true of Ernst. "Tell me, how is your friend Gerhard doing?"

"Nervous." Ernst sighed. "With von Puttkamer and the others making for South America, Gerhard is worried he'll be blamed once the Allies take the city."

"If necessary, we will vouch for him," Franz reassured.

"You would do that?" Ernst asked incredulously.

"Of course. For you, not him."

"Thank you." An awkward silence followed, broken by Ernst. "How are my girls coping?"

"Better. It's been a very trying few months for both Hannah and Sunny."

"Trust me, I've known my share of Freddies." Ernst snorted in disgust. "It always ends the same way with them. Hannah is far better off without him."

"You don't need to convince me of that."

"As for Jia-Li . . ." Ernst exhaled heavily. "She was special, that one. My heart goes out to Sunny."

Not wanting to dwell on his wife's pain or his daughter's heartache, he asked instead, "So tell me, Ernst. Why the hospital?"

"Why have I chosen to paint there?"

"Yes."

"The pathos. The vulnerability. It's perfect, really."

"I suppose so."

Ernst grimaced. "You suppose? Tell me, where could you possibly find more anguish?"

"You do realize you must get the patients' consent before you paint anywhere near them," Franz cautioned. "Many of them will prefer to just be left alone."

"Yes, yes, naturally," Ernst said with little concern.

"And it is still a hospital. You cannot bother anyone else while you are working there."

Ernst scoffed. "An artist who influences his setting is nothing more than a fraud."

"Regardless, Ernst—I know you."

The monkey started to hop up and down on Ernst's shoulder. He hooted and cried, in obvious agitation. Ernst reached up to stroke the animal's chest again. "It's all right, Wilhelm.

It's just the planes. They come every day. Papa won't let them harm you."

Franz looked up. The skies were clear. A few more seconds passed before he became aware of the soft vibration under his feet. Then he faintly detected the distant rumble. "Come," he said. "We'd better find shelter."

"Shelter from what?" Ernst asked. "The heat?"

"The planes."

"The planes?" Ernst laughed. "They come every day. What threat are they to us?"

"I promised Sunny," Franz muttered.

"You go ahead and find shelter. Wilhelm and I are going to find a drink somewhere."

"All right. I'll see you later at the hospital," said Franz.

The hum of the planes intensified. The volume suggested that they had to be flying lower than usual. Suddenly, a whistling noise pierced the roar. Franz glanced up and saw dark objects falling from the underbellies of several of the bombers. In moments, explosions boomed and violently shook the ground at his feet. A series of other denotations followed. Franz spotted fire and smoke only a few blocks away. "The ghetto, Ernst," he cried. "They're bombing the ghetto."

Franz raced over and grabbed the stunned artist by the arm. Frantic, the monkey leapt onto Franz's back and bit him on the shoulder. He shook the animal off without letting go of Ernst or slowing his pace.

They ran for the Ward Road shelter, a block over, the pavement beneath them undulating constantly from the aftershocks of the man-made earthquakes. Explosions seemed to be detonating everywhere at once. The taste and smell of smoke filled Franz's mouth and nostrils. He kept checking over his shoulder in the direction of his apartment. He didn't see any smoke rising from there, but he was still desperate with worry. "Please, God, please," he mumbled under his breath.

By the time they reached the shelter, refugees and Chinese were streaming into the cramped space from every direction. Those inside cried in protest as more and more people squeezed themselves into the already full space. Franz didn't even bother trying to get inside. Instead, he scanned the nearby buildings and chose the one with the sturdiest-looking entrance archway. A number of Chinese men and women stood clustered beneath it. Franz took a step toward it, but Ernst seemed stuck on the sidewalk, his expression dazed. "Kaiser Wilhelm," he cried. "Wilhelm! Where are you?"

Franz flashed back to the sight of Helen dashing along the pathway at the field hospital as the planes chased her down. He roughly shoved Ernst toward the protection of the archway. "The monkey will be fine. We need to get under cover. *Now.*"

They tucked themselves into the corner of the entryway. The noise was deafening: the relentless roar of the bombers, the terrifying whistling of the falling munitions and the intermittent booms of explosions near and far. The nervous chatter in Chinese beside them never let up. Franz's breath caught in his throat each time he heard the rumbling of a detonating bomb, followed, all too often, by the bone-chilling whoosh of a building collapsing. He couldn't help but imagine his own flat imploding, his family trapped inside.

The bombers came in wave after wave, undeterred by the screaming air-raid sirens and the ineffective Japanese anti-aircraft fire. A few anemic squadrons of Zeroes zipped out to defend the attack but, as best Franz could tell, none even reached the bombers before being knocked out of the sky by the American fighter planes.

Franz was watching one such lopsided dogfight when Ernst tapped him on the shoulder. Eyes wide, the artist pointed in the direction of the Adlers' apartment. Franz's gaze followed. The moment he saw the plume of rising smoke, he jostled free of the people around him and sprinted for home.

CHAPTER 48

As usual, the rumble reminded Sunny of Father Diego's warning. But for the past two months, the American planes had passed overhead almost daily without posing any threat to the ghetto and, gradually, Sunny's sense of urgency about the aircraft had receded. However, as the low-pitched sounds grew louder, she dutifully changed Joey's diaper and packed a bottle of water for him, conscious of how stifling hot it would be inside the shelter.

Esther and Jakob had gone off to visit Simon, but Hannah was still in the loft. How the girl coped in the furnace-like heat up there was a mystery to Sunny. "Hannah, the planes," she called to her. "We have to go."

"You and Joey go ahead," Hannah replied. "I have to change. I'll meet you there."

"You will come soon?"

"In a few minutes. I promise."

"All right. Don't dawdle, please."

Sunny lifted Joey off the floor. He offered her one of his placid smiles and reached for her face, gently exploring her cheek with his fingers, as he liked to do. She felt the familiar stirrings in her chest and kissed him on the forehead, wondering again how her world had ever existed without him in it.

Supporting Joey on her hip, she headed out the door. On the street, she had the odd sense of an approaching storm. Looking up, she noticed the dense formation of aircraft heading straight toward the city. She had never seen as many planes together or heard such a thundering. She assumed the Allies must have a major target in mind, and she silently wished them success in their mission.

As she made her way toward the shelter, she heard an unfamiliar whistling. Then she heard three booms somewhere behind her. *The transmitter!* she thought as the ground shifted beneath her feet and Joey cried out in surprise.

Sunny wheeled around and rushed back toward the flat, Joey in her arms. She burst through the door. "Hannah, come! *Now.*"

Hannah had already come down from the loft and was dashing, wide-eyed, toward her. Without another word, they raced out the door and down the block toward the shelter. Bombers and fighter planes filled the skies like a mass of hungry crows. Bombs were falling everywhere, the din deafening.

The shelter was already teeming with locals, but Sunny elbowed her way through a group of Chinese women and found a spot against the wall for the three of them. There must have been at least fifty people in the confined space, Sunny thought. It reeked of bodies and cooking oil, and the fear was palpable. Several children were whimpering; even a few adults were crying. One old Chinese woman was muttering hysterically over and over in Shanghainese, "Today we meet our ancestors."

Sunny glanced over to Hannah who, despite being pale with fear, looked composed. "Where is Papa?" she asked.

"He was meeting Ernst at the hospital."

"What if . . ."

"Don't even think it, Hannah. He promised me he would seek shelter at the first sign of the planes," Sunny said, trying to convince herself as well as her stepdaughter.

Hannah lapsed into silence. Sunny rocked Joey back and forth while humming a Chinese lullaby in his ear. After a few minutes, she heard a voice tentatively calling, "Hannah? Are you here, Hannah?"

Hannah straightened, almost bumping her head on the low roof of the shelter. "Herschel, is that you?"

Herschel squeezed into view between the others. "What are you doing here?" Hannah demanded.

His face reddened. "I was not far away when the bombing began and . . ."

"You decided to check on Hannah," Sunny said.

"Yes . . . no . . . I didn't know of any other shelters near me," he stuttered.

Hannah squeezed his shoulder and smiled. "Thank you."

The blasts intensified and the shelter shook with each new detonation. Sunny tucked Joey under one arm and cradled his head with the other. The woman beside her began to wail in distress. A few others yelled at her to shut up.

Three ear-splitting booms rocked the shelter in rapid succession. The force of the blasts propelled Hannah into Sunny. More cries and sobs filled the shelter, silenced only by the thunderous whoosh that came next. Sunny realized that one of the nearby apartment buildings must have collapsed, but she could not tell which one.

"There's a fire, Sunny!" Hannah said, her eyes filling with fear.

Smoke drifted into the shelter. Through the crack in the sandbags, Sunny saw flames.

"What if the shelter catches fire?" Hannah asked.

"It can't," Herschel reassured her before turning to Sunny for confirmation. "Can it?"

"No." Sunny shook her head confidently without actually knowing the answer.

More explosions shook the ground but, from the diminished volume of the blasts, Sunny could tell that the bombing had moved a few blocks away. The smoke, however, continued to thicken. The air tasted acrid. Sunny fanned the fumes away from Joey's face, concerned he could asphyxiate inside the poorly vented shelter. People began to cough. Several climbed out of the shelter. Sunny decided that she needed to get Joey into the open air too, despite the risk. "Stay here," she instructed Hannah and Herschel. As she shouldered her way toward the steps, she heard Franz's frantic voice. *"Sunny? Hannah? Are you down there?"*

"Yes, here, Franz," Sunny cried, overcome with relief.

Franz jumped down into the pit. He swallowed Sunny and Joey in a tight embrace. "Where's Hannah?" he demanded.

"Here too. With Herschel. He came to find her."

"Oh, thank God. Thank God." Franz closed his eyes and looked up. "And Esther and Jakob?"

"They went over to see Simon earlier."

"Oh, thank God," he repeated.

"What is it, Franz?"

"Our apartment—it's gone."

* * *

The smoke cleared, but they were forced to huddle underground for another taut half hour before the explosions finally petered out and it was safe to leave the shelter.

Sunny's legs felt rubbery as she stared at the pile of rubble where, an hour before, her home had been. The sight was surreal. The buildings on either side of theirs stood undamaged, but their apartment must have taken a direct hit. Sunny thought, with sudden concern, of the quiet old Chinese couple who lived in the flat next door. She gagged at the thought of how close she and Hannah had come to being crushed under their own roof.

Franz draped an arm over her shoulder. "Unlike families, new apartments are not difficult to find."

Sunny swallowed. "I suppose, yes."

Franz pointed up the street. One dazed man stumbled along, clutching his lacerated head as blood dripped between his fingers. Another was tying his shirt around his own thigh in an effort to stop the bleeding below. "The victims," he said. "They will need us at the hospital."

"If there still is a hospital."

"We must go find out."

"And if the bombers come back?"

Franz glanced up at the sky. It was clear of everything besides a few puffs of cloud. "What could be left for them to bomb?"

Sunny nodded. "All right. But first let's check on Essie and Simon."

"Yes, good idea."

Hannah went off with Herschel to find his grandparents, promising to meet Franz and Sunny at the hospital in an hour—sooner if the bombers returned.

Franz carried Joey in his arms. As they walked the half mile to

Herr Lessner's flat, Sunny was surprised to see how random the bomb damage was. One block was entirely spared. On another, every building on one side of the street had partially or fully collapsed. People wandered up and down what was left of the sidewalk, calling out for loved ones. Others lay on the pavement. Some writhed and moaned from the pain of new injuries. Several were still and lifeless. Sunny hated the sense of helplessness, her inability to offer any measure of comfort to the victims. What good were all her training and experience when she couldn't assist in the time of greatest need?

Her nerves were raw as they reached the block where Simon was staying. The street had been hit hard, the building on the corner partially collapsed. Still holding Joey, Franz ran ahead. He stopped halfway down the street, his shoulders slumped and his chin falling to his chest.

Sunny raced to catch up to him. She gasped when she caught sight of the Lessners' building. Only half of it was standing, and the roof on the far side had caved in.

Franz handed Joey over to her and headed for the building. "Where are you going, Franz?" Sunny demanded.

"I have to go find Simon."

"It's not safe," she cried. "The rest of the roof could collapse at any moment."

"I must, darling."

Sunny heard a cry and recognized Esther's voice. She looked over her shoulder and saw her sister-in-law on the other side of the street. Clutching Jakob's hand, Esther dodged across the roadway, waving frantically and calling out in German for help.

"Essie!" Sunny shouted to her.

Spotting Sunny and Franz, Esther rushed toward them. "Simon is inside," she cried. "We must get him out!"

Franz nodded hopelessly. “I will go see, Essie.”

“I will too,” Sunny said.

“No,” Franz said.

But Sunny didn’t even respond. Instead, she passed Joey to Esther, who took him in her arms without looking down. “I begged him not to go back inside,” Esther mumbled, sounding stunned. “He insisted. He said he had to help Herr Lessner. Then the roof just . . .”

Sunny and Franz warily approached the entrance to the building. They listened intently, as much for the sound of the walls or the roof creaking as for signs of life.

“Simon?” Franz called. “Are you in there?”

Nothing.

“Simon? Can you hear me? Say something!”

After a moment, Sunny heard a muffled voice. She listened carefully and made out the words “I can’t move.”

“I’m coming, Simon,” Franz called. With a quick glance over his shoulder, he added, “Wait here, Sunny,” then disappeared inside the building.

She was tempted to follow him, but she restrained herself for a tense minute or two until Franz called to her. “All right, I think it’s safe.”

Sunny stepped into the Lessners’ flat. The floor was strewn with broken dishes, overturned furniture and fallen pictures. Franz was next to a wall that had partially given way. “Where are you, Simon?” he called.

“Here,” Simon’s voice was louder and came from the next room. “I can’t move.”

Franz turned sideways and manoeuvered through a small opening in the damaged wall. “I’m coming, Simon.”

Sunny took a deep breath and followed her husband through the gap. On the other side, the ceiling had partially collapsed and she had to crouch to her knees. Heart pounding in her throat, Sunny felt claustrophobic, as if she had just crawled into a narrow cave. She navigated around chunks of roof and wall before she spotted Simon. He was lying on his back, his arms and chest free but covered from the waist down by a heavy oak chest of drawers.

Franz crawled over to him. His fingers darted to Simon's neck, feeling for the pulse.

"I'm still alive, Franz." Simon sputtered a laugh. "I just can't move my legs."

"Are you in much pain?" Franz asked.

"No. None."

Franz nodded gravely. "We will get this off you."

Franz pushed hard at the dresser, struggling to move it. Sunny crawled up beside him and shoved too. The dresser hardly budged. She was shocked by its weight. Finally, with both of them grunting and heaving, they were able to shift it aside. It fell free of Simon's legs with a loud clunk.

Sunny winced as she glimpsed Simon's right ankle, grotesquely twisted and obviously broken. "Simon, your foot," she whispered.

Simon grabbed her by the wrist. "It doesn't hurt at all, Sunny," he said, his voice fearful. Her stomach sank even before he added the words "I can't feel my legs."

CHAPTER 49

Although the refugee hospital had been spared from the bombs, nothing Franz had seen in his time at the front prepared him for the pandemonium that greeted them there. People were lined up out on the street, refugees and locals jostling for space and yelling for attention.

"My arm is broken," one man cried.

"My grandmother has terrible pain in her chest," shouted another.

Some of the wounded were too weak to stand and had to kneel or lie beside their relatives.

Franz tried to elbow his way through the crowd, but a few men angrily blocked his path. "I am a doctor here," he shouted over the din. "I need to pass now."

One of the two young Chinese men who had agreed to help carry Simon in—after Esther offered them her mother's watch—translated his words into Chinese. Finally, the reluctant crowd parted so that they could all snake their way into the hospital, carrying Simon on the blown-out door that passed for a stretcher.

The scene inside was even more chaotic. Injured people were everywhere, filling every stretcher and covering almost all of the floor space. Berta and the other nurses were a blur of activity, darting from patient to patient, slapping on dressings and administering shots of painkiller. Two older doctors—one of them the psychiatrist, Dr. Freiberg—looked lost as they tended to wounds that neither had likely seen since their days in medical school.

"Berta," Franz called to the head nurse, "we need to find a space for this man. Urgently."

Berta turned to Franz with an incredulous expression, as though he had just asked her to find him the Holy Grail. She raised her shoulders and shook her head helplessly.

"Please, please, you must," Esther begged. She was ghostly pale as she stood beside her husband's stretcher, gripping his hand fiercely.

"It's Simon, Berta. Simon Lehrer," Franz added, aware that the New Yorker had found housing for Berta's family when they had first arrived in Shanghai.

"*Ja*, of course," Berta said, spinning away. "I will find somewhere."

Franz looked down at his friend. "How are you?"

"I'm okay." Simon raised a thumb. "I am luckier than most, certainly luckier than Herr Lessner."

No one had found Lessner's body in the rubble. It wasn't possible he had survived, and no one had time to take more than a cursory look. They were far too concerned with extracting Simon before the rest of the ceiling caved in on them. Franz had reset Simon's dislocated ankle and used the sleeve of his shirt to splint it to the other foot. Esther had commented on how stoic her husband had been, but Franz and Sunny just shared a look, acknowledging that Simon's lack of discomfort during what should have been an agonizing procedure was an ominous sign. Franz could see that Simon too understood the gravity of his spinal injury, but he had remained upbeat during the journey to hospital, even joking that he needed to find a lighter chest of drawers for their new flat.

Berta waved them over to a bed she had freed up in the far corner of the room. Once Simon had been moved onto it, he looked up at Franz. "No offence, buddy, but I'd rather stare into my wife's beautiful eyes than yours. Go. Go help the others."

Esther grabbed Franz's wrist with her free hand, her fingers trembling with worry. "His back, Franz," she implored. "You must do something to fix it."

Franz summoned the most encouraging look he could. "The fractures will heal on their own, Essie. Right now, what he needs is bed rest."

"But his legs—he can't move them."

"Time will tell, Essie."

Franz reluctantly turned away and wove among the patients on the floor until he reached the nursing station. The surrounding moans, cries and wails formed a cacophony of suffering. Franz's hopelessness only deepened. Shouldering his way between staff members and haphazard stacks of supplies, Franz pulled Berta aside. There was no privacy, so they spoke in hushed tones, their faces almost touching. "How are our supplies holding up?" he asked.

Berta shook her head gravely. "We will run out of morphine soon. And we are very low on dressings and catgut."

"And anesthetic?"

"We still have a full bottle of ether but . . ." She flapped a hand toward the masses of new patients. "We will never keep up."

"The bombing has ended," Franz pointed out.

"More people keep arriving." Berta sighed. "Soon, we will have nothing left to offer."

Franz knew she was right, but he mustered a brave face. "We can do only what we can do."

She cleared her throat. "Dr. Adler, if we were to just focus on our own people, then perhaps . . ."

"Are you suggesting we turn away the Chinese?"

Her shoulders straightened. "This is a hospital for refugees. Today, we cannot even cope with the number of them who need our help. Surely those other people must have a hospital of their own somewhere, or perhaps—"

"Enough," Franz snapped. "Remember Europe before the war? There were many—too many—who used to refer to us as 'those other people.' That's how it begins."

"Dr. Adler, you can hardly compare what I am saying to—"

"Of course not." Franz softened his tone. He had known the nurse long enough to appreciate that she wasn't in the least malicious, and no more racist than most of the refugees. "But we will treat people on the basis of their need and urgency. We will do what we can. It's what we must do. Do you understand, Berta?"

Her face reddening, Berta looked down and mumbled, "I do, Herr Doktor. I am sorry."

Franz stuck two fingers into his mouth and whistled loud enough to draw the attention of the nearby staff members. "We will set up a station outside," he shouted. "To triage victims. Only those who require surgery or absolutely immediate treatment will be brought inside. We'll tend to everyone else outside. We must ration the morphine and dressings. Only for those whose bleeding will not stop or . . ." He lowered his voice, embarrassed by his own words. "Or a single shot for those whose pain is beyond bearable."

Several nurses nodded, thankful for the direction.

Just then, Sunny appeared on the other side of the ward. "The boys?" Franz demanded as soon as he reached her.

"Are with Hannah and Herschel."

"Where?"

"At the synagogue," Sunny said. "The street there was untouched by the bombs. It's safe there."

Franz quickly updated her on the plan for triaging casualties and then asked, "Would you prefer to triage or to operate?"

"You perform the surgery, I will triage." She smiled sadly. "After all, my Mandarin and Shanghainese are still slightly more proficient than yours."

* * *

Franz didn't leave the operating room for the next twelve hours. He lost track of how many fractures he had reset and limbs he had amputated. He could only imagine the scores of casualties that Sunny must have turned away at the front door. He rationed every single item at his disposal, using the fewest possible number of stitches to close his incisions and applying dressings that were more appropriate for scrapes and bruises than for major surgery.

Just as he had expended their last inch of catgut, Sunny stepped into the operating room to announce that there were no more patients waiting for surgery. "Thank God," Franz muttered, feeling exhaustion overcome him like a drug. "How is everyone holding up?"

"I am so proud of them," she said. "The nurses were amazing. And Dr. Freiberg never slowed down. He just kept putting on casts and stitching cuts." She laughed. "From psychiatry to surgery at his age."

"How many did we lose?"

Sunny's expression turned grim. "I didn't even count. Many were already dead by the time they got to us. Others, they never stood a chance."

"No one died in the operating room," Franz pointed out. "Only because of your skill in selecting appropriate patients."

Sunny was impervious to his praise. "With more help and more supplies, we could have done so much more."

"And yet, if we weren't here at all . . ."

She nodded but appeared unconvinced. "Yes, I suppose it could have been worse."

"How is Simon doing?"

"I haven't had a chance to visit him," Sunny said. "Essie left an hour or two ago to check on Jakob and Joey. She told me he was sleeping."

"Let's go see him now."

Simon's eyes were open when they reached his bedside. He viewed them with unbridled admiration. "I've had nothing to do but watch all day. I can't believe the work you all do. It's miraculous."

Sunny squeezed his shoulder. "You built this hospital, Simon. Remember?"

"That was a thousand years ago. Besides, anyone can renovate an old building and call it a hospital. It takes what you two do to make it real."

"How are you?" Franz asked.

"A little thirsty. Don't suppose you serve cold beer here, do you?" Simon forced a laugh. "There's no pain. I can't feel anything from my waist down." He looked from Franz to Sunny, then back to Franz. "I guess I'd better get used to that."

Franz cleared his throat. "With spinal injuries, you can never tell in the first few days how much recovery one will make."

Simon eyed him knowingly. "I'm more concerned about how Essie will take this."

Sunny swallowed. "She's very strong, Simon."

"My little Austrian ox." Simon laughed wistfully. "I never expected to get out of this war unscathed, but I never guessed it would be my own countrymen who would collapse the roof in on me."

"You must give it a little time," Sunny encouraged.

"Believe me, I'll be the last one to give up on my legs." The smile seeped from his lips. "But I don't regret it."

"Regret what?" Sunny asked.

"Any of it. Leaving Ernst's place. Coming back to the ghetto. Even staying with Herr Lessner. I don't regret a single thing."

Confused, Franz glanced over to Sunny. She seemed to understand better than he did what Simon was saying. "You were incredibly brave going back for Herr Lessner," she said.

"I was just so tired of being a coward. Hiding when my family needed me most." He locked eyes with Sunny. "If I had to choose again, I would still trade my legs for my dignity."

CHAPTER 50

The synagogue was the closest thing to a home that Sunny and her family had left in the world. She was hopeful that would soon change, but for the past week they had slept, or at least tried to sleep, on the hard wooden benches inside the temple. During the daylight hours, when the American bombers filled the skies like unrelenting storm clouds, they had been forced to spend much of their time crowded in the overheated bomb shelters. Inevitably, people would pass out from heat stroke; a few never woke up.

The Americans had continued to bomb Shanghai, their planes paying special attention to the Hongkew district that housed the transmitter. Sunny was amazed to hear that it was still standing after the barrage. The ghetto itself had suffered less collateral damage since the initial assault, but the memory of that day still caused her waking nightmares. Over fifty refugees had died in the air raid, and although the death toll among the Chinese was unknown, it was reputed to be several thousand.

The Adlers were just one of many families who had lost their home in the bombing. But the community had rallied. Word of the humanitarian efforts at the hospital spread beyond the borders of the ghetto; sensationalized in the city's newspapers, it quickly became the stuff of Shanghai legend. Even Ghoya publicly acknowledged the hospital's staff and sent fresh medical supplies to help them cope with the casualties.

The refugees, from the community leaders to those living in the hostels, showered gratitude upon Franz and Sunny. After it became known that the Adlers' apartment had been destroyed in the bombing, a more spacious flat was made available—the older couple who had been living there having agreed to move in with their grown son. A group of young volunteers had already furnished and repainted the apartment, which was conveniently housed in the building directly across the street from the hospital.

But Sunny was most touched by the thanks from her own native Shanghainese. She had long ago realized that her people were insular, prioritizing family over community. However, the locals now couldn't express enough gratitude to the refugees for their help, which had extended beyond medical care to firefighting and even search-and-rescue work. Every day, dozens of Chinese would show up at the hospital, synagogue and heime with baskets full of fruit, vegetables, rice and meat. They also left blankets, woks and even impractical gifts such as ornamental fans and elaborate banners stencilled with calligraphy.

Sunny was sitting inside the synagogue, watching Joey stack wooden blocks on the floor, when the rabbi approached carrying a basket that overflowed with Chinese pastries. "I cannot believe such generosity." Hiltmann chuckled. "Before the bombing, you couldn't leave your garbage outside without it being stolen. Now, every day they leave anonymous gifts on our steps."

Sunny nodded. "It's incredible to think that something so devastating as the bombing could bring people together as it has."

The rabbi sat down beside her. "If there's one thing we Jews have learned over the past few thousand years, it's that nothing brings people closer than suffering."

"It shouldn't have to be that way."

"It is the way it is." Hiltmann watched Joey rise to his feet and take a few tentative steps toward a block that had rolled away. "He's a sweet *boychik*, that one, but very timid."

"I love his caution," she said. "After all, we live in such reckless times."

The rabbi jutted his lower lip. "Yet our people have learned a very hard lesson about being too cautious."

"He's just a baby, Rabbi."

"I suppose I can wait another year or two to pass judgment." He arched an eyebrow. "You will raise him Jewish, will you not?

"I imagine so, yes."

Hiltmann nodded approvingly. "I only hope that, when the time comes, you will consider joining us in Palestine."

"My husband is considering it."

He scratched his beard. "Not you, Sunny? You do not want to leave Shanghai because it is your home?"

Sunny considered the question. "Shanghai is the only home I've ever known, but I've already lost the people who meant the most to me. If my old amah, Yang, doesn't come home from the detention camp, then all I will have left here is my family." She chuckled. "My very Jewish family."

"So then what would stop you from coming to Palestine with us?"

She looked down at Joey, who was gently banging the blocks together. She wished he could remain like that forever: safe and happily oblivious to all the terrible turmoil in the world around him. "I am worried, Rabbi."

"For the boy?"

She nodded. "For all of us, really. Hannah, Franz, Esther, Simon, Jakob, and me too."

"You think it will be nothing but more war in Palestine?"

"Won't it?"

"I have no idea," Hiltmann admitted. "I do know that once we have established our homeland, it will be the safest and most blissful place in the world for any Jew to live."

"And if none of us lives to see that day, Rabbi?"

He tapped his chest. "I doubt this old man will live to see it, but that hardly matters. I believe we owe it to God and, perhaps more importantly, to ourselves to try." He frowned. "Besides, you do realize, Sunny, that once the Japanese are finally defeated, *be'ezrat hashem*—God willing—Shanghai will never be as it once was."

"It will be free again."

"Is that so? I hear that the Chinese in the countryside are already fighting among themselves. The national army, the Kuomintang . . ." he stumbled over the pronunciation. "Is that how you say it? Them and the Communists. It could be like the Russian Civil War all over again."

Sunny had heard these rumours too. "It is a concern," she conceded.

"The British are not going to come back here after the war. The world is changing. What if the fighting spreads to Shanghai?"

Sunny couldn't argue with him. She sensed the winds of unrest without knowing much about the infighting beyond the city. "Rabbi, we have choices other than just staying here or going to Palestine."

"America?"

"Or England or Canada."

"*If* any of those countries will even take you." Hiltmann shook his head. "You probably don't remember before the war. The Evian Conference? Nobody wanted Jewish refugees. 'One is too many' was the charming remark made by one Canadian official."

"It will be different now. The camps . . ."

"You think? Ah, to be young and optimistic again." Hiltmann rolled his eyes affectionately. "Even so. You, Franz, Hannah and Joey will always be outsiders, even in America. Especially you and Joey. Will that be so much better?"

"Look at me, Rabbi. I'm neither Chinese nor Caucasian. Now I live among Jews. I have been an outsider my whole life. I don't know what it's like to be anything else." She paused. "But as long as we can live safely and freely, I don't care where we go."

The rabbi smiled widely. "So in that case, why not be an outsider in Eretz Yisrael?"

"It has nothing to do with being an outsider, Rabbi. Or even where I want to live."

"What is it, then?"

"The children. After all they have been through." She shook her head. "We must do what is best for them."

CHAPTER 51

August 14, 1945

It's as if the Japanese had never been here," Hannah said with awe as she walked between her father and Herschel along the riverside Bund. Hannah hadn't seen the grand boulevard in over two years, but the last time she had, Japanese soldiers were everywhere, and the Rising Sun flapped from every flagpole and rooftop. But now, the soldiers had melted away overnight like snow into a river, and the Japanese flags had all been torn down, replaced in many cases with the Stars and Stripes. The Americans were ubiquitous in Shanghai now, but they couldn't have been more different from the previous occupiers. Infantrymen and Marines mingled gregariously among the crowds, shopping at street stalls, often stopping to offer cigarettes to adults and chocolates to the children. Their jeeps and transport trucks roared around the city, giving rides to Chinese youths and honking happily at pedestrians.

The mood on the street was jubilant. Civilians of all ethnicities gathered on the sidewalk and in the middle of roadways, laughing, dancing and hooting in celebration. Although it wasn't yet noon, Hannah noticed that a number of revellers were drunk to the point of staggering.

"I doubt the Japanese will be missed terribly much." Franz laughed as he laid an arm affectionately across her shoulders. "The war is over, Hannah-*chen*. And we survived it!"

"It was those terrifying bombs—the atomic ones—that made them surrender, wasn't it?" Hannah said. "What if they had dropped one on Shanghai?"

"They never would have done that," Herschel piped up. "Not here. Not on us."

"I agree," Franz said. "At least, I hope not. The Japanese had lost long ago. Those atomic bombs only made them finally realize it."

"I am just glad they're gone." Hannah couldn't remember seeing her father look so relaxed or carefree. As relieved as she felt, she didn't fully share in the celebratory mood. Like everyone else, she had been anticipating the Japanese defeat for so long, but now that it had come, she experienced a discombobulating sense of limbo. She picked up on a nervous undercurrent to all the festivity. It was as though the city were collectively waiting for something, but no one quite knew what it would be.

"Were you serious when we spoke about moving, Hannah-*chen*?" Franz asked. "Would you really want us to go to Palestine?"

Hannah held her father's gaze. "Yes, Papa. I would."

Franz said nothing, but she could see in his eyes that he wanted to also.

She eased her shoulder free of her father's arm and reached for Herschel's hand. He squeezed hers back, his confidence in her feelings for him growing. She would never forget Herschel's bravery on the day of the bombing, when he came to find her in the shelter. That had banished the last of her lingering doubts. She would always be able to count on Herschel. That meant more to her than anything else.

Franz's eyes focused on the teenagers' interlocked hands, and he winked at Hannah. His approval elated her. "Shall we go see our old apartment, Papa?"

"I would love to see our neighbourhood again." Franz clicked his tongue. "But I think we had better get back home to Sunny and your brother."

"I guess we should," Hannah agreed.

They doubled back and crossed over the Garden Bridge into Hongkew. The celebration on Broadway was even more frantic than it had been on the Bund, the muggy air thick with the scent of frying meat. The tinkling sounds of Chinese music filled the street. Firecrackers popped as loud as gunfire. Impromptu parades appeared. The joy was contagious and washed away much of Hannah's circumspection.

They strolled past the now-abandoned checkpoint at the Muirhead Road intersection. With its rickety wooden gate and graffiti, it struck Hannah as so innocuous. She found it hard to believe that just the day before it had been as fierce a deterrent as an electrified fence.

As they walked down Ward Road, Hannah slowed at the sound of shouting. She immediately recognized it as distinct from the festive noises. Her father heard it too. He turned and headed into a nearby laneway.

A group of boys had formed a semicircle at the end of the lane. Their backs were turned, and Hannah couldn't tell what had drawn their attention, or their ire.

"King of the Jews?" she heard one of them yell. "More like king of the fools!" A chorus of laughter and jeers echoed.

As the three neared the group, one of the boys turned toward them. Hannah recognized him as an older boy from school. "This doesn't concern you," he said a cautionary tone.

Several of the others also looked over their shoulders at them. She recognized them too from school; a few had already graduated. She spotted Freddy standing beside Avi. Freddy looked away in embarrassment, but Avi glared defiantly at Hannah and Franz as he tapped a small wooden club against his open palm.

Now Hannah could see the small man who was the centre of attention. His back was pressed against the wall. He held his arms up to protect his face, but Hannah recognized his pinstriped suit, which was torn and bloodied.

"Please, please boys. I was good to your families." Ghoya sputtered in his distinctive nasal tone. "You have no idea of the pressure I was facing."

Avi raised his weapon above his head. "And you have no idea how much pressure you're going to face from my club."

"Show him, Avi," a boy yelled. Several others chimed in their encouragement.

Ghoya lowered his arms enough to expose his face. His eyes lit with recognition as he spotted Franz standing behind the boys. "Dr. Adler," Ghoya cried. "Oh, Dr. Adler! You must tell them. Yes, yes. Tell them."

"And what precisely shall I tell them, Mr. Ghoya?" Franz's voice was calm, quiet even, but Hannah sensed the rage behind her father's words.

"That I was a fair man." Ghoya shook his hands wildly above his head. "Yes, yes. Very fair. And that I only did what I had to. To protect you. All of you. Yes, yes. I only came back here to tell you how pleased I was for you. My people, my people!"

"Your people? *Your people?*" Avi scoffed. "Why, you stupid Jap." He swung the club, catching Ghoya on his forearm.

Ghoya screamed. "*No! No!* Stop it. Please, please." His voice squeaked with panic. "Dr. Adler. Tell them. You must, Dr. Adler. You must!"

Franz stared at the cowering little man. Hannah could only imagine what was going through her father's mind as he listened to Ghoya beg for help. This, from the man who had ordered Franz's flogging and who had kept their family imprisoned in the ghetto for over two years, forcing Esther and Simon apart. The man who had dispatched him to the front lines and would have happily left him there to die.

But Franz didn't say a word.

The silence was broken by a stocky boy next to Avi. He punched Ghoya heavily in the abdomen. The little man groaned and crumpled to his knees.

"You aren't the king of anything or anyone," another boy said as he stepped up to the kneeling Ghoya. "You remember my uncles? Felix and Isaac Cron? Do you, Ghoya?"

Ghoya looked up fearfully. He raised his uninjured hand and waved it frantically. "They . . . they were smugglers."

"Their families were starving," the teen cried. "You executed them. For what? For bringing a few cheap pens and watches into the ghetto? For just trying to feed their children?" He smashed his elbow into Ghoya's jaw. The little man toppled over.

"Time to end the king's reign," cried yet another boy as he stepped up and kicked Ghoya in the chest.

The other youths closed in like wolves. Hannah noticed that Freddy was hanging back. The violence reminded her of those terrifying final nights in Vienna. She couldn't even see Ghoya through the maze of bodies in front of her. She was relieved to feel a hand on her elbow, gently pulling her away. "We had better go, Hannah," Herschel uttered in a low voice.

"Enough," Franz suddenly shouted, rushing into the fray. "That's enough. Stop it!"

He grabbed at the nearest of the boys and yanked him back. Surprised, the others halted their assault and turned their attention to Franz.

"What's it to you?" Avi demanded as he shook the club at Franz. "Why should we?"

"This is barbaric," Franz said.

"This is *justice*," one of the boys retorted.

Franz shook his head. "No. This is a street mob. No different from how the Japanese used to behave. Or the Nazis. Do any of you remember Kristallnacht?"

"How can you compare it?" one boy cried as he motioned to Ghoya, who was rolling on the ground, clearly in pain. "This man is getting exactly what he deserves. He did so much worse to most of us."

"Let a judge decide what he deserves. Not a mob."

Avi came closer, his eyes brimming with anger. "Collaborators are just as guilty as he is."

"Careful with your accusation, son," Franz said. "After all, I have more reason to harm this man than any of you."

"Then why don't you?" Avi challenged.

Franz only smiled. "Because we are better than him."

Freddy stepped toward Avi and snatched the club out of his hand.

"Hey, Herzberg," Avi snapped. "What's the big idea?"

"Dr. Adler is right," Freddy said quietly.

"This is none of his business—"

Freddy shoved Avi backwards. "It's enough."

Avi looked about to strike back, but then his shoulders sagged. His face turned contrite, and he looked like a dog scolded by its master. The other boys shared uncertain glances. After a few moments, they began to turn away from Ghoya.

Hannah looked over to Freddy and their eyes met. His gaze was full of affection. His sheepish expression told her how sorry he was for what he had done to her.

Then Hannah reached for Herschel's hand. She broke off the eye contact and spun away from Freddy.

CHAPTER 52

September 20, 1945

Franz and Sunny stood side by side in the ward, watching an American nurse change the dressing on a woman's abdomen while a young uniformed doctor kneeled at the next bed, applying a plaster cast to another patient's knee.

Franz had never worked anywhere as skeletally staffed, poorly designed or underequipped as the refugee hospital, yet he had never felt more at home. He found it surreal, and mildly bittersweet, to see the American doctors and nurses assuming the roles that he and his team had performed for so long.

Sensing his melancholy, Sunny leaned her head into his shoulder. "They will care for them as well as we could have," she reassured him.

"Better, no doubt."

"No one could offer better care than we did with what we had," she said with certainty.

"We did the best we could, didn't we?"

Colonel Findlay, the U.S. forces' chief medical officer in Shanghai, had assured Franz that the army would maintain the hospital and continue to care for the refugees and the locals. So far, the colonel had been true to his word. Never had Franz seen the supply cupboard so fully stocked. Even the antibiotics and antimalarial medications were plentiful. He felt gratitude toward the Americans, but none of it negated his mixed emotions.

Sunny smiled tenderly. "It's time, Franz."

"Can you believe it's been almost seven years?" He stroked his wife's cheek, comforted by her proximity. "We met right here, darling. Practically on this very spot."

"Coming here was the best decision of my life," she chuckled. "And to think I only volunteered here to improve my German."

"There are easier ways to accomplish that than marrying an Austrian Jew."

She laughed again and kissed his neck. "Now you tell me."

"Dr. Adler! Sunny!" a familiar voice called.

Franz turned to see Berta striding down the corridor. He almost didn't recognize the head nurse in her hat and overcoat, instead of her usual matron's uniform. "You look so elegant, Berta."

"Yes, well, my Otto and me, we are leaving."

Sunny tilted her head. "Leaving Shanghai?"

"Our visas came through," Berta said. "There's a ship leaving for Hong Kong today. And from there to England. We have to stop in Holland to pick up my sister, Frieda." She lowered her voice to a hush. "Frieda was the only one in her family to survive the camps. Her husband and her two daughters, such beautiful girls." She sighed heavily and then touched her temple. "Frieda is not doing well. Not well at all."

"I'm so sorry," Sunny said.

Franz only nodded, unable to say the same words. He had worn out the phrase in the past month, and now it sounded to him like a meaningless platitude. The news from Europe had been as bad as the refugees had feared. Ever since the Red Cross had begun posting lists of the extermination camps' victims, Shanghai's Jews had fallen into collective mourning. Many wept in public. Others wandered the streets like zombies. The grief was palpable, wiping away the elation over the city's liberation. And another unexpected emotion had crept into the community: guilt—for surviving when so few of their relatives had. It was as if people were now ashamed of having fled to Shanghai. Franz wondered if that helped explain why so many were, like Berta's family, making hasty plans to leave the city. It saddened him to realize that, in many ways, war and oppression had been the glue that held their community together.

Berta reached out and, uncharacteristically, took hold of Franz's and Sunny's wrists. "I wanted to tell you how proud I am to have worked with you at the hospital. Both of you. What you did here with nothing really . . ." Her voice cracked and, on the verge of tears, she couldn't finish.

"I feel the same about you, Berta," Sunny said as she hugged the woman.

"Me as well." Franz squeezed the back of Berta's hand. "It was an honour. You are an exceptional nurse."

"Yes, well, I . . . Goodbye, then." Embarrassed, Berta turned and hurried off to say the rest of her farewells.

"We had better go too, Franz," Sunny pointed out. "The others will be at the port by now."

* * *

Franz held Joey while Sunny, Hannah and Herschel walked beside him, each lugging a heavy suitcase. The trusting look in Joey's eyes gratified Franz, but he was still ashamed to remember how hard he had once tried to persuade Sunny to give the boy up. He could never have imagined how rewarding being a father for a second time would be. Franz couldn't imagine life now without his son.

The port was as busy as it had been on the day the Adlers had first arrived. Only the uniforms had changed. American soldiers and sailors stood among the coolies and other locals, radiating an infectious vitality. Franz found their loud brashness utterly forgivable in light of their warmth and friendliness.

"Even the wild pheasants are out early." Ernst indicated the young dockside prostitutes who were aggressively soliciting the men in uniform while families with children strolled past in the midday sunshine.

Ernst pushed Simon's wooden wheelchair as Jakob rode happily on his father's lap. Esther clung, as usual, to her husband's side. She had been hovering over him so constantly since his injury that Ernst had teased her, "Who knew one fallen building could create a set of Siamese twins?"

Simon was smiling ear to ear. As he had predicted, he had never recovered any sensation in his legs, but he hadn't shown a flicker of self-pity or dejection, at least not in Esther's presence. The only time Franz had seen any cracks in his friend's optimism was one afternoon when they had been alone together. Simon had voiced his worries over how he would be able to care and provide for his family from the confines of his wheelchair. But even then, he had ended the conversation on a hopeful note: "On the plus side, Jake is going to have to learn to be a real accurate throw when he plays catch with his pop."

The group slowed to a halt in front of the gangplank. Soldiers, sailors and civilians were already boarding the imposing naval transport ship that would take the Lehrer family on the first leg of their journey to New York, via Singapore and San Francisco.

"Can't believe I'm going to be back in the Bronx within the month." Simon looked over his shoulder. "You sure you won't come with us, Ernst? I hear there's no better art scene in the world than in New York right now."

"The art is not the issue. It's the people." Ernst tossed a hand up dramatically. "If they are anything at all like my roommate of the past two years, I would lose my mind among them."

Simon laughed. "No one is going to miss me more than you, pal."

"I sincerely hope, for your sake, that is not the case." Ernst smiled.

"So where will you go?" Esther asked him.

Ernst shrugged. "Nowhere for now. It's going to be a fascinating time in this city. Change is in the wind. Kaiser Wilhelm and I can't wait to see what happens next."

"Where is your monkey, Onkel Ernst?" Hannah asked.

"I left him at home." Ernst nodded in Jakob's direction. "He's terrified of that one. He thinks the child is wild. Rabid, possibly."

Herschel and Hannah shared a laugh as he took his hand in hers.

Simon turned to Sunny. "Since you're half American, Sunny, we could get your whole family American visas today. Piece of cake." He snapped his fingers. "We've got a ton of room in our new place. My brother has rigged up the ground floor, so you don't even need legs to get around. You would have the whole upstairs to yourselves. The Bronx won't know what hit it."

Franz admired his friend's courage and enthusiasm, suspecting that at least part of it was put on for his wife's benefit. "We still have not decided on our ultimate destination," he said.

Sunny slipped her arm through the crook of Franz's elbow and leaned against him. "We are getting closer, though, aren't we, darling?"

Hannah turned to Sunny with wide eyes. Herschel's grandparents had already committed to going to Palestine on a ship that would be leaving in early October, and she had been lobbying hard for the Adlers to join them. "Palestine, Sunny?" she asked tentatively.

Sunny looked from Franz to Joey and back again. "I am warming to the idea," she said. "Especially now that Yang has moved to the countryside with her sister's family. There is not much left to keep me here. A fresh start might be the best thing for our family."

"You could have a fresh start in America too," Esther pointed out.

"That's true, Essie, but it sounds as though we might be needed more in Palestine." Sunny smiled at her stepdaughter and then turned back to Franz with a look of pure love.

Hannah threw her arms around her boyfriend and hugged him tightly. "Do you hear that, Herschel? We might be coming with you."

Franz's chest felt as if it might burst with joy. Tears welled as he gazed into his wife's eyes. He repositioned Joey to his side, so he could kiss her. As his lips found hers, it occurred to him that he could be the luckiest man alive. He had arrived in Shanghai with practically nothing—little hope and no prospects—and soon, he would be leaving with everything.

ACKNOWLEDGEMENTS

I owe far too many debts of gratitude to acknowledge everyone who has enriched and facilitated the development of the Adlers' story, which is so near to my heart.

I do wish to thank my family for their unwavering support and belief. I also want to acknowledge Kit Schindell, who has been at my side from the very first manuscript. She sees my work at its rawest and refines it like the artist she is. I want to thank my agent, Henry Morrison, for his guidance, and my manager, Jon Karas, for his inspiration. And I would like to recognize my wonderful editor, Lorissa Sengara, who has steered me from the first to the last page of this journey, contributing irreplaceably every step along the way.

Finally, I must acknowledge the people who survived in Shanghai under brutal conditions during the Second World War. The refugee Jews, the native Chinese and so many other nationals endured oppression with dignity, bravery and a degree of mutual tolerance that was rare for the era.